YOUR MISSION, WHETHER OR NOT
YOU CHOOSE TO ACCEPT IT...

Freki pulled a photo out of his pocket and pushed it across the table toward me. "This is one of the people we know was on the *Icarus*," he said. "We want you to find her."

The picture was that of a young woman: collar-length black hair, hazel eyes, lightly tanned in an outdoorsy sort of way. "Nice-looking lady," I said, passing the photo to Selene. "What's her name?"

"We know her as Tera C," Freki said. "Last name unknown. We think she was the *Icarus*'s computer expert."

Definitely not just a pretty face, then. "So how is finding a single human female supposed to be easier than finding a single missing ship?"

"Because she was seen three days ago in Havershem City on Pinnkus," Geri said.

"What makes you think she's still there?" I asked, noting out of the corner of my eye that Selene was working at her pad.

"We don't," Geri said. "But that's where she was seen, so that's where you start."

"Okay," I said. "So to summarize. You want us to find someone who *might* have been wandering around a city of—" I looked at Selene and raised my eyebrows in question.

"Eight million humans," she reported. "Three million aliens."

"—but who might or might not still be there," I finished. "That about cover it?"

BAEN BOOKS by TIMOTHY ZAHN

THE ICARUS PLOT

TIMOTHY ZAHN

THE ICARUS PLOT

This is a work of fiction. All the characters and events portrayed in this book are fictional, and any resemblance to real people or incidents is purely coincidental.

A Baen Books Original

Baen Publishing Enterprises
P.O. Box 1403
Riverdale, NY 10471
www.baen.com

ISBN: 978-1-9821-9280-8

Cover art by Dave Seeley

First printing, July 2022
First mass market printing, July 2023

Distributed by Simon & Schuster
1230 Avenue of the Americas
New York, NY 10020

Library of Congress Control Number: 2022013760

Printed in the United States of America

10 9 8 7 6 5 4 3 2 1

For Tera and James,
and their merry band of pirates.

CHAPTER ONE

———— ❖ ————

The four Grumpfers had been sitting at their table for nearly an hour, making the kind of rude noise their species liked to make, tossing back liters of the rum-based liquor their species liked to drink, and emitting increasingly acidic aromas as the ethanol in their blood sifted into their lungs and breath. So far they'd mostly behaved themselves, which for Grumpfers meant leaving the glassware and condiment bottles unbroken, but I knew it was only a matter of time before something went diagonal. My best chance was that my shift would be over and I would be long gone before that happened, or that the two Yavanni playing bouncer at the door would handle the situation.

As my father used to say, *Chance is a funny thing. A fat one and a slim one are the same thing.* Unfortunately, the way luck was breaking for me these days my chances here were likely going to run to one or the other.

It started almost exactly an hour after they first lumbered in, as if they'd set their watches for the occasion. One of them made the same kind of obnoxious-sounding comment all four had been tossing around the table, but this time someone apparently took offense. Two seconds and an angry roar later, with a multiple clatter of kicked-back chairs, all four of the big aliens were on their feet, two of them glaring across the table at each other, their fists bunched, while the other two looked on like they'd been roped in as observers or seconds to the challenge.

I looked at the door. The Yavanni were watching the standoff closely, but neither was making any move to intervene. At the bar Josmith, the bartender, was trying hard to pretend he wasn't there. Zayli had disappeared, either done with her shift or else gone to ground in the back room. That left only one person standing between the Grumpfers and a brawl that could completely wreck the taverno: the waiter who'd spent the last hour serving them.

Me.

It wasn't my bar. It wasn't my furniture. Ergo, it wasn't my problem. I was glancing around the room, picking a good spot to ride out the coming storm, when one of the standby Grumpfers pulled an orange-edged card from the aggressor's shirt pocket, waved it in front of the offended party's eyes, and then slapped it down on the table in front of him. Carefully, trying to be as invisible as Josmith and the sorry excuses for bouncers, I took a couple of steps forward and craned my neck to look.

It was, as I'd already guessed from the orange border, a med-warning card. The particular disease label was typical opaque medicalese, but one of the profile icons was all too familiar: a warning against overserving him with alcohol.

A second later the aggressor snatched the card back from the table and shoved it back into his pocket. But I'd seen enough. Never mind that the law said he was supposed to present that card before he so much as ordered. Never mind that his buddies knew perfectly well what would happen if he drank too much. The crucial point was that I'd served the drinks, and barring a long, leisurely tour through the Commonwealth's legal system I was the one everyone would blame.

And with that, unfortunately, it *was* my problem.

"Gentlebeings, please," I said, hurrying forward. I had a standing plan for handling drunks, which usually worked out pretty well, and right now it was the only card I had. Unfortunately, I'd never used it on even a healthy Grumpfer, let alone one with a medical condition, and I had no idea whether or not there would be any unpleasant side effects.

But if the coming fight resulted in any injuries, I'd be on the hook for those as well as for illegal alcohol service. At the moment, keeping my skin and internal organs intact trumped any fears over what might happen to the Grumpfer. "Please," I said again. "I think I have a way to resolve this."

The two antagonists stopped their snarling and all four aliens stared at me. Probably astonished that a puny human would dare butt into their argument, but I didn't care about the *why* as long as they stopped. "I apologize if the rumakaf isn't up to your usual standards," I continued. Holding my hands together, the left hand over the right, I surreptitiously loosened the hidden access panel just below my inside left wrist.

The six knockout pills were nestled together in the little hollowed-out space behind the wrist; pulling out two of them with my first two right-hand fingers, I transferred them invisibly to my left-hand palm as I pulled my hands apart.

"The rumakaf is not the problem," the offended party growled.

"Caleb's Drinkhouse always stands behind its products," I said, ignoring the interruption. I picked up the aggressor's glass with my right hand and sniffed the contents. "It smells all right to me." I transferred it to my left hand, my fingers holding the top of the glass as I let the pills drop into the liquid. "Tell you what," I added, offering the glass to him. "Finish up, and the next round of drinks will be on me."

One of the bystander Grumpfers stiffened and tried to reach across the table. But the aggressor was too fast. Before his friend could reach him he'd put the glass to his mouth and downed the contents. He slammed the glass back on the table—there it was, finally: the broken glassware I'd anticipated ever since they came in—and opened his mouth to resume his side of the argument.

He never got there. For a moment he remained standing upright, his mouth open, nothing coming out. Then, his knees unlocked and, almost in slow motion, he collapsed straight down onto the floor.

As my father used to say, *My friend and I had words, but I never got to use mine.* When dealing with Grumpfers, not having to argue or even talk was always the best outcome.

For another moment the other Grumpfers just

stared at him. Not a long moment, but long enough for Josmith to abandon his safe spot behind the bar and come trotting toward me. As if that was the signal the Yavanni at the door had been waiting for, they unglued themselves from their own sections of tile and likewise came clomping over. "Puke, what's going on here?" Josmith demanded.

"It's *Roarke*, not Puke," I corrected him. "And I don't know."

"What the hell's *that* supposed to mean?" he demanded. "You were here. You were serving them. Why *don't* you know?"

"Because I don't know," I repeated, putting on the bewildered expression I'd gotten a lot of use out of over the years. "He was drinking, and then suddenly he collapsed."

"Did he, now?" Josmith said, his own expression a sort of sarcastic suspicion that settled onto his face as effortlessly as my bewilderment settled onto mine. "You wouldn't have helped the process along, would you?"

"How?" I countered, holding out my bare hands. "You were standing right there. I just picked up his drink and handed it to him."

"Mm." Abruptly, he squatted down and pulled the card from the Grumpfer's pocket. "And what is *this*—?" He broke off, his eyes going wide, the sarcasm vanishing from his face. "The *hell*? Roarke—did you see this?"

So he *could* remember my name when he wanted to. "What the—? That's a *serving limiter*," I said, jabbing my finger at it like we'd just spotted the Rockabay emerald. "Where did—*when* did—?"

"Like you've never seen one before," Josmith bit out, straightening up and shoving the card at me. "You telling me you didn't see this?"

"Of course not," I snapped back, trying to figure out if his anger was real or if he was just playing to the audience. Loudly proclaiming our innocence would help us if the Grumpfer or his buddies decided to call a badgeman. But it wouldn't help as much as—

"You're fired," Josmith snarled.

—as kicking me out.

"That's not fair," I objected. As he turned and started to hand the card to the nearest Grumpfer, I snaked out my left hand and plucked it away from him. He made as if to grab it back; I took a step backward and peered closely at it. "He's supposed to show this to me before he orders. It says so right here on the card. It's not my fault."

"I said you're fired," Josmith repeated, his voice suddenly gone very quiet.

As my father used to say, *When a man goes all quiet, he's either deadly furious or is trying to lure you into range for a sucker punch. Either way, run.* "It's not my fault," I repeated, my voice just as quiet.

He held out his hand. I put the card back in it, and for a moment we faced each other in silence. The corners of his eyes wrinkled a little, and it occurred to me that he might have heard stories of my past.

But even if I'd felt like taking this further, it was pointless. It wasn't my bar, it wasn't my business liability that was on the line, and it clearly wasn't my business anymore. Not even on an hourly basis.

I gave each of the Grumpfers a polite nod, just to

look professional about it, then turned, walked past the two Yavanni, and headed into the back room.

Zayli was still nowhere in sight. Just as well. I rolled down my shirt sleeves and collected my jacket, info pad, and wallet from my locker. I grabbed one of the kitchen pads and tagged today's shortened hours so the boss could send my final wages into my account. Slipping on my jacket, stuffing my hands into the pockets, I shouldered the back door open and walked out into the city. The spaceport where the *Ruth* was currently berthed was a good five kilometers away, but busses cost money, and I was out of a job, and anyway right now I felt like walking.

Besides, the man following me looked like he could use the exercise.

The wind was at my back as I approached the *Ruth*, so I wasn't surprised to find Selene waiting for me at the open entryway, her long pure-white hair glistening in the sunlight and waving slightly in the breeze. "You're early," she said in the soft, delicate voice that went so well with her soft, delicate Kadolian features.

"Ran into a bit of a situation," I said, starting up the ramp toward her.

"Not a good one, I gather?" she asked. Her deep-set gray cats' eyes flicked over me like she was looking for knife wounds or plasmic burns. Probably she was, if only from force of habit.

"Well, the good news is that I didn't get hurt," I told her. "The less good news is that I got fired."

Her eyes' vertical pupils widened visibly, despite the bright sunlight beating down on us. Her nostrils flared, then contracted almost shut, then flared again.

Surprised *and* upset. A wonderful combination to come home to. "What happened?" she asked, reaching out her hand to me.

"Let's talk about it inside," I said, leaving my hands in my pockets. She stepped back through the entryway into the airlock as I reached the top of the ramp—

"Gregory Roarke?" a voice called from behind me.

I turned. The man who'd been following me was standing at the foot of the ramp, looking up at us. He was a large man, half a head taller than me, with a bulk that I'd assumed was fat but which I saw now was mostly muscle. He was wearing a plain brown overcoat over a suit that looked to be in the same price range as my entire modest wardrobe.

And now that I finally had a good look at him, I realized I'd seen him before. "Do you really have to ask?" I countered.

His forehead furrowed. "Excuse me?" He waved a hand before I could answer. "Never mind. Can I come up? We need to talk."

My first, fleeting, thought was that he might be a lawyer, here to rain subpoenas and summonses on me. But I'd known a lot of lawyers in my time, and none of them had been built like that. "What's on your mind?" I asked, heading down the ramp toward him.

His lip might have twitched as I approached. Probably he'd hoped to have this meeting out of the public eye. But the twitch might have been my imagination. "I'm looking for a croquette," he said as I stopped in front of him. "I'm told you're one of the best."

As my father used to say, *Never laugh at someone bigger than you are unless he's just told a joke.* But I couldn't let that one pass without at least a smile. "I believe there's an Old French café a few blocks west of the spaceport," I offered helpfully.

This time the forehead furrowing was accompanied by a narrowing of his eyes. "Excuse me?" he said again, his voice a shade more menacing.

"Sorry," I apologized. "It's a common mistake, but it still amuses me. *Croquette*, with the emphasis on the second syllable, is a French dish. *Crockett*, emphasis on the first, refers to those of us in the Association of Planetary Trailblazers." I raised my eyebrows. "I'm guessing you don't know much about us?"

The forehead smoothed, and he gave me a small smile. "Ah," he said. "*Mea culpa*. Yes, this is the first time I've looked to hire a crockett."

Mea culpa. Latin. With all the languages of all the peoples across the Spiral, there wasn't much call for dead languages these days. Maybe he was just a well-muscled lawyer.

Though given how aggressively the Patthaaunutth and their fancy Talariac Drive were working to monopolize the Spiral's shipping, Patth might soon become the unofficial lingua franca, kicking English into the dustbin of dead languages right beside Latin.

"So are you available?" he asked.

"Absolutely," I assured him. "But I have to tell you that I don't come cheap. Especially not at this particular moment."

"Oh?" He peered up at the *Ruth*, shading his eyes with his hand. "Trouble with your ship?"

"Nothing an infusion of money wouldn't fix."

"In that case, you *definitely* need the job," he said. This time his smile looked a little more genuine. "Ever hear of the Bonvere cluster?"

"I don't think so." I half turned. "Selene? Check the library for the Bonvere cluster, will you?"

"Certainly," she called back down, pulling out her pad. "A minute, please."

"Interesting," the man said, his hand once again shading his eyes as he looked at Selene. "You don't see many Kadolians these days."

"You never did," I said. "They've always been rare. Not sure anyone even knows where they came from." I cocked an eyebrow. "I'm surprised you recognized her."

He shrugged. "You were on my list of potential crocketts. I did a little research on you."

"Research is good," I said. "Next time, you might also want to take a quick run through the pronunciation guides."

For a second his face went rigid. Then, he smiled again. "Touché."

I smiled back. More Latin, or possibly French. "Did you enjoy your drinks?" I asked.

"My drinks?"

"The ones back at Caleb's," I said. "You came in about twenty minutes after the Grumpfers. Zayli was your server, though if you'd stayed much longer her shift would have ended and I would have taken over. You were still sitting there when I got fired, but were already outside ready to follow me when I finished my last bit of paperwork and left. Did I miss anything?"

For a moment he seemed to be considering whether or not to lie to me. Then he smiled again. He seemed to like doing the smiles, though he really wasn't very good at it. "I don't suppose you'd like to tell me what I was drinking?" he asked.

"It was a pale amber something," I said. "I never got

close enough to identify it, but given you had two glasses and aren't showing any effects I'm guessing it was a light cognac or possibly Germania ale. Also light, of course."

"Of course," he said. "You're quite observant."

"Comes with the territory," I said. "Sadly, I didn't get a chance to get your name from the charge tally."

"Well, we should rectify that." He stuck out his hand. "Call me Geri."

I should have known this was coming. People who sprinkled dead languages into their conversation also tended to like old-world gestures and customs. Handshakes were one of those.

Unfortunately, there was nothing I could do about it. Reluctantly pulling my right hand out of my pocket, I took the proffered hand and shook it. His grip was strong but not overwhelming, the grip of someone who's confident in his strength but knows when and where to use it. "Geri what?" I asked, letting go and returning my hand to its pocket.

"Just Geri," he said. "My employers like to keep things loose."

"Ah," I said. That kind of secrecy wasn't common, but it was hardly unknown, either. "I assume you represent one of the big developers?"

"There's big, there's small, and there's small but rising," he said. "Mine is one of the latter." He cocked an eyebrow. "Which isn't to say we're not well-funded. There are a couple of planets in the Bonvere cluster we think are ripe for development and colonization. A clean survey from a reputable crockett and we'll be ready to move."

"Sounds interesting." I half turned my head. "Selene?" I prompted.

"The Bonvere cluster is a group of eight neighboring

systems with promising spectral data and planetary reflectives," Selene called down. "A Commonwealth survey team did oxy/water confirmation fly-bys of six of the systems sixteen years ago, but the records don't show any follow-up visits since then."

"Probably because Lacklin happened," Geri said. "That system was opened up for exploration and claims right on top of the Bonvere fly-bys."

"Yes, I remember Lacklin," I said, nodding. "The aftermath wasn't very pretty."

"No, but for a while it was the shiny pebble of the Spiral," Geri agreed. "Pulled a lot of attention that direction." His eyes shifted to something over my shoulder. "Especially from *them*."

I turned to look. Walking toward the port's exit as if they owned the place were three Patth, wrapped in their usual gray hooded cloaks, the electronic implants in their mahogany-red faces glinting in the sunlight. Behind them walked four Drilies, with a frog-eyed Ihmisit port official bringing up the rear. "Must have just inaugurated a new ship," Geri said. "Usually they only run two pilots to a ship these days."

"Unless it was one of the larger corporate transports," I pointed out. "They still put three pilots on some of those."

"What, with *Drilies* as the crew?" he countered scornfully. "Not a chance."

"Oh, I don't know," I said, studying the squat, gorilla-armed aliens, their prehensile neck tentacles currently draped across their shoulders. "I heard a rumor a few years back that the Patth were considering licensing the Talariac to other species. The Drilies were supposedly at the front of the line."

"*Rumor* and *supposedly* being the key words," Geri growled. "Do you seriously think the Patth would let their monopoly go to slub-buckets who look like *that*?"

"They may not look like the ancient Greek gods, but they're smart enough," I said, wondering vaguely why I was defending the Drilies. They'd certainly been a pain in the butt to me more times than I cared to remember. "Besides, those tentacles would be a perfect place to implant Talariac locking gear."

"Hardly," Geri said. "You want to get hold of Talariac gear, you'd have to chop off a Patth pilot's whole head. With a Drilie, all you'd have to do is slice off the tentacles."

"Which would also probably kill him."

"What's a little murder if there's a stolen Talariac at the end of the rainbow?" Geri asked with an icy sort of casualness. "I'm just saying that with a Drilie at least you wouldn't need a bone cutter."

"Sure," I said, feeling my stomach churn. Even my own dislike of Drilies didn't go *that* far. "So are you hiring us to take a look at one of the Bonvere planets?"

"One, or possibly all of them," Geri said. "How long would that take?"

"For one, three days' travel each way and two more for the survey," I said. "All eight, you can add another two to three days each."

"Sounds reasonable," Geri said. "I'll call my partner and we can be aboard whenever you want. I assume you'll first need—"

"Whoa," I interrupted. "Selene and I travel alone."

"Not if you want me to pay to get your ship fueled and your drive brought up to code." He smiled. "Like I said, I checked up on you."

"How very thorough of you," I said. "Did all that research happen to mention that a Gemini-class ship is designed for a crew of two?"

"So you and the Kadolian can bunk together."

"There's not enough room in either of the cabins for two people," I explained as patiently as I could. "There's a dayroom foldout, but it will also sleep exactly one person." I gestured up and down his bulk. "With someone your size, even that would be pushing it."

For a long moment he gazed at me. Out of the corner of my eye I saw the three Patth and their entourage pass by, still looking like they owned the port. Eventually, inevitably, they probably would. "Fine," Geri said at last. "I'll tell my partner I'll do this one solo. What do you need to get the ship ready to go?"

"Like I said: an infusion of money," I told him. "Twenty thousand commarks ought to do it."

He raised his eyebrows. "That's a *lot* of engine work."

"That also includes our fee for eight systems."

"Ah," he said, nodding. "Better. What if we only do one?"

"You'll be due a refund."

He considered, then nodded. "Good enough. What's your timeline for getting out of here?"

"Four days, maybe five," I said. "Another two thousand would drop that to three."

"Yeah, I get it," he said, looking around. "Alien ports. Got to love them. How much to get us out of here tomorrow?"

"An extra twenty." I considered. "An extra thirty would probably have us ready in six hours."

"Tempting," he said, pulling out a wallet. Inside were a collection of gold-edged certified bank checks. He selected four of them and handed them to me. "We'll make it twenty. I'll be here this same time tomorrow. Here's my number." He slipped a business card onto the top of the stack.

An actual, physical card, on top of the Latin and French and the handshake. He definitely was pulling out all the classic stops. "We appreciate the business," I said, glancing at the card and then peering at the checks. Ten thousand commarks each, all right. "What if the ship isn't ready by then?"

"Just make sure it is," he said, a hint of threat in his tone. He looked up at Selene one last time, then again offered his hand. "Tomorrow."

"See you then," I said, giving his hand another brief shake.

He turned—not the precise spin of an ex-military man, but a good copy of the global-awareness movements of a trained fighter—and strode off toward the exit. I kept watching, and twenty paces later he pulled out his phone and started talking into it.

Selene was putting away her own phone when I joined her at the top of the ramp. "The tech department?" I asked.

She nodded. "They said they'll get started as soon as you deposit the money."

"Did you emphasize the need for some of that legendary Ihmis efficiency?" I asked, handing over the checks and nudging her backwards off the ramp into the less visible airlock.

"I did," she said, taking the checks. "I'll get these scanned across."

"In a minute," I said, touching her slender arm to stop her as she started to leave. "Pull up *Grumpfer dehydrogenase syndrome*, will you?"

There was puzzlement in her pupils, but she merely nodded and got out her pad. A moment to key it in— "It's a group of diseases that make Grumpfers ultra-susceptible to alcohol," she said, looking up at me. "Is that why you got fired?"

"Let's find out." I pulled my left hand out of my jacket pocket and held it out. "I held his med-warning card for a second right after he'd touched it. Well, right after Josmith touched it, anyway," I amended. "Sorry."

"Not a problem," she assured me. Taking my hand in both of hers, she held it to her nostrils and began slowly inhaling, taking each fingertip in turn, then working her way down to the palm. Once she held the hand to her eyes, her long eyelashes gently beating and then sampling the nearly undetectable odors clinging to the hand's artificial skin. I kept still, waiting for her extraordinary sense of smell to do its job. "Three humans touched the card," she said slowly. "You and Josmith and another I don't recognize. Also, two Grumpfers."

"Right," I said. "Did one of them have this dehydrogenase syndrome?"

"No," she said, still inhaling. "Both were completely healthy."

"So it was a frame-up right from the start," I growled. "Our mystery man probably gave him the card with a promise that he and his buddies could go into Caleb's and drink for free for the next hour."

"Josmith cancelled their bill?"

"Don't know—I left before he finished with them,"

I said. "But probably." I offered my right hand. "Our friend Geri. Was he the third human?"

She did a quick sniff of my palm where I'd shaken Geri's hand. "No."

"You sure?" I asked, frowning. "He was in the bar watching. He'd have been the perfect one to—oh," I said with a sigh. "Right. Check those bank checks."

Her pupils twitched in a frown, and she brought the bank checks up to her nostrils. Again, a single quick sniff was all it took. "That's him."

"So, Geri's partner," I said. "No money, freshly kicked out of my job; and then Geri conveniently happens by looking for someone to check out these Bonvere worlds. I do so like a well-constructed trapbox."

"But why get you fired?" Selene asked, her eyes frowning. "Why not just come here and hire you? Did they think you were *that* attached to life as a bar server?"

"If they did, they're fools," I said. "On the other hand, I've never yet seen a fool with that much money."

"He had more than these?" Selene asked, holding up the bank checks. "I couldn't see into his wallet from here."

"Lots more," I assured her. "If all the checks were the same denomination as those, he could probably buy any ship in the port and still have enough left for a nice vacation somewhere."

"Then *why*?" she persisted.

"No idea," I said. "But I'm sure Geri will let us in on the joke somewhere along the way. Be sure to have a good hearty laugh ready to go."

I gestured her toward the bridge. "In the meantime,

go scan those in and get some work crews out here.
I'll start running the rest of the checklists."

I looked back out at the port grounds. Geri and the
Patth group were long gone. "Geri said we'd better
be ready to go when he gets here," I added. "I'd just
as soon not find out if there was an *or else* attached
to that request."

CHAPTER TWO

— ❖❖❖ —

Geri showed up exactly on time, wearing a jumpsuit-type outfit that was far more appropriate for shipboard use than the suit and overcoat he'd been wearing the day before. He was rolling a medium-sized carrybag, which really wasn't much luggage for a month away from civilization. Either he was planning to avail himself of the *Ruth*'s limited laundry facilities or else the bag was filled with high-end self-cleaning clothing. From the look I'd had earlier into his wallet, I was betting on the latter.

Fortunately for me and whatever *or elses* he might have been holding in reserve, the work crews finished exactly forty-four minutes before his arrival, and I'd completed the final preflight checks thirty-two minutes after that. By the time he reached the airlock I was ready to welcome him in, show him where to stow his bag, and get him strapped down on the dayroom foldout. Selene had already gotten us a lift slot from the tower, and barely ten minutes after I sealed the entryway the landing pad repulsor boost nudged us off the ground and into range of the perimeter grav beams. They in turn lifted us up to where we could safely engage the thrusters, and we were off.

Geri was unstrapped and sorting his things onto one of the empty pantry shelves when I arrived in the dayroom. "Nice lift," he commented. "Very smooth."

"Thanks," I said, passing up the fact that the trickiest part of any spaceship lift was handled by the port's grav operators, not the pilot. "I assumed you'd want to start with the closest of the Bonvere systems, which is number four, so that's where we're heading."

"Let's start with number seven instead," Geri said. "That one showed the most promise."

"Okay," I said. I hadn't seen anything in the original fly-by data to suggest any of the planets was better than any of the others, but Geri was the boss. "Any particular order you want for the rest of them?"

"Not really," he said. "Let's go with whichever's most efficient."

"Okay," I said. "See you later." I turned back toward the dayroom hatch—

"So what did you do before you were a crockett?" he called after me.

I turned back. He was still arranging his things on the shelf, his back to me. "I thought you already researched me."

"I did," he said, still not turning around. "I mostly wondered if you would lie to me."

"There's nothing to lie about," I said, feeling a stirring of annoyance. First a setup to get me fired from my job, and now the world's most casual interrogation? "Bounty hunter is a perfectly legitimate profession."

"I'm not arguing," he assured me. "I'm guessing it pays better than this job, though. Why did you quit?"

"It's called the retrospective of age," I told him.

"Really." Deliberately, he turned to face me. "I thought it was because you nearly got yourself and your Kadolian killed five years ago."

My stomach formed into a knot, and I felt a flicker of ghost pain at my left elbow where the artificial arm connected to flesh and bone. "Like I said: retrospective of age," I repeated, managing to keep my voice calm. "See, when you die you don't age anymore."

"Very deep," he said, not quite sarcastically. "Personally, I like to think that anything that doesn't kill you outright makes you stronger." He nodded toward my left arm. "Literally, in this case. You *do* know you can get models that are way stronger than human bone and muscle, right? Not to mention versions that can hold a knife or even a two-shot plasmic."

"And I'm sure they're wonderful Mother's Day gifts." I pointed at the shelf he was loading up. "Incidentally, I'd put some padding around anything breakable if I were you. Things can get a little energetic when we hit atmosphere." Without waiting for any further comments, I turned and left the room.

Selene was seated at the plotting table when I arrived on the bridge, sifting through the nav database's records on the Bonvere cluster. "You're angry," she said as I dropped into the pilot's seat.

"Just annoyed," I said, checking our vector. The newly tuned drive was running a little hot, but otherwise we were bang on course. "I'm starting to think our passenger is going to be a major pain in the butt."

"He *did* pay to get our engines fixed," she pointed out. "That should earn him a certain degree of patience on your part."

"Maybe," I said. "On the other hand, as my father used to say, *It doesn't take much to morph a gift horse into a white elephant.*"

"We'll be dealing with him for a month at the most," she soothed, "a month during which our bills will all be paid. And now that our engines are up to code, we can start submitting bids again on new sampling runs."

"I suppose," I said. "Going to be a long month, though."

"If you'd like, I could handle our day-to-day interactions," she offered. "You'd only have to talk to him after we finished the sampling analysis."

"Tempting," I said. "But no, I'll deal with him. Like you said, it's only for a month."

"As you wish." She paused, and I looked over to see her eyes fluttering as her lashes sifted through the air. "Much better."

"Glad to hear I'm calming down," I said. "You might be amazed how many people would find that really creepy."

"I suppose they would," she said, a hint of concern in her pupils. "You don't, do you? Find it creepy?"

"Not a bit," I assured her. "Actually, reading my mind that way saves a lot of time during conversations."

"It's not reading your mind."

"I know."

For a moment she was silent. "Does Geri know?" she asked at last.

"No idea," I said. "He recognized you as a Kadolian, which most people wouldn't. But even those who know about the Kadolian sense of smell usually don't know how good it really is."

"I was just wondering if he would find it creepy."

"If he does, that's his problem," I said firmly. "He invited himself along on this little outing. Anything interesting in those records?"

"You mean the Bonvere planets?" Her pupils twitched a negative. "Not really. As I told you yesterday, they've just had a single fly-by. Geri said they were ripe for colonization, didn't he?"

"Yes. Why? Was he lying?"

"I don't know," she said. "It's just that the cluster is so far away from anywhere. Unless there are some really valuable resources there, I'm not sure how economical it would be to develop them."

"Unless the only ships traveling there had Talari-acs," I said as I finally got it. "Geri and his mysterious development group aren't looking to work these planets. They're looking to find something they can sell to the Patth for a quick turnaround." I snorted in disgust. "It's Lacklin all over again."

"You mentioned Lacklin yesterday," Selene said, sliding the Bonvere data off the screen and punching for a new search. "I never had time to look it up."

"It won't take you long," I said. "Lacklin was a newly opened system, with lots of people getting excited about it. The Patth saw the hype and decided they wanted to be the big dogs on the block. So they started arm-twisting and underbidding and managed to take over all the trade and passenger routes."

"And once everyone else had been pushed away,

they ran it into the ground," Selene said, peering at the screen as she scrolled down. "The other developers pulled out, the Patth didn't have any replacements lined up, and no one else would move in without huge guarantees."

"Leaving them with a half-built world which they then wrote off and mostly abandoned," I said. "Pretty much only other Patth live there now, though I hear other people may be starting to drift back in. The point is that if Geri is shilling for the Patth, maybe they're going to try starting from square one with the Bonvere systems. If they can buy them outright and then open bids for development, they may be able to avoid the confusion and resentment they bought themselves at Lacklin."

"Maybe," Selene said, sounding doubtful.

"You don't think that's what they're doing?"

"I'm not sure it necessarily has to be the Patth," she said. "Maybe Geri's looking for an out-of-the-way place for some other reason."

I frowned off into space. With my thoughts and resentments already pointed at the Patth, my conclusions had naturally ended up pointed that direction, too. Come to think of it, Geri had done all that pointing himself, first with the three Patth who were passing by the *Ruth* and then by bringing up Lacklin.

"Could be," I said. "Maybe some megamil is bored with his private island and wants a private planet."

"Or some criminal megamil is looking for a place to hide out," Selene suggested, turning to look at me.

"Which would be none of our business," I told her firmly. "We're retired from hunting, remember?"

"We don't have to be."

The artificial nerves in my artificial arm gave an unpleasant little twinge, and in my mind's eye I saw Selene fighting for her life in that hospital intensive care pod. "This is our job now," I said. "Our *only* job."

For a long moment we just looked at each other. Then, she lowered her eyes and turned back to the computer. "It's been a long day," she said. "If you'd like to go rest, I'll watch things here."

I wasn't really tired, but at this point letting her have some solitude would probably be the better part of discretion. "Thanks," I said, getting up and heading for the door. "I'll be back in two hours."

"No rush," she called back over her shoulder.

She was right, of course. Targets were always on the run, and bounty hunters were always in a rush to catch up with them. Hunting might pay better, but it was a frantic business, wearing on both body and soul. Planets waiting to be surveyed, on the other hand, always just sat patiently.

And planets never took a shot at you.

Yes, I reminded myself firmly. This was a *much* better job.

Two days later, we arrived at Bonvere Seven.

"You really don't have to be here," I told Geri as he leaned over my shoulder in the bioprobe control room. He was close enough that I could feel his radiated heat on the back of my neck, with little puffs of air from his breathing ruffling my hair. Neither was at all pleasant. "The dayroom has repeater displays, and we can hook up the intercom so you can hear everything that goes on."

"This is fine," he assured me, as if it was his comfort

I was worried about. "I'm a hands-on sort of person. When do the probes go?"

I clenched my teeth. *Paid for the engines. Only a month.* "We typically come in over the equator," I told him. "Some crocketts like to come in with the rotation; Selene and I usually come in against it. We drop to an altitude of between fifty and sixty kilometers, which puts us into the stratosphere, then launch both bioprobes simultaneously. They'll go out at forty-five-degree angles from the ship's vector, one angling north, the other angling south."

"Just two?" Geri asked. "I understood the usual pattern involved six to ten probes."

"We'll be happy to do follow-ups if these first two passes show any promise," I said. A random gust of stratospheric wind buffeted the *Ruth*, and I heard the slight hiss of maneuvering jets as Selene damped down the vibrations. "Typically, though, they come up pretty dry."

The extra puff of air from his snort ruffled my hair. "I wouldn't think you'd get much data from a couple of three-hour passes."

"You might be surprised," I said. "A fair selection of seeds, spores, and other vegetable matter gets thrown up into the atmosphere, where it can travel hundreds or even thousands of kilometers. The probes will get some of that, and of course they'll scoop up more localized samples at the lower altitudes. By the time they head up again, we'll have a fair idea of what's down there that might be of interest to a developer."

"Or to a pharmacologist?"

I felt my throat tighten. That one was *way* too close to the mark. "There are sometimes spores or seeds that contain chemicals adaptable to medical purposes," I said, choosing my words carefully.

"*Just* medical purposes?"

The *Ruth* rocked through another couple of seconds of buffeting. "Selene?" I called. "Everything okay up there?"

"We're fine," she assured me. "And we're now at altitude. Drop whenever you're ready."

"Thanks," I said, lifting the protective covers and arming the launchers. "Hang onto something," I warned Geri. "They've got a bit of a kick." Without waiting to see if he obeyed, I turned the locking keys and pushed the buttons.

Once, when we'd had to launch into an extreme wind-shear pattern, the jolt of the bioprobe launch had sent us into a spin that came damn close to dropping us into a stall. Compared to that, this was more like a friendly tap on the shoulder. The bioprobes shot off to both sides, angling away from the *Ruth* as they simultaneously dropped lower into the atmosphere, eventually disappearing from sight through layers of cloud. "And we're off," I said. "Timer set; reacquisition in three hours."

I turned to look over my shoulder at Geri. "Which means nothing to look at for three hours," I said. "If you want a snack, this would be a great time to go get one."

"Maybe later," Geri said. His eyes, I could see, were shifting between the tracking display and the two screens linked to the probes' video cameras. "Actually, it looks to me like there'll be plenty to look at."

"Not for much longer," I said. "The transmitters have a limited range, especially when they get into thicker air and humidity. They'll keep recording, but we won't know what they saw until we get them back up."

"How do you control them when that happens?"

"I don't," I said. "But then, I'm not controlling them now, either. They're running on pre-programmed courses."

"I see," he said. "Well, if there's nothing for you to do, I suppose *you* could go have a snack."

Fleetingly, I wondered if he'd had to learn how to be irritating or whether it was an inborn talent. "Sadly, I need to stay here in case something happens that I *can* do something about."

"Ah." He paused. "Why *Ruth*?"

I frowned. "What?"

"Your ship," he said. "Why's it named *Ruth*? Was she an old girlfriend?"

I took a deep breath. Pretending he wanted to watch two bioprobes collect airborne flora samples was bad enough. Digging into my life's trivia was starting to seriously push against the edges. "It's named after Ruth from the Bible," I said. "The story says she got a job gleaning the corners of Boaz's fields. That's what we do."

"Because the big survey groups get all the important jobs and you're left with the scraps?"

"Something like that."

"Ah," he said. "Still, there's something to be said for working the corners. They're quiet. Remote. Peaceful."

"They're certainly uncrowded," I said pointedly. If he wasn't going to take the hint, I was just going to have to drop a brick on him. "Speaking of *uncrowded*...?"

"Oh. Sorry," he said, as if he'd just noticed how close he was standing to me. "Sorry," he repeated as he finally took a step back out of the hatchway. "I think maybe I'll go have that snack you mentioned. Maybe grab a quick nap after that. Call me when the probes are on their way back up."

"You'll be the first," I promised.

He left. I took a few deep breaths in lieu of uncorking the expletive I'd been holding back for the past half hour and turned toward the intercom. "You hear all of that?" I asked quietly.

"Most of it," Selene's voice came back. "I'm rather impressed you didn't kick him out sooner."

"It was close, I'll give you that," I said. "Anything unusual going on out there?"

"Nothing I can see," she said. "Why, were you expecting something?"

"Not really," I said. "But I've been thinking about our conversation a couple of days ago, the one where we wondered if Geri was looking for an out-of-the-way place as a future hideout for someone. It's occurred to me that we might have had that backwards. He could just as easily be looking for someone who'd already had that idea and gone to ground on one of the Bonvere planets."

"And he thinks we and our two probes can search eight whole worlds for him?"

"Sounds ridiculous, I know," I agreed. "On the other hand, if there are specific tags he's looking for, and if those tags are light enough to get to the upper atmosphere, it might be barely possible."

"I assume you're talking about tags that shouldn't exist on an unexplored planet?"

"Exactly," I said. "Like chrysanthemum seeds, say, if his target is a flower enthusiast. Or maybe ash residue if he likes big cookouts."

"Interesting," she said thoughtfully. "Something we'll want to keep an eye out for when we get the probes back."

"Agreed," I said. "Well, stay on them. I'm going to make sure he's settled in comfortably, preferably out of our hair, then go run another tuning check on the engines."

"All right," she said. "May I suggest you also pipe in a live feed from the probes to the dayroom so he doesn't have to come stand over your shoulder while we bring them up?"

"Way ahead of you."

I was back in the probe control room half an hour before the scheduled retrieval, running final tests, double-checking the bioprobes' positions and status feeds, and generally awaiting the critical minutes looming ahead.

Geri, to my silent annoyance, was back hovering at my shoulder ten minutes after I arrived.

Still, as my father used to say, *When there's a bad penny you can't get rid of, at least you're never completely broke.*

Retrieval was always the trickiest part of the job. The bioprobes couldn't make it high enough on their own to just be plucked out of the air, and they couldn't maintain their maximum altitude more than a few minutes. That meant the ship had to dip farther into the atmosphere, get its tight-core grav beams locked on the probes before they began to sink, then reel them to safety without the buffeting winds knocking either the probes or the ship off-target. Since the typical trailblazer ship only had two beams, if more than two bioprobes had been sent the crocketts had to perform the operation multiple times in rapid succession.

Fortunately, for once everything went off without a hitch. Both probes surfaced within double-grab range, held steady vectors while the ship pinged their transponders, and the grav beams locked on with our first try. It was almost as if the *Ruth* was putting on its best behavior for its visitor.

"And that," I announced as the status board confirmed both bioprobes were secured in their bays, "is that. Selene will get us up into a stable orbit, and we'll go see what we've got."

"Congratulations on an excellent job," Geri said, stepping back. "I'm ready when you are. The clean room's aft, right?"

"Clean room's aft; dayroom, where you're going to be, is forward," I said, standing up and turning my best official stare on him. "The clean room's only big enough for two people."

"No problem," he said. "Selene can wait in the dayroom while you and I run the analysis."

"Not if you want the clean survey you asked for," I said. "She and I are licensed crocketts. You're not."

For a long moment we locked eyes. Then, he gave a small shrug. "The joys of bureaucracy. I presume I can at least watch the procedure?"

"Of course," I said. "Everything has to be recorded anyway. I just have to set up a feed to the dayroom."

"Good," he said, heading forward. "I'm anxious to see what you find."

The *Ruth*'s clean room was hardly a Class One facility, and in some ways it barely qualified as *clean*.

But it was good enough for trailblazer standards, at least for a first approximation. By the time Selene got us into a parking orbit and came to join me I had the probes open and their various containers neatly laid out on the examination table.

Now came the crucial part. The part that occasionally made this whole job worth the time and effort. The part that occasionally made us enough money to keep going.

The part Geri absolutely couldn't be allowed to see.

"Ready?" I asked as Selene settled herself on the opposite side of the table.

"Ready," she said, her pupils showing a heightened level of concern. She understood the risk here as much as I did.

Fortunately, I'd had plenty of time during the three hours the probes were away from the ship to come up with a plan. Trailblazer regs said the entire exam table had to be visible on the recording, but they *didn't* say anything about the whole room or, more importantly, the crocketts themselves. A small adjustment to the camera's angle earlier while Geri was having his nap, and we had the blind spot we needed.

As my father used to say, *The hand doesn't have to be quicker than the eye if the hand is out of sight.* Giving Selene a reassuring wink, I picked up the first sample container and we got to work.

The first fifteen went by as smoothly as any regulator could have wanted. I pulled a bit of each sample from its container and gave it to Selene. She ran a quick scan to categorize it, then handed me a small rectangular glass ampule. I carefully tweezed out a few of the feathers, seeds, dead insects, or whatever from the container and placed them inside the ampule. While I did that, she printed a time/place/category stamp to attach to the side. I sealed the ampule neck and affixed the stamp, she logged the whole thing into the computer, the ampule was stacked on top of the others in the shockproof collection basket, and it was on to the next container.

Fifteen went by as normal. On the sixteenth, we finally hit pay dirt.

I saw it in Selene's eyes as I eased out one of the seeds inside and handed it to her for scanning. She moved the sample out of camera range; but instead of taking it straight to the scanner she first raised it to her nose. A quick flaring of her nostrils, a brief flutter of the seed with her eyelashes, and she looked at me with her pupils showing cautious excitement. Only then did she run it by the scanner.

And this time, instead of handing me a single ampule, she handed me two of the little glass boxes pressed together.

I was ready. Holding them together, making sure they were angled so that the camera wouldn't show the double thickness, I started transferring the seeds, alternating between the two ampules. By the time she was ready with the stamp I had loaded ten seeds in each. I fastened the tag to one of them, then lifted them out of camera range just long enough to palm the second, unmarked ampule before putting the marked one in the collection bin. As I picked up the next container in line, I slipped the spare ampule into the collar of my exam smock and dropped it down my shirt.

There were fifty more containers, and I ran through them hoping lightning would strike twice. Unfortunately, it didn't.

But that was okay. Most of our crockett runs didn't glean us even one.

We purged the rest of the containers of the residual flora and fauna, started the sterilization process on them, the bioprobes, and the clean room itself, and were finally finished.

To my complete lack of surprise, we found Geri waiting for us in the corridor. "Well?" he asked.

"Lots of life churning around down there," I told him. "Preliminary indications are that everything is amino-based, so even if humans can't eat anything there are probably sentients out there who can. No evidence of any civilization—no combustion byproducts, refined metal or ceramic microbits; that sort of thing. As you said when you first offered us this job, it looks promising."

"Sounds good," Geri said. "What about microorganisms?"

"Those were sealed in their own containers before the probes reattached," Selene told him. "You'll have to take those to a Trailblazer Class One clean room once we're back in civilization to get them analyzed. The macro samples we tested were thoroughly sterilized before we brought them aboard, of course."

"I wondered why you weren't wearing full isolation suits," he said, his eyes narrowing slightly. "Anything else?"

"At this stage, there usually isn't," I said. Which, I noted with a certain degree of virtuous satisfaction, was a completely truthful statement. "Our report's available on the computer whenever you want to take a look. You also need to decide whether you want us to do a second sample run across a different part of the planet or move on to the next system."

"In that case, I'd better start reading," Geri said. "I'll let you know when I've made a decision."

"Whenever you're ready," I said. "We'll be on the bridge."

It took a moment for us to strip off our gloves and smocks and dump them in the laundry hopper. While Selene headed to the bridge I stopped by the dayroom, partly to snag a couple of drink boxes for us, mainly to make sure Geri was settled in at the computer terminal there. I continued on to the bridge, sealed the hatch behind me, and settled into the pilot's seat.

"So," I said as I dug the ampule out from my shirt. "Animal, vegetable, or mineral?"

"Vegetable, of course," Selene said, her pupils giving me a frown. "They're *seeds*."

"I know," I said. Not one of my better attempts at a joke. "I suppose I should have said legit or illegit?"

"Probably a bit of both," she said. "They smell very much like an opioid comparative."

"Definitely a bit of both," I agreed soberly, staring at the ampule and the tiny, innocent-looking seeds sealed inside. The pharmaceutical companies were always on the lookout for new pain-relief drugs, and one of them would probably pay well for a leg up on this potential new player in the analgesic game.

So would any number of the evil people out there who pushed their own versions of such drugs on the more miserable, lonely, hopeless people of the Spiral. Especially since drugs that weren't yet identified and codified were by definition not illegal and had no official restrictions on their sale and use.

"You're going to take them to Mr. Varsi?" Selene asked into my thoughts.

"You know he'll ask," I said with a sigh. Selene didn't like our occasional employer Luko Varsi, and absolutely hated working with him.

I could hardly blame her for her attitude. I wasn't all that thrilled about the man and his organization, either. But Geri had been right. Gleaning the corners of the trailblazer industry was just profitable enough to keep us alive as we took a downward drift toward financial ruin. At this point, our side deal with Varsi was all that was keeping us afloat.

"What if we don't go back to Xathru?" Selene asked. "It's not like there's anything to hold us there. If we don't go back, how would he even find us?"

"Oh, please," I said scornfully. "You think an organization with someone like Varsi at the top wouldn't have access to every banking, travel, business, and shipping data network in the Spiral? We so much as poke our heads out of the rabbit hole and Varsi will know it."

"What if we changed our identities?" Selene persisted. "We've seen targets do that. Couldn't we do the same?"

"Sure," I said. "But then how would we put bread and bitters on the table? Without our crockett licenses we've got nothing."

She didn't answer, but just watched in silence as I pushed up my left sleeve. The little storage space I'd created among the electronics and wiring behind the wrist access panel was too small for anything but my collection of knockout pills. But the larger space, the one that opened up just forward of the elbow, was longer, with enough room to hold a sampling ampule. I popped it open, snugged the ampule into the hole, and resealed the panel.

"You once said that without our bounty hunter licenses we were also nothing," Selene reminded me. "We found this job. We can find something else."

"You still need an identity and a history," I said. "Without our names, we don't have a history. *With* our names, we have people like Varsi."

"There must be something else."

"You find it, and I'll take it," I promised. "But until then, we do what we have to."

There was a ping from the intercom. "Roarke?" Geri's voice came.

I keyed the intercom from my end. "Yes?"

"I think we're done here," he said. "Time to head back."

I frowned at Selene. "You mean on to the next Bonvere system?"

"No, I mean *back*, as in back to civilization," Geri said. "How far away is Ringbar?"

I frowned a little harder. *Ringbar?* What the hell was on Ringbar? "Hold on, I'll check," I said, gesturing to Selene.

"That's where my partner said he would meet us," Geri went on. "I talked to him just before we left Xathru. He said he'd head to Ringbar and we should contact him there when we arrived."

"What about the Bonvere systems?" I asked. On the nav screen Ringbar's coordinates popped up, along with the course and time from our current position. "You *did* pay us for a whole month."

"The situation has changed," Geri said. "Don't worry, I'm not asking for a refund."

I frowned at Selene, saw the same frown in her pupils. If Geri and his partner had talked before we left Xathru, and he'd known then that the situation—whatever it was—had changed, why had we come here in the first place? Why hadn't we headed straight to Ringbar? "You're the boss," I said. "Looks like it's about a twenty-six-hour trip from here."

"What if you run the drive to plus-ten percent?"

"That'll get us there ten percent faster," I said cautiously. "But it'll burn thirty percent more fuel."

"Will another ten thousand commarks cover the extra fuel?"

"And then some," I said cautiously. "But running a drive hot isn't recommended."

"You just had an upgrade," he pointed out. "That should be good for at least a thousand hours of reckless driving. So do it."

I glared at the intercom. Still, he was right. And it wasn't like I hadn't abused the *Ruth*'s engines before. "You're the boss," I said. "Whatever you want."

"I want," Geri said. "In fact, go ahead and run it to plus-twenty if the tanks have enough fuel to cover it. I'm going to go take a shower; I'll give you another bank check when I'm finished. Well, don't just sit there—get us moving."

"Right away," I said. I keyed off the intercom. "Your wish is my command," I added under my breath. "Selene?"

"Course set at plus-twenty," she said, the altered course and fuel profile appearing on my display. "We could actually do plus-thirty if we wanted to."

"Well, we don't," I said, standing up. "Plus-twenty is as far as I want to push it. Do me a favor and pull up the shower's water-flow reading, will you? Beep me if it stops."

"All right," she said, her pupils showing another frown. "Any particular reason?"

"I'm going to go search his stuff," I told her. "I'd like to not be there when he comes back."

CHAPTER THREE

— ◈◈◈ —

The dayroom was deserted when I arrived. I took a few more steps down the corridor, confirmed that the water in the shower was running, and headed back.

Up to now, I'd timed Geri's showers as running between ten and fifteen minutes. I planned to be out of the dayroom in five.

He'd packed light, as I'd already noted, and the search didn't take very long. He had four changes of clothing—self-cleaning, as I'd suspected—plus a toiletries kit, which I'd seen on the shelf earlier but was probably back in the bathroom with him right now. There was an odd-looking but clearly high-end phone, a music player/recorder, a flashlight, and a couple of tubes with the cheerful labels of pain-relief tablets. And, of course, a wallet stuffed with multiple-thousand-commark bank checks.

It wasn't until I noticed the barely discernable seams running up the flashlight's cylindrical sides that I realized something wasn't right. Keeping an ear out for Selene's signal, I made a second pass through everything.

Two minutes later, I was back on the bridge.

"He has a gun," I told Selene grimly. "Specifically, a breakaway dart gun, compressed-air powered, with two curare darts and six vertigos. I didn't see any serial numbers, so I'm guessing it's a custom job."

"I see," Selene said. The words were calm enough, but her pupils showed her emotions were on a real spin-dizzy of a ride. It had been a long time, after all, since either of us had been shot at.

And neither of us would ever forget what had happened at that last shooting.

"So what do we do?" she asked.

"Right now?" I shrugged. "Nothing, I guess. He hasn't pulled a weapon on us, or even threatened us. Actually, considering the amount of money he carries around, I'd probably find it surprising if he *wasn't* armed."

"I suppose," she said reluctantly. "So we continue on as if nothing has happened?"

"Nothing *has* happened," I reminded her. "And yes. We go to Ringbar, we give Geri a hearty handshake and a cheerful wave goodbye, and we get the hell off the planet. Whatever else he might have in mind, we're done."

Geri was big, muscular, and reasonably chatty. He also at least made an effort to smile at people, even if he wasn't very good at it.

His partner, Freki, was pretty much the polar opposite. He was short, barely taller than Selene, with a thin and wiry build. His face seemed to be set in a permanent scowl, and aside from acknowledging Geri's introductions he hadn't said a word as we spread the final hardcopy results of our Bonvere survey across the low coffee shop table and went through the analysis with them.

"Yes, very interesting," Geri said, picking one of the ampules out of the collection basket and peering through the glass side. "So everything there is amino-based?"

"So it appears," I said. "We were able to get a partial sequencing on two of the samples—one was a feather, the other a spore—and it looks like we're starting with a fifteen percent chance that the fauna and flora will be human-digestible."

"A more complete analysis will almost certainly raise that number," Selene added.

"Absolutely," I said. "You can take the samples to a Trailblazer Class One—I think there's one on Ringbar—or to a lab of your own choice."

"Yes, we could certainly do that," Geri agreed. He raised his eyes to look steadily at me over the ampule. "Or we could take them to whoever is going to analyze your stolen sample."

I swallowed a curse. I'd have bet heavily that there was no way he could have spotted the extra ampule while we were bagging the samples. "What do you mean?" I asked, shoveling on all the puzzlement I could manage.

"I watched you load twenty of this type of seed," he said, wiggling the ampule he was holding. "There are only ten in here."

I shook my head. "No offense, but you're mistaken."

"I don't think so," Geri said. "So let's cut to the chase. Option One: You sit here while I call up the badgemen and the local Trailblazer rep, file my charges, tell them I think you stole some of my samples and insist they do a full search of your ship. When they find the lost seeds—and they *will* find them—you'll lose your license and probably your last chance at any kind of a decent life." He raised his eyebrows. "Of course, that doesn't factor in your private buyer's penalty for failing to deliver his merchandise. Does that option sound like fun?"

I looked at Freki. He looked like he was choosing which part of me he would hit first if I tried anything. "Not really," I said.

"Good," Geri said. "Here's Option Two."

He tossed the ampule carelessly onto the table. "We forget all this nonsense, ashcan this garbage, and move on to the *real* job. That sound better?"

"Probably depends on what the real job is," I said cautiously, the warning bells in the back of my head all going off at once. What the *hell* was going on?

"Trust me, you're going to like it," Geri promised. "Are you familiar with a ship called the *Icarus*?"

Nine years spent as a bounty hunter interrogating suspects, conning bureaucrats out of information, and bluffing criminals and law enforcement officials had given me a pretty good poker face. But even with that depth of experience it was a near thing. "I've heard a little about it," I said. "It came and went, what, six years ago?"

"About that," Geri said. "What else do you know?"

"I don't actually *know* anything," I said, stalling. How much did they know? More crucially, how much were they expecting *me* to know? "All I've ever heard are rumors. I'm guessing you're all hot and ready to enlighten us?"

For a moment Geri just looked at me, maybe trying to decide if he'd made a mistake in picking me for this scheme, whatever the hell it was. I held his gaze, staying quiet, watching Freki out of the corner of my eye. Both of his hands were visible, so if he went for a weapon I'd at least have some warning. Maybe only half a second, but it was better than nothing.

"You wouldn't be much use to us otherwise, I suppose," Geri said at last. "All right. Six years ago, a freighter named the *Icarus* left a planet called Meima and headed to Earth. It never made it."

"Lost?"

"Disappeared."

"Any idea where?"

Geri shrugged. "Somewhere in the Commonwealth, we think."

"Oh, yeah, *that's* helpful," I growled. "What are we up to now, two-hundred-odd inhabited systems?"

"It'll be exclusively human, with no significant alien presence," Geri said, ignoring the sarcasm. "That cuts the numbers down considerably. It'll probably also have a significant military presence, which means military supply lines and data trails."

"Theoretically, yes," I said. "Unfortunately, six years is more than enough time to set up a post from scratch, and not enough time to guarantee its existence will leak out to the Spiral at large."

"Do you always start a job sounding like you don't want it?" Freki asked softly. "Because we can still go back to Option One."

"It's not that we don't want the job," I explained patiently. "It's that the task your partner here has laid out is physically impossible. There are too many worlds, and *way* too much empty space between those worlds." I looked back at Geri. "Plus the fact that the price the Patth put on the ship had every bounty hunter in the Spiral on the lookout for it. If they couldn't find it then, we're not likely to find it now."

"I thought you didn't know anything about the *Icarus*," Geri said.

"I didn't think it was worth belaboring the obvious," I said. "So what was it carrying?"

Geri shook his head. "Irrelevant. Now—"

"Excuse me," I interrupted, folding my arms across my chest. "If you want me to find your missing ship, *I* get to decide what is or isn't relevant."

"We don't want you to find—" Geri broke off, throwing a glower at Freki before looking back at me. "Fine. The fact is, we don't know exactly what the *Icarus* was carrying. It had something to do with a supposedly revolutionary new stardrive, but whether it was just something that would boost a normal drive to be equal or better than the Talariac or something entirely new has never come to light."

"Hence, that other rumor," I said, nodding as a minor mystery from the past finally clicked.

"What other rumor?" Geri asked.

"The one you mentioned yourself a few days ago," I said. "The Patth plan to license their drive to other species and corporations who didn't want to have to hire Patth babysitters. I'm guessing they were worried about the *Icarus* stardrive and wanted to shore up their clientele before something new hit the market."

"Only it never did," Selene said.

"Which was why the plan was never more than a rumor," I agreed. "So if you don't want us to find the *Icarus*, what *do* you want us to find?"

Again, Geri and Freki exchanged looks. Then, Freki pulled a photo out of his pocket and pushed it across the table toward me. "This is one of the people we know was on the *Icarus*," he said. "We want you to find her."

The picture was that of a young woman: collar-length black hair, hazel eyes, lightly tanned in an outdoorsy sort of way. She was reasonably attractive, but there was a depth to her expression that suggested she was more than just a pretty face. "Nice-looking lady," I said, passing the photo to Selene. "What's her name?"

"We know her as Tera C," Freki said. "Last name unknown. We think she was the *Icarus*'s computer expert."

Definitely not just a pretty face, then. "It's nice when young people have careers," I said. "So how is finding a single human female supposed to be easier than finding a single missing ship?"

"Because she was seen three days ago in Havershem City on Pinnkus," Geri said.

I felt an unpleasant chill run up my back. Havershem City was *the* tourist and business destination for Pinnkus and most of that surrounding sector. But underneath the glitz it was about as corrupt a place as you could find anywhere. "What makes you think she's still there?" I asked, noting out of the corner of my eye that Selene was working at her pad.

"We don't," Geri said. "But that's where she was seen, so that's where you start."

"Okay," I said. "So to summarize. You want us to

find someone who *might* have been wandering around
a city of—" I looked at Selene and raised my eyebrows
in question.

"Eight million humans," she reported. "Three million aliens."

"—but who might or might not still be there," I
finished. "That about cover it?"

"Be thankful she's not still on Melayse," Geri said.
"The rat-holes there are just as crowded as Havershem
City and not nearly as civilized."

Civilized and *Havershem City*. Right. As my father
used to say, *Beware of people who put two words that
don't belong in the same breath together, whether it's
grammar or unhinged logic.* "I'm always grateful for
small favors," I said. "But it seems to me we've just
moved from the job of lifting a whale with our bare
hands to *only* lifting an elephant. It's progress, but it
doesn't make the job any less impossible."

Geri leaned back and gave me a thin smile. "Please,
Mr. Roarke. You don't seriously think we didn't check
your reputation before we hired you, do you?"

"You don't seriously think you can believe bounty
hunter reputations, do you?" I countered.

"Of course not," Geri said. "Why do you think
we ran that little test back on Xathru with the bank
checks and the Grumpfers?"

I felt my eyes narrow. "And then on Bonvere Seven
with the seeds."

"Exactly." Geri looked at Selene. "I presume you've
already determined that Freki was the other person
who touched those checks?"

"I don't know what you mean," Selene said, her
pupils showing uncertainly.

"It's okay," I told her. "It sounds like they already know."

"Thank you for not belaboring the obvious." Geri inclined his head to Selene. "You have a remarkable talent, Selene. Even better, a remarkably well-hidden one. I doubt more than one person in a billion has ever even heard of Kadolians, and only a few of those know how incredibly keen your sense of smell is. If anyone can pick up Tera C's trail on Pinnkus, it's you."

"A trail that's three days cold and still cooling," I reminded him.

Geri looked at Freki and gestured in invitation. "Freki?"

"I held the checks for one minute, a week before Geri handed them to you," the little man said. "If you can still smell my scent there, you won't have any trouble with Tera's."

"And as you said, the trail goes colder with every minute you sit here trying to weasel out of the job," Geri said. "So. We have a deal?"

I looked at Freki. Once again, he looked like he was deciding which part of me to break first. "I'm not a licensed bounty hunter anymore," I reminded them.

"I think you'll find you are," Geri said. He gestured, and Freki slid an envelope from inside his jacket and pushed it across the table to me. "Freki is quite good at cutting through bureaucratic paperwork."

"So I see," I said, opening the envelope and peering inside. The bounty hunter ID and license had my picture and all the pertinent data. Freki had even gone the extra mile and gotten Selene a hunter's assistant ID. "We'll also need traveling money."

"You won't need any," Geri said. "Besides, we've already been more than generous."

"I'm sure you think so," I said. "But I don't think you have any idea of the kind of costs a job like this can generate."

For a moment he just eyed me. Then, with a small shrug, he opened his wallet and pulled out three more ten-thousand-commark checks. "That's your up-front payment. Seven more of them when you hand her over to us."

"Sounds reasonable," I murmured as I put the checks away. Between the two payments, a total of a hundred thousand commarks. Whoever Geri and Freki worked for, he *really* wanted Tera C found. "I'm almost afraid to ask why we won't need traveling money."

"It's not that hard a concept," Geri assured me. "Obviously, you'll want that final payment as soon as possible. For our part, we don't want you to have to hold Tera any longer than necessary once you've caught her."

My stomach knotted. That was exactly where I was afraid this conversation was going. "You're already seen the *Ruth* has barely enough room for one extra person, let alone two."

"On the contrary," Geri said. "All we need to do is pull the exam table out of the clean room. There should be plenty of space on the deck for a roll-up bed." He nodded sideways at his partner. "Especially for someone of Freki's size."

"It's not open to negotiation," Freki added quietly.

"Oh, come on, don't look at us like that," Geri admonished me with another of his forced smiles. "A day to get there, a day or two tops to locate Tera, and you can settle back and take a well-earned rest. It'll be a simple moonlight walk."

"Shall we go?" Freki prompted.

A simple moonlight walk. I looked back and forth between them, my left arm aching in memory. Did they know the rest of the story? If they'd really checked us out, they surely knew what had happened five years ago, a year after *Icarus*'s disappearance, when Selene and I tried to collect on the bounty.

But even if they did, it was abundantly clear they didn't give a damn. "Sure," I said. "Whenever you're ready."

Removing the examination room table wasn't nearly as straightforward as Geri had seemed to think. There was a complete set of storage cabinets underneath it, and the contents of all those cabinets had to find homes elsewhere in the ship. The whole project took a couple of hours, which was probably a tenth of the time it would take later to put everything back together and bring it up to Trailblazer code.

But at this point, tables and cabinets and codes were the least of my concerns.

"Do you want to talk about it?" Selene asked when we were once again in hyperspace.

"Talk about what?" I asked.

"Whatever it is that's bothering you." She paused, and looking over at her I saw her nostrils flare twice as she sampled the air and my scent. "You're worried. You're fearful." She hesitated. "You're angry. Are you angry at me?"

"No, not at all," I assured her. "I'm never mad at you."

"But it has to do with me," she persisted. "I *know* it has something to do with me."

I turned back to my control board, feeling a fresh dose of old pain and anger swirling inside me, knowing that Selene was riding that same wave as my odor subtly changed in time with the turmoil.

What could I tell her? What *should* I tell her?

She didn't remember the last few hours of that day. As far as her memory was concerned, her life went straight from us heading out into the city to chase down our target to waking up in a hospital pod three days later with slowly healing holes from a pair of 3mm slugs in her left lung and a bad case of retrograde amnesia.

I'd been deliberately vague about the incident, mainly because the whole thing had been traumatic enough for her without piling on details that her brain had clearly tried to hide from her. In fact, I wasn't even sure she remembered who it was we'd been chasing.

But I remembered. The man's name was Jordan McKell, and he'd been one of the crew of the *Icarus*.

And now, one of his partners had surfaced. Tera C, the *Icarus*'s computer expert, was apparently strolling through Havershem City as if she didn't have a care in the world.

Geri and Freki were welcome to the *Icarus*. All I wanted was for Tera to lead me to McKell.

So I could kill him.

CHAPTER FOUR

—— ◆◆◆ ——

Pinnkus wasn't far from Ringbar, only a thirty-hour trip, probably the reason Geri and Freki had picked the latter as our rendezvous point in the first place. Following standard bounty hunter protocol, I transmitted my new credentials and my imminent arrival to the authorities as we headed in for a landing.

I was a bit concerned that Freki might have forgotten about the deep-record aspects of Commonwealth paperwork when he created my fake ID, and I had a couple of explanations ready in case I was called on it. But the accreditation went straight through without a hiccup, and the controller welcomed me to Pinnkus with about as much enthusiasm as bounty hunters were ever welcomed anywhere.

Not only did my new employers have money, they also apparently had some decent connections.

Most of the Spiral's major cities utilized a mixture of cabs and quick-rent runaround cars, trucks, and vans for citizens and visitors to use. Havershem City was somewhat unusual in that quick-rents constituted nearly the entire public transportation sector, with virtually no cabs anywhere.

The official explanation was that Pinnkus citizens *really* liked to drive themselves. Given Havershem City's reputation as a popular place for criminal organizations to make deals and hammer out disagreements, I was more inclined to assume it was so that there were no inquisitive cab drivers playing unwanted witness to the city's shadier activities.

Still, the needs of privacy notwithstanding, there were a fair number of surveillance cameras scattered through the metropolitan area, mostly at the edges of privately owned businesses. Freki's disclosure that Tera C had been seen in the city had been accompanied by a video clip from one of them, which meant we knew exactly where to start looking.

Where to start looking and, more importantly from our standpoint, where to start sniffing.

"Do you really think you can pick up her scent here?" Geri asked as he, Selene, and I worked our way through the pedestrians toward the taverno in the video clip.

"Your own video shows she was here," I reminded him. "Unless Freki's able to find another shot of her elsewhere, this is where we start."

"Right, but that was several days ago," Geri reminded me. "Even on Pinnkus the tavernos wash the tableware and napkins and scrub down the tables more often than that."

"But they probably don't clean the chairs," I said. "A single brush of her hand against the leg of the chair she was sitting on, and we'll have her."

He pondered that one a moment. "Except that our only shot shows her outside the place," he said. "We don't have anything from inside, so we don't know where she was sitting."

"See, that's why we're the professionals and you're just the one with the money," I said, smiling at Selene. We'd already come up with our jump-off plan, one that fortunately didn't involve any chair leg guesswork.

But sometimes stealth was part of the job, and Geri didn't strike me as the stealthy type. The more we could keep him out of the loop, the better.

"Right. The professionals." Geri snorted. "So why are we *really* here? Don't give me that crap about getting a scent off some damn chair leg. No one on the run is going to come back to the same taverno just because she likes the appetizers."

"Actually, that's not the case," I told him. "Targets often fall into patterns without realizing they're doing it. Plus, we don't know that she *is* on the run."

"With a six-year-old bounty on her head?" Geri asked pointedly. "Either she's on the run, or she's abysmally stupid."

"Or she came here looking for something," Selene offered.

"Like what?"

"Who knows?" I said. "Maybe they came through here six years ago and lost or hid something important. Maybe they met someone here and Tera's trying to reestablish contact."

"The *Icarus* never came anywhere near Pinnkus."

"How do you know?" I countered. "You said the ship disappeared. It could have done a six-week grand farewell tour of the Spiral, complete with synchronized cartwheels, for all you know." I pointed to the small awning and the four outside tables just ahead. "Here we are."

Freki's video had only shown a bit of the taverno's exterior, which hadn't looked all that impressive, and seeing the whole façade didn't improve my assessment of the place very much. The door was serviceable but nothing special, though it looked like it could take a pretty good impact without breaking. The white-brick walls on either side were mostly intact, though some of the bricks closest to the door had clearly taken a stray shot or two over the years. Two of the outside tables were occupied by couples, and I could hear enough conversational buzz drifting through the open door to suggest there were also a fair number of patrons inside.

"Selene's going to wait out here while you and I make sure it's safe," I told Geri. I stepped into the doorway—

And braked to a sudden stop as Selene grabbed my arm. "Fear," she whispered urgently in my ear. "There's fear in there. Terrible fear."

I peered into the taverno's gloomy interior. As my eyes adjusted from the bright sunlight outside, I could make out a dozen or more figures gathered together around a table near the taverno's center. Farther out toward the edges were a few more figures, apparently uninterested in whatever the big attraction was in the middle. "Human?" I whispered back.

I heard the subtle sounds of fluttering nostrils as she sniffed at the air. "Ulkomaals," she said. "One male, one female. It's overwhelming everything else. I'm sorry."

"That's okay," I assured her. "Surprises can be fun, too."

"Are we going in, or aren't we?" Geri growled from behind me.

"We're going in," I said, gently unwrapping Selene's fingers from my arm and giving her an equally gentle push out of the doorway. Her job was out here.

Mine, apparently, was in there. Making sure my Fafnir 4 plasmic was riding loose in its holster, I walked inside.

I'd seen the people gathered around the table from the door. What I hadn't seen until I was a few steps inside was that the table itself was only occupied by two men, facing each other from opposite sides with a deck of cards and a mess of poker chips in the middle. Seated midway around one side of the table and about a meter back from it was a pair of Ulkomaals, the male and female Selene had identified, their hands clasped tightly together. As I moved closer, I saw the dull white of plastic restraints connecting their wrists.

Prisoners, in other words. Not all that surprising for a place like Havershem City. Neither of the poker players was wearing a uniform or a security company badge or armband, which probably made them bounty hunters.

So why had they paused in the middle of delivering a package to play cards?

One of the men standing between me and the table was wearing a very familiar jacket. I angled to the side until I could see enough of his profile to be sure it was really him. It was.

Damn.

But I needed information, and he was the most likely source. "Hey, Jasper," I greeted him as I stepped casually to his side.

He looked at me, the dramatic frown he liked to give strangers to prove he was a serious badass dissolving into wide-eyed disbelief. *"Roarke?"* he demanded. His eyes dropped briefly to my left arm, then came back to my face. "You—I heard you were *dead.*"

"Nice to see you, too," I said. "Who told you that?"

"I—well—everyone." His eyes flicked to the door, paused for a second look as he presumably caught sight of my new shadow. "Your new partner?"

"My new employer," I corrected. "What's going on?"

Jasper looked back at the card game as if resetting his brain. "Right. Okay. On the left is Boff. He caught those two Ulkomaals you can see straight back from the table."

"Yeah, they're not hard to pick out of the crowd," I said. "What were they wanted for?"

"Escaped house slaves," Jasper said. "They were trying to get to Buulviv. That's their City of Refuge on Pinnkus."

I nodded. Every Ulko enclave throughout the Spiral had a City of Refuge where Ulkomaals could petition for a judicial hearing before the local elders. Until that petition was heard and adjudicated, no other species or governmental authorities could interfere. "Do they have a case?"

Jasper shrugged. "Don't know. Don't care. On the right is Oberon. You may have heard of him."

I winced. Every bounty hunter in the Spiral had heard of Oberon. His specialty was recruiting participants for the death matches so dearly beloved by some of the nastier criminal kingpins. The badgemen had been after him for years, but he'd always managed to stay just far enough inside the law that no one had been able to take him down. The fact that a lot of his clients were aliens who operated under vastly different legal structures than the Commonwealth didn't help.

Luko Varsi, I knew, also had a hand in some of those operations. Yet another good reason for us to hate working for him. "Let me guess," I said. "He's trying to steal the Ulkomaals from Boff?"

"He's trying to *buy* them," Jasper said, as if that was an important distinction. I doubt it mattered much to the Ulkomaals. "Boff's one of those hunters"—he sent me a significant look—"who gives, you know, half a damn about the packages he picks up."

"Like me?"

His lip twitched. Apparently, I wasn't supposed to have picked up on the look he'd given me. "Yeah, something like you," he said. "Or maybe he just cares about his reputation. Anyway, he didn't want to sell. Oberon offered to play him a little poker—loser gets the pot, winner gets the Ulkomaals."

I peered at the table. Between the players' stacks and the scattering in the current pot, there were a *lot* of chips out there. "Any idea what the table stakes are?"

"About ten thousand more than the bounty on the happy couple," Jasper said. "Why, you thinking about getting into the game?"

I smiled. With ten thousand in my wallet and another fifty thousand or so back at the *Ruth*, getting into a high-stakes game was actually possible for once.

But doing a head-to-head against a man like Oberon was never a good idea. Especially when there were better ways. "Whose deck are they playing with?" I asked.

Jasper frowned at me. "Why?"

"Whose deck?" I repeated.

"The bartender had one," he said, still frowning. "I hope you're not thinking of trying something stupid."

"I thought you liked watching people get hurt."

"Not when Oberon's involved," he said. "Especially not when I'm in the line of fire."

"There's the door," I said, pointing past Geri. "See you around."

I'd gotten three steps toward the table when a heavy hand on my right shoulder brought me to a stop. "What do you think you're doing?" Geri growled in my ear. "Focus on the prize. Tera's not here, so let's go."

"Right behind you," I said, reaching up with my other hand and digging at his grip. The artificial fingers were purported to be five to ten percent stronger than the ones they'd replaced, but even so I found myself not making a single iota of headway against him. "Three minutes," I promised. "If it doesn't happen by then, it's not going to."

For another moment he didn't move. Then, reluctantly, he loosened his grip. "Three minutes," he agreed. "And don't expect me to back you up."

"Wouldn't think of it," I assured him. I stepped forward, stopping at the inner ring of the observers.

For a minute I just watched, gauging the players' expressions and body language and getting a feel for the intensity of the play. Boff was the cooler of the two, playing with his head instead of his emotions, while Oberon seemed to be putting more of his ego into the game.

Something brushed against my foot. I looked down, catching a glimpse of an animal as it scampered under the edge of the table. I was just regretting not getting a better look when it unwittingly solved my problem by hopping onto the chair beside Boff and then up onto the table. For a second it seemed to be considering what to do, and then skittered to the edge of the table closest to the Ulkomaals, where some previous customer had abandoned a small plate half filled with crunch nuts. Hunching up on its haunches, it dug in.

I squinted, trying to figure out just what it was. It was furry, bigger than a rat and only slightly smaller than a ferret, with small but dexterous paws. It looked too well-groomed to be a stray or some breed of local vermin. Possibly someone's pet, then. Boff had glanced over when it first arrived on the table, but had returned his attention to his cards without further reaction. Oberon ignored the creature completely.

So had all the rest of the people watching the game, as far as I could tell. Either they all knew the animal, or else knew enough about the species not to worry about it.

Or, rather, worry about *them*. Even as I finished my brief visual once-over a second animal hopped up on the table from Oberon's side. For a moment they faced off over the crunch nuts, as if deciding which one had squatter's rights to the treats, and then the newcomer made an impressive leap off the table onto the Ulkomaals' combined lap. The winner shifted position, swiveling its body around to the far side of the plate, probably with the objective of blocking any new attempts by the second ferret to hop back and take another crack at the crunch nuts.

The hand ended, the pot going to Oberon. Boff collected the cards and shuffled, Oberon cut, and Boff dealt the next hand. If this hand and pot were representative of the game as a whole, I estimated they could be at it for another hour before the matter was resolved.

Unfortunately, I only had three minutes.

I waited until they'd gone through the initial bet-and-call phase, drawn their replacement cards, and settled into the serious art of betting. Then, taking a deep breath, I left the circle of observers and started toward the table. As I walked, I casually put my hands together in front of me and gave my left thumbnail a gentle double stroke with my right thumb.

Both players looked at me as I walked up to them. "You have a problem, bubbo?" Oberon growled, glaring at me from under bushy eyebrows.

"No, not at all," I assured him, flicking a glance at Boff. He seemed more bemused than irritated by my sudden audacity, about the same reaction he'd showed toward the ferret that had hopped up beside him a minute ago. The initial betting had been brisk, I'd already noted, and from my new perspective I could estimate that maybe a quarter of the table's total number of chips were currently in the pot.

An important hand for both of them, then. Perfect. "Just go on with what you were doing," I continued. "I'm just curious." Coming to a halt, I rested my left hand casually on the edge of the table, palm down, then picked up one of Boff's two discards with my right hand and peered at its back.

I hadn't gone in for one of the fancy weaponized arms that Geri had talked about earlier, the ones with concealed knives or plasmics. But I *had* added a couple of modifications that I'd figured would be useful if and when I decided to return to the bounty hunter life. Since one of the highest casualty rates in the profession stemmed from unwarily stepping around corners, I'd put in a thumbnail that could be transformed into a mirror.

It was also quite serviceable for reading the faces of cards turned toward it. The six of diamonds I was holding, for instance.

I nodded, as if to myself, and set the card back onto the table. Picking up Boff's other discard—this one the three of spades—I looked at the back and did the nodding thing again, this time adding a sort of under-the-breath *uh-huh*. I set the card on top of the other, smiled genially at the two players, and started to turn away.

And froze at the familiar sound of a gun being drawn from a holster. "Freeze," Oberon said softly.

Make that *two* guns being drawn, I mentally corrected myself as I heard a similar sound from Boff's side of the table. "Easy, gentlemen," I cautioned, holding my hands chest high where both of the players could see them, also making sure the left thumbnail was pointed straight at the ceiling where no one could see its reflectivity. It was designed to look mostly opaque except from straight on, but this was no time to take unnecessary chances. "I was just curious about whether or not the cards were marked."

"They're not," Oberon growled. "So get out of here."

"Sure," I said. I took a step— "But they *are*, you know," I added over my shoulder.

"Stop," Boff said, his voice *very* soft. "Who are you?"

"Name's Gregory Roarke," I said.

"Really," Boff said. "I've heard of you. Also heard you'd retired."

I shrugged. "It didn't take."

Boff snorted gently. "Does it ever? Turn around."

I turned back to face them, still keeping my hands up. Both were pointing guns at me, all right, Oberon with a Golden 6mm, Boff with a Victori plasmic. With his free hand, Boff cut the deck and slid off the top card. "What is it?"

I picked it up, again setting my left hand where the thumbnail could catch the reflection. "Nine of clubs," I said, holding it up where the two players could see it. I glanced over the top of the card—

And felt my breath catch in my throat. On the far side of the table, past the ferret that was nibbling on the crunch nuts and partially blocking the players' view, I saw that the second ferret was still nestled in the Ulkomaals' combined lap.

Chewing industriously on the plastic restraints holding the two aliens' wrists together.

It made no sense. None. I'd used those restraints dozens of times in my years of securing prisoners, and while I'd never tried licking or biting one of them I didn't believe for a single second that the plastic could possibly taste good. Not even to street animals, where the need to scrounge questionable food encouraged lowered gastric standards.

But it was happening. The ferret was gnawing away, its relatively tiny mouth and teeth able to bite into the plastic without shredding the neighboring skin the way a prisoner's own teeth certainly would.

"This one," Boff said, sliding another card off the deck.

I snapped my attention back to him. "Sure," I said. I reached over to pick it up—

And stopped short as Oberon wrapped his fingers around my wrist. "Enough," he said. "I don't know what your game is, but it's over. Chucks?"

"Yeah, boss?" one of the onlookers standing behind him replied, taking a step forward.

"Take this hopper outside," Oberon said. "Explain to him why interrupting me is a bad idea."

"Sure, boss." Smiling unpleasantly, Chucks drew his own gun and took another step forward—

"No, let's explain instead why rigged games are an even worse idea," an authoritative voice came from directly behind me.

I turned. Geri was standing there, straight and tall, his whole muscular bulk poised defiantly against the two weapons still pointed at me. Unfortunately, all that muscle wouldn't do a damn bit of good against a plasmic and a 6mm.

Fortunately, the gold InterSpiral Law Enforcement badge displayed in his hand would.

I looked at his face, my brain trying to wrap around this new development. Were Geri and Freki really...?

No, of course they weren't. The badge was a phony, the authoritative voice a carefully constructed affectation, the whole scene nothing but a last-second plan to extricate their tame bounty hunter before I lost another limb. Or worse.

Only now Geri had stepped *way* over the line. Impersonating an ISLE officer was a serious felony. Even worse, on a world with as much organized crime as Pinnkus, faking official credentials without having any official authority or backup could be quickly fatal.

"So here's what you're going to do," Geri continued into the crowd's sudden silence. "You're going to split the money back to the two of you, back to whatever the situation was before you came in here. Got it?" He gestured with the badge. "Oh, and you're going to start by putting those guns away. Do it fast enough and I'll forget to run your permits."

Boff and Oberon looked across the table at each other. Then, with the strained grace of men who don't have much choice, they returned their weapons to their holsters and started counting their chips. It was all over, or nearly so.

There was only one problem. The ferret chewing on the Ulkomaals' wrist restraints hadn't finished.

"That's fine," I said, raising my voice. "Officer," I belatedly remembered to add. "But I, for one, would like to know exactly how a marked deck got into this game in the first place." I turned, putting my back to the table, and pointed toward the bar at the far end of the room. "You—bartender—where did those cards come from?"

The look on Geri's face was priceless, though I probably would have found it far more entertaining if I hadn't been the one it was directed toward. He'd had the situation wrapped up in a neat bow, and now here I was threatening to open it back up again.

And not just the wager, but also the temporary and probably unstable inactivity the crowd had been forced into. A number of these patrons were probably locals, and if they thought the staff had taken sides in a bounty hunter confrontation there could be unpleasant consequences.

But I needed to buy the ferret some time. Oberon wasn't going to give up on throwing the Ulkomaals into a death-combat cage just because some badgeman had told him to. One way or another, he'd get the aliens away from Boff. Unless they got out of here right now, they were dead.

"They came from the bar," someone spoke up. "The bartender—that one there—he got the deck from under the bar."

"Dani brought it over," someone else said, pointing to a large woman in an apron with tired eyes and a defiant set to her mouth. "She brought the chips, too."

"I didn't do anything," Dani protested. "Louie gave me the cards. I just delivered them."

But it was too late. The crowd was stirring, the unpleasant mutterings starting to become louder and more focused. I had the impression Dani wasn't one of the taverno's favorite servers, possibly with the kind of attitude or smart mouth—or even just a steadfast refusal to be dumped on or hit on by the customers—that encouraged people to think the worst of her.

And now, too late, I realized that freeing the Ulkomaals at the cost of endangering an innocent bartender and server was nowhere near the high moral ground I thought I'd been occupying.

Some of the customers were starting to get to their feet now even as the group surrounding the card table began moving toward the bar. The crowd was getting ugly, and it was up to me to stop them, however I had to do it. I opened my mouth, ignoring the warning look on Geri's face—

"No," a deep, cultured voice cut through the rising din.

I turned toward the voice. Seated alone at a table near the bar was a squat, broad-shouldered creature with a sort of squashed lizard face. A Kalix, I tentatively identified him, though I'd never actually met one. A reasonable enough species, if I remembered correctly, though not above shady activities like smuggling or bounty hunting.

The crowd's advance seemed to falter a little. "Neither is to blame," the Kalix continued. "After the human male set the card box on the bar, but before the human female picked it up, another human male took the box and replaced it with another."

"Sure he did," someone said scornfully. "And you're just saying something *now*?"

"I do not know all the customs of humans," he said. "In Kalixiri card games, the dealer discards the first two cards before dealing. I thought perhaps humans discarded the entire deck."

"Don't be stupid," the same voice bit out.

"What did he look like?" someone else asked.

The Kalix shrugged. "He was human," he said, sounding embarrassed. "Beyond that, I cannot say. Sadly, all of you look alike to me. I only know he immediately exited the establishment."

Someone snarled something derogatory. A couple of others flung curses or insults at the alien.

But the situation had been defused. With no clear target for their anger and bloodlust, the crowd reluctantly started to dissipate back to their chairs.

I looked back at the table. Boff and Oberon were still sorting through the chips, both clearly intent on making sure neither of the others swiped more than his fair share from the pot. The two ferrets were nowhere to be seen.

Neither were the Ulkomaals.

I turned to Geri. His eyes were hard, his expression

that of someone who would gladly forego the money he'd already paid out in exchange for the satisfaction of bouncing me a few times off the taverno's brick wall. "That went well," I said.

Geri's eyes flicked back over my shoulder toward the two bounty hunters and the Ulkomaals' empty chairs then returned to me. "You pull something like that again," he warned softly, "and I mean *ever* again, and I will cut you into small pieces and feed you to the street rats. Do I make myself clear?"

"Completely," I assured him, feeling a shiver run up my back. So, even angrier than just ready to bounce me off a wall. Good to know. "Though if you do that, you won't ever get a line on Tera."

He snorted. "I don't have a line on her *now*."

"Of course you do," I said. "Come on—Selene's probably already halfway to her place by now."

We made our way to the door...and as we reached it something made me look back at the table where the Kalix was sitting.

Just in time to see the two ferrets hop up on the table and scamper up his arms, where one of them settled comfortably on each shoulder. The alien spotted me looking at him, and I could swear he gave me a microscopic nod.

And then we were outside, and Geri was looking around. "So?" he demanded. "Where is she?"

"No idea," I said, pulling out my phone. "Let's find out."

CHAPTER FIVE

—❖—

Selene, as it turned out, had only made it half a block away. But that distance represented a satisfying degree of progress.

"She touched the wall outside the taverno four times after leaving," she explained when Geri and I were once again with her. "I got a good sense of her odor."

"So you'll be able to track her?" I asked.

"Assuming it hasn't been too long since she's been through this area, yes."

"Wait a minute," Geri put in. "When did she touch the wall?"

"It's on the video you showed us," I said, frowning. I'd seen Tera touch the wall once, just as she walked out of range of the camera, which was why I'd left Selene out here while I took Geri into the taverno on a wild goose chase.

But *four* times? Why would Tera have touched the wall that many times?

The only thing I could think of was that she was fighting to keep her balance. But she hadn't looked drunk or even tipsy on the video. Drugged, maybe? "Selene, how close together were the touches?" I asked.

"Very close," Selene said, her pupils giving me a frown. "Perhaps half a meter apart."

"Like she was leaving a trail?" Geri asked.

"For who?" I countered. "She couldn't possibly know a Kadolian was going to be on the hunt."

"There are other scent detectors," Selene said.

"Not nearly as good at the job as you are."

"Doesn't matter," Geri said, suddenly sounding impatient. "Certainly not worth wasting time on." Which was rather unfair of him, considering he was the one who'd brought up the subject of a trail in the first place. "You said you can track her. Fine. Start tracking."

Selene looked at me, her pupils framing a silent question. "You heard the man," I said with a sigh. "Let's do it."

We set off down the walkway, staying close to the storefront walls along the side where the scent that came off Tera as she passed would be more likely to linger. The street we were on was a major thoroughfare, with vehicular traffic and bustling pedestrians sweeping past us in both directions, and Selene didn't buy herself much good will with her habit of stopping every few steps for a closer examination of the walls before continuing on. A couple of times she stopped dead and dropped to her knees to check out a crack in the pavement, and it required quick deflection work from Geri and me to keep her from causing a citizen pileup. That stunt made her—and us—even less popular.

We reached the first cross street, more of a wide alley than an actual street, and she turned that direction for a few steps, again checking the walls and the walkway. Reversing direction, she took us back across the intersection to the other branch of the side street and repeated the process, sampling the mix of aromas on that side before deciding Tera had stayed with the main avenue.

We crossed back to our original side and continued on. At the next intersection—this street was a little wider and better traveled than the last one—she went through the same routine before continuing on along our original path.

Through it all Geri's attitude fluctuated between curious, impatient, disbelieving, and suspicious. For once, though, at least the glowering came wrapped in a blanket of silence. It was a nice change from his usual, more verbal expressions of curiosity, impatience, disbelief, or suspicion.

We'd reached the third intersection, and Selene was doing her round-the-corner survey, when one of my casual look-arounds caught something new. Half a block away from the intersection, the other direction along the cross street Selene was currently testing, was Jasper. He was standing in front of a restaurant façade, pretending to look at their menu post, but I could tell by the angle of his head and face that he was actually and very surreptitiously peering down the street in our direction.

Given how slow our progress had been since leaving the taverno, it was highly unlikely he'd been traveling at that same halting speed. That made it pretty obvious that Selene, Geri, and I were the current focus of his attention.

Unless it wasn't us he was watching, but someone behind us.

I turned back around, looking past Selene at the clumps of people farther down the street. There were three open-air cafés in the next two blocks, each one hosting a scattering of patrons lounging at the tables with drinks or small snack plates. A few loiterers stood clear of the pedestrian traffic, some of them peering at info pads, others chatting idly with each other, others just leaning against the walls and presumably contemplating humanity's place in the universe.

But no matter how casual they all looked, I could tell every single one of them was paying close attention to what was going on around them. Their eyes drifted across the windows of the apartments above the cafés and shops, coming back down again to linger on everyone who walked or drove past them.

I hissed out a breath. No, they weren't looking at *everyone*. Just the women.

They were looking for Tera.

I stepped up close behind Selene, casually confirming first that Geri was waiting for us back at the intersection and out of earshot. "You okay?" I asked quietly. "Do you need a break?"

"No, I'm fine," she assured me. "I think this is where we need to turn."

"I don't think that would be a good idea right now," I said. "So we're going to turn around, and you'll tell Geri we need to keep going straight."

It had been a long time since Selene and I had been professional bounty hunters. Even so, she still remembered how to not react visibly when I dropped something unexpected on her. "Trouble?" she murmured.

"Could be," I said. Of course, the fact that Kadolians didn't go in much for facial expression or body language made that lack of reaction a lot easier for her to pull off. "We can check out this area later."

"Okay." She knelt down and sniffed at the pavement a moment, making it look good. Then, she stood up again and we headed back together toward Geri. As we walked, I saw that Jasper had abandoned his pretend menu survey and was apparently talking to some unseen person standing out of my view in the doorway.

I didn't know Jasper all that well. But I *did* recognize his current posture as the subservient body language of someone talking to their boss or someone equally important.

And finding out who Jasper was working for would probably be worth a little extra exercise. "Change in plans," I told Selene. "We're going to cross the street and head up the other side. There's someone up that way I want to check out."

"All right." She craned her neck. "Is that *Jasper*?"

"Yes, and he was also in the taverno," I told her. "I want to find out what he's doing here. Havershem City in general; this street in particular."

"I'd almost forgotten his scent," she muttered.

"I'd like to forget everything about him," I said sourly. "The man's always been a pain in the butt."

"Well?" Geri asked as we once again joined him.

"Nothing there," I told him. "We'll try up the other way."

"Really?" Geri asked, his eyes narrowing slightly.

"Really," I confirmed, frowning at his reaction. "Why?"

He nodded behind us. "Sure looks like a stakeout

going on down there." He nodded his head back in Jasper's direction. "Not so much on that side."

"Interesting logic," I said. "But as my father used to say, *If fifty million people believe a foolish thing, it's still a foolish thing.*"

"You're saying all those other people are wrong?"

"I wouldn't dream of impugning the abilities of my fellow bounty hunters," I assured him. "If you want to go join the crowd, be my guest." I gave him my best cheerful smile, took Selene's arm, and headed across the intersection.

We were barely halfway across when Geri caught up with us. "This had better be good," he warned. "His name's Jasper, right?"

I winced. Geri didn't miss much. "Yes," I said. "Let's find out what he's doing here."

Jasper was still having his one-sided conversation. So far he didn't seem to have noticed us bearing down on him among the other pedestrians, but I knew that wouldn't last long. I picked up my pace, hoping to get a look of the mystery man before he slipped back out of sight.

We were fifteen paces from Jasper when I saw the sudden tension that meant we'd been spotted. His lips moved one last time and then stopped, and I had the impression he was getting instructions from his still unseen conversational partner. We were almost in sight of the doorway—

"Excuse me?" a voice came from behind us.

It was a voice I'd only heard once. I'd never expected to hear it again, and with a tantalizing mystery hanging like low fruit in front of me I didn't want to hear it now. I caught Selene's upper arm and kept walking, hoping

I could pretend long enough that I hadn't heard him to take the last few steps I needed...

A hand fell on my shoulder, not hard enough to forcibly stop me but hard enough to put an end to my oblivious act. Swearing under my breath, I stopped and turned around.

It was the Kalix from the taverno, his two pet ferrets still crouched on his shoulders like gargoyles on some neo-Gothic mansion. He snatched back his hand as I turned, perhaps suddenly realizing the gesture might have been taken as a threat or, worse, a rudeness. "What?" I snapped.

"Forgive my presumption," he said, shrinking back from my tone. "But I was in the taverno and saw your InterSpiral badges—"

"Not me—him," I interrupted, jerking a thumb at Geri. The last thing I needed right now was for someone on a public street to suggest I'd been impersonating a badgeman.

"—and there is someone who appears—" The Kalix broke off, looking back and forth between us. "Oh. Yes. I see now. My apologies." He made a show of turning toward Geri. "An acquaintance of mine is in danger," he said. "I hoped you could offer assistance."

"I'm sorry, but we're on special assignment," Geri said, surface politeness mixed with an undercoating of impatience. "You need to call the local badgemen."

"But this particular young woman is afraid of the locals," the Kalix objected.

Geri had started to turn back toward Jasper. Now, abruptly, he reversed direction. "A young woman?" he echoed, digging into his inside jacket pocket. "What does she look like?"

"She looks human," the Kalix said. "I don't...human faces are difficult to distinguish between."

"Was her hair black?" I pointed to my jacket. "This color."

"I understand the meaning of *black*," the Kalix said, a little stiffly. "Yes, her hair was that color."

"Did she look like this?" Geri said, producing the picture of Tera C he'd showed me.

The Kalix took the picture and frowned at it.

Selene plucked at my sleeve. "Gregory, he's here," she said urgently.

"Who?"

"Mr. Varsi," she said. "He's here. He's very close."

In a star-thriller that would be the cue for a sudden startled reaction, or at least a dramatic narrowing of the eyes. I passed on both options in favor of keeping my face expressionless. If Selene was right...

Of course she was right. There were plenty of times when she couldn't identify a particular scent, or lost one that had been buried under a hundred others. But when she made a positive identification she was always on target.

What the hell was the head of a drug cartel from Xathru doing on Pinnkus?

Xathru was Varsi's home. That was where he always was when we brought back some exotic seed or spore that Selene thought might form the basis for some new drug that Varsi's organization could exploit. In the three years we'd been working for him he'd never mentioned traveling anywhere off-world.

The Kalix was still studying Tera's picture. Keeping my movements casual, I gave my left thumbnail the double stroke that would turn it into a mirror and then lifted my left hand to my face to rub at a pretend itch on my forehead. With the thumbnail now in front of my right eye, I focused on Jasper. Now that our backs were turned, maybe his mystery conversationalist would risk a quick peek out of his sheltered position.

He did. And Selene was right.

It was Varsi.

I stared at his image, trying to figure it out. I'd registered with the Pinnkus authorities on our way in, but even if someone there had tagged my name and sent word to Xathru, Varsi couldn't possibly have made it all the way here in that time. Clearly, he'd known somehow that the *Ruth* was coming here and that we'd collected some promising seeds for him. But that made even less sense.

Unless he'd been tipped off before we arrived at Pinnkus.

I looked sideways at Geri. I'd assumed he and Freki were on their own, or maybe hunting for the *Icarus* on behalf of some government or private patron. The possibility that they might be working with Varsi's organization had never occurred to me.

"I don't know," the Kalix conceded, tapping the photo with a large finger. "The hair is the same color. But the face . . . I don't know. But it could be her. Does this female fear for her life?"

"Yes, very much," Geri said, taking the picture back and putting it away.

"Then they may indeed be one and the same," the Kalix concluded.

"Glad you agree," Geri said, not bothering to hide his sarcasm. It would have been a waste of time anyway—if human faces were a mystery to the Kalix, verbal nuances probably were, too. "Can you take us to her?"

"Yes, of course," the Kalix said. "She's near the spaceport. We shall need to find a cab or a runaround if we're to arrive before—"

And right in the middle of his sentence all hell broke loose.

The only warning was the faint, high-pitched shriek of a descending mortar shell. Reflexively, I dropped into a crouch, yanking my plasmic from its holster and attempting to do a complete three-sixty scan without twisting my neck off. Out of the corner of my eye I spotted three objects dropping toward the stakeout gang stationed in and around the cafés on the far side of the main thoroughfare and turned to face them.

The stakeout gang had spotted the attack, too. Most of them were already on the move, some diving for the minimal safety of the tables, others trying to reach the more substantial cover of nearby doorways, others just hitting the ground where they stood and hoping for the best. Two of them were fast enough to draw down on the falling objects, firing what looked to be 6mm sniper pistols into the sky. One of the shots actually connected, bouncing the target shell a meter sideways like it had been kicked by an invisible boot. An instant later, the objects hit the ground—

And that whole section of street erupted in billowing clouds of white smoke.

The Kalix gave a startled little squeak. "Oh, my!" he exclaimed, grabbing my wrist in one hand and Selene's in the other. "Come, please—we must hurry. A runaround—where's a runaround?"

"Stay put!" Geri snarled. He had a weapon in his hand now, too, not the breakaway dart gun I'd found in his luggage aboard the *Ruth*, but a muted black Libra 3mm semiauto. He turned to look at the line of cars parked along the curb beside us, his free hand digging into his jacket pocket.

With the cacophony of panic shouts from down the street filling the air, I never even heard the whistling of the mortar shell that slammed to the pavement no more than ten meters away from us.

The Kalix shrieked as the white smoke exploded outward, a longer version of the high-pitched squeak he'd made when the first bombs had started falling the next block over. "We are attacked!" he shouted. "We are attacked!"

"Don't panic," Geri ordered, turning a brief warning glare at the three of us. "Just stay there." He turned back toward the line of parked cars, gun still in hand, and disappeared into the smoke.

"Gregory?" Selene asked, her voice shaking.

"It's all right," I said, trying to calm the sudden pounding of my own heart. The cloud was moving way too fast to outrun, even if there hadn't been another batch of the stuff already flowing toward us from the opposite direction. All we could do was stand our ground and cross our fingers. "You can hear them still shouting, right? Not screaming or gasping for breath, just shouting. This stuff isn't poisonous—it's just designed to keep people from seeing what's happening."

"I understand," she said in a small voice.

"So just relax," I said, wishing I could do the same. The leading edge of the cloud was nearly on us; taking a deep breath, I held it as the smoke rolled over us and the street was swallowed up in white haze.

The breath-holding was pure reflex—I knew I couldn't maintain it long enough for the cloud to dissipate. More to the point, gas weapons like this were specifically designed to circumvent that tactic. A bit of the gas snuck into my nostrils, bringing with it an aroma of carbonized sugar.

And as it did so, I felt some of my tension disappear into a sense of relief. I knew that smell, and I'd been right: the fog was indeed of the nonlethal, non-incapacitating sort. Slow, steady breaths were the key to making sure enough oxygen got into the lungs. I opened my mouth to reassure Selene and coach her in the necessary breathing pattern—

The shouts of frightened and confused pedestrians were erupting from inside our part of the cloud when Selene gave a heart-wrenching, gasping scream.

"What is it?" the Kalix demanded, his own voice none too calm. "Is she hurt?"

"It's the smell," I bit out, cursing myself for not anticipating this. Burnt sugar might bring most people pleasant memories of crème brûlée, but the sheer intensity of the aroma was hitting Selene like a brick to the face. "We have to get her to the ship and the clean room."

"The what?"

"The—never mind," I said. His hand was still gripping my wrist; shaking it off, I pulled Selene away from him and wrapped my arms around her to try to steady her shaking body. "Geri knows where it is. The fans and air filters will help clear her lungs and clean off any residue."

"But there's no runaround," the Kalix protested. "How do we get her to your ship?"

"Here!" Geri called out of the blank whiteness, and I felt the puff of stirred air as a car door swung open toward me. "Come on—I've got us a van."

I didn't pause to wonder how he'd gotten into a presumably locked vehicle. I shifted to a one-armed grip around Selene's shoulders and headed toward his voice, my other hand waving blindly in front of me. Four steps into my run my palm slammed into something hard, which a couple of exploratory taps confirmed was an open door. I got to the proper side of it, now waving my hand up and down, and two steps later found the top of the doorway. "In here," I said, putting one hand on each of Selene's shoulders and guiding her through the doorway into the van. "Kalix?"

"I'm here," the alien said, and I felt a second puff of air as he opened the door in front of ours. Selene's shoulders shifted in my grip as she got her hands on the seat backs and pulled herself inside—

And without warning a fumbling hand found my upper left arm, closed tightly around it, and yanked me backward.

"Go!" I shouted toward Geri. Using my last bit of distance and leverage I caught the edge of the door with my right hand and slammed it shut, hoping desperately that I hadn't caught Selene's arm or foot. A second hand found my right arm. I had just enough distance left to deliver a double toe-kick to the door with my right foot as I was pulled away. Geri must have gotten the message, because even as I was dragged backward and the cloud swirled with fresh bodies charging toward the van I heard it screech away from the curb and roar off into the smoke.

Selene was safe, or at least as safe as I could make her under the circumstances. Me, not so much.

But I still had one slender chance to remedy that. Mentally crossing my fingers, I let my knees buckle, collapsing my legs out from under me.

A pair of average street assailants probably would have been taken by surprise enough to lose their grip on my arms. This pair weren't average, or else they knew that if I broke free in the middle of all this smoke I'd be making tracks elsewhere before they could ever find me again.

Still, just because they were strong enough to maintain their hold didn't mean they were strong enough to catch my weight and suspend me in midair, at least not when that sudden weight had been handed to them without warning. My buckled knees sent me butt-first toward the ground, forcing them to bend toward me as they followed me down.

And as my rear hit the ground, I leaned backward, lifted both legs, and swung them as hard as I could toward the unseen bodies now towering over me.

Without knowing which direction the two men were facing I had no way of knowing whether my slashing feet would land on their heads or shoulders. From the feel of the impacts, I guessed it was one of each. But all that really mattered was that my counterattack jarred both grips loose. Half a second later I'd rolled over onto my stomach, shoved myself up into a hunched-over vertical, and headed as fast as I dared toward the street.

A smart man in my position would probably have

bet on the traffic out there having ground to a halt, sprinted across the street, and tried to disappear into the surrounding buildings before the smoke cleared. But I'd seldom been accused of being smart. More than that, assuming it was a set of Varsi's goons who'd just tried to grab me, maybe some judicious eavesdropping would give me a clue as to what he was doing here.

Still, not being smart enough to run away didn't mean I was stupid enough to just find a car hood to sit on. At the very least, the two I'd just kicked would want some degree of retribution for their pain and suffering.

Fortunately, there was another option. Just as I knew this kind of smokescreen chemical was nonlethal, I also knew it was a bit heavier than air. That meant it would clear out from the top down, with the stuff floating just over the pavement dissipating last. Right behind the van Geri had stolen, I remembered, was a sedan-type vehicle, smaller than the van but with a similar axle track and ground clearance. My flailing hand found the front bumper, and three seconds later I was flat on my back beneath it, waiting patiently for the smoke to clear out.

I quickly found out that, whatever the normal tranquility quota was for the neighborhood, it had sold out long before Varsi's thugs got here.

"Damn it, where'd he go?"

"The *hell*—he *kicked* me!"

"Hey—your cheek's bleeding."

"You think I don't damn well *know* that?"

"Oh, *damn* it all—they got our van!"

I frowned at that last one. From bits and pieces Varsi had dropped during past conversations I'd assumed he and his minions used the Everlock protocol on their vehicles and offices. Even the handful of professional thieves who maintained that Everlock was not, in fact, unhackable conceded that it would take at least ten minutes and a backpack full of specialized equipment to do it.

Yet Geri had gotten the van open in only a handful of seconds. Either I'd been wrong about Varsi's security standards or Geri was something unique in the world of master thieves.

"How the *hell* did they—"

"Quiet."

The voice was Varsi's, and the word was delivered without inflection, volume, or implied threat. But the escalating ranting instantly died into silence. Even without being in a position to look into Varsi's face and those cold, dead eyes, that word in that tone sent a chill up my back.

Though speaking of that face and eyes...

Right now, all I could see from my vantage point was a bunch of shoes as Varsi's men finished whatever brief recon they'd conducted as the smoke cleared and gathered again around their boss. But I still had my thumbnail mirror, and it seemed a shame to waste the opportunity. Cautiously, knowing full well that if any of the thugs out there spotted it I would be instantly dragged onto the slowest, most painful road to death, I eased the thumb toward the edge of the car I was hiding under. A small gust of wind pushed aside the last bit of white smoke, and there they were.

It was a tableau I'd seen many a time at the luxurious lair that was Varsi's office. There were half a dozen thugs in overcoats and expensive suits standing around, their expensive guns currently half hidden beneath those coats. Two of them were clutching at shoulder and head where my flailing kicks had landed. All the thugs looked nasty, while those two in particular looked murderous. Standing just off the center of the group was Jasper, looking almost frail by comparison with the thugs. His gun was still holstered at his side, and I found myself vaguely surprised they'd let him keep it.

And at the exact center of the ring was Varsi.

He was of only average height and build, several centimeters shorter than his men, possibly even a centimeter shorter than Jasper. He had no visible weapon, and in fact his hands were buried in his coat pockets.

But even the most casual observer would have no trouble recognizing that he was the one in charge. Varsi dominated every meeting, every discussion, every confrontation. I could still vividly remember the first time I'd been escorted into his office, and the complete lack of emotion on his face as he informed me that I would henceforth be working for him.

"Did you call our people at the spaceport?" Varsi asked in that same calm voice.

"Yes, sir," one of the thugs said. "But with everyone else on encirclement duty—"

"There are two there, correct?"

"Yes, sir."

"Two of them against three targets incoming plus whoever's on the ship," Varsi said, fixing the thug with cold eyes. "Do you still wish to lodge a concern?"

The thug's shoulders seemed to tense up. "No, sir."

"Good." Varsi's head shifted slightly. "You said he never spoke to the Kalix in the taverno."

"He didn't, Mr. Varsi," Jasper said. "Neither of them did."

"But you say the one showed a badge?"

"Yes, sir," Jasper confirmed. "It looked like ISLE, but I wasn't at the right angle to see it."

The cold eyes frosted over a little more. "And you didn't make the effort to correct that deficiency?"

Standing inside the thug circle, there was nowhere Jasper could back up to. But the sudden look on his face told me he really, really wanted to. "I was . . . I didn't think . . ."

Varsi turned away from him toward one of the other thugs, provoking another twitch from Jasper's expression. "Find out who he is, and who he's associated with. Now."

The thug nodded. "Yes, sir."

Varsi paused, and I could feel the sudden increase in the group's tension. "There's a bottle of Roma Blue and a plate of steamers waiting for me at my table," he said. "I expect the woman to be brought to me in time for us to have her final drink together."

"Yes, sir," one of the thugs said. Varsi gave a small nod; and with that silent signal they scattered, a couple heading away up the street, the rest heading down toward the stakeout that had been so badly disrupted by the smoke mortars. Jasper hesitated, apparently unclear as to his role, then hurried to catch up with the latter group. Varsi watched them go, then turned and disappeared back through the doorway he'd emerged from earlier.

And as the crowd of thugs passed by, and I was able to get a better look at their faces and body language, I realized it hadn't been tension I'd seen in them. Rather, it had been anticipation.

I eased my thumb away from the edge of the car, watching the shoes as the thugs headed off on their mission, trying to figure out what to do. If the woman Varsi had mentioned was Tera C—and it would be the height of absurd coincidence if there was an entirely different woman in his crosshairs—the lady was in serious trouble. So was I, though in a much more limited sense, since I'd already been paid to bring her in.

So what had Varsi meant by Tera having her final drink with him?

Maybe it was just a turn of phrase. Maybe he just meant that he wanted to meet Tera before his goons took her off to sweat the location of the *Icarus* out of her. She and the ship were clearly valuable properties; he surely wasn't planning to just kill her.

Unless Geri had lied to me about her. Tera had been valuable once—the bounty that had been put on her and her shipmates six years ago had proved that much.

But things change. Maybe there was no longer any profit to be had here. Maybe all that was left was some kind of revenge.

My left arm gave a twinge of remembered pain. And if revenge was the order of the day, I was definitely aboard.

Unfortunately, there was only one place I might be able to get any of these new details. Varsi had already had his meal interrupted once, and he probably wouldn't appreciate it if he was interrupted a second time. Still, with the bulk of his force off hunting Tera, this was the best time for us to have a quiet chat.

Though I was pretty sure he wouldn't be offering me a glass of that Roma Blue.

CHAPTER SIX

$$\diamond\!\!\!\!\blacklozenge\!\!\!\!\diamond$$

The thugs' shoes moved down the street, disappearing into the pedestrian and vehicle traffic that was finally starting to move again. Picking my moment, I rolled out from under the car into the street, stood up, and returned to the walkway.

From my earlier, more limited vantage point, I'd assumed Jasper was looking at the menu post of a restaurant. Now, from this angle, I could see that the modest doorway Varsi had disappeared into was in fact the entrance to a private club. It was the placard giving the name and membership requirements that Jasper had been pretending to study.

I didn't bother to read the placard as I strolled past the door. No matter what the restrictions were, I was a hundred percent sure I wouldn't fit them.

The main entrance was never the only way into places like this, of course. Rear exits and service doors were the two most obvious avenues for the aspiring sneak, but their very popularity meant that any security system worth its promotionals already had them solidly covered. Less obvious were air ducts and sewers, the former impractical for a whole host of reasons, the latter so utterly disgusting that only the very desperate ever tried it.

Fortunately, I was nowhere near that desperate.

Three mortar shells had been dropped on the stakeout crowd a block away, but our block had only been hit with one. That suggested either that the person who'd been lobbing them off the rooftops decided we didn't merit that many shells, or that he hadn't had time to drop all of them before he had to run.

Of course, it could also be that he'd only had one shell left after dealing with the other crowd. But that option left me with nothing, so I decided not to think too much about it. I continued down the street to the end of the block, where I found a small curio shop with inattentive clerks. Slipping into their back room, I found the stairs leading upward and climbed the three flights to the roof.

All of the block's buildings were joined by a common roof, as I'd already concluded from the street-level design. Setting off through the forest of vent tubes, rain channels, and low eave walls, I backtracked toward the scene of our attack.

For once, the most pessimistic option turned out not to be right. There were indeed two unused smoke shells waiting abandoned for me on the roof. Not left behind because the attacker had lost interest or run out of time, but because two of the disposable launcher's three tubes had malfunctioned.

Perfect.

Carefully, I cut the tubes open with my multitool and removed the shells. They were nicely compact, about twenty-five centimeters long and seven in diameter, though such things always looked a hell of a lot bigger when they were coming straight down at you. Like most mortar rounds they were impact triggered, with safety catches that would be opened as they traveled through the tubes. Picking up both shells, I continued my trek back to the private club.

Varsi's comments about Roma Blue and steamers had implied that part of the draw of the place was high-end cuisine, and as I got within range of the cooking vents I could tell that guess had been correct. From the aroma wafting up onto the roof I tentatively identified the dish of the day being something that included butter, olive oil, and tomato. Selene, had she been here, could have rattled off the full list of ingredients, how many cubic centimeters there were of each, and possibly come up with the dish's recipe.

Fortunately, I didn't need any of that. All I needed was to get the weather cap off so I could drop one of the shells down the vent tube.

Since I couldn't get in to see Varsi, I'd simply get him to come out to see me.

As my father used to say, *If you can't raise the bridge, lower the river.*

I'd been a bit concerned that the shell might be too wide to fit into the tube, but once again that worry was for nothing. Once the weather cap was off, the shell fit into the opening with a good millimeter or two to spare. There was probably a mesh or filter of some sort at the bottom of the vent to keep anything from landing in the soup, but that was okay—the impact would trigger the shell, and with the smoke being heavier than air it would flow into the kitchen without a problem. As a nice bonus, mixing the smoke with the kitchen odors should help disguise the telltale burnt-sugar smell that Varsi might recognize.

By the time the first whiffs of smoke came drifting up the vent tube, I was already halfway back to the curio shop and my path back down to the street.

There was theoretically a fifty-fifty chance as to which door Varsi would pick for his exit. But knowing the man's ego, I couldn't imagine him voluntarily stepping out of an upscale establishment into a service alley. Not unless he was specifically and repeatedly being shot at. Possibly not even then.

So I was waiting a dozen meters down the street from the main door when he appeared, moving along among the other patrons and staff as they fled from the smoke.

"Mr. Varsi," I called. I started to move toward him.

And came to a quick halt as one of the two bodyguards who'd apparently been left inside during the earlier street meeting moved protectively in front of him. "I just want to talk to him," I said soothingly, making sure my open hands were visible.

"Well," Varsi said, stepping out from behind him and giving me one of those soulless looks he did so well. "I thought that might be you. You ruined what was left of my steamers."

"I'm sorry about that, sir," I apologized. "But I needed to talk to you, and I didn't think they'd let me inside."

"Indeed they wouldn't have." He cocked his head slightly. "You should know that Billings and Coolidge are rather annoyed with you right now."

The two thugs I'd kicked during my escape, no

doubt. "I'm sorry about that, too," I said. "I didn't know at the time that they were with you."

"After today, they may not be," Varsi said, his voice sending a fresh shiver up my back. Varsi generally allowed his people a single mistake each. Today's incident may have put Billings and Coolidge over their quota. Hopefully, it hadn't put me over mine. "You said you wanted to talk?"

"Yes, sir." I looked around at the knots of people gazing in fear or bemusement at the smoke drifting out the door, and at the other, less curious, people who were just trying to get around them. "Could we go somewhere with a bit more privacy?"

He eyed me another moment. "There's a small park a block over," he said. "Riley?"

"Yes, sir." The man who'd stepped in front of him inclined his head toward the street. "That way," he said. "Straight across."

"And then?"

"And then just keep walking."

My first, biggest fear was that Varsi would let me get halfway across the street and then have Riley shoot me in the back. To my relief, he didn't. My next, slightly smaller fear was that I would make it to the park, discover that Varsi hadn't followed, and then spend the rest of my short life looking over my shoulder until Varsi's men found a less conspicuous time and place to shoot me in the back.

Once again, my pessimism proved to be overstated, or at least premature. For Varsi, finding out what I had to say apparently outweighed whatever damage my smoke bomb had done to his steamers.

I'd assumed the park would be a casual open space nestled in among the city's buildings, stocked with grass or other ground greenery, small trees, and maybe benches and a child's play structure. It turned out instead to be a walled combination of a Zen garden and fernery, complete with a neatly dressed door steward at each of the two entrances and a special ID card required for entry, the whole thing rising out of the center of the grassy space I'd originally expected. In retrospect, it seemed likely that the park and the exclusive club we'd just left were probably a package thing.

Varsi was passed through the door with a courteous nod, the steward reaching to a control beneath his lapel to buzz us in. Varsi's bodyguards didn't get any such nods, but I spotted the sort of knowing look pass between them and the steward that I'd often seen exchanged when professional soldiers or ex-soldiers ran into each other. For me, it was neither the nod nor the look, but rather a long and unpleasantly suspicious stare.

A minute later Varsi and I were seated alone on one of the benches, gazing out at patterns of stone, fern, and delicately raked sand.

"Tell me first what you're doing here," Varsi opened the conversation. "I admit to a certain degree of surprise when I was told of your arrival. Especially when I was also told you were in the company of a badgeman."

"There was no intent of deception or subterfuge," I assured him. So he *wasn't* here for me, after all. That was both a relief and, oddly enough, a bit of a letdown. "I was hired to do a crockett job by a man named Geri. When the job was finished, he asked me to bring him here."

"His full name?"

"He never gave it."

"You didn't ask?"

"I've met other people who wouldn't give me their names," I said. "They're never the sort you feel comfortable pressing with questions like that."

"Yet you said yes to his job?"

"He paid very well. We needed the money."

"As usual," Varsi said. "I assume he's the badgeman you were seen with in the taverno?"

"Well, he's *got* a badge, anyway," I said. "But he never mentioned any InterSpiral connections until he flashed it."

"You think he's an imposter?"

"Probably," I said. "Actually, I'd say almost certainly. If he was sticking to an undercover role hard enough not to identify himself to me when he first brought us to Pinnkus, I can't see the situation in the taverno being worth blowing his cover over."

"Perhaps the situation was more dire than you realized."

"Could be," I conceded. "But there's also the thing with the van he stole when the smoke mortar hit. I've never heard of even a badgeman with a warrant being able to override an Everlock protocol as fast as he did."

"Someone special, then," Varsi said. "Why did he bring you to Pinnkus?"

I hesitated. But the fact that Varsi had been willing to travel all the way to Pinnkus strongly suggested he already knew what was going on. "He said there was a woman hiding here who had a valuable secret," I said. "He wanted me to find her."

"Did you?"

I shook my head. "No."

"Are you certain?"

I looked sideways at him. His eyes were still on the garden, but there was an ominous tightness along his jawline. "We hadn't found her as of the point where we were smoke-bombed and the others left me here," I said. "Has something happened since then?"

He was silent another few seconds. I looked at the sand, noticing for the first time that there was an almost eerie luminescence that swept periodically across the furrows, presumably stimulated by hidden lasers or focused ultraviolet lights. The glow varied in intensity as it flowed across the landscape, sometimes barely visible, other times bright enough to rival the cloud-muted sunlight from above.

And in one of those brighter surges, as I looked back at Varsi, I saw something I hadn't seen before: small lines and curves etched faintly into sections of the skin of his face. The reflection from the sand faded away, and as normal light regained its prominence the lines vanished.

But they were there. More than that, I'd seen that sort of thing before in the preliminary layout surgeons used in preparation for reconstructive surgery.

Only there was nothing wrong with Varsi's face that required reconstruction. If anything, the idea of changing his face went in the exact opposite direction. For many in the criminal underworld, his was a face that demanded instant respect and servitude. The only reason he might want it changed was if he didn't want or need it anymore.

Like if he was preparing to run?

"I received news from the spaceport while we were

walking from the club," he said into my thoughts. "Your ship, the *Ruth*, took off ten minutes ago."

I stared at him, questions about his future abruptly forgotten. What the *hell*? "You're sure?"

An instant later I wished I could call back the words. People like Varsi didn't like having their statements questioned.

Fortunately, he seemed more interested in my reaction than in taking personal offense at my question. "You didn't know they were leaving?"

"No, of course not," I said. "Why would Selene—?" I broke off. "No. Of course it wasn't Selene. It was one of the others." I frowned. "But didn't I hear you say you had people at the spaceport?"

"I did," Varsi said, his voice somehow going even colder. "Both of them are dead."

"Oh," I said awkwardly. Dead, and probably not from natural causes.

Also probably not from the kind of carelessness that would induce them to turn their backs on Selene, Geri, and the Kalix. If their deaths were connected to the *Ruth*, that only left— "Freki," I muttered. "Geri's partner. He stayed with the ship."

"Does he also masquerade as a badgeman?"

"I don't know," I said. "If he has a badge, he never showed it to me."

"You seem to know very little about these people," Varsi said with a hint of contempt. "What about the Kalix?"

"I know even less about him," I said. "He was in the taverno when Geri and I went in. He popped up again while Selene was trying to track down our target, claiming he knew a woman who was in danger somewhere near the spaceport and asking for Geri's help."

"This woman being Tera C?"

So she was indeed the woman Varsi and his people were looking for. I'd never really doubted that, but it was nice to have it confirmed. "I don't know," I said. "He couldn't identify her picture. Geri had decided we'd go check it out when that smoke bomb hit." I shrugged. "You know everything else."

"Do I?" he countered. "Everything else?"

"I just meant—"

"Do I know who these two men are or who they work for?" Varsi demanded. "Do I know who this Kalix and his female friend are? Do I know whether the Kalix and your other friends are secretly working together?" His eyes narrowed. "Do I know whether or not Selene found Tera C?"

"I've told you everything I know, sir," I said, trying to keep my voice level and sincere.

"Perhaps," he said, his tone not giving any clue as to whether or not he actually believed that. "I assume that if further information comes your way you won't hesitate to share it with me."

"Of course," I assured him quickly.

"Good." He held out his hand. "And as long as we're here . . . ?"

I frowned. "Sir?"

"You said your new employer gave you a crockett job."

For a split second I considered telling him that the Bonvere Seven survey had come up dry. It certainly wouldn't be the first or last time something like that happened. Furthermore, with the sample ampules back on Ringbar where Geri had left them, there was no way for Varsi to prove otherwise.

More to the point, if he was on the cusp of changing his face and vanishing into the ether, it might be smart to hold onto the last of the Bonvere seeds until the next boss emerged from the scramble and I could make a deal with him.

But people like Varsi didn't concern themselves with concepts like proof or reasonable doubt. And as I looked into his eyes I realized that there were *lots* of other planets out there with interesting seeds.

Unfortunately, giving in to the inevitable was going to cost me the literal ace up my sleeve. But there was nothing for it. Varsi wanted the seeds, and he wanted them now.

As my father used to say, *Three people can keep a secret if one is you, the second is trustworthy, and the third is dead.*

In Selene, I'd found someone in the second category. If Varsi thought he could actually walk away from a major criminal organization, even one he was in charge of, he might well end up in the third.

I glanced over my shoulder as I took off my jacket, noting that Varsi's two bodyguards were still back by the door. If I turned a little ways toward Varsi, they wouldn't see what I was doing. I turned the necessary few degrees, pushed up my sleeve, and popped the rear access panel in my arm.

"Interesting," Varsi said thoughtfully as I pried out the ampule and handed it to him. "I always suspected you had a special hiding place in the event that customs or Trailblazer inspectors became curious. But I didn't expect something like that."

"Hopefully, no one else will, either," I said, sealing the panel again. "I don't know how useful those will be. Selene just said they showed promise."

"Perhaps," Varsi said. "I'll have them examined and the appropriate payment entered into your account on Xathru."

"Thank you." I braced myself. "Though under the circumstance, perhaps this one time we could make it cash?"

"Under the circumstances?"

I'd been thinking about his imminent and presumably unannounced departure into the misty void. Belatedly, I realized that was a topic best left untouched. "My ship leaving Pinnkus without me," I said instead. "I need to figure out where they went and get after them, and credit transfers from off-world tend to be pretty slow."

"I see." Varsi reached into his jacket, dropping the ampule into a pocket and emerging with a billfold. "Shall we say ten thousand?"

"That would be good, yes," I agreed. A seed that Varsi's organization could extract a new street drug from would be worth at least ten times that amount, I knew. But I was hardly in a position to bargain.

"Excellent." He pulled out two five-thousand-commark bank checks and handed them to me. "And just as a reminder: when you find Tera C, you'll contact me immediately."

"Of course," I said with a fresh tightening of my throat. Not *if* we found her, but *when*. He fully expected me to deliver, and he wouldn't be happy if I didn't.

"Excellent." He stood up, waving me back as I started to do likewise. "No—stay here a while. As long as you want, in fact. Meditate, calm your heart and soul, and plan your next move."

"Thank you, sir." In other words, he'd already been seen entering with me and apparently didn't want to risk that connection being reinforced by us also leaving together. Varsi's commitment to employee loyalty only went one direction.

I watched him collect his bodyguards and exit through the door we'd entered by, then started a mental countdown. I'd wait until he had time to get back to the club, I decided, then get out of here and see what I could find out about the *Ruth*.

Another two minutes should do it. I turned back to the garden for one final look at the sculpted sand—

I frowned. Half hidden beneath a particularly shaggy cluster of ferns at the near edge of the sand pit, staring right at me, was a small furry creature.

My first thought was that a rat had gotten into the garden, or possibly that it was a permanent resident. But it was too big for that, too long. More like a ferret.

And then, I got it. The animal wasn't a ferret, at least not one of the Earth variety. It was one of the Kalix's two shoulder pets.

But that was impossible. The Kalix had been in the van with Selene and Geri when they all roared off together. How could one of his ferrets be here now?

Could Geri have kicked everyone out before he and Freki absconded with the *Ruth*? But the spaceport was a good thirty kilometers away. How could the ferret have made it all the way back here already?

Unless in the mad scramble to get in the van he'd gotten lost.

I sighed. Bad enough that I was stuck here on my own. Now I had another lost soul to take care of.

"Come here," I said, leaning toward him and beckoning. "Are you lost? Come on, I won't hurt you. Are you hungry? I'll bet you're hungry."

For a moment he didn't move. Then, cautiously, he crawled out from under his fern canopy and skittered toward me. "Come on," I said again, wondering if he would remember me. Some animals could make connections that quickly, but I had no idea whether this was one of those.

But he was still coming. "That's right," I said, beckoning again. "Come on."

He stopped at my feet and looked expectantly up at me. Mentally crossing my fingers, I reached my right hand down to pick him up, switching at the last moment to my left. If he was a biter, he might as well get it out of his system with my artificial hand instead of the flesh-and-blood one.

But he didn't bite, or claw, or even squirm. I got him up and onto my lap, and for a moment we just looked into each other's eyes. I'd heard you could gauge the intelligence of an animal that way, but if so I was damned if I could do it.

In the meantime, I'd promised him something to eat. "Come on," I said, standing up. I thought about putting him on my shoulder the way the Kalix had, realized he would either fall off or dig in with that impressive set of claws, and instead crooked my left arm across my stomach and settled him there.

The door steward was still standing guard as I opened the door, staring off into the distance. I gave him a friendly nod as I passed, didn't get so much as a glance in return, and turned toward the street. I would find a runaround, I decided, head over to the spaceport, and see if I could cajole someone into giving me some details about the *Ruth*'s departure. If I spotted a food cart along the way, I'd stop and try to find something the ferret liked.

"Hey! You!"

I looked toward the voice. Three men were standing beside one of the buildings across the open green area a dozen meters from the walled garden. Two of them were keeping a wary eye on the steward—and vice versa, which I now realized was where he'd been staring and why he hadn't acknowledged my nod—and the third glaring at me.

"Yeah, you," he growled. The spokesman detached himself from the wall and stalked toward me, his two buddies right behind him. "You. Roarke.

"Traitor."

CHAPTER SEVEN

———— ❖ ————

My first thought was to wonder how the hell I could be a traitor to people I'd never even met. My second thought was that I'd better figure out a way out of this, and fast.

All three of them were armed, of course. That much was obvious from the way their hands were hovering near belts or half-open jackets. Even if it hadn't been three-to-one odds, the right flap of my jacket and the plasmic concealed beneath it were currently trapped by my arm and the ferret currently lounging there.

The only thing that was keeping them from drawing right then and there was the presence of the steward at the garden door behind me, and my assailants' obvious suspicion that he, too, was armed. Given the garden's clientele, I would bet heavily that way myself.

Unfortunately, I would also bet that he had instructions not to get involved unless he or one of his patrons was in imminent danger. As someone who'd just been inside I might qualify for that protection; as someone who'd only been in there as someone else's guest, I might not. Either way, it wasn't a hill I wanted to pitch a tent on.

"Have we met?" I called, keeping my voice pleasant. Aside from the fact that I needed more intel on this situation, I'd found that most people didn't like to talk and shoot at the same time. If I could keep them talking, I might be able to forestall the shooting part.

"Name's Fulbright," the spokesman said. "And yeah, a long time ago. You poached one of my targets."

"Sorry about that," I said. So, a fellow bounty hunter. "If it helps, I probably didn't know you were after him, too."

"You mean like Jasper didn't know when *he* went poaching my targets?"

"What does Jasper have to do with it?" I asked, frowning. "I have nothing to do with him."

"Oh, yeah, right," Fulbright said sarcastically. He strode to within a couple of paces of me, glanced furtively at the steward, and stopped, his buddies stopping along with him. "You've got nothing to do with the butt-brain you were just talking to."

"Okay, look, let's back up a minute," I said, easing a casual step backward toward the garden. "You called me a traitor. How am I a traitor?"

"You know damn well," Fulbright said, countering my backward step with a forward one of his own. "You *and* Jasper. Don't deny it—I saw you talking to him."

"Yes, we've established that," I said. "How does talking to Jasper make me a traitor?"

"Don't play stupid," Fulbright bit out. "The Patth offer a hundred thousand commarks for this Tera C flooz. Varsi comes along and says if we hand her over to him instead of the Patth we get *two* hundred thousand." He jabbed a finger at my chest. "Only you and Jasper already work for him. So if *you* find her he doesn't have to pay anyone. Poaching my target. *Again.*"

"Yeah, well, just wait a second," I said, frowning. Given what Geri had said about the *Icarus* being some sort of new stardrive, it had been pretty obvious that the Patth were behind the hunt.

But Varsi was in the business of selling weapons and illicit drugs, not personally flying them around the Spiral. Why in the world would he shell out two hundred thousand for Tera, especially when he could sell her to the Patth for only one? Was he hoping to buy himself some goodwill?

If so, he was sadly mistaken. I'd dealt with the Patth on occasion, and they didn't have any goodwill to sell. "He's offering to pay *double* the Patth bounty?"

"Yeah, except you're going to—"

"Yes, right, right," I cut him off. "Then what? Varsi turns around and hands her to the Patth?"

"Or sells her to someone else," Fulbright said, his tone going all dark and ominous. "*Or* just kills her to make sure no one steals her back from him."

"Why would he kill her?" I asked. "Two hundred thousand is a lot of pocket change for a corpse."

"Then why don't the job specs say he wants her alive?" Fulbright countered. "Man wants a target alive, he says so right in the specs. Man doesn't say, you figure he doesn't care."

I frowned. That was indeed the way the bounty business worked. "Maybe it was just an oversight," I said. "So what exactly do you want me to do? Deliver a message of protest to Mr. Varsi?"

Fulbright grinned, showing me a mouthful of crooked teeth. "Oh, yeah, we want you to deliver a message," he said softly. "The message is that sometimes you get corpses without having to pay for them."

"Ah," I said, nodding. "Well, here's the thing—"

Spinning around, I took off at top speed toward the Zen garden door.

I'd only started with a couple of meters' head start, but I gained another three before Fulbright's brain was able to switch from *threaten* to *chase*. I heard them belatedly scrambling after me as I ran, keeping my eye on the steward. His expression changed from startled to alarmed to determined as the pack of us raced toward him. He reached into his jacket, not toward the upper lapel that held the door buzzer, but lower down on the other side where a holster would be—

Grabbing the ferret around the ribs with both hands, I lobbed him straight at the steward's face.

The man was quick. Seeing the squirming mass of fur and claws flying toward him, he dropped instantly into a crouch, abandoning any effort to draw his gun in favor of putting both forearms protectively in front of his face. I veered out of my path just far enough to stiff-arm my left palm into his shoulder, toppling him backwards out of the ferret's arc, and just long enough to dip my fingers into his jacket and key the door release. I kept going, hitting the door shoulder-first and shoving it open, then spinning back around on my heel to shove it closed before Fulbright and his playmates could charge in behind me. I got a look into three angry faces at eye level, plus a glimpse at ankle-level of the ferret darting through the closing gap behind me—

And then the door closed, and the lock clicked, and three shoulders slammed into it just a fraction of a second too late.

"*Dammit!*" I heard Fulbright's breathless curse over the wall. "You two, go around—there's another door back there."

I muttered a somewhat breathless curse of my own. So much for sprinting across the garden and slipping out that way. Though maybe if I hurried, I might still beat them out.

But no. There was undoubtedly another steward on that door, and with all the noise back here he was unlikely to be taken by surprise the way his fellow guard had. I had no idea what kind of marksmen Fulbright and his buddies were, but a door steward at a place like this would likely be *very* good with a gun.

So that door was out. So was this door, at least as long as Fulbright was on the other side of it.

Unfortunately, staying put also wasn't an option. Even if Fulbright hadn't seen how I got the door open, it probably wouldn't take him long to figure it out. Unless I could learn how to teleport in the next thirty seconds, there was likely to be a gun battle in my near future.

The ferret was nosing at one of the fern clumps at the edge of the rippled sand field, a larger patch than the one he'd been hiding in earlier. Looking for something to eat, probably, his tiny brain completely oblivious to the predicament we were in. Another wave of luminosity swept over the sand...

The lasers.

I was at the ferret's side in an instant, carefully digging into the ferns. The kind of laser or UV light that would be used for the garden's visual effects would be too weak to be an effective weapon. But Fulbright wouldn't know that. Besides, all I needed was something that looked mean and dangerous enough to draw his attention for a couple of crucial seconds.

There it was, buried beneath three layers of fronds: a flat, black box with a projector lens facing the sand and a power cord snaking out of the other end. Shooing the ferret away, I pulled the box up out of the ferns and started fiddling with the power cord end.

I'd barely started when I heard the door lock click open behind me.

I stayed where I was, crouched by the ferns, balancing the box on my right hand and pulling at the power cord with the other, making sure the lens was pointed away from the door. I heard Fulbright's steps as he charged across the short stretch of ground toward me, hoping he was looking at the box and wondering if it was dangerous. As he trotted to a stop a couple of meters away, I half turned toward him, letting my eyes widen with surprise and chagrin at the Clandise 4mm semiauto in his hand. I took my left hand off the power cord, turning it toward him with the fingers spread wide, showing it was empty—

And as his eyes reflexively shifted from the box to the empty hand, I let the box roll back to the ground and hurled the sand that had been hidden in my right hand into his face.

He bellowed a roar of pain, his gun hand flailing, his free hand clawing at his eyes. I was already in motion, leaping sideways away from the sand, trying to get out of his line of fire.

I needn't have bothered. Fulbright might be loud and angry, but he was smart enough not to shoot when he couldn't see what he was shooting at. He was still trying to clear the sand out of his eyes when I rolled back up to my feet and introduced him to the ground.

A minute later I had his hands and feet secured with the same kind of plastic wrist restraints Boff had used on the Ulkomaals back at the taverno. My new ferret friend came up while I was working and sniffed at the restraints, and I watched to see if he would settle down for a snack the way he had back there. But he just sniffed the plastic once and hopped off Fulbright's back. Apparently, the brand Boff used tasted better than mine.

"You're dead, Roarke," Fulbright snarled as I finished and stood up. "You and Jasper and Varsi. You're all dead."

"Eventually, yes, that'll happen," I agreed, reaching down and scooping up the ferret. "But if I were you I wouldn't try to hurry the process along. Be good and maybe I'll let you know when I've delivered Tera C to the Patth."

The steward was pulling himself groggily off the ground as I slipped out the door, some blood trickling down his cheek. Apparently, Fulbright had wanted to make sure he had me all to himself once he got into the garden. I dropped Fulbright's gun on the ground beside him, then made quick tracks out of there.

I reached the main street grid without further trouble and turned back onto the thoroughfare Selene and I had walked after leaving the taverno. I had no idea whether I would find anything useful in that direction, but at least it had the virtue of taking me farther from all the various people and groups who were currently mad at me.

I'd gone three blocks and still hadn't spotted either a runaround or a decent food cart when my phone vibed.

I thought it might be Fulbright, freshly freed by his buddies and mad as a scorched cat. Second guess was that it was Varsi wanting to know if I'd found Tera yet.

Instead, it was Selene.

"Where are you?" I asked, trying not to show my annoyance at having been left behind and knowing I wasn't completely succeeding.

"We're back at the spaceport," she said. "I'm so sorry we abandoned you. Geri said we had to convince everyone we'd found Tera, and the only way to do that was to make a big show of leaving. He said you'd be fine, that Mr. Varsi wouldn't be a problem once the rest of us were gone."

I glared at the world. But there was a certain level of logic to it. Though I would have felt differently if Varsi *had* decided to be a problem. "So you just circled the planet and landed again?"

"Yes, but we came in with a different ship's ID," she said. "Kifri's idea. We're the *Sleeping Beauty* now."

"Who's Kifri?"

"He's the Kalix," she said. "He said he left one of his outriders behind when you were captured so he could keep an eye on you. Did you find him?"

"More like he found me," I said. I looked down at the ferret, who'd given up looking around at the cityscape and had settled in for a nap. Not exactly the kind of bodyguard I'd have offered if our situations had been reversed. "But yes, I've got him. So what now?"

"Geri says you need to get back here so we can figure out how to continue the search," Selene said. "Can you find a runaround, or should I get one and come pick you up?"

I looked around the nearby streets, trying to spot any of the flavors of quick-rent vehicles we'd seen tooling around the Havershem City streets. Nothing. No runarounds, no vans, and no trucks.

But there was a large building halfway down the next block that I hadn't spotted before. A building sporting a very familiar logo.

"Let's go with option three," I told Selene. "No point in me coming there when the hunt is here. I'm on the main street, four blocks due west of where we were when all the smoke bombs went off. Call me when you get close and I'll guide you in."

"But Geri says we need a plan."

"We *have* a plan," I said patiently. "I do, anyway. If Geri wants to stay there and plan, he's more than welcome. But you get yourself over here. I'd like to have Tera in hand before sunrise tomorrow."

There was a brief pause. "Really?" she asked.

"Really," I assured her.

"All right," Selene said, still sounding a little uncertain. "We'll be right there."

As my father used to say, *When you lie down with dogs, you risk being picked up along with them when it's time for the neutering.* Between Fulbright, Varsi, and the Patth, I had no intention of hanging around this case and this planet long enough for that to happen.

The ferret draped along my arm gave an inquisitive sort of squeak. "No, I'm not joking," I assured him, eyeing the building I'd spotted, the three-story whitestone with the big *StarrComm* logo over the entryway. "I know exactly how to find her."

I'd planted myself at a nicely shaded outdoor café table and was sipping a cola when a spaceport runaround stopped at the curb and they piled out.

All of them, including Geri and Freki. Apparently, my employers had decided they didn't need to stay behind and plan after all.

"Are you all right?" Selene asked anxiously as she hurried toward me. Behind her, the Kalix snapped his fingers twice. "I'm so sorry, Gregory. I shouldn't have let them take off."

"I'm fine," I assured her, watching as the ferret abandoned the nut bar he'd been chewing on, bounded off the table, and scurried over to the Kalix. Apparently, a double finger snap was the signal to come. "I doubt you could have stopped them even if you'd tried."

"Thank you for taking care of Pax," Kifri said. The ferret reached him, leaped to the top of his boot, then clawed his way up trousers and tunic to the Kalix's right shoulder. With a contented-sounding squeak, he dug his claws into the tunic and settled down.

"My pleasure," I said. The other ferret, already settled on Kifri's left shoulder, leaned forward a little and gave a couple of small squeaks. Welcoming back the prodigal, or possibly chewing him out for desertion. "I wasn't sure what to feed him, and he seemed interested in one of the café's nut bars, so I got him one. I hope that was all right."

"Yes, very much so," Kifri assured me. He reached up and stroked the ferret's head, then did the same for the other one. "I trust you had interesting adventures together?"

"Actually, I could have done with a little less excitement," I said. "What happened with your lady friend at the spaceport?"

"I tried to contact her," Kifri said with a heavy sigh. "Alas, she did not answer."

"Well, don't worry about it," I said. "I'm guessing we'll have her all safe and sound within the next twelve hours."

He brightened. "We will?"

"I think so." I shifted my attention to Geri and Freki, who'd been standing silently on the sidelines watching all the byplay. "Welcome back. I hope you didn't damage my ship."

"I hope *you* didn't damage our chances of finding Tera C," Geri countered. "So what's this big exciting plan of yours?"

"Let's start with why she's here," I said. "Actually, as long as we're using the café's table let's start with you ordering drinks or something."

"Let's start with the plan," Geri countered. He waved at the server for his attention, then dropped two hundred-commark bills on the next table, pointed to the money, and gestured for the server to take it and leave us alone. "Not really interested in drinks or company."

"Fine," I said. "As I said, why is Tera here? Not on Pinnkus, not even in Havershem City, but why is she here in this particular neighborhood?"

"Why don't you tell us?" Geri asked with strained patience.

"Because she's not just hiding." I pointed at the StarrComm building down the street. "She's looking for something. Something that requires quick interstellar communication."

Geri and Freki exchanged looks. "Not some*thing*," Geri said reluctantly. "Some*one*."

I raised my eyebrows. "Come again?"

Again, they looked at each other. Freki gave a microscopic nod, and Geri turned back to me. "I told you Tera had left the Icarus project," he said. "What I didn't tell you—"

"So Icarus is a whole project now?"

"What I didn't tell you," Geri continued, ignoring my question, "was that before she left one of the other members also disappeared. We think she's looking for him."

"Really," I said. Which would more than explain my tentative guess that she wanted to stick around a StarrComm building. If she had feelers out on other planets—or if she expected her quarry to try to contact her—StarrComm's huge communications arrays were the only way to gather information short of hopping a ship and going everywhere in person. "And you didn't think this was something Selene and I needed to know?"

"It was classified," Geri said. "*Extremely* classified."

"Let me guess," I said, leaning back in my seat and favoring the two of them with my best cynical smile. "The Path want Tera alive. They want this other runaway dead, and they want to handle that part of the job themselves."

"Something like that," Geri said in an extremely neutral tone. "May I also say that it's a tribute to your skills that you figured that out without being told."

"I appreciate the compliment," I said. "I appreciate saving time and effort even more. Can I get this walking corpse's name?"

Geri's lips twitched. "Jordan McKell. He was the captain of the *Icarus* when it vanished."

"Really," I said, trying to keep my face and tone calm. McKell. And of course, the Patth wanted him dead.

There wasn't a lot the Patth and I agreed on. But for once, at least, we were on the same page.

Apparently my calm act hadn't been as good as I'd hoped. "Sounds like you know the man," Geri suggested. He was gazing closely at me, and it wasn't just with idle curiosity. Freki was eyeing me, too.

As were Kifri and his two ferrets. The ferrets, especially, suddenly seemed highly interested in the conversation. Or maybe they were just looking at the half-eaten nut bar.

"McKell and I had a run-in once," I said briefly, picking up the nut bar and handing it to Kifri, noting as I did so that both ferrets immediately lost interest in me. As my father used to say, *Food and money always trump news and drama*. "But that's beside the point. The fact that Tera's on the hunt supports my theory that she needs access to the StarrComm building for her search."

"So you're saying she never left for the spaceport at all?" Kifri asked hesitantly. "That I was misinformed?"

"You mean that she lied to you?" Geri said bluntly.

"Probably not," I said. "There's another StarrComm facility near the port, but that one probably has way too much traffic for her to feel comfortable going there. Especially since a lot of its clients will be Patth."

"Good point," Geri said, nodding. "The average Patth usually doesn't work very hard at distinguishing between human faces, but two hundred thousand commarks is a great incentive for them to make the effort."

"So it is," I said, an odd feeling creeping up my back. According to Fulbright, the Patth were offering only a hundred thousand for Tera. It was *Varsi* who had supposedly upped the ante to two.

Unless the Patth had decided to match his offer. But I doubted a local official could authorize that kind of monetary jump on his own, and we were running pretty tight numbers for something like that to have worked its way up the ladder and back down again. Odds were that Geri was simply quoting Varsi's offer.

Varsi, who Fulbright was also convinced wanted Tera dead. "All the more reason we need to get on this right away," I added.

"About time you figured that out," Geri rumbled. "*Now* can we hear your plan?"

"Sure," I said. "We start with you and Freki hunting down the local quick-rent vehicle records." That would be a complete waste of time, I suspected, but I'd rather have them poring over date/time listings than standing around looking over my shoulder. "While you do that, Selene and I will head over to StarrComm and look for a pattern of calls."

"I thought caller information was confidential," Kifri said, busily offering bites from the nut bar to each of his ferrets.

"All it takes is money," I told him. I raised my eyebrows at Geri. "Speaking of which...?"

He glared a little harder at me, and I could see the numbers shifting behind his eyes as he updated the running total of just how much cash he and his partner were already into me for. But he dug three hundred-commark bills from his wallet and handed them over without argument. "You'd just better get some results this time," he warned as I tucked them away.

"Guaranteed," I promised.

"What about me?" Kifri asked. "What do you want me to do?"

"Whatever you want," I said. "Go home, or hang out here. It's up to you. But I'll warn that it'll probably take some time."

"I'll wait," the Kalix decided. "We still haven't established that your endangered friend is the same as mine, and I'd like to find out for sure. Though it would be an interesting coincidence if there were two such human females in such distress."

"It would indeed," I agreed, deciding it wasn't worth an argument or even an extension of the conversation. In a place like Havershem City, especially this close to a major spaceport, there were probably ten people per block in some kind of trouble.

Though probably not many of them in danger for their lives. "I saw a quick-rent office when I was passing that last side street," I said, turning back to Geri.

"Yeah, we saw it, too," Geri said, tapping Freki's arm. "Call if you find anything."

"You, too," I said as they left the table and headed down the street. Standing up, I offered my hand to Selene. "Come on, Selene. Let's go find our missing lady."

CHAPTER EIGHT

———— ❖ ————

I'd told Kifri that all it took to get StarrComm records was money. In general that was only true if you had enough of it and were lucky enough to find someone willing to accept a bribe. Otherwise, you needed a fistful of warrants, discovery writs, or data summons, plus the badges that went along with those orders.

Fortunately, if you had a Kadolian for a partner, sometimes you could bypass some of the process. Our first job wasn't going to be gathering data, but checking to see when Tera had been in here last.

Usually that involved waiting for whichever booth she'd last used to be empty. That didn't cost commarks so much as it cost minutes. As my father used to say, *Time is like money you can't lend out or get back.*

In this particular case, that investment wasn't going to be too bad. Normally, StarrComm liked to spread out their facilities across a given planet, and with their major center being at the spaceport it was unusual to find a second one this close. From what I'd read about Pinnkus on the trip from Ringbar, there'd once been a large import/export office complex in this part of Havershem City, and StarrComm had put in this satellite station to accommodate their needs and ease pressure on the main facility.

But as the Patth gathered more and more of the shipping business to themselves, the office complex had steadily lost clients until it was now a bare shadow of its former self. There was apparently still enough of it left to keep StarrComm from closing the satellite center entirely, but no one expected it to last more than a few more years.

The whole damn Spiral was just waiting for a stardrive breakthrough that would let the rest of us compete with the smug little aliens. If this Icarus project really was that breakthrough, and if Tera C was the key, it was no wonder the Patth wanted her.

Most StarrComm centers I'd seen had anywhere from eighty to two hundred booths, and even then a potential caller could wait up to an hour for a turn at one of them. This particular center, in contrast, had a mere forty booths, only half of which were still active. Even better, of that half only seven were in use when Selene and I checked in at the desk.

The desk crew's procedure was as minimalist as the facility itself. They accepted our sign-in sheets without bothering to ask for IDs, told us we could have any empty booth, and pointed us down the hallway.

I'd wondered how much longer this place would keep going before StarrComm shut it down. If today's profile was any indication, its lifespan was more likely to be measured in months than years. Maybe even weeks.

It took us half an hour to surreptitiously check all

the functioning booths that weren't already in use. About two-thirds of that time was spent making a pair of interstellar calls from a couple of them so that the desk crew wouldn't wonder what we were doing back here. Both calls were to Xathru: one to my mail drop—not surprisingly, there were no waiting messages—and the other to Varsi's.

Given Varsi was on Pinnkus, I'd expected he would set up his drop to do an automatic echo relay to him here, the way most traveling people did. On the assumption that he would answer the call I had an enthusiastic *working-on-it* speech all prepared. But the drop merely acknowledged I'd reached the correct number and asked me to leave a message. Either Varsi hadn't set up a relay, or he'd simply had enough of me for one day and decided to pass on my call.

I was fine either way. I'd only made the call to keep the StarrComm desk crew happy, and this way I got to save my speech for another time. With Varsi, enthusiastic *working-on-it* assurances always eventually got used.

After that, it took another half hour of waiting as each of the occupied booths became empty, checking it, then waiting for the next to be clear. Most of the conversations were short—not surprisingly, given StarrComm's prices—and I opted to make one additional call while we waited for a particularly long-winded business type to finish his conversation. Again, my call was to Xathru, and I still had no messages. Finally, we'd cleared them all.

And after all that, we had nothing.

"She *was* here," Selene said as we sat at a table in the building's deserted snack bar, an unneeded amenity in a place with nonexistent wait times. "We know she opened the door to Booth Eight."

"But not recently," I reminded her. "You said, what, no less than five or six days ago?"

"Possibly even seven," she said. "But even that long ago, if she'd been inside I would have found some of her scent. Why would she touch the door and not go in?"

"Good question," I conceded, scowling through the snack bar's glass walls at the line of booths across the hallway. The first set, Booths One through Ten, were visible from where we sat, with Eleven through Twenty on the far side, back-to-back with them. The other group, Twenty-One through Forty, were arranged similarly down the hallway that ran past the other side of the snack bar. Only the booths facing the snack bar, One through Ten and Twenty-One through Thirty, were operational, the two sets back-to-back with them having been closed down.

Still, just because something was closed down didn't mean it was no longer useful. In fact, sometimes it was even more so. "Come on," I said, standing up.

"Where are we going?" Selene asked as she followed suit.

"*You're* going to Booth Eight," I said. "*I'm* going to Booth Eighteen."

It took some fancy work with my multitool, and a couple of trips back and forth to Selene's side of the line of booths. But in the end, we figured it out.

"Hi, there," I said, waving cheerfully at Selene through the gap I'd opened between our two booths by taking out the pair of corresponding wall panels and a thick wad of sound insulation. "Welcome to Tera's back door."

"I don't know what any of this is," Selene said, craning her neck to study the two small black boxes and assorted connecting cables that had been wedged into the insulation.

"No reason why you should," I said. "I only know because I ran into something like it once in the days before you and I teamed up. Though pulling this in a StarrComm building is definitely an elevated level of chutzpah. Okay; here's the deal."

I pointed to one of the small boxes. "This one links the transceiver in my booth to the one in yours. That lets a person sit in this otherwise unused booth and make StarrComm calls for free. In this case, of course, that person being Tera C." That wasn't just a guess—Selene had picked up Tera's recent scent all over this particular booth.

"But wouldn't there still be a record showing the number being called?" Selene asked. "Even if it's not from Booth Eighteen, won't there be a charge stemming from Booth Eight?"

"There would," I agreed, "except that the connection from Eighteen links in *after* the register. Now, there would be a problem if someone else was already using Eight, which would show up as either a mixed signal or some bad interference. But if she picks her time right she should be able to avoid that."

"That emergency exit," Selene said, nodding toward the big orange door at the end of the corridor. "If she can bypass all the trip sensors she could get in without even having to check in at the desk."

"Right." I tapped the other box with my multitool. "But here's the real genius. This is an echo relay that'll take an incoming StarrComm signal and route it to a local phone. Assuming she's got a StarrComm connection set up out there, she can call out *and* someone else on Pinnkus can call back to her the same way. Both signals will route instantaneously through the other StarrComm booth and back through to this one."

"Sounds like an expensive way to make a local call."

"Normally, it would be absurdly expensive," I agreed. "But remember, she's got the billing part of the system bypassed. So not only can she make interstellar calls, but she can also talk locally without any of those calls showing up on the Pinnkus servers or recorders."

Selene's pupils reacted as she suddenly got it. "She's invisible," she breathed. "So is whoever she's talking to."

"Exactly," I said. "Theoretically, I suppose you could still trace the calls here and to the echo and get that information that way. But since StarrComm is an interstellar corporation, legal access to its records come under far stricter rules." I considered. "Actually, if the echo repeater they're using is tagged as an unknown number, a trace might not be able to glean anything at all, warrants or no warrants."

"So she's calling off-planet *and* talking to people here on Pinnkus," Selene said slowly, her pupils showing she was still working it through. "Does that mean she is indeed the person Kifri is in contact with?"

"Possibly," I said. "In which case that makes Kifri... what? Local contact? Diversion? Muscle?"

"Or all three," Selene said. "You remember that the reason he approached us in the first place was because he saw Geri's ISLE badge in the taverno."

"Right," I said, nodding. "Maybe he wanted to attach himself to Geri to see what he was up to."

"And perhaps to monitor his investigation if he was looking for Tera."

"Good point," I said. "Which raises another interesting

question. Kifri said his lady friend was in trouble, and Geri told us Tera was looking for McKell. But people in trouble or on the hunt usually like to keep moving, or at least need to keep mobile. And not just on a planetary level."

Selene's eyes flicked back to the black boxes in the gap. "This looks rather...permanent."

"If not permanent, at least it took a fair amount of time, effort, and planning," I agreed. "*And* money—electronics like these don't come cheap. If you're only sticking around a few days, there are easier ways of getting the same results."

"Except that after those few days she'd have to start running again."

"Exactly," I said. "What she has set up here sure looks like a base of operations. That's not usually what you do when you're hunting a missing colleague on the run. It's what you do when you're making and receiving interstellar calls."

I watched Selene's pupils, noting the interplay of logic and emotion there, feeling the same mix churning through me. "I don't like what I'm thinking," she said at last.

"Neither do I," I agreed heavily. "But given everything else we've heard, it's a possibility we can't ignore. She may not be looking for McKell at all. She may well be looking for a buyer."

I ran a finger over one of the connector cables. "I think she's put the Icarus project on the market."

For a long moment we just looked at each other. "But that doesn't make sense," Selene said, her pupils shifting between disbelief and confusion. "If Earth has a chance to break the Patth stranglehold on Spiral shipping, why would she betray you that way?"

I winced a little. *Betray* you *that way*. Selene might be my partner, but neither of us could ever forget that I was human and she wasn't. "Money is the usual reason," I said. "Power runs a close second. But there may be other possibilities."

"Such as?"

"Let's save that conversation for later," I said, suddenly remembering where we were. Even with business as light as it was—or maybe *because* business was so light—sooner or later the desk crew would start wondering what had happened to the two of us and probably send someone to check. "Right now, we need to get this buttoned up again."

"Right." Selene held out her hand. "Multitool?"

I handed it through the gap. My current booth might be currently unavailable, but Selene's wasn't. If business stayed light enough for the desk to just point people in the right direction we should be all right. But if things got busier and they started assigning customers to specific booths, we would have a lot of explaining to do if and when someone showed up at Booth Eight.

Selene vanished from my view as she set the panel on that side over the hole and started reattaching it. Two minutes later, she joined me in my booth; two minutes after that, both booths were back to normal and she and I were walking casually back toward the main exit.

As usual in such situations, I made sure we were engaged in an animated conversation as we passed the desk, a tactic I'd learned was an effective buffer against unwanted questions from people who were curious but didn't like to interrupt. I smiled and nodded to the crew as we passed, ignored the questions hovering in their faces, and we made it out without any problems.

Just the same, I took us another couple of blocks and around two corners before heading back to the café and our rendezvous with Kifri.

The Kalix was waiting patiently when we arrived, sipping from some monster-sized mug of something while his ferrets sat on the table busily working their way through individual nut cups. "They didn't like the nut bars?" I asked as we sat down across from him.

"Ah—you're back," he said, his squashed lizard face brightening. "I was beginning to be concerned. Did you have any difficulty?"

"None at all," I assured him.

"And my friend?"

"I'm afraid I was a little off in my estimate," I admitted. If he was reporting to Tera, the last thing we wanted was for him to have an accurate picture of our progress. "StarrComm was a bust, so we shifted to checking the nearby residence buildings."

"Oh," he said, looking around us. "It looks like there are a lot of them."

"There are indeed," I agreed. "On the plus side, we've eliminated a couple of neighborhoods and I expect we'll sort out the rest by this time tomorrow. Once we've narrowed it to one or two buildings, it'll just be a matter of waiting for her to show herself."

"So you're thinking the day after tomorrow?" he suggested.

"Or possibly the night after tomorrow," I said.

"Yes," he said, his voice sounding troubled. "That can be a long time for a person in danger."

"I know," I said. "But as long as she's in hiding

there's not much else we can do. We'll pick up the hunt again tomorrow morning. In the meantime, it's been a long day, and we're going to pack it in."

"Do you need a place to sleep?" Kifri asked. "My rented room is small, but you're welcome to share it."

"That's okay—our beds on the *Ruth* are pretty comfortable," I said. "Have you heard from Geri or Freki?"

"No," Kifri said. "I take it they haven't called you, either?"

"No, but I wasn't expecting them to make much progress on the quick-rentals today," I said. "We'll check in with them on our way back to the ship. Though *they* may want to find accommodations elsewhere."

"Yes, I was able to experience something of your dayroom facilities while we were circling the planet," he said, a little ruefully. "They were not as comfortable as I'm told humans generally prefer."

"The mattress on the floor of the clean room is even worse," I said. "We'll get started again about eight tomorrow morning—we can meet here then if you'd like, or you can just call me when you're ready to join us. If you *want* to join us, that is. Again, you don't have to."

"I'd be honored to be a part of this effort," he said eagerly. "I'll be here at eight. A pleasant good night to you both."

"And to you," I said. "Sleep well."

We found a runaround three blocks away, loaded in some cash, and headed for the spaceport. Along the way I called Geri, who told me he and Freki had rented a hotel room in the search area for the night, and also informed me that he'd collected their luggage from the ship while Selene and I were in the StarrComm building. He made a point of assuring me that he'd locked up behind himself.

I hadn't specifically given him an access code, but given all the times he'd been present when either Selene or I opened up I wasn't surprised he had it.

The fact that he and Geri weren't going to be aboard ship was, for a variety of reasons, a good thing. My only regret on that score was that I'd hoped to get a quick look into their luggage and see if Freki had the same kind of breakaway dart gun I'd found earlier in Geri's carrybag. Even if both men currently had all their weapons on them—as I certainly did—it wouldn't be hard for Selene to tell whether or not a given bag had recently played host to a given weapon. But without having the bags at hand that wasn't going to happen.

We had a quick meal in the dayroom and picked up a few other items, and within two hours of leaving the StarrComm building we were back again. The sun had already set behind the taller buildings, and the sky was darkening, with Havershem City rapidly approaching the optimum time for skulking and mischief.

For once, our timing was perfect.

The StarrComm center fronted onto the major thoroughfare that we'd first followed from the taverno in our search for Tera C. The main entrance was at the center of that wall, facing north, with an inconspicuous emergency exit tucked away near the northwest corner. The building's eastern and western sides were bordered by wide access drives, each of which was in turn bordered by a tastefully landscaped double row of trees and tall bushes. The southern wall was similarly bounded by a double tree row, but with a gap left open for a narrow service drive leading to the street south of the building.

The fancy tree encirclement was a standard feature of StarrComm centers on a lot of human-run worlds. I'd never been able to decide whether that was because the locals were proud of the buildings and wanted to draw attention to them, or if they were less than enthusiastic and had planted the trees in an effort to hide them.

Selene and I circled the building, marking the locations of the west-side exit door we'd theorized Tera used to sneak into the building plus five additional emergency exits that would be available to her in a pinch.

Unfortunately, adding in the main entrance and the emergency exit on the northern side, that gave us a pair of access doors on each side of the building, with only two of us to cover all of them. Geri and Freki would round out the number nicely, and would probably come if I asked. But I didn't really want either of them around right now.

Fortunately, we had an advantage most stakeout teams didn't. Along with the exit doors, our search had also revealed that the east side of the building was where the air circulation system emptied out into the general atmosphere.

I set up Selene there in one of the collapsible camp chairs we'd brought from the *Ruth*, picking a nice spot between two of the bushier trees where she'd be mostly out of view of the city's badgemen patrols but free to sniff the air coming out of the building.

She wasn't completely hidden, but wrapped in dark clothing and with a scarf covering her white Kadolian hair she shouldn't attract unwelcome attention. I took the other chair and retraced my steps to the building's far side, setting up among the trees at the southwest corner where I could simultaneously watch both the south and west sides. With Selene covering the east side, that left only the north side unguarded. Still, given the high traffic flow on that avenue, and the correspondingly high number of streetlights, it was the least likely choice for a clandestine entrance or exit. Or so I hoped.

I strapped on my night-vision monocular, opened one of the bottles of water I'd brought, and settled in to wait. A gentle breeze was drifting in from the north; hopefully, it wouldn't get blustery enough to interfere with Selene's analysis.

It was exactly ten minutes to midnight, and the breeze was still just a breeze, when my phone vibed. I keyed it on and held it to my ear. "Selene?"

"She's here," her voice came tautly.

I frowned. No one had gone into the four doors I could see from my position, including the one we'd assumed was her usual. "You sure?"

"Yes," she said. "But no one used either of the doors on this side."

"Ditto for these two sides," I said, frowning a little harder. So much for the well-lit side being the least likely choice. "So she went with the main entrance, after all. Is she alone in there?"

"No." There was a brief pause, and I heard the faint sounds of Selene sniffing the air flowing past her position. "There are three other humans—"

"Desk crew, plus probably a client," I interjected.

"—one Ulkomaal—"

"Another client."

"—and . . ." Another pause. "Gregory, have you seen Kifri? I think he's somewhere nearby."

I looked around. There wasn't anyone in sight. I opened my mouth to tell Selene that.

And then, a hint of movement right at the top of my monocular's field of view caught my eye. I looked up.

There was something moving along the edge of the StarrComm building's eave wall. Moving quickly for a couple of seconds, then pausing for a quick look down off the edge, then running a couple of seconds more. My first thought was that it was a squirrel, or Pinnkus's equivalent of that animal. And then, abruptly, it clicked.

It was one of Kifri's ferrets.

I turned my eyes away from the scampering creature, giving the rooftop a slow, careful scan. If the ferret was up there, then Kifri probably was, too. That must be what Selene was smelling, his scent rolling off the roof and mixing with the odors from the building. Apparently, his job while Tera was making her clandestine calls was to find a convenient catbird seat and watch for potential intruders.

I was just about to tell Selene about it when I heard footsteps coming from the south.

Heading directly toward me.

CHAPTER NINE

———— ✦ ————

I couldn't tell if they were close enough yet to hear me if I kept my voice low. But I had to risk it. "Intruders," I whispered into the phone. "Stay put. I'll come get you."

I slipped the phone away, straining my ears. It had been only those three or four incautious footsteps that had been loud enough to penetrate my distracted concentration, but now that I was focused I could hear more, softer steps. There were two of them, moving along the tree line toward me, probably having come up along the service road back there.

The first crucial question was whether they were coming specifically for me. If so, and if they'd already spotted me, I was in a world of trouble. Seated flat-footed in a chair, with my plasmic and knife both inconveniently wedged between my belt and jacket, I was in no position to take on double-team odds.

But I was still half hidden by the trees, with no movement that would attract the eye. Furthermore, the steady, slightly hurried pace of the footsteps held nothing of stealth or murderous intent. More likely they'd decided the corner was a good place for whatever they had planned—whether standing guard or launching an attack—and they were merely hurrying to get in position.

And if *that* was the scenario, I was more than ready to play along.

I waited until they were four or five meters away and just about to a place where they couldn't help but spot me, then cleared my throat. "About time," I growled. "I put in the call an hour ago."

The footsteps abruptly halted. "Who's there?" one of them demanded.

I smiled to myself. Even with the growl I had no trouble recognizing that voice. "Well, hello, Jasper," I greeted him smugly.

For a second he seemed speechless. Then, I heard the soft sound of a weapon being drawn from its holster. "What the hell are you doing here?" he bit out, stepping into view.

"I told you—I'm the one who called it in," I said patiently, keeping my hands casually in view where he could see they were empty. He was holding a dart gun, I saw, not one of the fancy breakaway ones like Geri had, but larger and probably sporting a larger magazine.

Naturally, it was pointed directly at my face. Briefly, I wondered what the gun's vertigo-to-curare ratio was. "And would you mind pointing that thing somewhere else?" I added.

"I'll point it wherever the hell I want," he growled. His partner, the second set of footsteps I'd heard, now stepped into view, one pace behind him and also with a dart gun in hand. Unlike Jasper, he wasn't pointing his weapon directly at me, but rather at the ground in front of me. Interestingly, it seemed to be also angled just slightly toward Jasper.

Just because Jasper worked for Varsi didn't mean Varsi's people entirely trusted the little weasel. To be honest, I couldn't really blame them.

"What do you mean, you're the one who called this in?" the second man asked. "Since when does Mr. Varsi listen to you?"

"Since when does he tell you everything?" I countered. "Never mind. You'll see how it is later tonight when he hands out the bonuses." I stood up, set my water bottle on the ground, and picked up the camp chair. A quick twist and inward press of the back supports, and I'd collapsed it into its storage form, with the seat and back folded up into a wad and the legs bunched together like a four-barrel minigun. "Now that you're finally here, you can take over sentry duty." I went on, "I'm supposed to meet Mr. Varsi at—"

Jasper's gun was pointed at me. His partner's wasn't. It seemed only fair, then, that I hit Jasper first.

My first hard jab with the chair was straight into his gun, the bunched legs hitting the weapon's barrel and shoving it backward, possibly breaking one of Jasper's fingers as it was wrenched out of his grip. My second jab was lower, slamming the ends of the chair legs into his stomach. He gasped as the wind was knocked out of him, doubling over and falling to the ground.

His partner was still gaping in shock at the unexpected attack, and was only just starting to bring his gun into firing position when I repeated the attack in reverse order, first burying the chair legs into his stomach. The gun went off with a soft chuff, and even as I slapped the chair legs against his hand, knocking the gun to the ground, I waited in tense anticipation for whatever drug had been in the dart to take effect.

To my relief, I felt nothing. A regular slug or flech-ette would have torn through the bunched fabric of the chair without even noticing, but darts designed to merely penetrate clothing deeply enough to deliver an injection didn't have enough momentum to get through.

Dropping the chair, I retrieved the two dart guns and checked their magazines. Both had the same loads: two vertigo darts on top, the rest of each thirty-round magazine filled with curare darts.

According to Fulbright, Varsi wanted Tera dead. I'd argued against that conclusion, even if only in my own mind. But I couldn't argue against the evidence in my hands. The vertigo darts on top were there to get rid of whatever escort Tera might have, or maybe to clear unwanted bystanders from the area. The curare darts were meant for the lady herself.

I looked down at my assailants, trying to sort out my options. I needed to get Tera out of the StarrComm building alive, but I couldn't just leave Jasper and his friend as they were. They might be temporarily out of commission, but neither was fully unconscious, and the minute they caught their breath they'd be right back to being trouble. I had restraints ready in my pocket, but that wouldn't keep them from yelling their lungs out to warn Varsi that his plan had gone sideways. Neither would the vertigo darts, which were great for putting someone flat on their back for half an hour or more but didn't do anything to the vocal cords.

Which left me only one choice.

The nice thing about curare darts—or the nasty thing, depending on your point of view—was that while a full dose would kill the target a partial dose would only slow him down, with the degree of that incapacitation depending on how much of the drug had penetrated the various layers of clothing and skin. For the hunter, that meant even a grazing wound would do the job, even though it might take a little extra exercise to chase him down.

Here, exercise wasn't the issue. What was crucial was that I give the two of them enough to sedate them for an hour or two but not enough to kill them.

I didn't have any of the relevant numbers, and there was no time to look them up. Popping out one of the curare darts, mentally crossing my fingers, I stuck the needle end in Jasper's neck and squeezed gently on the plunger. He had just enough time to glare at me before his eyes rolled backwards and he collapsed into a limp heap.

I repeated the performance with the second man. His glare was even more impressive than Jasper's, but in the end he was just as unconscious.

There was no way to tell if I'd overdone it, and nothing I could do if I had. At least both of them were still breathing steadily. I stuck one of the dart guns in my belt, held the other one pressed against my leg where it wouldn't be too conspicuous, and headed around the south side of the building at the best compromise I could manage between speed and silence. I reached the end of the south side and cautiously rounded the corner.

Twenty meters ahead, a visibly shaking figure was standing just to my side of the nearest exit door, head bowed, right hand braced against the side of the building as if for support or balance. My first, horrible, thought was that it was Selene, but an instant later I realized the figure wasn't wearing a scarf, and didn't have Selene's distinctive white hair. In the open space between us were two men, hurrying toward the figure with their backs to me, dart guns like the ones I'd taken from Jasper and his buddy ready in their hands. One of the men had a set of wrist restraints in his free hand, while the other was pulling out a phone.

But at this particular moment their attention wasn't on the target. Instead, they were both staring at Selene, freshly emerged from her hiding place and charging at them with her folded camp chair in one hand and her water bottle in the other.

Back when I'd been a working bounty hunter there'd been an official code of conduct that prohibited collateral damage unless there was no way to avoid it. I didn't know what rules Varsi's men were working under, but I doubted they would worry very much about shooting innocent bystanders if they needed to, or even if they just felt like it. They certainly wouldn't hesitate to gun down a perceived threat charging toward them, even if that threat consisted of a folded camp chair and a water bottle.

Fortunately, we weren't going to have to learn their rules of conduct the hard way. Selene could see me coming up behind them, and I wasn't so far out of practice that I couldn't recognize a diversion when one was handed to me on a platter.

The top darts in both of my borrowed dart guns were vertigos, which meant I didn't have to kill anyone. Unfortunately, I was facing the same problem here that I'd just had with Jasper, that merely dropping them to the ground without also shutting them up would gain us nothing but a couple of minutes of free time. Against a crowd of thugs, that wasn't nearly enough of a head start.

And so, instead of shooting them, I simply came silently up behind them and whacked each of them behind the ear with the butt end of my gun.

They went down without so much as a whimper, though the clatter of their guns as they hit the pavement made me wince. But at this distance, and without a steady wind to carry the sound, it was unlikely the noise had made it to the street and whoever else Varsi had in the area.

I turned to the swaying figure still leaning against the building. To my complete lack of surprise it was Varsi's target and mine, Tera C. "Are you all right?" I asked, stepping to her side.

She started to nod, winced with the movement, and went back to the better policy of holding her head completely level. "Yes," she said. "Vertigo dart. Who are you?"

"Name's Roarke," I said. "Hang on, we're getting you out of here." I looked around as Selene trotted up to us. "You okay?"

"I'm fine," she said, her pupils registering interest as she peered at Tera's face. "I saw her come out, and saw them shoot her, but I was too far away to do anything. Your timing was excellent."

"As was your diversion," I said. "Let's get moving before anyone else decides to join the party."

"They're already gathering," Selene said, sniffing the breeze. "Several more humans have arrived in the past few minutes to the north of the building. I don't know how we're going to get to our runaround."

"We're not," I said. "I can handle Tera. You head

south and see if you can find a quick-rent on the street over there. Runaround, van—anything. You need cash?"

"I have enough." She stooped briefly over the unconscious thugs, collected their dart guns and stuffed them into the folds of her camp chair, then straightened up and hurried on ahead toward the service road.

Taking Tera's left arm and easing it over my shoulder, I put my right arm around her waist and followed. For a moment her hand remained pressed against the wall, as if she feared losing contact with it would rob her of her last bit of equilibrium. Then, reluctantly, she lowered her arm, her hand fumbling for and then gripping the hand I had around her waist. "Where are we going?" she asked.

"Someplace safe," I assured her.

"You're going to give me to the Patth?"

I winced at the weariness in her voice. "We need to keep moving," I said.

"Are you a bounty hunter?"

"Used to be," I said. We reached the end of the tree line and I started us down the service road. Selene, I noted, had already disappeared around the buildings lining the street. "I mostly do other work now."

"I'm told there's a bounty on me," she said. "Are you going to collect it?"

"We'll talk about that later. Easy," I added as she swayed against me. For a second I thought the unsteadiness might be a ruse, and that she was about to try to break free.

But the swaying settled down, and we kept going. "I just . . . do you know how much?" she asked.

I shook my head. "Bounty hunters don't share that information with other people."

"It's *my* bounty," she said, a bit of black humor peeking through the fatigue and dizziness. "I'm just curious to know what I'm worth."

"It's a lot," I conceded. "Let's just concentrate on getting back to our ship."

By the time Tera and I reached the end of the service road Selene was waiting with a runaround. I got Tera into the back seat, put Selene in beside her to make sure she didn't try something stupid like jumping out, then hopped into the driver's seat and headed toward the high-speed turnpike that would take us to the spaceport.

And with that, I could finally relax a little. Even at this hour the turnpike was reasonably busy—people and cargoes left Havershem Spaceport at all hours— and since Selene had rented the runaround with cash there was no record anyone could access as to which one we were in. Without that, there was no way Varsi or anyone else could pick us out of the traffic flow.

Granted, even with the new ID Selene had said the *Ruth* was running under he might be able to figure out where it was and rush enough people and guns there in time to block the ramp. But there was another way to get aboard the *Ruth* than the main entryway, and I would bet large sums of money that neither Varsi nor any of his thugs knew about it.

We were home free. A few more minutes to get to the *Ruth*, a call to the control tower to set up a lift slot, and we'd be on our way.

And then all I had to do was figure out what we were going to do with Tera.

As my father used to say, *A bird in the hand is only worth what a buyer is willing to pay.*

I had the bird. I had the buyer.

But as my father also used to say, *The easy answer isn't always the right one.*

I'd been mulling it over for about ten minutes, and Tera had finally taken the hint and stopped asking questions I didn't want to answer, when I heard Selene stir on the seat behind me. "Gregory, can you give me your monocular?"

"Sure," I said, digging it out of the pocket where I'd stashed it and handing it over my shoulder. "What's up?"

"I'm not sure," she said, and I saw in the mirror that she was leaning close to the side window. "There's something flying around overhead."

I felt my throat tighten. "What kind of something?"

"I don't—there it goes," she said. "Heading toward the spaceport."

I leaned forward over the wheel and looked up through the windshield. Sure enough, there was something flying rapidly away ahead of us. "Could you tell what it was?"

"I don't know," Selene said, her voice gone suddenly dark. "But I think it was one of the *Ruth*'s bioprobes."

"What's a bioprobe?" Tera asked.

"Drones for sampling planetary atmospheres," I told her absently, my mind suddenly spinning onto an entirely new set of unpleasant thoughts. What the hell would one of our bioprobes be doing here? Never mind the fact that flying an unlicensed aircraft around the city was probably illegal. Who could have programmed it to leave the *Ruth* in the first place?

I clenched my teeth. Or, more likely, who was currently sitting in the control room manually flying the damn thing?

"They didn't go to a hotel," Selene murmured. "They're in the ship."

"Who's in the ship?" Tera asked.

"Our employers," I said shortly.

"That's a good thing, isn't it?" Tera persisted. "If your partners are aboard, we'll be able to leave faster."

With a supreme effort, I refrained from verbally taking her head off. I didn't have the time or the brainpower right now for a game of Twenty Questions. "I didn't say they're our partners," I said. "I didn't even say we were on the same side. Selene, find me the number of the tower scheduler."

"All right." There was a short pause. "Got it."

"Call it," I said, reaching back over the seat again. "What was the name again on our new ID?"

"The *Sleeping Beauty*."

"Thanks." The phone's weight settled into my hand, and I held it to my ear. Four vibes...

"Havershem Spaceport Control," a voice came on.

"This is the *Sleeping Beauty*," I said. "Just wanted to make sure our lift slot was still on schedule."

"Of course," the controller said, sounding a bit miffed that I would even have to ask. "You're lifting at oh-two-fifteen."

"So, twenty minutes from now?"

"That's how *my* math works," he said. "Don't know about yours. Is there a problem?"

"No, not at all," I assured him. "I've run into glitches at some ports I've visited, that's all."

"Not on Pinnkus you haven't."

"Indeed not," I agreed. "Thank you."

I keyed off and handed back the phone. "Twenty minutes to lift," I relayed to Selene. "According to

this"—I pointed at the runaround's status display—
"we're twelve minutes from our landing cradle."

"Only eight minutes to spare," she said. "Maybe
that's why they were watching us."

"Maybe," I said, easing down a little harder on the
accelerator. "Right now, I'm less interested in the *why*
as I am in the *what the hell*. They have no business
even being in our ship, let alone playing with our
equipment. What the hell are they thinking?"

"I suppose you'll have to ask them," Selene said.

I grunted. "I suppose I will."

With the extra speed I'd nursed out of the runaround,
we screeched to a halt beside our docking cradle exactly
ten and a half minutes later. Selene and I piled out,
Selene still lugging the folded camp chair, and I spent
one of our precious minutes maneuvering a still wobbly
Tera C out of the vehicle and onto the ramp.

Fortunately Havershem Spaceport had landing cradles, which put our hatch at more or less ground level,
which meant that we only had to negotiate a short ramp
instead of the much longer zigzag we'd have to climb
on a flat-pad landing field. Tera and I headed in, Selene
staying behind another moment to collect our change
from the rental before following.

I was three steps from the entryway when the
hatch opened and Geri stepped into view. "*There*
you are," he said, his fingers waggling at me in an
imperious manner. "Come on—come *on*. We're almost
ready to lift."

"Who the hell gave you permission to make arrangements for my ship?" I demanded, resisting the impulse
to walk right straight up into his face and have this

out right here and now. We had bare minutes to get the *Ruth* buttoned up before we lost our lift slot, and Varsi and his thugs were undoubtedly on their way. A detailed diatribe on why exactly an employer didn't get to override an owner would have to wait. Giving him a serious glare, I started to brush past him—

"Whoa," he said, catching my arm and bringing me to an abrupt halt. The same motion brushed up the hem of my jacket, revealing one of my borrowed dart guns. "Is that a *curare gun*?"

"It's got some curare in it," I confirmed, trying to pull free.

"No, no, no," he said, keeping his grip. With his free hand he plucked the gun from my belt.

And to my astonishment tossed it over the edge of the ramp to disappear into the depths of the landing cradle.

"What the *hell*?" I demanded. I twisted my arm back again, this time putting some shoulder and hip into the movement, and finally managed to break Geri's hold.

But not before he got to the second dart gun and sent it spinning away after the first. "Geri—!"

"Curare darts are illegal on Pinnkus," he cut me off. "You get caught with one, you're in big trouble."

"We're eight minutes from *leaving* the damn planet."

"Better safe than sorry," he said calmly. Grabbing my arm again, he shoved me through the entryway. "Come on, come on. You too, Selene. Hello, Tera C— nice to finally meet you."

"The pleasure's all yours," Tera said icily as Selene helped guide her into the ship.

"Better us than Varsi," Geri replied. "Okay, get

to your seats and strap in. We're ready to go." He stepped over to the entryway controls—

"Not yet we're not," I said.

And reaching into the folds of Selene's camp chair, I pulled out one of the two dart guns she'd stuffed in there. "First, you and Freki are getting off."

Geri turned back to me, his eyes on my gun, his expression a well-steamed mixture of chagrin, betrayal, and anger. "Roarke, what the *hell*—?"

"You said earlier that two hundred thousand commarks was a great incentive," I reminded him. "But the Patth are only offering one. *Varsi's* the one who's offering two."

"So?" Geri demanded.

"So I figure you're actually working for Varsi," I said, watching Tera out of the corner of my eye, "and Varsi wants her dead. Sorry, but I'm not going to be a party to murder."

Tera's eyes went wide, her face paling. She'd heard there was a bounty on her; apparently, she hadn't heard this latest variant on the deal.

Geri's eyes and face, in almost comical contrast, narrowed and reddened in the same reverse degree. "Don't be ridiculous," he snarled. "The Patth upped their bounty to two hundred thousand this afternoon."

"I'll be sure to check on that," I promised. "You and Freki are still getting off."

"Roarke—"

"Did I mention that I haven't had a chance to check the mag on this gun?" I interrupted. "The ones you just tossed down the rabbit hole came with a couple of vertigos on top of a whole pack of curares. This one might have the same loading, or it might all be curares. If I were you, I wouldn't want to find out the hard way."

Clearly, Geri wasn't me. I was still getting out my last word when he leaped at me, his hand darting out to try to slap my gun to the side.

Unfortunately for him, I already knew he wasn't me. I snapped my elbow up, flipping up my forearm and letting his slashing hand pass uselessly beneath it, then dropped the arm back into position and pulled the trigger. There was a soft *crack* as the dart shot out and I saw the slight jerk as it slammed into his chest.

An instant later I had to dodge to the side as his charge nearly ran him into me. He stumbled past and toppled to the deck, barely getting his hands beneath him in time to break his fall. There he stayed, crouched on all hands and knees, making little retching noises.

"I guess it *was* a vertigo," I commented, looking at Tera and Selene. Tera's color had come back, though her eyes were still wide as she stared down at Geri. Selene, without any reaction I could read in her pupils, was already digging out the other dart gun from inside the camp chair. "Stay here and watch him," I instructed her, waving my gun at Geri. "Watch *both* of them," I amended. "Same mystery package with that one, by the way. Be back in a minute."

Freki was on the bridge, running through the final launch checklist. He reacted to my gun with somewhat less facial reaction than Geri had, though he more than made up for it with sheer visual shrivel power. I disarmed him and marched him back to the entryway, to find that Selene had already disarmed Geri. The latter, I noted, had been carrying both his Libra 3mm and his breakaway dart gun. I thought about reminding him the gun was illegal, decided we didn't have time for either irony or sarcasm, and just nudged the two of them out onto the ramp.

Theoretically, they could stand there and beat on the hatch after I sealed it. As a practical matter, if they did that they'd end up at the bottom of the cradle once I pulled in the ramp, which would be both painful and difficult to explain to the port badgemen who'd be sent to haul them out.

Fortunately, they were smart enough to know that. The last view I had as the hatch closed was the two of them making tracks for the edge of the cradle, Freki running, Geri doing a sort of unsteady waddle that was probably the best he could manage under the circumstances.

I was in the pilot's seat on the bridge, ready to go, when the tower signaled my clearance. Fifteen minutes after that, the *Ruth* was out of Pinnkus's gravity well, and I'd sliced us into hyperspace. We had Tera, and she was still alive. Win-win for us all.

Now all we had to do was keep her that way while we figured out what the hell we were going to do with her.

CHAPTER TEN

◆◆◆

Selene and Tera were waiting in the dayroom when I arrived, Tera sitting on the foldout, Selene on one of the fold-down seats across from her, her dart gun ready in her lap. Tera looked mostly recovered from the effects of the vertigo dart. Selene, as always, looked mostly unreadable.

"We're on our way," I announced as I unfolded one of the other seats and sat down. "How are you feeling?"

"I'm fine," Tera said, watching unblinkingly as I made a show of pulling out my own dart gun and checking the magazine. One vertigo dart, twenty-eight curares. "Where are we going?"

"That's the question, isn't it?" I agreed. "Right now, we're heading to Chaclari, mainly because it's close and easy to program in. That gives us two hours to find a better location." I raised my eyebrows at her. "That's your cue."

"My cue for what?"

"Your cue to tell us what's going on," I said.

She lowered her eyes. "I'm looking for someone," she said with a hint of embarrassment. "A friend who disappeared."

"Ah," I said. At least her story meshed with Geri's on that part.

On the other hand, given that I didn't especially trust either of them, that wasn't a huge step forward. "Seems to be a lot of that going around," I pointed out. "Your friend jumps ship on the Icarus project. *You* jump ship. What is it about this thing that makes everybody want to be somewhere else?"

"I don't know what you're talking about," she said, looking up again, her face settling into an impressive poker mode.

"Of course not," I said. "Though in my experience, people try to know at least a little about an item they're trying to sell."

Finally; a reaction. For a second I saw a flash of astonishment cross her face. Then the mask slid down again. "I already told you I don't know anything about any Icarus project."

"Right. I forgot." I looked over at Selene. "You get all that? I'd call it surprise mixed with some chagrin. Don't forget there's probably an overall dislike of me layered on top of everything else."

"Noted," Selene said, her pupils showing a dark amusement. We'd played this game before with suspects and informants, and even though the last time we'd worked it had been several years ago she'd picked right back up on the technique.

I returned my attention to Tera. The poker face was

still there, but there was some apprehension lurking behind her eyes as she looked at Selene. "Sorry—I guess I didn't mention that," I said, as if the thought had just occurred to me. And as if I was genuinely sorry. "Selene's something of a living emotion detector. Comes in handy when I want to know if someone's lying to me. What she does is—well, that doesn't matter," I said off-handedly. In general, undefined threats were more frightening than defined ones. "Where were we? Oh, right—selling Icarus. Do you already have a buyer, or were you working some kind of auction?"

"I still don't know what you're talking about," Tera said. "Shouldn't be surprised, I suppose, since spouting gibberish seems to be your specialty. That nonsense about someone wanting me dead, for instance."

"Why would you think that's crazy?"

"You said yourself that the Patth are offering a hundred thousand commarks for me," she pointed out. "Why would anyone want to pay for me to be dead when I'm worth that much alive?"

"You might be surprised," I said. We could have this discussion now, or I could let her sweat a little. The latter, I decided. "Right now, though, we need to figure out what to do with you."

Again, a flicker of surprise crossed her face. "A hundred thousand commarks, remember?"

"Well, yes, giving you to the Patth is the most fiscally responsible move," I agreed. "But even if we go with that, there are a few hurdles in the way. We can't just grab a Patth off the street, restraint-lock you to his wrist, and ask him to empty his wallet. We need to find out who's got the money, and where they want you delivered."

"Ah," she murmured. "Of course."

"Or it might be worth seeing if someone else would pay more for you," I continued. "Your Icarus friends, for instance." I raised my eyebrows. "Unless, as I said a minute ago, you're trying to sell them out."

"Yes, I heard you a minute ago," Tera said.

"And?"

"And what?" Tera asked patiently. "I told you, I'm just looking for a friend."

"Right," I said, as if I'd forgotten that. "Even so, Icarus might still be interested in talking to us. Assuming anyone's still left there."

Another hint of something slipped past her mask. "I trust you're not expecting me to rattle off names and StarrComm numbers."

"Hoping, but not expecting," I conceded. "Still, you've got time to come up with those. Right now, I'd settle for a few explanations, if you felt so motivated."

"I've already told you I'm out here—"

"I was thinking more of explanations of the Icarus stardrive," I interrupted. "What it is, how it works—that sort of thing. I assume that's what the Patth want to chat with you about."

She favored me with a thin smile. "According to you, they're willing to pay a hundred thousand for that privilege. What's *your* offer?"

"Again, a conversation for another time," I said. "Right now, you've got about an hour and a half to offer your recommendation of where we should take you. After that, Selene and I will have to figure it out ourselves." I stood up. "So. Let's get you settled."

The *Ruth* wasn't nearly big enough to have any kind of dedicated brig, of course. On the other hand, transporting a prisoner required more security than just a set of wrist restraints and a pinky-swear that he would stay put.

My solution had been to convert a section of the dayroom into a sort of open-air cell. The foldout itself was included in that zone, as were a small locker within reach stocked with water and snacks and a concealed vacuum toilet that swung out of the wall. More hidden panels opened to reveal magnetic hack-proof shackles with enough slack in the chains to allow the guest the necessary freedom of motion. Privacy was minimal to nonexistent, but the life of a prisoner wasn't supposed to be pleasant.

There was no shower, but in a pinch prisoners could be unlocked and escorted down the corridor. Most of the time, given the options and the class of prisoner we'd usually worked with, I preferred to deliver them dirty.

Selene watched, dart gun at the ready, while I got Tera set up with the wrist cuffs. I double-checked everything, made sure the chains were secure, and made sure the locker was stocked. Then we left her to her thoughts and broodings and headed to the bridge.

"I presume you checked to make sure you had a vertigo on top?" I asked, nodding at Selene's dart gun as we settled into our seats.

"Yes," she confirmed. "But there was only one of those. The rest were curare."

I nodded heavily. "So Varsi's thugs really *didn't* care whether she ended up alive or dead."

"I was hoping you were wrong about that."

"Me, too," I said. "Obviously, Tera knows something—or has something—that Varsi doesn't want getting out into the Spiral. Not even to him."

"But if Geri and Freki want her dead, why did Geri throw the other guns away?" Selene asked. "He could have taken one, fired the vertigos down into the cradle, and shot her with a curare right there."

"Maybe the bounty specs offered a bonus if they delivered her to Varsi alive," I said, keying on the hidden camera that focused on the foldout. Tera had settled herself into the chair and was staring across the dayroom, thinking or brooding. "Varsi told his own thugs to bring her in so she could have her last drink with him, so maybe he wants to kill her personally if he can."

"And if he can't, he'll pay for a body?"

"Something like that," I said, my stomach tightening. Selene and I had hunted our share of dead-or-alive targets, but with the understanding between us that we would bring them in alive or not at all. "Either way, I'm pretty sure his claim that curare darts are illegal on Pinnkus was complete crab dip. Plasmics and flechette guns are just as deadly, and we saw those all over the place down there."

At least there would be nothing there the authorities could trace back to us. A lot of people passed within gun-dumping distance of a given landing cradle, and close exposure to grav boost equipment was very bad for delicate things like biochemical traces. And of course, any registration numbers and certificates would point to Varsi and his goons, not us.

"I was just thinking," Selene said slowly. "Jasper and the others are probably awake by now."

"Yeah," I agreed, wincing. Varsi would be *very* unhappy with us when he found out what we'd done, and he didn't have a reputation for letting go of grudges. I would need to figure out something to ease him off our back, and that peace offering had better be good. "Maybe after this is over we can slip over to some unexplored world and find something that'll make him forget this little hiccough."

"You were the one who taught *me* not to bet on an inside straight," Selene pointed out, her pupils showing a brief flicker of dark amusement.

The amusement faded. "Gregory, this doesn't make any sense. What could she possibly know that would be worth two hundred thousand commarks to keep secret?"

"If I knew, it wouldn't be a secret anymore," I said. "You're right—on the surface it seems colossally wasteful, especially with the Patth ready to shell out a hundred thousand for her alive. But Fulbright was right. If a target's wanted alive, the bounty specs always clearly state that. I can't imagine someone like Varsi making that kind of mistake."

"Especially since the Patth might also read it," Selene pointed out.

"Oh, I'm sure they did," I said. "I'm equally sure they didn't notice the difference between their specs and Varsi's. The wording would be obvious to professionals like Fulbright, but it might be subtle enough that aliens wouldn't pick up on it. Even humans who aren't familiar with the business would probably miss it."

A movement caught my eye, and I looked at the dayroom monitor. Tera was staring straight at me and waving a hand for attention.

Scowling, I keyed the intercom. So much for the camera being hidden. "What?" I called.

"I've changed my mind," she said. "You're right,

there's someone at Icarus I should call. Are we going to be landing near a StarrComm center?"

"I can make that happen," I confirmed. "I'll get you a pad and pen so you can write out the number and message."

"I'll need to talk to them myself."

"Actually, no, you probably won't," I said.

"Roarke—"

I keyed off. For a few more seconds her mouth moved, then she apparently noticed the intercom light was off and stopped. She sent the camera a scorching look that was probably designed for deployment at a much closer range, then settled back into the foldout.

"If there are code words and responses, she may need to be there in person," Selene pointed out.

"I know," I said. "I'll cave on that eventually, but I want to see first what I can bargain out of her."

Selene's pupils frowned. "She's alone and a prisoner. What kind of bargaining chips does she have?"

"The best kind of all," I said. "The kind we're sorely lacking in. Information."

When I'd first returned to the bridge after kicking Geri and Freki off the *Ruth* at Pinnkus I'd found that Freki had programmed in a course for Kashmir, and for a while after that I considered going back to that course. Whatever they'd had planned for Tera, it was on that world, and it might be interesting to get a peek at the setup. Especially if it was some of Varsi's people waiting with two hundred thousand commarks for them and a shallow grave for Tera. In theory, at least, we could get close enough to such a trap to see it without falling in.

But Kashmir was eighteen hours away, which would give everyone we'd left behind on Pinnkus way too much time to crowd into the StarrComm centers screaming alerts to everyone on their contacts lists. The last thing I wanted was to find a whole array of reception committees—Patth, Varsi, and anyone else who'd gotten the memo—waiting when we tried to walk off the ship.

Granted, those screams into the night might also offer Chaclari as one of our possible destinations, in which case we might land to find that same gaggle of trouble waiting for us. But even if someone inexplicably decided to bet all their chips that we were going there, two hours wasn't a lot of time to organize a response. Whatever anyone threw at us would have to have been thrown together on the fly, and operations like that were usually the exact opposite of airtight. For all those reasons, a nice two-hour flight to Chaclari seemed our best option right now.

It was therefore with a very unpleasant sense of foreboding when, two hours after leaving Pinnkus, we found ourselves still driving through hyperspace. It was with an even more ominous sense of impending doom that I dug deeper into the numbers and discovered we were in fact tracing out Freki's original course.

It took another hour, and a partial dismantling of the navigational console, to find out why.

"It seems we're going to Kashmir after all," I growled at Selene as I pulled myself up from the bridge floor into a sitting position. "Freki somehow managed to freeze the helm/navigation computer interface with his course already locked in."

"I thought you'd changed it to Chaclari."

"I thought I had, too," I said. "The table still works,

and I can still plot and program. The problem is my plotting never gets any farther than the nav displays."

"I didn't know that was even possible," Selene said, crouching down and peering up into the equipment racks.

"Neither did I," I said. "On the other hand, breaking into an Everlock-equipped van is also supposed to be impossible. Geri did that, too." I hissed out a breath. "Who the hell *are* these people, Selene?"

"I don't know," she said. "What are we going to do?"

"Go to Kashmir, I guess," I said. "On the plus side, we shouldn't have to land—the cutter array is completely independent of the space-normal control system. But even just being in Kashmir space is going to be problematic. I assume we're still broadcasting the *Sleeping Beauty* ID that Kifri put in, but given that Geri and Freki know about that means they'll be looking for it."

"There's no way to shut it off?"

"Sure, lots of ways," I said. "Up to and including taking a hammer to the transmitter. The problem is that showing up without an ID will trigger even more alarms."

"But at least it would buy us some time."

"True," I said. "But with our hyperdrive refresh cycle hovering at fifty minutes, probably not enough."

"I thought we were down to forty."

"That was before the capacitor recharge time started slipping again," I said. "Actually, now that I think about it, there's no reason Freki couldn't have gimmicked the capacitors or cutter array, too. We might hit Kashmir to find the hyperdrive won't cycle at all."

"And, of course, they already know we're going to be there," Selene said, her pupils wincing. "They'll have a trap all ready."

I nodded heavily. Going to Chaclari was supposed to throw everyone off the scent while we topped off the fuel tanks, gathered whatever intel we could, and then got the hell out. Now, Freki's sabotage had cut that plan off at the knees.

"Unless..." Selene said slowly.

I looked at her, expecting to find her looking back at me. Instead, she was gazing at the dayroom monitor. "Unless what?" I prompted.

"Didn't Freki say Tera was the *Icarus*'s computer expert?"

I looked at the monitor. "Yes," I said softly. "Yes, he did."

"I think," Selene said, "that we may have found the bargaining chip you were looking for."

Lying flat on her back on the bridge floor, Tera set down her light and probe and shifted her focus from the open access panel to Selene and me. "I wish I could do something," she said. "I really wish I could. But I'm afraid this isn't my area of expertise."

"Why not?" I demanded, feeling an unreasonable surge of anger. Tera had been poking around in there for a good thirty minutes, and against all my years of carefully cultivated prudence I'd started mentally loading way too much of my hopes onto her. Now she was saying she'd failed? "This is a nav system. It's a computer. You're a computer expert. Fix the damn thing."

"I can't," she said, meeting my glare evenly. "I'm only an expert on certain systems, mostly archaic ones at that. This doesn't fit either of those—" She paused, peering up again into the open panel. "Well, okay, it's archaic enough. But it's still nothing I can handle."

"Terrific," I growled. The *Ruth's* nav equipment and computer had been state of the art when I'd bought them. But that had been eight years ago, and with the progression rate in that industry I might as well be using a stone abacus. "No need to be insulting about it."

"I'm just stating facts."

"What if we came out of hyperspace, reset the course, and then went back in?" Selene asked. "Would that work?"

"Probably not," Tera said. "The system is still bypassed somewhere this side of the cutter array. If you can't change the settings now, you won't be able to do it then, either. You'll just go back in with the same course you've already got."

"Besides, if they rigged the hyperdrive to fail when we came out at Kashmir, we'd be stuck dead in space," I said.

"Why would they do that?" Tera asked, frowning. "What if you'd gotten a hull ridge or something and had to come out to repair it? With a ruined hyperdrive, we'd have been stuck in the middle of nowhere."

"Can you think of a better way to make sure you're dead?"

Her jaw tightened briefly. Maybe she still didn't believe that her death was Varsi's end game. Or just didn't *want* to believe it. "Okay, granted," she conceded. "But without a body, how do you collect the bounty? Is Varsi the type to take people's word for things?"

"Not even close," I conceded. "And for the record, ships this small don't usually get hull ridges."

"There are other reasons you might need to take a breather along the way."

"Whatever," I said, suddenly tired of this conversation. "Come on—I'll let you wash up and then get you locked down again."

"Exactly," Tera said, not moving.

I frowned at Selene, got the same frown back from her pupils. "Excuse me?"

"I said *exactly*," Tera said. "As you said: wash up."

"You've lost me."

"Don't worry, I'll find you again," she said. "If I could point you in a direction that might keep you away from Kashmir, what would it be worth to you?"

"What do you *want* it to be worth?" I countered. Maybe my bargaining chip gambit wasn't quite dead yet.

"I want you to take me to a StarrComm center of my choosing," she said. "Someplace I know I'll be safe. In person—not a message or recording."

"You want this conversation to be private? Because that's off the table."

She studied me. "Fine," she said. "You can sit in if you want."

I hesitated, just long enough to make it look like I was being forced into a deal and not like it was one I'd already planned to make. Getting to know where she felt safe, and where she would presumably find allies, was an even better deal than I'd hoped. "All right," I said. "If this new direction works, you've got a deal."

I raised a finger warningly. "If it *doesn't*, I don't plan on hanging around Kashmir a microsecond longer than it takes the hyperdrive to cycle."

"I wouldn't want you to," Tera assured me. Hoisting herself up into a sitting position, she held out her hands, palms upward. "Take a look. What do you see?"

I frowned. Hands. Fingers. Thumbs. Manicured nails that hadn't been properly tended to for at least a few weeks.

"Dust," Selene said quietly.

I looked closer. Dust, and dirt.

Dust.

I raised my eyes to her face. She had a faint smile on her lips, a smile tempered by the knowledge that I could easily renege on my promise and there would be nothing she could do about it. "You're saying Freki never opened that cabinet," I said, just to prove I'd gotten the correct answer.

"Exactly," Tera said. "There are also dark circles around the screw heads, swirls that only go one way. Like they were unscrewed only once in the past few years and not screwed back in again."

"Which is what I just did," I said, trying to visualize the *Ruth*'s control circuitry layout. Out of the corner of my eye I saw Selene move to the pilot's seat and start pulling up schematics. If I was right . . .

"The Number Two equipment bay," she announced.

"Right," I agreed. Number Two was behind a two-by-one-meter panel on the bow-ventral part of the hull where a lot of the hyperspace cutter array circuitry was housed. It was designed to be accessible only from the outside, since the board-certified techs who worked out of spaceports were generally the only ones licensed and qualified to deal with it.

On most ships, I would need to stop the ship, put on our single vac suit, and head out for a risky and reasonably unpleasant spacewalk.

Luckily, the *Ruth* wasn't most ships.

❖   ❖   ❖

We got Tera cleaned up—she did all the work but Selene watched her—and got her back into her restraints on the foldout. I sent Selene back to the bridge to keep an eye on her, then switched to a set of coveralls and got into the subdeck crawlway beneath the *Ruth*'s main deck. Getting a roll platform under my chest, I worked my way through the narrow passageway to the bow and the section of hull on the inner side of the equipment bay.

Every bounty hunter, at one time or another, found himself in a situation where his ship's entryway was blocked. Usually the obstruction was either local law enforcement officers who wanted the glory of the capture or rival hunters who wanted the money. Occasionally it was friends of the captive with visions of undying gratitude, though that didn't happen very often and the undying gratitude part was even rarer. The point was that experienced hunters were always on the lookout for ways to smuggle a chunk of valuable human cargo aboard without getting into potentially lethal arguments.

With some hunters, it was a set of collapsible freight crates prelabeled with false customs stickers that could be lifted into a cargo hold among other, more legitimate cargo. With other hunters, it was a set of equally bogus warrants and credentials designed to intimidate or drive off any entryway opposition.

With me, it was the Number Two equipment bay.

The disguised inner hull plate's hidden catches, designed to work from either side, were easy to unfasten if you knew the trick. I swung the plate into the crawlway, being careful not to bump or otherwise damage the cutter array equipment that was fastened to the plate's other side. Beyond the equipment and the gap was the outer hull plate. With the *Ruth* sitting in a docking cradle that plate would also be openable from either side, though with vacuum on the far side the ship's internal air pressure currently kept it snugly in place. I pulled out my light, clipped it to the edge of the opening, and turned it on.

And there it was: a small box with half a dozen wires snaking out of it that had been soldered to various spots on the layered mass of cutter array electronics.

I spent a few minutes studying the setup, tracing the wires and making careful notes of where each of them ended up. Then, I turned myself carefully around and rolled my way back to the crawlway hatch.

Selene had the various strata of the equipment bay's schematics up on three of the displays by the time I reached the bridge. Between the two of us, we worked out where each of the mystery box's cables was going, what it was doing, and the order in which we needed to disconnect them.

Two hours later, the *Ruth* was ours again.

Tera had finished her nap or whatever and was working on a nut bar and bottle of water when Selene and I arrived in the dayroom. "Okay, it seems to have worked," I said. "Time for your part of the deal. Where are we going?"

"Melayse," she said. "There's a StarrComm center south of the New Sandio Spaceport that will work. About a kilometer away—quick walk there, quick walk back."

"And?" I asked.

"And what?" she asked. "I make my call, and then..." She hesitated. "And then I guess you do whatever you want with me."

"What if that means returning you to Icarus?" I asked.

Her lip twitched. "I don't think Icarus wants me back," she said. "But if you can find them, you're welcome to try."

"We'll find them after they tell us what they're willing to pay," I said. "For that, I'll need a number."

She shook her head. "I can't give you that."

"I could always give you to Varsi."

She studied my face. "I can't give you a number," she repeated. "But I could punch it in out of your sight and let you talk to them. Good enough?"

"As long as I get to talk to them," I said. "Okay, I'll get us on our way. You get some rest."

"What if I'm not tired?"

"Get some rest anyway."

I waited until Selene and I were back on the bridge with the dayroom camera going before asking the obvious question. "What did you get?" I asked as I called up Melayse on the nav table.

"Nothing from Melayse or the StarrComm call," Selene said. "But there *was* a reaction when you talked about sending her back to Icarus."

"Yeah, I got that, too," I said. "You think she's afraid of going back?"

"Sorry, but I don't know her well enough for that kind of fine-tuning. All I can say is that she reacted to that suggestion."

"So Icarus is still playing on her mind," I said. "Then, there's Melayse itself. Recognize the name?"

"Yes," Selene said. "Back on Ringbar, Geri said she'd been there before they spotted her on Pinnkus."

"That's the place," I confirmed. "Like Havershem

City but less civilized, I believe he also said. I wonder why she'd want to go back."

"Either because she has friends there or else had to leave something valuable behind," Selene said. "Or perhaps there's some unfinished business."

"I'd say you have the possibilities covered," I acknowledged. "Let's go see which one it is."

CHAPTER ELEVEN

———— ❖ ————

Melayse was one of those worlds that liked to call itself *cosmopolitan*, by which it meant it was comfortably wealthy, pompously artistic, welcoming of all species, and smugly pleased with itself over all of it. Its inhabitants believed, or at least pretended to believe, that they were far and away above the rest of the common herd: healthier, smarter, more caring, and better able to handle life in general.

And they tried very hard not to notice that their world had places like the New Sandio Commons.

The Commons wasn't a slum, exactly, at least not like slums on poorer, less cosmopolitan worlds. It was crowded and noisy and definitely not artistic, but it didn't have the dirt and poverty and hollow-eyed sense of hopelessness that characterized slums throughout the Spiral.

But it had the same mass of people as a slum, and it was pretty clear that the majority of those living there weren't exactly thriving.

The Commons had started out innocently enough, as a market and business area that had grown up around the New Sandio Spaceport as a convenient place for interstellar travelers to get the various items and services they needed or wanted. StarrComm's later decision to put a center on the market's other side had accelerated development, giving those same travelers a location where they could now communicate with the outside worlds.

The problem was that there was only so much the business area could expand outward without opening up the distance and thereby losing the convenience that was its main reason for existence. So as the competition for space grew, the wide thoroughfares that had been filled with cabs and runarounds slowly narrowed as kiosks and portable stands began encroaching on the edges. As the roads became less passable, more and more travelers decided to skip the high-priced vehicle rentals in favor of a brisk walk to the StarrComm center, which encouraged even more kiosks and more narrowing.

Eventually, the roads had shrunk to narrow pedestrian walkways that would handle small service and supply vehicles but not much else. As the profits rolling into any individual shop continued to shrink, semipermanent single-person huts began to join the kiosks as the owners tried to cut their living expenses as much as they had their business outlay. Slowly, every other space in the area filled in, and the people adapted to the compact living that had exhausted the centers of so many other major cities across the Spiral.

Fortunately, that effect only encompassed the area between the spaceport and the StarrComm center. In the rest of the area around the Commons and the spaceport, Melayse life continued in its usual glorious way, with stretched-out spaces and wide roads and a multitude of vehicles to serve them.

Inside the Commons, it might as well have been an entirely different planet.

Claustrophobic congestion apart, the place maintained the multicultural aspects of the general Melayse experience. Not surprising, really, considering that many alien ships passed through the spaceport and the local businesses had always made an effort to cater to them. As Tera and I worked our way down the main street, I could see food kiosks representing four different species, and could smell the cooking aromas of at least three others. Pedestrians were everywhere: moving past us on errands, pausing at kiosks to peruse the wares, slipping between the booths and huts en route to the more established and permanent stores and eateries along the street, or simply stopping dead in the middle of the traffic flow to greet friends or hold animated conversations.

It was, in short, the perfect place for a prisoner to try slipping the leash. Presumably, Tera knew that, though she also presumably knew that *I* knew it and would be ready for her to make a bid for freedom.

But as we walked along I realized that wasn't how things were playing out. Prisoners planning to run usually first tested their boundaries a few times by easing away from their keepers, then easing back to their mandated positions, gauging the keepers' reactions and trying to judge when and where to turn that random drift into a mad dash.

Tera wasn't doing any of that. On the contrary, she

was sticking to me like she was glued there, her arm all but pressed against mine.

At first I assumed she knew the standard prisoner rabbiting pattern and was simply trying something new in hopes of lulling me into a false sense of security. But after passing through a concentrated knot of Drilies, a brief tangle that put Tera out of my reach and even out of my sight for a second or two, I reluctantly concluded that she genuinely had no plans to ditch me.

It wouldn't have helped her anyway, not with Selene invisibly working her own way through the crowd a short ways behind us, ready to use her magic tracking skills to catch up with our wayward prisoner. But Tera didn't know that.

We were about halfway to the StarrComm building when I first realized that it wasn't just Selene following us.

They were fairly unobtrusive, as tails went: lumpy-faced creatures with mostly human height and build, though with shortened torsos and extra-long arms, wearing open-front hooded brown cloaks over long neo-Greek tunics. There were three of them marching together a few pedestrians behind us, with one more each on our flanks keeping casual pace with us. Their cloaks covered all the usual places where people carried weapons, but from the purposeful manner of their stride I had no doubt all five of them were armed.

Of course, so was I. I had my plasmic holstered beneath my jacket on my right hip and one of our new dart guns stuck into my waistband on my front left.

The problem was that I was facing five potential opponents and I only had two vertigo darts. I could theoretically aim my plasmic to injure, but any clean shot with a fully-loaded curare dart would be fatal to most oxygen-breathing species.

That meant that in a full-out battle, Tera and I would either end up dead or I'd be on the hook for a bunch of violent deaths. I was a bit hazy on the specifics of Melayse law, but on most planets in the Spiral any killing had damn well better be provable as justified.

Normally, a bounty hunter didn't bother a prisoner with such trivia as the fact that someone else was trying to crowd in on the action. But given how hard Tera was clinging to me, I was pretty sure she'd already noticed our uninvited escort.

It might be interesting to find out just how much she knew about them.

"You hungry?" I asked as we approached a booth that was giving off the unmistakable aroma of Earth BBQ. "There's a spot just ahead that might be good."

"No, thank you," Tera said, a hint of stifled stress in her voice.

"You sure?" I pressed, casually taking her arm. "We could also invite your friends, if you'd like."

The muscles under my hand tensed. "Don't look at them," she warned, abandoning her efforts to hide her tension. She'd seen them, all right, and it was pretty clear she didn't consider them friends.

"Are they after the bounty?" I asked. "Or do they want you for some other reason entirely?"

"You've got it backwards," she said. "They're not after *me*. They're after *you*."

"Really? What for?"

She hissed out a breath. "They want to kill you."

I knew a fair number of people in the Spiral who would be more than happy to see me dead. But most of them were currently in prison, and of the remainder most had either learned caution or else were working down long lists that had lots of other names ahead of mine.

But at least with that crowd I knew what they looked like and could hopefully spot them in time to come up with a strategy. I'd never even seen this species before, let alone these individuals. "What for?" I asked. "I don't even know them."

"I don't think they know you, either," she said hesitantly. "I think they think you're someone else."

"Who?"

"Someone I used to know."

"Jordan McKell?"

A brief pause. "Yes."

I ground my teeth. Like a bad penny, the name that kept sliding in and out of all these conversations. "The other fugitive from the *Icarus.*"

"The *only* fugitive," she corrected stiffly. "I'm out here hunting him, remember?"

"Right. I forgot. So why do they want McKell?"

Another brief pause. "A few years ago he killed two of them."

I winced. "Great."

We passed the booth—it was BBQ, all right, advertising both Texas and New Kansas City blends—and for a moment I was tempted to stop and buy a rack of ribs anyway, just to see how our escorts responded.

But all other things being equal, this would be a terrible place for a shoot-out. There was little effective cover, zero freedom of movement, and a lot of collateral damage waiting to happen.

As my father used to say, *All things being equal usually means the odds are on the other guy's side.*

"I don't suppose there's any chance McKell's lurking around somewhere," I suggested. "Waiting to pop up at the last second, star-thriller style, and shoot at them from ambush?"

"He's a fugitive," Tera said with strained patience. "The essence of being a fugitive is that you don't pop up and shoot at people."

"Pity," I said, looking around as best I could without moving my head. The key to preventing this kind of situation from boiling over was to keep the pursuers thinking they had the upper hand. If they knew I'd spotted them, they might be inclined to have things out here and now.

And then, a movement caught my eye. A small, longish creature was scampering toward us over the top of one of the kiosks. It reached the end of the roof and made an effortless leap to the next one in line, where it paused and peered down at us.

It was one of Kifri's ferrets.

"What about your pal Kifri?" I asked.

"What about him?" Tera countered. "And he wasn't exactly a pal. More of a convenient bumper."

"A bumper could be useful right about now," I said. "No chance he could be somewhere nearby, I suppose?"

"Not unless you brought him aboard in your luggage," Tera said. "We left him on Pinnkus, remember?"

"Right." The ferret, having had its look around, turned and scampered back the way it had come, leaping from booth to booth until it was lost to sight among the banners. "I guess in that case we'll just have to keep walking and wait for inspiration to strike."

"It had better strike fast," Tera warned. "There's a security substation about two minutes ahead."

"Really? Sounds good."

"Sounds terrible," she retorted tensely. "These guys don't want to be caught or even just questioned. We make a move toward any badgemen, and they'll be killed where they stand."

"Better them than me," I muttered.

"What was that?"

"Nothing," I said. I'd had my share of run-ins with the law, and I had no special love for the people tasked with enforcing it. But most of those times I'd probably deserved it, and at any rate I had no intention of setting anyone up to be slaughtered. "What's a block over to our right?"

"Past the permanent buildings? Just a service road."

"Busy?"

"Probably not at this time of day."

As my father used to say, Probably *is shorthand for no one wants to trouble you with the actual odds involved*. But at the moment, it was our best shot. "Good enough," I said. "Okay. See that alley about fifteen meters ahead? The one just past the whistle-snack kiosk? We're going to do a hard right-hand turn there and hit the service road. If we're fast enough, we might be able to get to the next corner ahead and possibly lose our new fan club."

"What about the Iykam on that side?"

So they were called Iykams. Not only had I never seen one, I'd never even heard of them. "If he keeps to his current pace, he should get an extra step or two before he can react to our change of direction," I said. "That should let us pass behind him. If he's instead on one of his drift-backs, we'll just have to cut in front of him and hope for the best. You game?"

She huffed out a breath. "All right. But be careful."

"Words to live by."

I kept watch on the Iykam out of the corner of my eye as we approached our turn. He drifted back... moved forward again... steadied on our flank. I resettled my grip on Tera's arm and got ready. We reached the alley—

Abruptly, I spun her to the right, giving her a small push as I made the same hard right beside her. The Iykam, as anticipated, took two more steps before he belatedly spotted our maneuver. He braked to a halt as we hurried past behind him, spinning around toward us. I gave Tera another push and let go of her arm, slowing slightly as the alien finished his turn. His hand darted to his left side, disappearing into his open-front robe.

And as it came back out I reached in, caught hold of the hand, twisted the weapon sharply against his thumb, and plucked it from his grip. A quick push against his chest to throw him off balance, and then I was in the alley, breaking into a full-on run as I charged after Tera.

Given the obsession everyone else who was chasing Tera seemed to have for dart guns, I was expecting to find that I'd just added another such weapon to my collection. But a quick glance as I ran showed it was something entirely different. It was roughly the size and shape of a flechette gun, but the barrel was all wrong for a projectile weapon and the grip's bottom plate looked more like that of a power pack than a cartridge magazine. Some kind of plasma gun, maybe, except that the barrel wasn't right for that, either.

"Roarke?"

I looked up from my study of my new toy. Tera had reached the end of the alley and was standing in the service road, waiting for me to point her the right direction. I waved her to her right, the direction we'd been going on the main street before taking this detour. She nodded and disappeared around the building at that intersection, and I put on an additional burst of speed to try to catch up. Whatever the Iykam's weapon did, I would prefer to get out of here before I got a private demonstration.

Unfortunately, achieving that noble goal depended on the Iykams being slow on the uptake, and I knew better than to count on that. Sure enough, as I rounded the corner a quick look down the alley showed three of the aliens charging after us, their hoods thrown back, their open robes flapping in rhythm with their pumping legs. Tera might barely be to the next alley by the time they came around the corner, but I would still be a good five meters away.

I'd already concluded that I couldn't kill any of them. Luckily for me, that didn't mean I couldn't let any of them get hurt.

My time and distance estimates proved to be right on the money. Tera was at the next street and waiting for further instructions, and I was five meters behind her, when I heard the shuffling of footsteps rounding the corner behind me.

"Stop, human!" a harsh voice ordered. "Stop, or die."

"Don't shoot!" I shouted back, braking to a halt with my arms held away from my body and my borrowed weapon pointing to the side away from them. "I'm not him!"

The footsteps stopped. "Face us," the same voice ordered.

At least none of them had shot me in the back. Small favors. Slowly, I turned around, my arms still held wide. "Whatever blood feud you're running, it has nothing to do with me," I said.

"The weapon you stole," one of them ordered. "Throw it to me."

"Sure," I said. All three were still standing there, I noted, keeping their distance instead of continuing forward. Did that mean these guns were short-range weapons, and that none of them wanted to get shot by the one I was holding?

I hoped so. My distance from them exactly equaled their distance from me, after all, and if they didn't want to get shot with one of these things neither did I. I swung my arm with deliberate slowness, tossing the gun to land at their feet.

"Here—you might as well have this one, too," I added as one of them bent over and picked it up. Brushing aside my jacket with my left hand, I pulled the dart gun from my waistband with two fingers. I turned slightly to my right, as if to get a better angle, and lobbed the dart gun toward them. This toss was much higher than my first one, the gun's arc topping off a good three meters above the ground.

And as it started back down, with the Iykams' eyes reflexively following its path and my partial turn half hiding my right hand, I drew my plasmic and fired a shot directly at the weapon.

Geri's breakaway gun had been designed for concealment, with a single compressed air cylinder and a magazine of eight darts. The more robust, full-sized weapons Selene and I had taken from Varsi's thugs had tripled down on both magazine load and propellant. The three compressed air cylinders, flash heated by my plasmic shot, exploded spectacularly.

One of the aliens shouted something vicious-sounding as the group was raked with high-speed pieces of the shattered weapon. One of the others gave a sort of screech of pain or rage or both.

The third, even as he ducked, managed to get off a shot.

I'd heard of coronal-discharge weapons. I'd never before seen one in operation, and I could have gone my whole life without that particular experience. The Iykam's aim wasn't perfect, but even with the focal point of the blast a meter to my side I still felt a horrible tingle in my hair and skin as a blazing blue-white aura sizzled from the gun into the air. For a second or two it swirled like an angry demon looking for a victim before it dissipated.

Leaving me with tingling skin, hair that felt like it had been singed but probably hadn't, and an artificial left arm's worth of artificial nerves screaming in agony.

But I didn't have the time to scream or cry or wrench at the arm to try to detach it. The aliens were still there, they were still armed, and if they recovered from their shrapnel shower fast enough to get a clear second shot it wouldn't just be my arm that felt like it was burning. I sprinted to Tera, grabbed her hand, and charged down the next alley and the crowded street beyond.

We braked to a fast walk, making our way through this new batch of kiosks, shops, and pedestrians. I kept an eye behind us and to both sides as we slipped through the crowds, watching for renewed pursuit. But if the Iykams had recovered and reorganized, there was no sign of it.

"What *was* that?" she breathed as we settled into a speedy walk.

"Coronal-discharge gun," I said. "A few nations have played around with them, but they're such short-range weapons that no one's ever bothered producing them in any serious numbers."

"Except the Iykams."

I rubbed my arm where the aftereffects still tingled. "Except the Iykams."

Five minutes later, still with no signs of Iykam pursuit, we finally came within sight of the Starr-Comm building.

"I trust you'll be able to keep it short and sweet," I warned Tera as we wove our way through the final few layers of the Commons gauntlet. "Even if our friends don't pause to pick out *all* the shrapnel, they'll be back on the case soon enough." Ahead, through the crowd of shoppers, I could see a sparse double stream of customers entering and exiting the main StarrComm entrance. One of the humans in the latter group was clearly in a hurry, brushing impatiently past a pair of k'Tra strolling down the steps in front of him—

Grabbing Tera's shoulders, I spun her around toward the scarf shop we were passing. "Face in, and hold still," I muttered. I grabbed a scarf at random and held it up to her cheek, as if I was checking its color against her skin tone. "Don't move."

"What is it?" she asked suspiciously. Still, whatever her doubts, she nevertheless took the cue and picked out two more scarf ends to hold against her other cheek.

"An old friend just came out of the StarrComm building," I told her. Of all the *damn* bits of bad luck... "Our buddy Freki."

"*Freki?*" she echoed, starting to turn to look.

I was faster, catching her cheek with my palm and turning her head back into the kiosk. "I said *don't move*," I growled. "If he sees us, this all goes up in smoke."

I could feel the tenseness in her cheek. But she obeyed, putting back one of the scarves and picking out another one. I kept my back to Freki's presumed approach line, watching out of the corner of my eye for him to pass by. If he didn't—if he recognized us and stopped—I was going to have a second fight on my hands.

I was trying to come up with a plan for that fight when, to my relief, I caught a glimpse of his back as he passed us by, heading in the direction of the spaceport. He had his phone to his ear, and while it was impossible to hear what he was saying with all the ambient noise I didn't doubt that the conversation had to do with us.

I waited until I'd had my last glimpse of him, then gave it another thirty seconds to be sure. Putting the scarves back, I guided Tera back into the stream of pedestrians.

But not toward the StarrComm center. Not anymore.

It didn't take her long to notice the change in plans. "Wait—where are we going?" she asked as I steered her down another alley. "The StarrComm center's *that* way."

"Freki just came out of there," I reminded her. "He may have left people behind or instructions to the staff to watch for us."

"But he—" She broke off, and I could see her fighting to get herself under control. "We have to get in there."

"Why?" I asked. "This big call of yours need to be done right this very minute?"

"But—" Again, she went silent. I looked at her, saw concern and frustration racing across her face. "Fine. So where *are* we going?"

"I'm working on it," I assured her.

"Work faster."

We continued on, Tera glowering with frustration, me checking down each street and alley as we passed for signs of the Iykams. Fortunately, they seemed to have had enough for one day.

Finally, I saw what I was looking for: a line of runarounds parked along the edge of the Commons, cars we could get to while still under the visual cover of all the people and aliens. Shifting my attention to the more open Melayse landscape beyond the Commons, I spotted a cluster of three tall hotels rising into the sky around a tube transport junction about a kilometer away. I flipped a mental coin, and the Pinnacle Arms won. "There," I told Tera, nodding ahead. "Those hotels over there."

"That's a long way to walk over open ground," she warned.

"Hence, the runaround," I said, steering her toward the second quick-rent in line. Not that I was paranoid, but I'd long ago learned to avoid both the first or last item in any sequence.

Besides, that particular runaround was right beside the notice board that listed the quick-rent prices.

"Over here," I told Tera, stopping beside the board. "Give me your finger."

"What?"

"Your finger," I repeated. I took her right hand, straightened out the forefinger and lifted it to the board. "Just relax your hand."

"What are you *doing*?"

"Leaving a message." Picking a clear spot on the board, I used her finger to trace out *P-I-N-N-A-C-L-E A-R-M-S* in large letters. "There," I said, letting go of her hand and opening the runaround's door. "Get in."

"A message for whom?" Tera asked, frowning at the board as she climbed into the runaround.

"Selene's tracking us," I explained as I went around to the driver's side. "Rather, she's tracking you. She can't track us in a runaround, so I told her where we were going."

"Oh." Tera settled into her seat, a puzzled expression on her face as I fed a hundred-commark bill into the runaround's slot. "So we're going to ground?"

"We're going to ground," I confirmed as I checked the displays and pulled out into the street. "We're going to rest, get something to eat, and try very hard to figure out what the hell we do next."

CHAPTER TWELVE

———— ❖ ————

The receptionist at the Pinnacle Arms greeted us the way every hotel desk clerk across the Spiral greeted a couple checking in without luggage: with a courteous smile layered over just enough smirk to get the point across without getting himself in trouble. The fact that I was paying for the room in cash prompted him to add a bit more leer to the mix; the fact that I was reserving the room for three days at least gained me a bit of grudging admiration.

I didn't care what he thought, of course. I certainly had no intention of staying longer than a few hours at the most. But if Freki or the Iykams came poking around the hotels' registers, the fact that this particular unidentified couple had apparently settled in for the long haul might at least put them off the scent a little.

We'd been there for half an hour, and Tera was in the shower, when Selene arrived.

"Any trouble?" I asked as I let her into the room.

"No," she said, her pupils holding a lingering uneasiness. "I found the runaround stand and your message, then tracked you to the room through the elevators. Did you shoot someone back there?"

"Sort of," I said. "Why, was there some commotion?"

"There was a lot of excited talk," Selene said. "I saw some people helping someone toward the spaceport, but I didn't want to get too close." Her pupils went a little accusatory. "It all happened across Tera's scent trail."

"At five-to-one odds, I didn't have much choice," I told her. "I didn't kill anyone, if that makes you feel better."

"It does," she said, the emotion in her pupils easing a little. "What happened?"

"There are some aliens out there called Iykams who apparently want Jordan McKell dead."

"And?"

"And because I was hanging around Tera they decided I must be him," I said. "Ironic, isn't it?"

"Ironic how?" Tera called from the bathroom doorway.

I looked at her. I'd half expected to find her wrapped in a towel, the way mystery women in star-thrillers always came out of showers. But while her hair was still wet she was fully dressed. "Never mind," I said, stepping toward the bar. "You want something to drink?"

"No, thanks."

I just stood there and stared silently at her. She stared back, and then her lip twitched. "Fine," she said. "Caff cola. So you found us."

"Of course," Selene said. "Your trail was quite clear."

"Not as clear as a phone call would have been," Tera pointed out. "Or would that have been too easy?"

"That would have been too hard," I said as I poured her cola, "given that both our phones are on the dayroom table next to yours."

"You didn't bring your *phones*?"

"Melayse likes to consider itself in the upper tier of Spiral worlds," I said. "Part of that is having an absolutely first-rate communications system. Part of *that* is the ability to locate, tap, record, and otherwise mess with any phone they think would benefit from being located, tapped, recorded, or messed with. Ergo, the phones stay on the ship."

She snorted. "Are *all* bounty hunters this paranoid?"

"The ones who are still alive are," I said. I poured a bourbon for myself and carried both drinks over to her. I generally didn't like to mix alcohol with interrogation, but while the worst of the pain in my artificial arm had faded away the thing still ached. Given a choice between the distraction of residual pain and the possible confusion of an alcohol buzz, I figured I might as well go with the latter. "Have a seat," I said, gesturing her to a cushion on the couch next to Selene.

"Thanks," she said, taking the cola and pointedly sitting down instead in the chair farthest from the couch.

Not that that would make much difference. With the almost imperceptible breeze from the room's air system coming from behind her, she was already too close to Selene to hide the changes in her scent. I sat down in the chair facing her and set my glass down on the table beside me. "Let's start with your name," I said. "Your *real* name."

"Tera."

"Last name?"

She looked sideways at Selene. "Let's just leave it at Tera," she said. "So who exactly are *you*?"

Already trying to control the conversation. But that was okay, too. The larger and broader the baseline Selene could gather, the better she'd be able to pick out the emotional twitches when Tera started lying to us. "Gregory Roarke, as I already told you," I said. "Former bounty hunter. I was hired to find you and deliver you to a couple of gentlemen named Geri and Freki. This is Selene—don't bother asking; her family name is eighteen syllables long, and I'm not about to repeat it here. She currently works crockett jobs with me. Tell me about the Icarus project."

"What about it?"

At least she wasn't going to waste time pretending she'd never heard of it. "What is it?"

Tera shook her head. "That's classified."

"By whom?"

"Also classified."

"Is it a stardrive?"

"Classified."

There was no change in her expression, but I'd caught the subtle indicator in Selene's pupils. "Okay, so it's a stardrive," I concluded.

"I never said—"

"You didn't have to." I nodded toward Selene. "Living emotion detector, remember?"

Tera's face went rigid, the telltale of people who realize they're in over their heads. Unfortunately, also the telltale of people on the edge of shutting down the conversation, at which point we would get nothing.

Time to lay out a couple more cards. "Look, Tera," I said, shifting to a more conciliatory, less confrontational tone. "You saw the Iykams. They're here, and they're gunning for your friend McKell."

"Perhaps," Tera murmured.

I frowned. There'd been another signal from Selene on my comment... "I stand corrected," I said, watching Tera's face closely. "*Not* McKell. Or rather, not *just* McKell. They're after Kifri, too, aren't they?"

Tera's eyes flicked to Selene, back to me. And then, her shoulders slumped, just enough. "Fine," she said in a low voice. "But if I tell you everything, you have to promise to keep it to yourselves."

"Of course," I said.

"I mean *really* to yourselves," she insisted. "You let any of this out, and I'll be dead. Probably you will be, too."

"Never my favorite outcome," I agreed. "Okay. We're listening."

She took a deep breath. The whole break-and-confess thing had been quite a good performance, I decided. It would be interesting to see how many lies she was about to drop on us.

"There was a woman named Tera connected to the Icarus project," she said, her eyes shifting one last time to Selene before settling in on me. "Last name was never released, but I know it began with a C. There was also a man named Jordan McKell on the project and a Kalix named Ixil."

"You talk about them as if they were all dead," I said.

"Dead?" Tera shrugged. "As far as I know they're

all alive, well, and still with the project. The point is that the stuff I just told you leaked out and...a couple of friends and I realized there might be some big money to be made."

I looked at Selene, noting the steadiness of her pupils. As far as she could tell, Tera was telling the truth. "So I was right," I said. "You *are* trying to sell the Icarus project. Only not the *real* project." I cocked an eyebrow at her. "You're nothing but con artists, are you?"

Her lip twitched. "That's rich, coming from a bounty hunter," she said. "Whatever. So anyway, we located a couple of Patth Expediters named—"

"A couple of who?"

"Expediters," she repeated. "Agents working directly under the Patth Director General, usually attached to a given director or sub-director, and carrying out special operations throughout the Spiral."

I nodded as the obvious connection finally hit me. "Geri and Freki."

"Yes." She gave a soft snort. "I'd have thought the names alone would have clued you in that they were being cute about their identities."

I must have looked blank, because her lip twitched again. "Geri and Freki. Odin's wolves in Old Earth Norse mythology."

"Right," I said, as if it had just slipped my mind. Deep studies into Earth myths hadn't exactly been a high priority throughout my life. "What about the Iykams? Are they also working for the Patth?"

"Yes, but on a much lower level," Tera said. "Expediters are the elite, while Iykams mostly just travel with Patth ships to protect the pilots. But they're sometimes also brought in when extra muscle is needed."

"Muscle with the charming ability to char their victims beyond any hope of identification," I muttered, wincing at the memory of that blast.

"I'm sure that comes in handy sometimes," Tera said, wincing a little herself. "I don't know why they're even here, unless Freki called them in." She fixed me with a sudden glare. "Assuming that he really *is* here, that you didn't lie about that."

"Oh, he's here, all right," I assured her. "And I have no intention of crossing his path again until I have a better idea of what I've gotten us into."

"You mean what *Geri* got us into," Selene corrected softly.

I frowned at her. That was an excellent point. "You're right," I said. "He and Freki *are* the ones who got this ball rolling. I wonder why they picked on us."

"You were probably convenient and stupid," Tera said with a touch of impatience. "Can we get on with this?"

"Sure," I said. "So you proclaimed yourself to be the real Tera C and started looking for a pair of suckers to invest in your soap cloud. What kind of deal did you make with them?"

"I didn't," Tera said. "We were still figuring out how to approach them when you popped up out of nowhere on Havershem City and grabbed me."

"Just as well we did," I reminded her. "I don't know what your friendly Norse wolves had in mind, but a man named Luko Varsi and his people were also there, and Varsi wants you dead."

"That doesn't make any sense," she insisted. "Why would anyone care if I run a con on the Patth?"

"What makes you think he cares a tinker's damn what you do to the Patth?" I countered. "You really don't recognize Varsi's name?"

"No. Who is he?"

"Oh, hang on to your hat, girl," I said sourly, picking up my glass. "You want wolves? I'll give you wolves."

I took a long sip from my drink. It seemed to help with the ache. "Let's start with a list of Varsi's interests. They include happyjam and other illegal drugs, weapons, legal and illegal servitude, illicit transport—do you need more?"

"No, I get the picture," Tera said grimly. "I've dealt with worse."

"You may have dealt with *bigger*," I corrected. "I doubt you've dealt with *worse*. Did I mention he's madly in love with money? That he'll do anything to gain it and keep it?"

"Fine—he's a bad man," she said, the words coming out with a shiny new coating of frost. "I get the picture. You still haven't explained why he would want me dead."

"You're not thinking," I said. "Do you really believe that in a lifetime of conning people you never took any of that dearly beloved money from something he's involved in?"

Tera frowned. "Are you're saying he'd kill me because I might have conned him out of a few commarks ten years ago? That's crazy."

"That's because you're not as psychotically invested in such things as money and pride as he is," I said. "But I know the man. Trust me—if you stepped on his fingers anytime in the past century, he wants payback. And ultimately, it really doesn't matter how petty the reason why that bullet or flechette is lodged in your chest. You'll still be dead."

"I get the point," she said. "Anything else about him that I should know?"

"There's one more thing," I said. "Maybe it impacts you, maybe it doesn't. Varsi appears to be prepping for some facial reconstructive surgery, which suggests to me that he may be planning to run."

"From who?"

"Who knows?" I said with a shrug. "Given the section of the ethical spectrum he hangs out in, he may have pissed off someone else as nasty as he is."

"Maybe one of those bigger dogs?"

"Could be," I said. "For all I know he could be running from some other criminal boss, EarthGuard, *and* the Patth. The point is that he could be going after you for injured pride, or possibly because you're a loose end he wants to clean up."

For a minute the room was silent. Tera seemed to suddenly notice the glass of cola beside her and took a long drink. "So what's next?" she asked.

"Well, the first thing you need to do is find a way to warn Kifri about the Iykams," I said.

"Kifri?"

"Your Kalixiri friend you tried to tell me was still on Pinnkus," I said. "No—don't bother; I saw one of his ferrets scouting along the tops of the kiosks."

"That outrider could have belonged to some other Kalix running around the Commons."

I raised my eyebrows. "Did it?"

Tera's eyes flicked again to Selene, and her mouth twitched. "I was hoping you hadn't spotted him," she said, giving up. "Fine. Yes, Kifri's here. But don't worry, he already knows about the Iykams."

I frowned. "How?"

"His outrider," she said, sounding puzzled. "You just said you saw him."

"Yes, I did. And?"

"You don't know about Kalixiri outriders?"

"Not really," I said. "What, they know Morse code or something?"

"It's way better than that," she assured me. "When the outriders are on a Kalix's shoulders they can link into his nervous system and transmit whatever they saw and heard directly into his brain."

I looked at Selene, saw the surprise in her pupils. Apparently, she'd never heard of that either. "So once the ferret got back he could show Kifri everything he'd seen?"

"Everything he saw, heard, touched, and smelled," Tera said. "It also works the other direction, with Kifri giving them orders and instructions before he sends them off to scout. Since the outriders were watching us, they would also have seen the Iykams. Ergo, Kifri knows about them."

"Never heard of that trick before," I said, looking again at Selene. Her pupils still showed wonderment at the idea, but there was no hint that she'd caught Tera in another lie. Crazy or not, it was apparently true.

"I'm not surprised," Tera said. "It's not a state secret, but the Kalixiri don't exactly proclaim it from the high places, either."

"I haven't had much experience with that species," I said. "People carrying bounties usually avoid their planets and enclaves. Kalixiri aren't much for letting criminal activity slide, and they're terrible at taking bribes from targets."

"Sounds about right," Tera said. "So Kifri's been alerted. What's next?"

"We declare your con blown and get you off this rock," I said bluntly. "I suggest—"

"Whoa," Tera cut me off. "It's not blown. Who said it was blown?"

"The lads with the corona guns were a pretty good indicator."

"They're hunting for *you*, not me," Tera countered. "So we get *you* off the rock."

I shook my head. "That's not how it works."

"It's *exactly* how it works," she retorted. "Look, I appreciate all your high-ground ethics, but this is *my* gig, and as of right now you're out of it. Thanks for saving my life and all, but you can go ahead and do that sunset fade now."

I looked at Selene. She wasn't any happier about leaving Tera at loose ends than I was. "What about Freki?" I asked. "What if he's working for Varsi?"

"I already told you Expediters work for the Patth."

"What if they're doing some freelancing?" I asked. "Remember, Geri mentioned a two-hundred-thousand-commark bounty. That number came from Varsi's bounty specs, not the Patth's."

"Maybe it was a special deal the Patth made for them," Tera said. "In fact, Geri said as much before you kicked them off the ship."

"And maybe he was lying," I said. "Either way, don't forget we also have new players in the game. Even if Freki wants you alive, that doesn't guarantee you'll get to keep all your body parts if the Iykams get to you first. As my father used to say, *Alive can also mean not quite dead.*"

"Paranoia," Tera said with a sniff.

"Survival," I corrected.

"What about my StarrComm call?"

"You mean the call from the place Freki was seen leaving?" I asked. "The Freki who can presumably snap his fingers and have Iykams come running?"

For a moment Tera just glared at me. "All right," she said at last. "I guess I can call from wherever we go next. So we get off Melayse?"

"As quickly as we can," I said. "Unfortunately, Freki knows about the *Ruth* and its new ID and probably has it staked out by now. I've reset the lock code, but I wouldn't count on that keeping them out more than a day or two."

"I don't understand why he's even here," Tera said. "If he programmed the *Ruth* to take us to Kashmir, why didn't he go there?"

"Standard tactical logic would agree with you," I said. "All I can think of is that he and Geri figured I might be able to break the programming and decided to split the difference."

"With Geri going to Kashmir and Freki coming here," Tera said, nodding thoughtfully. "I wonder why they picked Melayse."

"Because they knew you'd been here before and might be able to persuade me to bring you back."

"Which I did," Tera agreed. "So. Kashmir?"

"Kashmir," I confirmed. "Granted I haven't had a lot of experience with either of them, Geri strikes me as the marginally more easygoing of the two. Though that's *easygoing* in the sense of possibly being less likely to open fire before asking questions."

"Not exactly a ringing endorsement."

"Right now it's the best we've got. Unless you're

ready to pack it in and start a new game on someone less dangerous."

"Danger is half the fun," she said with a tight smile. "And there's way too much potential gain in this one to give it up."

"I figured you'd say that," I said. I'd known a few con artists in my time, and they were even crazier than bounty hunters when it came to taking risks.

But as my father used to say, *If everyone was the same, the geneticists would have a lot of explaining to do.* "One last question. How does Jordan McKell fit into all this?"

She shook her head. "Not at all."

"You went to all the work to impersonate Tera and Ixil and didn't bother to bring a McKell onto the team?"

"We didn't have anyone who could play the part," she said. "The whole team is just Kifri and me and a couple of others. But I had McKell's name, so I spread it around to give me an excuse to move around."

"And so you'd have an invisible bogeyman to invoke if things got tight?" I suggested. "Put that gun down or Jordan McKell will shoot you from the shadows?"

"That, too," Tera said. "So if we can't take the *Ruth*, how do we get to Kashmir?"

"Oh, please," I said, glancing at Selene. "Who said anything about not taking the *Ruth*?"

"Really?" Tera asked, frowning.

"Really," I promised, giving her my best, most innocent smile. Because she needed to think she'd pulled the wool completely over our eyes. Especially the wool that had been wrapped around that last big gaping lie.

The one about Jordan McKell.

CHAPTER THIRTEEN

———— ❖ ————

We waited until dark to leave the hotel. Partly that was because nighttime activities in the Commons eased enough to make travel easier but not enough to lose us sufficient visual cover to avoid any fresh Iykam attention, and partly it was because I wanted to give my left arm as much time as possible to recover. The tingling had long since faded away, but it had left behind an unpleasant numbness that felt like half the artificial nerves had been fried or otherwise shut down. If the system didn't reboot on its own, I was looking at a lot of expensive repair work down the line.

But both of those were minor considerations. Mostly, I'd seen how the spaceport lights were set, relatively low and sharp, and knew that after nightfall there would be lots of illumination on the walkways and ship ramps and lots of well-defined shadows elsewhere. That was the kind of situation that would work best with the plan I had in mind.

Tera's snide comments notwithstanding, the fact that the contents of the liquor cabinet came as part of the room's price and included both bourbon and Selene's favorite sauvignon had nothing to do with the decision.

Small survey ships the size of the *Ruth* invariably had only a single hatch and airlock, generally positioned amidships on the port side, with a ramp that could either extend to the edge of a convex landing cradle or be elongated into a zigzag stairway for landing fields that only had horizontal pads. Either way, unless the occupants had a hull survival pod they were willing and able to pop, the ramp was the only way in or out.

Defensively, that meant people inside the ship had only one spot they needed to guard if someone tried to break in. Offensively, that similarly meant a would-be intruder only needed to concentrate his firepower on that same one spot. For surveillance or siege, it meant the traditional encirclement strategy boiled down setting up camp outside that single hatch.

Presumably, Frcki knew all of that and had arrayed his Iykam goons accordingly. Which was fine with me, since I'd never intended to sneak Tera into the ship through the hatch anyway.

The New Sandio Spaceport was more compact than most, which meant that all of the usual support cables, hoses, tool lockers, and so on were laid out along the relatively narrow walkways between landing cradles. Adding in the various cargo and supply crates awaiting shipment elsewhere, either to warehouses or back onto the ships themselves, travel through the area became an ever-changing obstacle course.

Generally speaking, those were the kind of annoyances that made merchants look for better facilities.

But like the oddly angled lighting, all those hindrances worked in our favor. Entering the port a good half kilometer from the nearest and most likely approach point, Tera and I made our way through the mess with the goal of sneaking up on the *Ruth* from behind.

As I'd anticipated, the light fixtures that illuminated the walkways had left the back sides of the ships in relative darkness. We reached the *Ruth*'s cradle, slipped down to the bottom, and worked our way over to the Number Two equipment bay. I got the outer fasteners off, popped the inner catches and swung back the plate, then helped Tera climb inside and into the subdeck crawlway. Warning her to stay off her phone and just relax until Selene and I arrived in the morning, I closed everything up and retraced my steps back into the Commons.

Selene was waiting at the little all-night café near the edge of the spaceport where I'd pointed her before Tera and I headed to the ship. "Anything?" I asked as I motioned her to stand up.

"Freki passed me two streets over," she said. "He had two or possibly three Iykams with him. They headed in, and I think they set up at the two ships south of the *Ruth*."

Right where I would have set the front edge of a picket line if I'd been in charge of stopping a trio of fugitives. Freki knew what he was doing, all right. "Are they still there?"

She sniffed a couple of times. "Freki has moved once or twice, but I think the Iykams are still where they first settled in."

"Good," I said, and started walking. "Let's hope they have a relaxing night."

"Are we going back to the hotel?" she asked as she joined me.

"The StarrComm building," I corrected. "Now that Freki's settled down elsewhere, there are a couple of things there I want to check out."

As I'd anticipated, a lot of the kiosks were closed and boarded up at this hour, but there were enough places still open to keep the crowds comfortably dense. Even if our main opponents were hunkered down outside the *Ruth*, the Patth and Varsi bounties were still floating around out there, which would have half the bounty hunters in the Spiral on high alert. And given what had happened in Havershem City, I could well be listed by now as an additional bonus.

"I trust you realize there's nothing to keep Tera from opening the entryway and going outside to talk to Freki," Selene said as we walked. "She could also make some phone calls."

"Oh, I fully expect her to make a call or two," I said. "That was one of the things I wanted to check on, actually. But I don't think she'll leave the ship."

"Why not?"

"You may not have noticed, but our hotel bathroom had its own exit behind the towel rack," I told her. "If she'd wanted to run, to Freki or Kifri or anyone else, she could have done it while she pretended to take a shower."

"You think she's worried about the Iykams?"

"After they saw her standing there watching while I pumped shrapnel into them? *I* would be."

"But we're assuming Freki has them under control," Selene pointed out. "If Freki wants to make a deal with her, she should be safe enough."

"Except that according to her she hasn't approached him yet," I reminded her. "But on top of that, I have the feeling she wants us to be with her when she has that first meeting."

"Why do you say that?"

"Think back to Havershem City," I said. "You were first able to get a track on her by her handprints outside the taverno."

"Correct."

"Well-spaced handprints, as if she'd bounced her hand against the wall a few times before continuing on."

"Also correct."

"Okay," I said, glancing around. Just because Freki had parked some of the Iykams by the *Ruth* didn't mean all of them were there, and the last thing I wanted was to run into any spares he'd left lying around. "Now think about her outside the StarrComm center later that night. One vertigo dart, and she was leaning against the building like she was trying to push it over. Do you see what I'm seeing?"

Selene thought about it for a few more steps. "You're suggesting that she was shot with a vertigo a few days earlier outside the taverno," she said slowly. "But that it didn't affect her as badly that time."

"Actually, I don't think it affected her hardly at all," I said. "That strongly suggests she had an autoinjector of antidote ready to jab into her arm or leg. A few seconds after that, she'd be recovered and ready to sprint away."

"Perhaps," Selene said, her pupils brimming with thought and memory. "The aroma of those first hand-prints held a slight addition that could have been a mix of vertigo and antidote."

"So we agree she has an antidote," I concluded. "So why didn't she use it outside the StarrComm building?"

"Perhaps she ran out," Selene said doubtfully. "Though that seems a bit convenient."

"Agreed," I said. "The only other conclusion I've come up with is that she hung around because she *wanted* us to take her to the *Ruth*."

"That seems a bit of a stretch."

"Given that the only alternative right then was being picked up by Varsi's thugs, not really."

"*If* she knew they were there."

"She did," I said. "Kifri's ferrets were on the roof, and now that we know how they transfer information back and forth, we can be sure Kifri knew, too. New topic, or maybe same topic in different shoes. When you lifted from the Havershem City Spaceport and did that little loop-de-loop, where was everyone?"

"I was in the clean room."

I winced. Getting that mortar gas out of her system. "Geri and Freki?"

"On the bridge."

"Kifri?"

"They put him in the dayroom," she said. "I think they locked him in."

"Good. What about his remaining ferret?"

"It—" Selene broke off, and I could see the sudden revelation in her pupils. "The ventilation lines. They connect to the bridge."

"Exactly," I said, as if I'd been way ahead of her on that one instead of that possibility only belatedly occurring to me while I was putting Tera into the equipment bay. "Those lines are more than roomy enough for animals that size. If Tera's right about them being able to record and then download conversations, that means Kifri knew exactly what our two mythological wolves were doing and saying."

"Yes," Selene said, her pupils narrowed in concentration. "So the question becomes what did they say that would make Tera ready to trust us?"

"No idea." I nodded toward the StarrComm center that was now visible past the kiosks. "I'm hoping Kifri will tell us."

Selene followed my gaze. "You think he's in there?"

"Tera was here on Melayse before she went to Pinnkus," I reminded her. "Unless she was just passing through, I'm guessing she and Kifri gimmicked this StarrComm center the same way they did there."

"That seems reasonable," Selene said, nodding. "Let's find out."

Like the Commons itself, the StarrComm building was fairly quiet, but only in contrast to its daytime crowds. There was a line of people waiting to check in at the front desk, but my bounty hunter license and a scowl got us past them.

There was, however, no getting past the young woman at the desk.

"Name, please?" she asked, her eyes flicking only for a moment to my license before settling on my face. "I hope you're not expecting any preferential treatment. There are people who've been waiting an hour for a booth, and I won't put you ahead of them."

"You misunderstand," I said mildly. "We're not here to make a call. We're meeting someone."

"Are you, now," she said, her tone gone a little frosty. "This may come as a shock, but we're a StarrComm facility, not a neighborhood café. If you want to set up a meeting, do it at one of those."

"I'll remember that for next time," I promised. "But he asked to meet here, so here we are. Don't worry—we won't get in your way."

With a pleasant smile I turned, taking Selene's arm, and headed for the half-filled waiting area. "Well?" I asked quietly.

"He's here," she confirmed. "I smelled him as soon as we were inside."

"Good," I said, rubbing my left thumbnail to its mirror mode and checking behind us. I'd thought the receptionist might have her phone out, but she was merely talking with one of the other women from the desk crew. "Doesn't look like she's calling to warn him, though."

"Do you want me to go find him?" Selene asked.

I looked over the men, women, and aliens in the waiting area, trying to gauge their collective mood. Most of them looked like business or shipping types, and most seemed grouchy or at least somewhat resigned. Not surprising, really, given that at this hour they'd probably prefer a run at the New Sandio nightlife or even just settling down in their own warm beds instead of sitting in uncomfortable chairs waiting to make business calls.

And they might not be happy if they saw an alien apparently cutting the line in front of them. "We'll go together," I decided.

I put my scowl back on and we headed toward the door at the far end that led to the booths. I spotted a couple of glares from the corners of my eyes as we passed through the group, but no one tried to stop us or even spoke up. A minute later, we were through the door and out of their sight. We stepped to the first booth in line, and Selene got to work.

Three minutes after that, she'd found him.

"This one," she whispered, sniffing again at the door marked 114. "He's in here."

"Okay," I said, stepping close and pressing my ear against the door. But StarrComm prided itself on privacy, and its sound insulation was more than up to the task of blocking my attempted eavesdropping.

On the other hand, if Tera and Kifri had indeed pulled the same trick here that they had in Havershem City, booth 104 might be worth checking out.

"Come on," I whispered to Selene, heading around the end of this bank of booths. We found 104 and went in, locking the door behind us, and I went over to the panel separating our booth from Kifri's.

Normally, I wouldn't have been able to hear anything through that wall, either. But StarrComm's vaunted privacy depended on their booths having the standard thickness of sound-deadening material between their booths, and as we'd seen in Havershem City Tera's electronic black boxes required some of that material to be removed. I pressed my ear to the panel.

Kifri was in there, all right, busily at work. Not only could I hear the sounds of tools against metal and the scraping of cables on ceramic, but I could also hear a quiet scratching noise, the kind that might be made by claws against plastic or ceramic. The ferrets, doing a little exploring. Tera and Kifri had indeed pulled the same ghost comm game here, and as soon as I left Tera aboard the *Ruth* with her phone she'd called Kifri to come clean it out.

I frowned. Certainly a big con like the sale of alien

tech took some setup, which might be what all the free StarrComm calls were about. But at the same time, the longer our Tera masqueraded as the woman from the Icarus project the more likely someone would dig deeply enough into her story to expose her. She certainly wouldn't want to push her luck by leaving Melayse, taking the time to travel to an entirely different world only to set up shop there instead.

Unless someone had tumbled to her here and she'd had to make tracks off the planet. But in that case, why ask Selene and me to bring her back?

Selene was looking questioningly at me. I gave her a smile and nod, and started to move away from the wall.

And stopped as I heard a soft tap from the other side, like someone was knocking on 114's door. I pressed my ear a little tighter as I heard the door open ...

"Ixil, they're here," a woman's voice came through the panel.

"Roarke and Selene?"

I frowned. That was Kifri's voice ... but the woman had just called him Ixil. Wasn't that the name of the Kalix Tera had mentioned earlier in conjunction with Icarus?

One way to find out. I stepped away from the panel, gesturing Selene to the door. We left the booth and hurried back around the end of the bank.

I'd expected to find the woman I'd heard standing at the open booth door, probably still talking to the Kalix. But while the door was open, there was no one visible. Either she'd said all she had to say and left, or she'd gone inside for a more private conversation. Beckoning Selene to follow, I headed for the open door.

Selene's gasp was my only warning. Even then, I had only enough time to spin around and get my hand on my holstered plasmic before I saw the woman standing behind us, her gun already leveled at us.

It was Tera.

For a frozen second I just stared at the face behind that gun. I'd told Selene that Tera wouldn't leave the *Ruth* tonight, and I'd fully believed that. And yet, here she was.

And then that second of confusion cleared, and my eyes and brain started working again. The woman facing us had Tera's same short black hair, but her eyes were blue instead of hazel and her face was enough off for me to realize this was an entirely different person.

She was also pretty damn good on the observation front. She'd apparently followed my entire train of surprise, reaction, and recognition just by watching my face, and now congratulated me with a small smile. "Very good," she said.

"Gregory, it's the receptionist," Selene whispered anxiously.

"Yes, I know," I said. "You really *were* serious about us not cutting in line, weren't you?"

"Rules are rules," she said, matching my slightly flippant tone. "In the booth, please."

"Of course," I said, focusing on her gun. "Nice Forelock 3 mil, by the way. Not exactly the quietest weapon on the market."

"Then we'd better hope I don't have to use it," she said.

"It's all right, Jennifer," Kifri's voice came from behind us. "I think we've moved beyond threats here."

I half turned. The Kalix was standing in the booth

doorway, his ferrets on his shoulders, a messenger bag slung in his hand. "I'm good with that," I agreed. "Are you the Ixil that Tera said was on the Icarus project?"

Ixil's eyes flicked over my shoulder to Jennifer. "Let's say I'm a reasonable facsimile. If you don't mind, I'd prefer you continue to call me Kifri."

"If you'd like," I said. "Are you as reasonable a facsimile as Twin Tera here?"

"We don't have time for this," Jennifer growled before Ixil could answer. "Either take them with us or let me shoot them."

"I think our two friends here will be reasonable," Kifri said, eyeing me closely. "You don't have someplace you need to be, do you?"

"Not until morning," I said. "Before we head out, you should know there are some aliens out there who very likely want Ixil—the real Ixil—dead. Are you planning to continue the pretense to the point where you're a reasonable facsimile of a corpse?"

The squashed-lizard face didn't change, but both ferrets twitched. "Actually, there are quite a few beings out there who want me dead," he said calmly. "We'll try to avoid them. Come." He turned toward one of the emergency exits and set off at a brisk, if lumbering walk.

"Where are we going?" I asked as we followed.

"Spaceport," Jennifer said from behind us. "And we're in a bit of a hurry."

"So we walk fast?" I suggested.

"Don't be silly," she said. "We drive."

Given the distance to even the closest edge of the spaceport, I wasn't all that surprised to find that people in a hurry would want a vehicle. I assumed their car would be one of the quick-rent runarounds we'd used earlier. To my mild surprise, the vehicle turned out to be a produce delivery truck. "Moonlighting on the job?" I suggested as Jennifer nudged me into the front passenger seat beside Kifri and motioned Selene to get into the back. "I thought StarrComm paid better than this."

"You have to actually be an employee to get paid," Jennifer said as she got in behind me beside Selene. I thought about adjusting one of the mirrors to see if she was still holding her gun on me, decided all that would accomplish would be to irritate her further, and didn't bother. Irritating someone for no reason was always a bad move, especially when that person had already asked permission to shoot you.

"Good point," I said as Kifri got us moving. "Do we get an explanation, or do we have to figure it out for ourselves?"

"Let's go with the latter," Kifri said encouragingly. "I always like to know the caliber of the people I work with."

"You mean the people you con?"

He shrugged, his ferrets twitching in time with the motion. "Them, too," he conceded. "But not everyone is a mark, you know."

"Good to know," I said, not believing it for a minute. "Okay. You two are going to board some liner as Tera C and her faithful Kalixiri sidekick Ixil. Using false names, of course, but the Patth and the roughly eighty percent of the Spiral's bounty hunters who are currently on the case will see through that fast enough. While they try to beat the liner to its destination, Jennifer will lose the wig and you'll put fake mustaches on your ferrets or something, swap out IDs and walk off the ship as Mr. and Ms. Innocent Party. Meanwhile, with everyone else now decoyed to the back end of nowhere, Selene and I get Tera to Kashmir so she can spin her little web for Geri. How am I doing?"

"Pretty much on the money," Kifri said.

"Good," I said. "Speaking of money, now that I know what's going on, I think we're entitled to a percentage of the payoff."

"I thought Geri promised you a healthy sum for delivering Tera to him," Jennifer said.

"Times are hard," I said. "How much are you planning to con out of the Patth?"

"Five million at least," Jennifer said. "Probably closer to ten."

"Sounds good," I said. "We'll take ten percent."

Jennifer snorted. "You'll take three," she said flatly. "We've already put a lot of time and money into this thing."

"I've put a fair amount of time into it, too," I reminded her. "Plus I've got Iykams looking to shoot me down in the street. Hazard pay alone should bring it to eight."

"We've *all* got Iykams gunning for us," Jennifer countered. "Five."

"Geri and Freki are also mad at me, and you want me to walk straight up to them," I said. "Seven."

"*With* Tera in tow," Jennifer said. "That should wipe away any bad feelings they might have. Five."

"Six?"

"Five," she said firmly.

"Five," I agreed, putting some resignation into my tone. I didn't really care about any of that, but I'd wanted to see how well they bargained. "I presume we can talk to Tera about where and how we get our cut?"

"Excuse me," Selene spoke up. "We may have a problem."

I craned my neck to look over the seat. She was gazing at her pad, her pupils showing nervousness. "What's wrong?" I asked.

"Two hours ago a Patth freighter landed on Pad A47 in the northwest corner of the spaceport," she said. "A Class VII."

I felt my stomach tighten. That was a problem, all right. "Hell," I muttered. "How close is that to your liner?"

"Half a kilometer away," Jennifer said.

"That should be plenty of distance," Kifri said. "Patth usually stick fairly close to their ship while in port."

"You're missing the big picture," I said. "It's not the Patth you need to worry about. It's the Iykams."

"The—?" Kifri broke off. "Oh. Yes."

"Oh, yes," I mimicked darkly. "Tera said they're mostly guards for the Patth pilots, and there are three pilots on a Class VII. If we posit three to four Iykam guards per pilot, that means Freki now has an additional labor pool of nine to twelve Iykams to draw on."

"Yes, I see the problem," Kifri said. "You think they'll be gathering by our ship?"

"Depends on how transparent your fake IDs are," I said. "If you designed them so that you'd be long gone by the time they were tagged, and even then someone would have to go through the security records to be sure, you may be okay. But I'd hate to count on that."

"Especially with a Patth Expediter involved," Jennifer said, her voice more thoughtful than worried. "The Patth have backdoors into most port security systems. We should probably assume they've already got a campfire going by the liner."

"A definite problem," Kifri agreed. "We can't afford to let them see us go aboard. Perhaps we should consider switching to a different liner."

"No good," I said. "If Freki's already inside their system, switching ships won't help. Unless you're using opaque IDs he'll spot the switch."

"And we can't do that," Kifri said. "We need our IDs to be semitransparent in order to draw pursuit away from you and Tera."

"You have any suggestions?" Jennifer asked.

"Sure," I said. "Drop us off at the Patth freighter and go to ground somewhere. Give me half an hour, maybe forty minutes, and you should be clear to board without any Iykam interference."

It was hard to make a sideways glance deep and penetrating, especially while maneuvering a truck through spaceport traffic. But Kifri managed to pull it off. "All right," he said. "Anywhere in particular you want to be dropped?"

"Selene?" I prompted.

"There's a taverno called the Vennedrikk just south of the ship," she said, still studying her pad.

"You heard the lady," I confirmed. "The Vennedrikk taverno."

"All right," Kifri said. "Just don't jeopardize the task of getting Tera safely to Kashmir. Without her, this whole thing falls apart."

"No problem." I lifted a finger and looked back

over my shoulder at Jennifer. "Oh, and be advised that we're back up to ten percent."

Fifteen minutes later Selene and I were back on the spaceport streets, heading toward the tasteful *Vennedrikk* sign a block away. "I trust you have a plan," Selene said.

"I do," I assured her.

"And you think this is really something we should be doing?"

I nodded. "Absolutely."

Selene gave a sort of sigh. "Because Tera lied about Jordan McKell?"

So she had spotted Tera's lie, too. I'd figured she'd caught the subtle change in Tera's odor, but I hadn't wanted to ask. "Yes, because Tera lied," I confirmed. "I'll go further: I think she lied about everything. I don't think this is a con game at all, except for the part where they're trying to con us."

"I didn't smell any other lies from her."

"Creative wording, maybe," I said. "Or else she's so used to lying it doesn't usually come out in her scent anymore. Why the Vennedrikk?"

"There were four other pads the Patth ship could have chosen, all of them more convenient to the Starr-Comm center, fueling, or cargo unloading facilities," she said. "Since they chose this one, I assumed there was something of interest in the area."

And unlike everyone else, Patth ships generally got to tell the control tower where they were going to land instead of the other way around. "Nicely reasoned," I complimented her. "If that something isn't the Vennedrikk itself, it's bound to be nearby."

"Though if all their guards have been pulled away, the pilots may not be able to leave the ship," she pointed out.

"Not to worry," I said. "Just because the pilots are aboard doesn't mean the rest of the crew can't go out. We'll find someone we can make mischief on."

"I hope it works." She paused. "Why is Jordan McKell so important to you?"

Someday I would tell her, I promised myself. When it was all over and McKell had paid for what he'd done, I would tell her.

But not now. Not in the middle of a job. Especially not in the middle of a job that might finally bring McKell to that place of final judgment.

"It's personal," I said. "Come on. We've got a ship-load of Patth to scare."

CHAPTER FOURTEEN

◆◆◆

Compared to most spaceport tavernos I'd seen—certainly compared to Caleb's Drinkhouse on Xathru—the Vennedrikk was definitely on the upscale side of the spectrum. The overall atmosphere was dark, with small light globes at the center of each table and a handful of slightly brighter focused lights over the bar that stretched across two-thirds of the back wall. It was the kind of darkness designed to make the socializing patrons look better to each other, while at the same time shrouding the less gregarious types who'd come to drink anonymously and didn't want to be bothered by anyone else.

Tonight, both groups seemed to be well represented. Both the bar and the tables were occupied, though several of the smaller two-person tables had only one patron. From the doorway I couldn't get a good look into the booths lining the side walls, but they also seemed full. Waiters and waitresses hurried back and forth, carrying trays and drinks, moving with the kind of low-level agitation that came of having too much work spread over too few people.

For what I had in mind, it was the perfect setup.

"Are they here?" I asked Selene as we stepped to the side of the doorway out of the traffic flow.

"Yes," she said, nostrils and eyelashes both pumping like mad as she sampled the cacophony of aromas filling the room. "At least one Patth...at least one Iykam."

"Good," I said, taking off my jacket and handing it to her. The move exposed my holstered plasmic to view, but I wasn't planning on standing here long enough for anyone to notice. "Take this and find a place at the bar with the right airflow. Order a sauvignon or something. This may take a few minutes, so just sit tight."

She nodded as she draped my jacket over her arm. "Be careful."

I went back outside and rounded the building to the service entrance in the rear. The door was propped open, probably to help with air circulation, which should work nicely to Selene's advantage. I went inside, slipped past the buzz of conversation and rattling dishes coming from the kitchen, and found the employees' locker room. A couple of spare aprons hung on a hook by the door; snagging one, I put it on over my street clothing, made sure the bulge of my plasmic didn't show through, and pushed open the door leading into the main room.

The door opened up at one end of the bar, right beside a harried-looking bartender mixing a couple of ginger volcanoes. "I'm here," I called to him. "Where do you want me?"

He looked up, did a double take as he spotted the apron. "Who are you?" he asked.

"Wilson," I said, watching him closely. "Swing shift. Ahny called and said you needed help." With all the background noise, I knew, *Ahny* could sound like *Johnny*, *Lonnie*, *Bonnie*, *Arnie*, or any of a handful of other names. In a human-run bar the odds were pretty good that at least one of those would click.

Either the name sounded familiar or else the bartender was so overworked he would have taken in a stray cat if he thought it could handle drink orders and a tray. "Great," he said, pausing to pull a pad from under the bar and hand it to me. "Those Najik at table eight need their orders taken."

"Got it," I said, glancing around. I had no idea of their numbering system, but the four aliens were easy to spot. Giving the bartender a cheerful smile, I headed off across the crowded room.

In some ways, I reflected, it was rather like coming home.

I'd told Selene it might take a few minutes. In fact, it took nearly fifteen minutes of drink orders and deliveries before I'd covered enough of the room to spot the three Patth in one of the side booths and their lone Iykam guard at a two-person table nearby. The Iykam, I noted, was seated where he could see not only the Patth and the main entrance, but also the door beside the bar that I'd entered through. The creatures might be ugly and use nasty borderline-illegal weapons, but at least they were reasonably professional.

Except for the fact that there was only one of them instead of the minimum of two that were required to properly secure a room. But to be fair, the lack of available backup personnel was probably Freki's fault.

I waited until I'd served a round of drinks to a booth near the Path. Then, slipping my plasmic out of its holster and holding it out of sight underneath my now empty tray, I stepped over to the Iykam. "Can I get you something else, sir?" I asked, leaning close as if the conversational buzz around us was making it hard for me to hear him.

"I need nothing more," the Iykam said, glaring up at me as if wondering why this stupid human couldn't see that his glass was still three-quarters full.

"Just one question then," I said. "Here," I added, offering him the tray.

Most people, when something is shoved at them, automatically take it. The Iykam, fortunately, was one of that majority. He took the tray, his glare turning into a somewhat bemused frown—

And then became a rigid mask of impotent rage as I pressed the muzzle of my plasmic against his chest. "Easy," I warned. I leaned a little closer and reached into his robe with my left hand, watching his eyes for any sign that he was going to try something brave or stupid. Most of that arm was still numb, but the fingers were mostly back, and I was able to find the butt of his corona gun and draw it from its holster. "Easy," I said again, sticking the weapon into my waistband behind the apron where it wouldn't be visible and he couldn't easily get it back. "Like I said, a question." I took back the tray before it could occur to him to use it as a weapon and moved back a few centimeters, again using the tray to block anyone else's view of the plasmic still pointed at him.

"You will die for this," he said, his voice chillingly sincere.

"Maybe later," I said. "Here's the question: Is everyone off that Patth ship out there?"

"How should I know that?" he demanded. "Do I seem to you to be a Patth?"

"No, but you work for them," I said. "Don't be coy, and don't get cute. I need to know if they're all off. I don't want to hurt anyone."

Finally, that little flicker that showed the message was getting through. "I don't know," he said. "What is it you want?"

"What do I *want*?" I growled. "I want payback from the Patth for ruining my shipping business. Never mind. All I want is to take down the ship, but if you won't talk and if I have to kill a couple of the little bastards, I can do that."

"There are still Patth aboard," the Iykam said. "If they die, it will go far worse for you."

"Yeah, well, it's already as bad for me as it can get." I glanced past him, caught Selene's eye, and gave her a microscopic nod toward the door. "But it's going to get worse for them. And for you, too, if you don't get them the hell off."

"I cannot help you while you hold a weapon on me."

"That's *your* problem, not mine." I hesitated, like a revenge-seeking man who still had some shreds of conscience left might do. "Here's what I'll do. I'll give you three minutes after I leave this place to get everyone off. After that, it's on your hands."

I stepped back from his table, glancing at the three Patth in their booth to confirm they weren't watching our little drama, then headed for the bar, watching the Iykam out of the corner of my eye the whole way. The bartender was busy at the other end, and I slipped through the door without him even noticing.

Thirty seconds later, having divested myself of the apron, tray, and corona gun—dropping the latter into one of the garbage bins near the rear door—I was striding quickly back around the taverno toward the street.

Selene was waiting when I arrived, pressed against the side wall out of the way of the stream of other pedestrians. "Success?" she asked, handing me my jacket.

"I think so," I said, starting us back in the direction we'd come from earlier. Glancing around to make sure no one was watching, I holstered my plasmic and slipped on the jacket. "You get anything?"

"The Iykam's scent changed strongly while you were talking to him," she said. "The Patth scents remained the same. There were no other changes from anyone else except those consistent with alcohol consumption."

"So no one noticed anything. Good." Which wasn't to say someone might not remember something crucial afterward if the Patth decided to pursue the issue. Under the circumstances, though, I was pretty sure they wouldn't. "The Iykam's response, by the way, was probably anger, fear, frustration, or anger. You should probably catalog that for future reference."

"You said *anger* twice."

"He was pretty angry."

Selene nodded, her pupils showing understanding. For better or worse, she was used to that reaction to the way I did business. "What did you do to him?"

"Nothing," I assured her. "Took his gun and told

him I was going to attack his freighter. Offered him three minutes to get the rest of the crew out first."

She looked at me, the earlier understanding turned to horrified disbelief. "Gregory!"

"Don't worry, we're not going to touch it," I hastened to assure her. "But they can't be sure of that, wherein lies the problem. If I'm planning to destroy the ship, they have to get the rest of the Patth out of there before that happens. But if what I really want is to get everyone into the open where I can take sniper shots at them, having them outside is the last thing they can afford to do. Not without some protection in place."

"Yes," she said, her pupils settling down again. "Which means recalling all their Iykam guards."

"Just as fast as their lumpy little legs will take them," I agreed. "That should give Kifri and Jennifer a clear shot to slip onto that liner—"

"Watch out!" Selene interrupted, grabbing my arm and pulling me to the far side of the walkway as two vans roared into view, weaving in and out of traffic with complete disregard for anyone who might wander into their path, their screeching tires sending all the other pedestrians jumping for the edge along with us. I peered at the vans as they shot past, but it was too dark inside to see anyone.

On the other hand, given they were heading straight toward the Patth freighter, it wasn't hard to guess who they were. "And there they go," I said, looking back over my shoulder as they disappeared between a pair of small customs sheds flanking the freighter's main ramp. "Anything?"

"I'm sorry," Selene said. "The windows were closed."

"That's okay," I said. Sometimes I forgot that there were limits on what she could do. "Those vans weren't marked as spaceport security. So, process of elimination."

The foot traffic sorted itself back out, the people continuing on their way, Selene and I continuing on with them. I kept alert for the sounds of running footsteps behind us, and for vehicles heading our direction, or for the less subtle sounds of sirens and *Lawbreaker!* shouts.

But there was nothing. As I'd expected, the Patth didn't want to make any kind of commotion, especially one that would leave them looking vulnerable. A shipping and economic empire like theirs was far more susceptible to public image and rumor than, say, a group like EarthGuard that had lots of weapons and didn't much care what people thought about them.

"Are you going to phone Kifri?" Selene asked.

"I thought we'd let them figure it out for themselves."

"If they're in hiding, they may not realize the Iykams are gone," she pointed out.

"And if they don't, that'll tell us something about their intel capabilities, won't it?"

Out of the corner of my eye I saw her looking thoughtfully at me. "You really don't think they're con artists?"

I shook my head. "No."

"Then who are they?"

"You want my completely unsupported, wild-eyed theory?"

"I'll take whatever you have."

"Okay." I took a deep breath. "Tera—our Tera, the one aboard the *Ruth*—said she was masquerading as the real Tera C. I don't think so. I think she and Ixil *are* the real Tera and Ixil, straight from the Icarus project."

"I see," Selene said thoughtfully. "How does Jennifer fit in?"

"No idea," I said. "Someone else from the project, maybe, or some friend who got roped into it. You accepted that premise awfully easily."

"I agreed to hear your theory," she reminded me. "That means listening to all of it. I asked about Jennifer because Tera never mentioned her."

"Probably on purpose," I said. "That would let Jennifer play shadow backup, someone that neither we nor the Patth would know to watch out for."

"That seems reasonable," Selene said. "If they're not con artists, then what's their purpose? What are they trying to accomplish?"

"Here's where the theory gets iffy," I said. As if the first part hadn't been iffy enough. "If they're really part of Icarus, and if Icarus is important enough for the Patth to drool out a hundred thousand commarks to get hold of Tera, the government or EarthGuard or whoever should have corralled her and dropped her in a box long ago. The fact that they haven't tells me she's operating with their approval."

"Again, to what purpose?"

"Only one that I can see." I glanced around, making sure none of the other pedestrians were close enough to hear. "I think they've been studying the *Icarus* for six years, and have figured out the damned thing doesn't work. I think Tera and Ixil are out here trying to get some of their investment back by selling their white elephant to the Patth."

Selene digested that for another few steps. "A stardrive that doesn't work," she said. "And they think the Patth will buy that?"

"They've already put a hundred thousand on the table," I pointed out. "Yeah, I think they'll buy it."

"Interesting," she said. "So it *is* a con game."

I thought it over. Actually, she was right. "Okay, sure," I conceded. "But a government-sanctioned con game is more of a psych-ops thing."

"I'm not sure I see the difference," she said. "If you're right about this, what's our response? Do we still take Tera to Kashmir?"

"That seems like the direction everyone's pushing us," I said. "If Tera—whoever the hell she is—wants to connect with Geri, who are we to say otherwise? As my father used to say, *A man who gets in the way of a determined woman will just end up with a woman-shaped hole in him.*"

"That sounds painful," Selene murmured.

"Extremely," I agreed. "I don't suppose you had a chance while I was serving drinks to figure out which liner Ixil and Jennifer were going for?"

"There are three in the direction we were originally heading," she said. "The first leaves in half an hour, the second in two hours, the third in eight."

"They seemed too much in a hurry for it to be on the last one," I said. "Probably the first, possibly the second. Well. I was planning on spending the night at the hotel—it's already paid for, after all—and then heading out in the morning. But I think now we'll just wait until after that second liner takes off. No point dragging this out any longer than we have to."

"Hardly worth going back to the hotel for a couple

of hours," Selene said, an odd reluctance seeping into her voice.

"Agreed," I said. "So, a bite or a drink at one of the Commons booths or eateries, and then we'll head back to the *Ruth*. I know you're tired, but once we've got Tera safely in hyperspace you can get some sleep." I cocked an eyebrow at her. "Unless there was something back in the hotel you wanted."

"Not really," she said. "I was just remembering there were two of those little bottles of really good sauvignon left in the bar."

"Not to worry," I assured her, patting my jacket pocket. "I picked them up on my way out."

It wasn't until we settled down at one of the more mid-scale diners in the Commons that I realized that I was more hungry even than I was tired. This particular place didn't have the Earth BBQ we'd passed by earlier—that kiosk, sadly, was closed for the night—but it had a decent enough quintip roast and a passable bourbon. Selene had a glass of the house sauvignon, which she declared highly inferior to the bottles in our hotel bar—which, given the per-glass cost, constituted something of a con job in and of itself—and a baked fish whose name I couldn't pronounce but which she declared nearly as good as the best she'd ever had. Though whenever she raved about a meal I could never tell whether she was talking about its taste or its aroma.

Between the meal, the drinks, and the hunt for a quick-rent vehicle, we managed to burn the two hours necessary to let the first two liners get off the ground. If Ixil and Jennifer had failed to take advantage of our diversion, they deserved whatever the Iykams decided to dish out.

Selene was a bit tipsy as we left the diner, which with Kadolians translated as little more than a slight loss of balance. I found an unused runaround and got Selene inside, slid in yet another of our hundred-commark bills, and headed for the *Ruth*. I was hoping Freki and his Iykam entourage would be long gone by now, either blazing off in hot pursuit of their chosen liner or else standing by one of the empty pads waving impotent fists at the sky.

I was wrong on both counts.

I'd parked at the *Ruth*'s ramp and was helping Selene out when pretty much every single shadow erupted with an Iykam. Before I could even think about grabbing my plasmic or getting under cover we were surrounded by a ring of corona guns and lumpy aliens eager to use them.

"Well," a low voice came from behind me. "You two have had a busy night."

I turned. Freki was watching us from the top of the ramp, standing just outside the *Ruth*'s hatch with a Ryukind plasmic hanging casually at his side.

Outside the *open* hatch, I saw with a sinking heart. He hadn't just strolled up there while my back was turned. He'd already been inside, and was just now coming back out.

Inside the ship . . . where we'd left Tera.

As my father used to say, *Your best weapon is the truth. Your second-best is a carefully cultivated innocent stupidity.* "Hey, how did you get aboard?" I asked, throwing confusion and a hint of tipsiness into my voice. "I changed all the access codes."

"Working for the Patth has certain advantages,"

Freki said. "Did you know it was a Patth subsidiary that helped develop the Everlock protocols?"

It was hard to maintain an innocent expression when you're feeling like the biggest idiot in the Spiral, but my stupid expression was fortunately close enough to pass. I had of course heard those rumors over the years, which meant that the casual theft of Varsi's van back in Havershem City should have tipped me off then that Geri and Freki were a lot higher in Patth organizational structure than they'd let on. But of course, I'd long since dismissed the Everlock rumors and forgotten about them.

And, of course, the *Ruth*'s hatch lock was only a cheaper and slightly less secure version of those same protocols.

Carefully cultivated innocent stupidity. "What does that have to do with—? Oh," I interrupted myself as if the connection was only now dawning on me. "Right. Everlock. Well. I hope you didn't eat all the grainory chips while you were in there."

"I wasn't looking for snacks," he said coolly. Detaching himself from his position by the hatch, he walked down the ramp to face me. "You know, Roarke, you've been something of a disappointment to us."

He stopped, and for a moment just stared silently up at me. I stared back, maintaining my innocent look, struck by the incongruous and almost laughable scene of a short human and a group of even shorter lumpy-faced aliens trying to face down a much taller human.

But that short human had a drawn plasmic, and the short aliens had corona guns, and I for one didn't feel much like laughing.

"You had Tera right in your hand," Freki continued.

"Yet somehow she slipped through your fingers and escaped. How do you account for that, bounty hunter?"

"Maybe you should ask your associates here that question," I said, trying to keep my voice steady. Kifri had said the Iykams were under Freki's control, but the first indication that he'd been wrong about that would also be the last breath I ever took. "I had the situation—*and* Tera—under control until they charged in and tried to incinerate me."

"You fired on us first," one of the Iykams retorted.

"I didn't fire on you at all," I shot back. "The point is that if you hadn't been stalking us I wouldn't have lost track of her."

"We made no threatening move—"

"Enough," Freki said.

The Iykam subsided. But I could still sense a simmering anger there as he stared at me.

"But that's water under the bridge," I said. "The fact of the matter is that if we found her once, we can find her again."

"Really," Freki said, his voice going a few degrees colder. "Let me give you a hint. She's currently aboard an Ulko spaceliner bound for Rachna."

I let my eyes widen. "She's on a *liner*? How—?"

"How do I know?" Freki cut me off. "Because the Iykams saw her board, that's how."

"No, no, obviously someone saw her," I said. "What I was starting to ask was if she was seen getting aboard how is she still there instead of standing here in restraints?"

And only then did the crucial fact manage to push its way past the bourbon in my brain.

Freki had just come out of the *Ruth*, presumably

having searched it thoroughly. How could he possibly have missed finding Tera?

Because Tera wasn't there anymore, obviously. Sometime after I'd let her in through the equipment bay she'd slipped right back out again and made her way to the liner to wait for Kifri and Jennifer to show up.

No. Not Kifri *and* Jennifer. Just Kifri. The minute Selene and I left that pair to set up our diversion, Jennifer had faded off into the night, leaving Tera to join the Kalix in settling aboard that Ulkomaal ship.

"Because the Iykams weren't able to intercept her before she reached dock security," Freki said. "They were attempting to present the bounty documents when they were suddenly called away to an emergency at a Patth freighter." His eyes narrowed. "I don't suppose you had anything to do with that?"

"How could we possibly have anything to do with a Patth emergency?" I demanded, feeling the irritation of a one-two mental punch as a second stray fact popped up out of my memory. Havershem City, where Kifri and his ferrets had surreptitiously freed those two runaway Ulkomaals from slavery or worse. The whole Ulko species had a reputation for talking to each other, and remembering and repaying debts. No wonder the liner's security had made sure Kifri wasn't followed aboard by gun-wielding aliens.

"Are you denying you were there?" Freki demanded.

"Of course we weren't there," I said indignantly. "We spent some time looking for Tera in the Commons, then went to the StarrComm center to see if she'd made any calls, then went back and poked around the Commons some more."

"And?"

I shrugged slightly. "Selene picked up her scent twice, but both times the trail faded before we could follow it all the way."

"You never went to the northwest sector of the port?"

"No," I said. "Why? What's in the northwest sector?"

"That's where the Patth freighter is berthed."

"Of course we didn't go there," I said, daring to add a little scorn to my tone. "Why would we? The *Patth* are the ones who put out the bounty—why the hell would Tera hang out near one of their ships?"

For a long moment Freki just continued to stare up at me. Selene was standing very still at my side, I noted peripherally, her mild sauvignon buzz long gone. A couple of the Iykams were twitching just a bit underneath their hooded robes, and I wondered vaguely if I could take both of them before they got the two of us.

Then, very deliberately, Freki returned his plasmic to its holster. "As I said, a disappointment," he said. "I believe you've forfeited your thirty-thousand commark advance."

"I don't keep that kind of money on me," I said, still watching the twitching Iykams. "Wait a second and I'll go get it for you."

"No need." He patted his jacket. "I've already got it. Perhaps we can do business another time."

"Don't assume this time is over yet," I said. "Keep those bank checks warm, because you'll be handing them back to us soon enough."

He smiled faintly and turned away. "Come," he said as he strode away.

For a moment the Iykams stayed where they were, as if underlining the fact that they didn't *have* to obey him. Then, to my relief, they broke their encirclement and marched off behind him.

Beside me, Selene said something under her breath in her own language. "I don't understand," she murmured. "Do you think he . . . ?"

"What, killed her?" I shook my head. "You heard him. Tera got on the liner with Kifri. Ixil. Whoever."

"But—"

"In a minute," I cut her off. Freki and his entourage rounded the side of one of the other parked ships, and I took Selene's arm. "Okay, now," I said, walking us up the ramp toward the hatch. "Before he decides he wants his expenses money back, too."

Three minutes later I had the hatch sealed and was on the bridge starting the ramp-up from standby to full power. "Give the tower a call, will you?" I called over my shoulder. "See how soon we can get out of here."

"Yes, please," Tera's voice came from behind me.

CHAPTER FIFTEEN

◆

It wasn't easy to swivel around and draw while seated in a pilot's chair. But inspiration and sudden shock are remarkable enablers. An instant later I was facing the bridge hatchway, plasmic leveled at the woman standing there.

Standing motionlessly, with her hands visible. Luckily for her. "What the *hell* are you doing here?" I snarled, lowering my plasmic to my lap.

She raised her eyebrows with the same coolness as if I'd just asked for a weather report. "You invited me, remember?"

"You know what I mean." I raised my voice. "Selene? Come join the party."

There was a footstep from the corridor. Tera glanced over her shoulder, then returned her attention to me. "I assumed that just because Freki hadn't seen me come through the hatch didn't mean he wouldn't eventually want a look for himself," she said as if I should have expected that, too. "So I stayed in the crawlway ready to duck back out the rabbit hole and hide at the bottom of the cradle if I heard him work the lock." She sent a lopsided smile back over her shoulder at Selene. "Lucky for him, he doesn't have anyone with your abilities on the payroll."

"I'm sorry, Gregory," Selene's somewhat mortified voice came from behind her. "I should have smelled her. I wasn't paying enough attention."

"Don't worry about it," I assured her. "Anyway, there was probably enough of her scent already here even if you'd been specifically looking." I felt my eyes narrow as I focused on Tera again. "So it *was* Jennifer who got onto that liner with Kifri."

"Yes." Tera considered. "*And* no." She raised her eyebrows, silently inviting me to be clever.

Selene, for one, was apparently not interested in playing that game. "What does she mean?" she asked.

"She means that our diversion at the Patth freighter wasn't to let them sneak aboard," I said sourly, tasting bile and leftover bourbon. *Damn* these people, anyway. "Our diversion was to let them sneak *off*." I raised my eyebrows at Tera. "So the Iykams and everyone else are now chasing a complete red herring?"

"It's safer that way," she said. "We don't want either of them getting shot by some overeager bounty hunter."

"Or some overeager Iykam," I said. "By the way, Jennifer says Kifri's real name is Ixil."

"Yes, she told me you'd overheard that," she said ruefully. "We were saving that particular name to spring on Geri during the con. But I suppose it doesn't hurt that you also know it."

"Real names are always so handy," I said. And with

that, I had my opening. "Speaking of names, it's about time you gave us yours."

A frown flicked across her face. "I already did. I'm Tera."

"Fake Tera, anyway," I said. "But okay. Let's at least have the real Tera's real name. You said it's Tera C. What does the 'C' stand for?"

"As I said, it was never released."

"Probably true," I said. "At least, Selene didn't catch it as a lie."

"Of course it's true," Tera insisted.

"But it's also misleading as hell," I said. "Because you already know the name. Because you *are* the real Tera. The *real* Tera C." I paused dramatically, giving her a knowing smile. "The real Tera—"

I broke off. "The real Tera . . . ?" she prompted cautiously.

"Oh, I don't know," I said calmly. "But you do. Selene?"

"Surprise and fear," Selene said, her tone matching mine.

"Thank you." I looked down at my lap, noticed I was still holding my plasmic. Shifting in my seat, I returned the weapon to its holster. "You see, only the real Tera C would worry that her name had gotten out," I said quietly. "So, real Tera C from the Icarus project, here's what we're going to do. We're going to get this ship into space and on its way to Kashmir."

I swiveled back around to face the control board. "And then," I said, "you're going to tell us what the hell is *really* going on."

❖   ❖   ❖

I'd had some lingering suspicions that Freki hadn't really given up on us, and that we might find a nasty surprise or two waiting when we tried to leave Melayse. Once we were in the air, with no hidden emergency exit to slip out of or shadowy landing cradle to hide in, even a quick search would damn us in double-quick time.

But apparently his disgust at our incompetence had been real. The New Sandio control tower was quick and efficient, there were no last-minute blocks or return orders, and an hour later the cutter array sliced us into hyperspace, and we were safe. At least for the moment.

And then, as I'd promised, we sat Tera down on the dayroom foldout for a serious talk.

Because as my father used to say, *A threat is just a promise no one wants you to keep.*

"It starts with a man named Jordan McKell," she said, looking up from the steaming mug of tea she'd made for herself. It wasn't a blend I was familiar with, but the aroma was pleasant enough.

Though if it was designed to calm her nerves, it was doing a rotten job of it. I could see a slight trembling in her fingers, plus a smaller twitchiness in her cheeks and throat. Too much caffeine, possibly. That, or she was more nervous than I'd ever seen her before.

"I've mentioned him before," she continued. "He was our pilot on the original *Icarus*, the man who got us safely through all the Patth attempts to find us and take the ship for themselves."

"You're talking about the *Icarus* ship, now, right?" I asked.

"Yes," she said. "Now, we use the name for the

overall project. So you know McKell. What you may not know is that he has a somewhat...checkered past."

She paused for another sip from her mug. I looked sideways at Selene, saw her nostrils and eyelashes quivering as they sampled the airflow. If Tera was hoping the smell of the tea would mask any of her own subtle scent changes, she was in for an unwelcome surprise. The confidence I could see in Selene's pupils was my guarantee that she was fully on top of things.

And if Tera's latest story turned out to be yet another patch of spiderfloss, I was going to be dangerously annoyed.

"He started out well enough, I suppose," she said. "Five years in EarthGuard Auxiliary. But that ended in a court-martial for severe insubordination and a dishonorable discharge. After that came four years in Earth Customs, kicked out this time for taking bribes. A few other small jobs came and went"—she seemed to brace herself—"and he ended up working for one of the Spiral's biggest criminal organizations, using his ship to smuggle drugs and weapons."

Despite my promises to myself to keep emotion out of this, I felt a darkness drift across my vision. Defiance, bribery, and smuggling, all of it ultimately leading up to our own encounter with him five years ago.

Tera had said he'd killed a pair of Iykams. Given the rest of his history, I doubted it was self-defense.

"The point is that he always showed a tendency toward instability and rashness," Tera said. "Once we got the *Icarus* to safety, he was offered a place on the team working on it. He accepted, and up until a few months ago everything was fine. But then..."

She shook her head. "There are people who can't just sit by when unpleasant truths raise their ugly heads. McKell is one of them. I can't go into details, but . . . Bottom line: He's out there somewhere, and Ixil and I need to get him back safely."

"So McKell deserted Icarus," I said, "and you and Ixil deserted to track him down. This project must be heaps of joy to work for."

"It's not as bad as you make it sound," Tera said, mild protest in her voice.

"I'm just looking at the fact that it seems to inspire the stupid in people. So what was that nonsense story you spun about a con game and you and Ixil pretending to be entirely different people?"

"The Patth had a hundred-thousand-commark bounty on me, and your friend Mr. Varsi was offering twice that," she said. "The Iykams were already on Melayse, and there were bound to be a few bounty hunters also lurking around. I thought if I could dangle a potential reward bigger than anything anyone else was offering you wouldn't turn me over to any of them."

Again, I looked at Selene. She looked back, her pupils unchanged. So far, no lies that she could detect.

Though as always that didn't preclude the presence of carefully chosen weasel words that said one thing and implied something else entirely. "All right then," I said, turning back to Tera. "Change of subject. No more evasion, no more *classified* excuses. Your life's on the line; McKell's life is on the line; *our* lives are on the line. I know the rumors, but I want the truth. What the hell is the Icarus project?"

Tera's lips compressed, but she gave a reluctant nod. "You called it earlier," she said. "And for once the rumors were true. If we can get Icarus fully up and running, it will offer a way to get across space faster and more efficiently than anything we've ever seen."

"Better than the Talariac?"

"Far better," she assured me. "But Icarus isn't our problem right now. Our problem is to find McKell before something happens that we can't backtrack from."

"Such as?"

She gave me a look of strained patience. "The Patth know the truth about Icarus. McKell knows the truth about Icarus. Do I need to draw you a map?"

I looked one last time at Selene, wondering if any of that had been more of Tera's lies. But no. As far as Selene could tell, every bit of it was true. "So what's the plan?"

"We're assuming Geri went to Kashmir," Tera said. "I'm hoping McKell followed that same logic and headed there, too."

"So McKell's stalking Geri?"

"I don't know if he *stalking* him, exactly," Tera said. "But Geri's definitely the key to whatever crazy scheme McKell's got in mind."

"So if we find Geri, we find McKell?"

"That's the assumption."

"Good," I said grimly. "Lucky for us we know how to get Geri to come into the open."

Tera looked at Selene. "You can track him down?"

"Eventually, sure," I confirmed. "But it doesn't sound like we've got enough time for that."

Tera's lips compressed briefly, and from the look in her eyes I could tell we were on the same page. "We need to offer him something he wants," she said.

"Yes," I said.

"We need to offer him me."

I nodded. "Yes."

It was a six-day trip from Melayse to Kashmir. We mostly traveled in silence, with the bulk of our conversation revolving around basic ship's functions and a bit of overall planning of what we were going to do once we got there. Tera wasn't in a particularly conversational mood, while Selene reverted to her usual self-restraint of mostly talking only when someone else started the ball rolling.

For my part, I was working through what I was going to do once I finally came face-to-face with the man who'd cost me so much. For the past five years the desire for justice and payback had been a distant hunger in the back of my brain, seldom intruding on my daily life but never completely going away, either.

But now suddenly there was Icarus to be factored into my thinking, along with the awesome potential it represented for the Commonwealth and the other peoples of the Spiral. The Patth weren't on my personal vengeance list, but their rise to power certainly hadn't made them a lot of friends along the way. Whatever McKell was mixed up with, and whatever Tera did or didn't want him to do, they both were clearly vital parts to this whole thing.

I still hadn't figured out what I should do when we arrived.

There was always the chance that the number Geri had given me back on Xathru had been for a phone he'd since discarded. But it wasn't. Three vibes into the call, he answered.

"I've been expecting you," he said without greeting or other preamble. "Freki said you left Melayse rather like the scalded cat of legend."

"There didn't seem anything in New Sandio worth hanging around for," I said.

"Apparently not," he said. "I presume there's a connection between your departure and the fact that the Ulko liner he was interested in turned out to be empty?"

For a moment I was tempted to take his words at literal value and express my astonishment that every single passenger aboard had somehow vanished. But we both knew what he meant, and I preferred to save my innocent/stupid act for special occasions. "Can't say I'm surprised," I said. "Did he also tell you that I asked him to keep our advance payment warm?"

"He did," Geri confirmed, and in my mind's eye I could envision a sort of urbane predator's anticipation on his face. "Does that mean you're ready to deliver?"

"I am," I said. "When and where?"

"There's a private meditation club twenty kilometers west of the Shah Mir Spaceport called the Deodar Expanse," Geri said. "It has a landing field to the north of the main building complex that will accommodate the *Ruth*, and your names have been registered for entrance. I'll be in the Grand Hall at the center of the east residence wing in two hours. Do you need me to repeat any of that?"

"No, I've got it," I said. "We'll see you soon."

I keyed off and turned to Selene. "You pull it up?"

"Yes," she said, peering at her pad. "The Deodar Expanse truly lives up to its name. It includes six building complexes and ninety square kilometers of forest, grassland, sports venues and artistic interactive circles."

"Any Zen gardens?"

She looked up, her pupils frowning. "Probably. Is that important?"

"Not really," I said. "I got to visit one in Havershem City, that's all. Do you see the landing area?"

"Yes," she said. "It doesn't seem large enough for the number of people the residences seem capable of housing."

"That's because meditation clubs are playgrounds for the rich and powerful," Tera said, her voice and face betraying her tension. "Their private yachts drop them off and then go sit at one of the regular spaceports until they're called for."

"You've seen a lot of these clubs, have you?" I asked.

She shot me a quick look. "A few," she said. "Let's focus on finding McKell, shall we? Preferably before you have to hand me over to Geri."

"Well, he's not going to be anywhere on Deodar's grounds," I said. "You heard Geri—very exclusive place, very exclusive landing pad, very exclusive clientele. How could McKell even find a way in?"

"I'm sure he could figure out something."

"Maybe," I said. "But with the kind of security they're bound to have he's not going to be able to slip through the gate and then just sit around sipping cola for a few hours. I'm guessing he's parked at Shah Mir Spaceport waiting for Geri to show up."

"You could be right," Tera said, her voice thoughtful. "Can you pull up a list of ships currently berthed there?"

"Sure," I said. "Selene?"

"I have it," she confirmed. "What are we looking for?"

"A ship name with the initials SB," Tera said, stepping forward to look over Selene's shoulder. "McKell's ship is named the *Stormy Banks*, and his fake IDs all have the same initials."

"Let me guess," I said. "His flight jacket has an SB logo on the shoulder?"

She frowned at me. "How did you know?"

"I've known a few other ship captains who've done that," I said, wondering briefly what she would say if I told her I'd gotten a good look at that jacket five years ago when Selene and I nearly ran him to ground.

"Here's one," Selene announced. "The *Singing Banjo*."

"That sounds like McKell," Tera said. "Any open slots nearby?"

"There's one three slots to the south."

"Try to get it for us," I told her. "We'll put down, walk over, and see if he's there," I added to Tera. "If he is, we nab him there and do whatever's necessary to get him out of there. If he's not, we'll assume he's already in the meditation club and pick up with Plan B."

"He won't be easy to corral," Tera warned.

"I still have a couple of vertigo darts," I said. "Do you still have that autoinject antidote for the drug?"

"Yes, but I doubt he'll be shooting back with them," Tera said.

"I didn't think he would." So; confirmation that she did indeed have an antidote. And, by extension, that she'd deliberately allowed Selene and me to grab her at the Havershem City StarrComm center.

Problem was, I couldn't see how that fit in with her claimed goal of chasing down McKell before he got into trouble. Could Selene have been wrong about her latest story being the truth?

"Got it," Selene announced.

"Did you have to offer extra payment?" I asked.

"No, no bribes," she said. "The tower was very accommodating."

Right on cue, the approach path and destination popped up on my nav display. "Okay," I said. "Everyone strap in. Here we go."

In retrospect, that unexpected official cooperation should have set off a warning bell in the back of my brain. But focused as I was on Tera and her story, I never even noticed it.

Not until it was too late.

CHAPTER SIXTEEN

— ❖ —

I got us to our landing pad without trouble, and had Selene put a call in to the fuelers. Then, leaving the two women inside—under protest from both of them—I went outside and did a quick walk around the ship to check out our new neighborhood.

It was hot out here, hotter than I'd expected. Still, the place seemed quiet enough. There were a few humans and aliens in the area, but all of them seemed to be going about legitimate business. Most were port personnel working on equipment repairs or upgrades, but there were also a couple of small ship crews doing the kind of do-it-yourself thruster or cutter array adjustments that didn't require professionals. I didn't see anyone loitering around pretending to be busy, which given the heat wasn't surprising. There certainly weren't any lumpy Iykams lurking in the shadows.

At least, not in the shadows I could see on my limited tour. Given the amount of cover from ships and port equipment available to hide behind, the fact they weren't breathing down the *Ruth*'s intakes really didn't mean much. I would need Selene and her superhuman sense of smell to get a better read on that one.

The fuelers arrived just as I finished my recon. I got them started, handed over the advance fee that was always required when a ship was paying in cash, then went back inside. My single thigh-length vest wasn't in very good shape, but we weren't exactly heading out on a major social event, and the lighter garment would give my arms and torso some relief from the heat while still concealing my holster. Selene and Tera had meanwhile armed themselves with our two dart guns, concealed by two of Selene's much more respectable duster-vests, and the three of us headed out.

Given my partner's unique abilities, I usually tried to approach a target from downwind. Unfortunately, the breezes over Shah Mir today were light and shifting, which made it something of a crapshoot to match the air flow to our approach path. But we could only try. Tera had said the *Singing Banjo* should be due north; with the current breeze coming from the northwest, I took us one landing pad to the east to give us a route in from the southeast. Hopefully, the breeze wouldn't shift again before we got there.

For once, luck and the universe were with us. The breeze, though light, continued coming from the northwest, and as we rounded the final ship's stern and reached a stack of off-loaded cargo crates on the walkway we came into view of a slightly battered-looking Capricorn-class freighter.

Fifty meters away, standing beside the landing ramp with his back to us as he worked diligently on an info pad was a medium-built man with dark hair dressed in faded jeans and a black leather jacket.

I frowned. Given the heat, the fact that he was still wrapped in leather struck me as pretty damn suspicious.

I felt Tera step up beside me. "Well?" I whispered to her.

"I can't tell," she whispered back. "Looks like his jacket—I can see the edge of the shoulder patch—but I can't tell for sure."

"Is he usually this immune to heatstroke?"

She shrugged. "Heat doesn't bother him. He also has a certain macho streak."

"I know the type," I said, scowling. I'd hoped we could get at least a ninety-percent-positive ID before we had to come out in the open. "I'll take a look," I said. "You two wait here."

"No, I'd better go," Tera said, touching my arm as I started to take a step out of cover. "He won't trust a stranger."

Unfortunately, that was probably true. "Fine, but I'm coming, too," I said. "Selene? Anything?"

"I don't know," Selene said uncertainly. "I'm smelling a lot of spices coming from that direction."

I shifted my attention from the black-jacketed man to the ships and open space past him. The freighter parked to the west of the *Singing Banjo*, I noticed, had its main hatch open. "Cooking aromas?" I suggested.

"Maybe," Selene said, still sounding tentative. "I don't know. It doesn't smell...*warm* enough to be cooking." She muttered something. "And now the wind's shifted."

I focused on the breeze ruffling my hair. It had changed direction, all right, veering a bit more west.

On the other hand, if Selene crossed the pathway in front of us and took up position between the *Singing Banjo* and the freighter to the east of it, she should be back in the main air flow. The space was mostly open, but there was also a diagnostic cart sitting there with cables to the other ship that should give her enough cover. "Feel like a little walk?" I asked her.

"Across to that cart?"

"Yes," I said. "Keep it casual, and don't look at him along the way."

"Understood." Stepping past Tera and me, she walked across the walkway. She passed the cart as if she was heading to the next row of ships, then did a quick double-back and dropped into a crouch beside it. She leaned her head out a little, sniffing the air, then turned her face toward Tera and me. I raised my eyebrows in silent question, got a small shake of the head and equally small shrug in return.

"What's she saying?" Tera asked.

"Inconclusive," I said, wishing I was close enough to see her pupils. Even with extensive attempts at coaching, Selene was only marginal at sending body language signals. "Well, no sense putting this off. Let's go."

"No, I'd better go alone," Tera said. "He might think you're coercing me or holding me hostage. Let me confirm it's him and persuade him you're our friend, and then you can join us."

I felt a sour taste at the back of my mouth. So now the age-old hunter's dictum of always working in groups was going completely out the window as all three of us went in entirely different directions.

Still, I would at least be in plasmic range of both of

them. "Just make it fast," I said, drawing the weapon from my holster. "If it isn't him, get the hell back here."

"I will." Glancing once around the area, Tera slipped out from behind our cover and headed at a quick but casual-looking walk toward the still oblivious man. Raising my plasmic, I leveled it at the center of the black leather jacket, bracing the gun against the edge of the crate stack. Tera was nearly there, keeping to the side where she'd be out of my line of fire if I had to shoot. Another five steps...

And without the slightest hint of warning, a hand darted over my shoulder and grabbed my gun wrist.

I tried to twist out of his grip. But my attacker was already pulling my hand back, wrenching me off balance. I tried to shout a warning, but his left hand came around from the other side and clamped firmly over my mouth. My right arm was already stretched out, and with him spinning me around my left elbow was out of position to do anything. My only chance was to kick backward and try to take out a knee or shin, but my legs were already working full-time to keep me upright.

And so, as I'd done in Havershem City, I let my legs collapse under me.

Unfortunately, unlike Varsi's thugs, this attacker was ready for it. Even as I started to fall he dropped with me, giving me an extra shove downward that sent me slamming with additional force onto my butt. Even as the jolt rattled up my spine, he let go of my wrist and slid his hand up to my plasmic, twisting it against my thumb and wrenching it from my hand.

I jabbed back over my head with both hands, hoping to get to his eyes or nose or maybe grab an ear. But again he was ready, blocking my right arm with his and grabbing my left wrist with his left hand. I tried to roll away, but he twisted my left arm around at the elbow and slammed the forearm straight down onto the top of my head. There he held it, using my own arm to pin me to the ground. I tried to break free, but he shifted position to block my still flailing right arm with his shoulder and adding his right hand to the task of holding me down.

For a moment we struggled silently, me trying to force my way back up to my feet, my assailant trying to keep me sitting helplessly on the ground. But what he didn't know was that my part of the struggle was mostly just for show. In order to get both hands on my left arm, he'd been forced to drop my plasmic. It was lying there on the walkway, apparently forgotten, just out of reach of my right hand. If I could keep him focused on holding me down long enough to figure out a way to get to it, we would have ourselves a whole new ball game.

And then, suddenly, there was the opening I'd been hoping for. Most of the nerves in my left arm were still dead, but enough of the pressure sensors were left for me to recognize that he'd let go with his right hand and was only holding my arm in place with his left. Abandoning my pretend efforts to stand up, I turned my head to my left, letting his downward pressure now also drive me sideways.

The sudden change in position took enough of the weight off my right leg that I could now snap it out in front of me, then hook it back at the knee, catching my plasmic with my heel and bouncing it to within reach of my right hand. I grabbed the weapon, twisting around on my butt and shoulder to turn myself half-way around, making sure I kept the weapon tucked in close to my chest where he couldn't grab it or slap it out of my hand. I got a glimpse of his face as he abandoned his attack and leaped backward.

And even as I brought the plasmic around, the air exploded into a dense cloud of white, burnt-sugar-smelling smoke.

But that single look had been enough. The man who'd taken me down was Jordan McKell.

I scrambled to my feet, my nose filled with the smell of the smoke, my ears catching a hint of McKell's footsteps as he ran off, my mouth working with furious, helpless curses. If McKell had been sneaking up behind us, that meant the man we'd seen standing beside the *Singing Banjo* was an imposter.

And with the smoke blocking my view of everything, I had no way of knowing whether Tera had evaded the trap or fallen into it. Worse, I had no idea what had happened to Selene.

What I *did* know was the direction McKell had gone. Gripping my plasmic, praying I'd have a chance to use it, I headed off into the smoke.

I couldn't see a damn thing, but my extreme caution and watchfulness on the walk over from the *Ruth* was now paying off. I remembered every step of the way: the position of every ship, ramp, equipment cart, crate, even the handful of broken or uneven walkway stones we'd passed. I knew which direction McKell had taken, and if I needed to run blindly through a smoke screen to take him down, I should be able to do it without killing myself.

And even if it did—even if I ran full-tilt into

something—I needed to do this. I'd heard no shrieks or commotion from either Tera or Selene, which meant they'd either gotten away clean or had been efficiently and silently taken. With the cloud rolling their direction, I couldn't get to either of them without putting all of us in jeopardy.

But if I could chase down McKell, maybe I could trade him to Geri for at least Selene, maybe even Selene and Tera both. I picked up my pace, knowing that the kind of handheld smoke grenade McKell had used had more limited coverage than the mortar shells he'd hit us with in Havershem City. That meant he—and I—would soon be out in the open again. I reached out my free hand, swinging it back and forth in front of me, hoping I might catch a corner of his shirt. Abruptly, I ran clear of the cloud—

Just in time to see a figure disappear around the stern of the next freighter over.

I leaned forward into my run, pumping my legs for all they were worth. I'd only had a quick glimpse of McKell, and an even shorter glimpse of the man ahead of me, but there was no way it could be anyone but him. I kept running, wondering fleetingly if I should get out my phone and try to call Selene, decided that any distraction at this point might get me shot. I reached the freighter and ducked around it, alert for attack.

And found myself alone.

I slowed to a jog, eyes darting everywhere, trying to figure out where he could have disappeared to. The Shah Mir Spaceport used landing cradles, but the ships occupying the two closest had wide stabilizer fins that filled most of the gap between the edge of the cradle and the ships' hulls, making it highly unlikely that McKell had slipped down there. The freighter to my right had its ramp extended, the particular hatch position and cradle profile putting the ramp at a low angle, not much more than half a meter above the walkway. The hatch at the top of the ramp was closed and I could see the red indicator lights that showed it was locked.

The ship across from it, lying off to my left, also had a small height difference between hatch and walkway, though this one was more than a meter. Its exit ramp wasn't extended, but the hatch itself was open.

Farther down the walkway, as far as I could see, the entire rest of the area was deserted.

I headed toward the two freighter hatches, looking back and forth between them, trying to guess which one McKell had gone to ground in. Just because the hatch on the right-hand ship was closed didn't mean it hadn't been open when he tore around the corner, offering him the chance to run up the ramp and close it behind him.

Of course, the people inside might have had something to say about a sudden and uninvited guest. But McKell was undoubtedly armed, and anyway he'd just proved he didn't need a weapon to make someone's life unpleasant.

On the other hand, ship hatches were thick and heavy, and it was rare to find one that was both quick *and* silent. I hadn't heard the sound of a sealing hatch, and I certainly hadn't spotted any movement from that quarter as I rounded the ship's stern.

Which left the ship to my left.

I took a second, longer look. No ramp, but the

hatch was an easy enough jump for someone in decent shape. Even better, once he was inside there would be no sound or movement to give away his presence.

It was my best shot. I gave my left thumbnail the double stroke to turn it into a mirror and started warily forward, keeping one eye on the open hatch and the other on my raised thumbnail. I'd been attacked from behind once today, and I had no intention of going two for two. The freighter hatch to my right was still in my peripheral vision, should McKell be lurking behind it, and anyway he probably couldn't open it without making enough noise to alert me.

I was close enough now to the left-hand freighter to see into the shallow airlock. I shifted my full attention to it, searching the darkened chamber for movement.

"That's far enough."

I froze. The voice had come from behind and to my right, from the closed hatch I assumed McKell couldn't have slipped into or out of without my knowing about it. Keeping my eyes and plasmic pointed where they were, I eased my left thumb up and angled it for a look.

The hatch was still closed. McKell was lying flat on the walkway, half of him under the edge of the ramp where the shadows and low angle had hidden him during my approach.

The half of him that wasn't under the ramp was pointing a plasmic at me.

"So what now?" I called back to him. "You shoot me and go back to running from people like Tera and Ixil?"

"I'm not exactly running," McKell said, and in my thumbnail I saw him slide out from concealment and start to get up. If his plasmic's aim wavered for even a second . . .

But it didn't. "And I'm not going to shoot you," he added as he straightened up. "Not unless you insist on it."

"Didn't realize I had a say in the matter," I said. "I don't suppose you care that Tera is in danger."

Even in my limited view I could see a flicker of emotion cross his face. "Of course I care."

"Then why are you standing here holding a gun on me instead of doing something about it?" I demanded. "What the hell are you running around here for, anyway?"

"There are reasons," he said.

"Oh, right," I said sarcastically. "*Reasons.* The universal excuse of all irresponsible or incompetent people."

"Can't argue with that," he conceded. "But sometimes it's also the truth."

"What about Tera?" I demanded. "Or Selene? Or don't you even know about Selene?"

"I know about her," he said. "I'm sorry you and she are in this mess."

"This *mess*?" I snarled. "You call it a *mess*? *I* call it deadly danger."

"You want to go help her, nobody's stopping you."

"Except you."

"*Nobody's* stopping you," he repeated, leaning on the first word this time. "Keep your plasmic pointed away from me, and you're free to go anywhere you want. I won't interfere."

I hesitated. With him centered in my secret mirror I knew exactly where he was standing, *how* he was standing, how he was holding his plasmic, and everything else about his position. If I could take him by surprise—if I could spin around fast enough—I might be able to get off an incapacitating shot before he could react with one of his own. If I succeeded, I would finally have evened the score.

If I failed, Selene would be all alone.

"If it makes you feel any better, there *is* a plan," McKell said into my hesitation. "And getting yourself killed trying to get the drop on me won't help either you or Selene."

"Or the plan?"

"Or the plan."

"So I *am* part of the plan," I said. "What happened to your regrets about dragging us into this? Come on—I should at least get to hear what I'm supposed to do."

"You'll probably be getting a call soon," he said, ignoring the question.

"I'm sure I will," I said. "I'm a very popular guy. So, what, you want me to say hello for you?"

"If you think that's a good idea, go ahead," he said calmly. "Just...all I can say is you've got good instincts, Roarke. Go with that."

"Do you want me to tell you what my first instinct is to do right now?"

"Thanks, but I can guess," he said. "Just say the word, and you'll be on your way to a whole new world. Remember that."

I felt my lip twist. As threats went, that one had been delivered pretty casually. But there was an intensity beneath the calmness, a warning not to dismiss it. "Any particular word you had in mind?"

"*Artichoke* is a good one," he said. "It's catchy, memorable, and not one most people would ever think of."

"Artichoke," I said flatly.

"Artichoke," he confirmed. "Anyway, we're done here. I don't suppose you'd be willing to close your eyes and count to a hundred?"

I sifted rapidly through my extensive collection of expletives. Not a single one properly fit the absolute absurdity of that request. "What do *you* think?" I said instead.

"No, I suppose not," he said, a hint of regret in his voice. "I'll see you later. Good luck." In my mirror I saw him lift his other hand—

I spun around, dropping into a crouch, swinging my plasmic around. But I was too late. Even as McKell came into view at the corner of my eye the space between us exploded into more of the thrice-damned white smoke.

I thought about shooting anyway, fully aware that he was probably already on the move. I thought about trying to guess which direction he'd go and trying to continue my pursuit. I thought about screaming my rage and frustration at the sky.

What I actually did was wait, shaking with adrenaline reaction, until the cloud dissipated.

To find myself once again alone.

I looked around as the last remnants of the smoke swirled around my knees and ankles. No one. No McKell, no workers or ship's crew, not even the faint whine of distant runarounds or trucks. I might as well have been the last man on Kashmir.

That eerie thought was still echoing through my mind when my phone vibed.

I twitched in reaction. Muttering a curse, I jammed my plasmic back into its holster and yanked out my phone.

It was Selene's phone calling. But I was pretty sure it wasn't her at the other end. "Roarke," I said.

I was right. "My congratulations, Mr. Roarke," Geri's smoothly irritating voice came in my ear. "I'll admit I had my doubts that you'd be able to hand Tera off at the Deodar meditation club, given their high-end security and all. Bringing her to Shah Mir where we could intercept her without fuss or bother was sheer genius on your part."

I squeezed the phone hard. "I'm glad you're glad," I said. "So you got her?"

"We got her," he confirmed. "Where exactly have you wandered off to?"

I glared at the emptiness around me. "I was chasing down my attacker."

"McKell?" He gave a little snort. "Waste of time. He's too fast and too smart. Which is a good thing, of course. If he hadn't stayed on the run this long Tera would have found him long ago and we'd have lost our opportunity to get to know her better. Come on back—we're waiting for you beside the *Singing Banjo*."

I felt my stomach knot up at the thought of having to face Tera. "You go on ahead," I said.

"What about the hundred thousand commarks we owe you?"

"You can drop it in my account," I said. "I'll send you the deposit details."

"I'm afraid we're going to need to see you in person."

"Why?"

"For starters, as I said, we owe you money," he said. "But mostly, it's because of Selene."

For the second time in a minute I attempted to crush my phone in my hand. "What about her?"

"Have you forgotten so soon how bad that smoke is for her? While you were busy chasing McKell we were helping her escape his cowardly attack before she could suffer those effects a second time."

"I appreciate your thoughtfulness," I said. "If you can just drop her off at the *Ruth* we'll be on our way."

Geri's sigh was clearly audible. "Are you really going to play this game? Fine. Here's the reality: You and your lovely alien partner are coming with us, and you're coming with us now."

"You already have Tera," I reminded him. "We don't know anything about Icarus that she doesn't."

"I know that," he assured me. "But as you may have noticed, Tera can be rather stubborn. And while she may not hesitate to sacrifice her own life or health, I get the sense she wouldn't be nearly so cavalier with the lives of others."

With an effort, I forced down the furious panic bubbling up in my throat. "If you even *think* about hurting Selene—"

"Really, Mr. Roarke," he said reproachfully. "We have no interest in hurting anyone, I assure you. With someone of Selene's unique vulnerabilities there's no need. Imagine Tera's emotional agony as the two of them sit across from each other in the heavy atmosphere of some, let's say, exotic and spice-heavy cuisine. I'm sure we can find something that makes your partner thoroughly miserable without actually harming her."

"I'm going to kill you, Geri," I said softly. "You hear me? If you don't let Selene go right now, I'm going to kill you."

"I'd expect nothing less," he said calmly. "I'd also

note that a promise like that will be hard to keep if the two of us are at opposite ends of the Spiral."

I took a deep breath, inhaling the ghost of the burnt-sugar smoke. "I'll be right there," I said.

"I'll be waiting," he said. "Not me personally, of course—Tera and Selene and I are long gone. But the runaround and driver I've left will bring you to our ship."

So he was even denying me the chance to defy the odds of a long-distance kill shot. "You just make damn sure nothing happens to them," I said. "Either of them."

"Trust me," Geri promised, and even given the perverse satisfaction in his voice I could sense his sincerity. They were the key to the Icarus project and whatever glory or money his Patth masters were prepared to heap on him. Of course he wouldn't hurt them.

Not unless and until he had to.

"Now, be a good boy and hurry up," he continued. "Time is passing, and we still have a long ways to go."

Midway through my jog back to the ship, it occurred to me that I hadn't said hello to him from McKell. Probably just as well.

CHAPTER SEVENTEEN

——— ❖ ———

I watched for McKell all the way back, just in case he decided to pop his head up out of the gopher hole again. But there was no sign of him. Whatever this "plan" of his was, it apparently included leaving Tera, Selene, and me to the wolves.

About halfway back it occurred to me that I'd used that phrase a lot in my career. Now, with Geri and Freki's using Odin's two wolves as their aliases, it felt disturbingly like the universe was deliberately mocking me.

I didn't dawdle on my way to the *Singing Banjo*, and certainly the silent driver in the runaround didn't pause to see the sights on our way to the other end of the spaceport and the nondescript ship waiting for us there. Just the same, he and I had barely made it aboard before the hatch was sealed behind us, the repulsor boosts kicked in and nudged us up out of the landing cradle, and we were on our way. Wherever

we were off to next, it was clear Geri was in a hurry
to get there.

He was waiting for me inside the airlock, and after
relieving me of my phone and plasmic he escorted me
down the corridor to an aft suite. Tera and Selene
were already there, sitting on individual recliner
couches, neither of them with particularly enthusiastic
expressions.

Maybe they'd hoped I would mount a last-minute
rescue and my arrival brought that expectation to a
bitter end. More likely, they were just too emotionally
exhausted to even bother glaring at me for messing
up so badly.

Geri apparently wasn't interested in witnessing our
awkward reunion. Thankfully, he also wasn't interested
in gloating, at least for now. He told us a meal would
be delivered in two hours and that we'd be landing
eight hours after that, and then beat a hasty retreat,
resealing the hatch behind him.

For a few minutes Selene and I talked, comparing
notes on what had happened after McKell triggered
the smoke grenade. Remembering the similar attack in
Havershem City, and fearful of a repeat of the debil-
itating effects of the smoke, she'd run away from the
cloud as fast as she could. Unfortunately, her path of
escape had taken her straight into the arms of Geri's
thugs. To their credit, they'd then kept going, helping
her get away from the smoke and waiting until it had
dissipated before putting restraints on her wrists and
loading her aboard a runaround.

She'd reached Geri's ship about the same time
as Tera, the latter arriving in a different vehicle but
escorted by the same class of thug. They'd had their

phones and other equipment confiscated, then been unceremoniously dumped in our current group cell.

It was a reasonably nice cell, I had to admit, especially given the ship's rather shabby exterior. Geri might not want to draw unwelcome attention to his transport, but that didn't mean he was interested in roughing it, either. In retrospect, I could see why he and Freki had seemed less than thrilled by their accommodations aboard the *Ruth*.

Geri had said our trip would take ten hours. Except for our dinner break—which turned out to be the same upper-class caliber as our suite—I spent that entire time visualizing the local star map and trying to figure out where we were going.

But in the end, given Geri's masters, there really was only one obvious destination. By the time we arrived, I already knew where we were.

"There it is," Geri said, waving at the viewport as the ship headed in. "Lacklin. I've always thought of it as the unofficial Patth home away from home."

"It's everything the guide books say it is," I agreed sourly, gazing out at the cloud-speckled sky and green and blue patches beneath it.

"You laugh," Geri said, his voice almost introspective. "But that's indeed what it could have been. It's got a wide swath of decent climate, and the landscape and natural attractions are the match of anything in the Spiral. It could have been a thriving colony with an equally thriving tourist trade."

"So what went wrong?" I asked. "The planet not looking profitable enough for the Patth? They had to lock down all the travel and shipping routes, too?"

"Essentially," he said. "Only it wasn't *all* the Patth, but just one of the two directors who'd been tasked with developing the system. They had diametrically opposed visions of what they wanted Lacklin to be, and the"—he looked sideways at me—"more greedy of them won out. You already know the result."

"All non-Patth interest was strangled away, and the rest of the Spiral took their business elsewhere."

"Yes." Geri considered. "Though given how things subsequently turned out, that may have been a blessing in disguise."

"How so?"

He gave me a mysterious smile. "You'll see," he promised. "And then even you, Bounty Hunter Gregory Roarke, seasoned traveler of the Spiral, are going to be amazed."

There were still a couple of decent cities on Lacklin, probably more the result of Patth pigheadedness than any real demand for the real estate, plus a dozen or more small and no doubt underutilized lake and mountain resorts. We skipped past all of that, settling into one of a pair of isolated landing cradles set in an unremarkable stretch of grassland at the edge of an equally unremarkable strip of tangled forest. Completing the hat trick of dullness was a set of half a dozen dilapidated farm buildings, including a house, barn, three sheds, and a crop silo.

I'd hoped that, out in the middle of nowhere on a Patth-dominated planet, Geri might forego any extra security for the next leg of our journey. No such luck. He met us at the suite with three sets of restraints, and a minute later we were marched to the outer hatch with our wrists tied together in front of us. Either the man was even more paranoid than I'd thought or he was under strict orders from someone uphill from him in the Patth hierarchy.

I rather hoped it was the latter. I already had a pretty good feel for Geri's style and constraints. If I was going to make any deals, I probably needed someone higher up that mountain to talk to.

Not that I had anything to bargain with at the moment. But I always tried to keep my options open.

I'd naturally assumed we were going to one of the habitable structures, the house if Geri was feeling hospitable, the barn if he wasn't. Instead, he stepped off the landing ramp and turned to the right toward the crop silo. With three of his thugs paralleling Tera, Selene, and me on either side, we followed.

The view through the ventilation mesh showed the silo was about half full. Geri either didn't notice or didn't care. He walked up to a spot directly beneath the silo pipe and pulled open a hidden control panel. A handprint, optic scan, and muttered voice code, and an equally hidden door popped open from the silo wall. With an appraising look back at the three of us—probably wanting to see if we were sufficiently impressed by the cleverness of it all—he walked inside.

The room behind the door was narrow but long, leading to an elevator near the center of the silo. More security checks to get the elevator door open, and he headed in.

Unlike the corridor, the elevator car was quite roomy: good in that no one was going to have an attack of claustrophobia, bad in that it meant all our guards could pile inside with us without any of them getting close enough for me to help myself to one of their plasmics.

The floor selection panel had just two buttons. Geri punched the lower of the two, the doors closed, and we started down.

And down, and down, and down. The idea of the Patth putting a secret installation out in the middle of nowhere was crazy enough; the thought that they'd also apparently decided to put it deep enough to smell magma was edging on the ludicrous. An irreverent thought flicked through my mind, that some director's brother was probably in the mine-shaft-drilling business.

The trip seemed to take forever, but it probably lasted no more than a minute. The momentary relief that the doors were finally open was tempered by a sight that I could have gone my whole life without seeing: a pair of the lumpy-faced Iykams seated behind heavy full-auto flechette guns pointed straight toward us. Geri made some kind of hand signal; the Iykams responded by angling the muzzles of their weapons a few degrees away from us. Behind the guard post, a rock corridor stretched out, the walls far enough apart to accommodate both us and our phalanx of guards, the floor and ceiling lit only by subdued light sconces spaced every ten meters or so. With another glance over his shoulder to make sure we were following, Geri headed down the hall.

I knew the Iykam guards wouldn't be in a facility like this if they couldn't obey even orders they didn't like. Still, as I walked between them, I got the distinct feeling that they rather hoped I would give them an excuse to open fire. I passed up the temptation to offer them a smug smile, and moved on.

The corridor ended in a T-junction. Geri paused there, glanced right, then turned left. We followed, and as we rounded the corner I smelled a faint hint of something coming from the other direction. "Selene?" I murmured.

"Cooking aromas," she murmured back. "Patth and Iykams. Freshly laundered linens. Filtered water. Alcohol-based beverages."

"Living quarters?"

"Yes," she said. "Ahead . . . metal. Electronics. Iykams and Patth. Many Patth."

I nodded. The supervisor I'd been expecting, presumably, plus more minions. Now we were getting somewhere. A set of blast doors guarded by a pair of corona-gun-armed Iykams slid open as we approached, and Geri led the way through.

Into a large cavern buzzing with activity.

Selene had been right about there being a lot of Patth. The malicious little creatures were everywhere: monitoring consoles, working at equipment scanners and analyzers, or just sitting in circles with info pads propped up in front of them discussing or arguing among themselves. Spaced around the cavern walls, well clear of all the work areas, were more armed Iykams. At the center of the cavern was a cylindrical chimney a good five meters across, that disappeared upward into the rock. An industrial-sized lifter plate built into a heavy-duty framework lay ready on the floor beneath it, surrounded by four cable racks helping to organize the multitude of cables and wires snaking from the various consoles up into the chimney.

"I believe introductions are in order," a smooth voice came from the side.

I turned. The Patth walking sedately up to us looked like all the other members of his species, given that I'd never taken the time to learn how to distinguish between Patth faces. But his hooded robe told me all I needed to know. Instead of the usual unadorned gray, his had six royal blue slash marks set into each sleeve and the same number on the left and right edges of his hood.

This was no academic, equipment supervisor, or even high-level diplomat. This was a full sub-director, just two Patth ranks below that of Director General itself.

"Of course, Your Eminence," Geri said, his voice taking on a respectful tone that underlined what the Patth's outfit had already told me. "This is Bounty Hunter Gregory Roarke, his partner Selene, and Tera C, whom I believe you already know."

"I've not, in fact, had that pleasure," the Patth corrected, gazing into Tera's face. His attention shifted to me, and for another long moment his eyes traced across my features like he was looking for something specific. Then, he gave a small shake of his head. "No, you're not him. I thought perhaps...but no."

"Let me guess," I said. "You were wondering if I was Jordan McKell?"

"Indeed I was," the Patth agreed. "I see I was mistaken. I see, too, that you are insightful."

"No, it's just that I keep running into that problem," I told him. "Some of your Iykams wondered the same thing. Though I really don't know why. McKell and I don't look a thing alike."

"Human faces," the Patth said, an odd intensity drifting into his voice. "Difficult to distinguish between. You're acquainted with McKell, then?"

"He threatened to shoot me and tried to break my arm off," I said. "If that counts as acquaintanceship, I guess I'd have to say yes."

"He's being sarcastic, Your Eminence," Geri interjected.

"Thank you, Expediter," the Patth said. "I *am* familiar with human wordplay. Yes, that does seem the sort of social interaction McKell specializes in. You're fortunate to be alive, Mr. Roarke." He paused, as if reconsidering his statement. "Or perhaps not. Welcome, all of you, to the Firefall project. I'm Sub-Director Nask, whom you will be serving."

Serving. That didn't sound good.

Selene apparently didn't think it did, either. "May I inquire as to what our service will consist of?" she asked.

"For you and Mr. Roarke, there are two possibilities," Nask said. "The first is that you rest in your quarters for the next few days, coming out at meal times to the finest cuisine and alcoholic beverages the Patthaaunuth can provide. The second is that you spend those same days writhing in agony under the most exquisite torture the Patthaaunuth can devise."

Deliberately, he turned his gaze onto Tera. "Which of those paths you walk is entirely in the hands of your companion."

I looked at Selene, seeing the growing fear in her pupils. Geri had already stated that Selene and I were being brought along to ensure Tera's cooperation. But somehow, when he said it, the threat had sounded theoretical and distant.

Now, it was suddenly real, imminent, and utterly horrifying.

"No," Tera said flatly.

"You haven't yet heard my request," Nask said.

"I'm not saying *no* to your request," Tera corrected. "I'm rejecting the statement that anything that happens to them is on me. If you choose to torture or kill them, that is entirely your decision, and the consequences will be entirely on your hands."

"A difference without a distinction," Nask scoffed. "Their pain will be the same whether they blame you or me."

"Perhaps," Tera said. "But know that when the time comes for repayment, their view of whom to blame will be of critical importance."

For a moment the two of them held each other's gaze. Then, almost unwillingly, Nask broke contact, shifting his eyes again to me. "I doubt Mr. Roarke will ever be in position to seek retribution."

"You didn't think McKell would, either," Tera said.

Nask turned back sharply— "Yes, I know who you are," Tera continued, a small, grim smile twitching at her lips. "McKell was merciful and let you live. If I were you, I wouldn't count on such restraint from every human that falls into your hands."

"I also wouldn't count on every human you meet to be strong and righteous to the point of pigheadedness," I put in. Advance placement of blame for someone else's suffering wasn't the direction I wanted this conversation to go. "Personally, I'm a great believer in compromise and cooperation. What exactly is going on, and what can we do to make all this talk of torture go away?"

Nask looked at me, back at Tera, then back at me. "A reasonable request," he said. "Come."

He turned and headed toward the lifter. Someone

prodded me with a none-too-gentle jab in my back, and as I half-turned to glare at him I found to my surprise that somewhere in the past couple of minutes the human guards from Geri's ship had been replaced by Iykams from the cavern contingent. Here in the heart of whatever the hell this was, apparently, only Patth and their most loyal servants were acceptable.

The Iykam prodded me again, harder this time. Turning, I headed after Nask, noting that Tera and Selene were likewise under Iykam guard.

We reached the lifter, and as Nask and I stepped onto it I craned my neck to look up. At the top I could see a metal plate covering the top of the shaft, with an opening the size of our lifter in the center. Through the opening I could see that the space beyond was well lit. The rest of the group piled on behind us, the lifter's guardrails extended, and we headed up.

The lifter had three speeds, I noted, and Nask had chosen the slowest of them. Whatever was up there, he was going to milk as much drama out of it as possible.

"What you're seeing is one side of an alien artifact that has apparently lain buried on Lacklin for thousands or perhaps millions of years," Nask said as we rose sedately up the shaft. "Tell me, Mr. Roarke, are you familiar with Patthaaunutth mythology?"

"Not even familiar with the human version, I'm afraid," I said.

"Pity," he said. "Ancient literature tells so much about the basic hopes and fears of a species. Our myths include the story of Orammescka, a Patthaaunutth who flew high in the heavens to challenge the sun and subsequently fell to his death. Unlike the theme of foolish glory prevalent in so many of your human myths, though, his goal was the more noble one of capturing fire and bringing it to his people."

"Sort of like Prometheus," I said, a cold chill running up my back as I again looked up at the alien artifact above us. Tera had implied the Patth had been looking for McKell as a way of getting their hands on the Icarus project.

She'd been wrong. The Patth didn't need Icarus. They already had one of their own.

"I thought you didn't know human myths," Nask said.

"There are a few stories that have gotten stuck in popular culture," I said. "I know about Thor and Hercules, too. So if you've got your own super stardrive, what do you need with us?"

"Interesting," Nask said, eyeing me thoughtfully. "As I said, you have the gift of insight."

"Wasn't that hard, really," I said with a shrug. "The minute you invoked the Icarus myth, it was obvious where you were going."

"Obvious only to those who can connect the spots," he said. "As to what I need you for"—he turned his head toward where Tera was standing silently behind me—"perhaps Tera would be kind enough to enlighten you."

I turned, too. Tera's expression was wooden, but I could see subtle stress lines in her throat and at the corners of her mouth. I looked at Selene, saw in her pupils that she was smelling that same tension. "Tera?" I prompted.

She took a deep breath. "I don't know for sure," she said, her voice as wooden as her face. "But at a guess, I'd say Sub-Director Nask's people haven't been able to get Firefall working."

She looked at me. "I think he wants me to fix it for them," she added softly, "and is ready to sacrifice you and Selene if necessary to force me to do it."

There didn't seem to be much that needed to be said after that. Tera went silent, Selene didn't seem interested in adding to the topic, and Nask also seemed to be done for the moment. I had the impression he was pleased that Tera had been the one to drop that bomb instead of him. Part of his plan to shift as much responsibility for any pain we suffered into her lap, presumably.

Not that it had worked. I was smart enough to keep the blame on the people making the trouble, along with the people who'd given them their orders. Though that distinction probably wouldn't mean much to the rest of my nerve endings when the agony really got started.

We reached the top of the shaft; and as my head rose above the level of the metal I saw that it wasn't a flat plate but a slightly curved section of a sphere. A *large* sphere, too, a good forty meters in diameter. Across from us and about thirty degrees up the side was another rectangular gap, this one about one meter by two, that led through the wall into another area that was as well lit as the one we were just entering. That gap was also the destination for most of the cables from the cavern below us. Near the opening were another eight or nine pieces of analysis equipment welded to the inside of the sphere wall.

It wasn't until I belatedly focused on the operators casually sitting and standing—and walking—across the metal surface in total defiance of gravity that

I realized that the equipment wasn't welded to the metal but simply stacked there.

Somehow, the sphere had its own radial gravity field powerful enough to overcome and supplant that of the entire planet below us.

I looked at Nask, to find him looking intently back at me. "So you really *don't* know anything about Icarus," he said.

"Did you think I did?" I demanded, feeling my anger at his patronizing tone collide head-on with my churning dread at his threat of torture. The result, I knew from past experience, was a dangerously explosive mixture. "I got you your damn prize—where the *hell* do you get off threatening us?"

With my wrists tied together, I knew better than to try to get physical with him. But maybe Geri didn't know that. Or maybe Geri just felt like hurting someone, and I was his first choice. Regardless, a second later I found myself down on one knee, fighting for balance with my face pressed against the lower part of Nask's gray robe as Geri jabbed the edge of his foot into the back of my left knee. Behind me I heard Selene's startled whimper as Geri's hand closed in a painful grip on the top of my left shoulder.

"One doesn't speak to a Patth sub-director in that tone, Roarke," Geri said, his voice the calm of an approaching storm. "I believe you owe him an apology."

With my judgment half blinded by pain and rage, my first instinct was to shrug off his hand, leap up, and throw everything I had into the most devastating punch I could manage. But with my hands restraint-locked, and a circle of armed Iykams watching, I knew any resistance would be futile.

Back on Kashmir, my awareness of what my death would do to Selene had kept me from launching a suicidal attack at McKell. Now, that same concern dictated that I swallow my pride, play their game, and wait for a better opportunity.

As my father used to say, *Getting your enemy to overestimate you is good. Getting him to underestimate you is better.*

I craned my neck, looking up. Geri was standing over me, his expression that of someone eyeing a disgusting bug and wondering if it was still useful or simply needed to be stepped on. "My apologies, Sub-Director Nask," I said, forcing a humility into my voice that I absolutely didn't feel. "I spoke without considering the consequences."

"Apology accepted," Nask said. "Help Mr. Roarke up, will you, Geri?"

"Of course, Your Eminence." Shifting his paralyzing grip on my shoulder to my upper arm, Geri pulled me to my feet. "He is, after all, only a bounty hunter."

"But still a useful one," Nask said. The lifter came to a final halt, fitting neatly into the rectangular hole in the sphere. "Come, Mr. Roarke. Let me introduce you to Firefall."

CHAPTER EIGHTEEN

❖

Between my aching leg and the sphere's vertigo-inducing gravity I expected the trip to be pretty unpleasant. As it turned out, as long as I kept my eyes on the metal at my feet, with occasional glances at Nask as he strode along in front of me toward the rectangular opening I'd seen from the lifter, the unsteadiness I'd anticipated didn't occur.

My leg still hurt, though.

"Now, this is the challenging part," Nask said as we gathered around the opening, Geri close behind me and to the side, the Iykam guards forming a circle around all of us. "As we stand out here, the gravity points into the opening. On the other side, the smaller sphere also has a radial gravity field pointing outward toward *its* wall. Here at the opening, the fields therefore point in opposite directions."

"So you're saying that if we jumped straight in, we'd just bounce up and down?" I asked.

I felt a touch of air on the side of my neck as Geri took a step closer— "That would indeed be the case," Nask said. His fingertips made a small gesture away from me, and out of the corner of my eye I saw Geri retreat. Apparently, I'd already had my lesson in proper groveling for the day. "So we of course will not do that. What we will do is this."

He lay down on the floor, settling onto his back parallel to the long edge of the opening. Then, he rolled over the edge, his hand reaching in to something on that side, and disappeared from sight as he completed the roll. "The operation is easier than it looks, I assure you," his voice came through the opening. "Geri will be next, followed by Mr. Roarke and then the ladies."

"Looks to me like there's a handhold somewhere on that side," I pointed out as Geri lay down on the floor. "It would be a lot easier if you took off the restraints."

"I'm sure it would," he agreed, making no move to actually do so. "Make it quick, and don't forget how many corona guns are pointed at your back." He rolled into the opening and disappeared.

"Gregory?" Selene asked as I got down on the floor, her pupils showing anxiety.

"It'll be okay," I told her, wishing I actually believed that. "I'll be waiting on the other side to help you through." Bracing myself, I rolled.

Nask's assurances notwithstanding, the maneuver wasn't quite as easy as it looked. But it wasn't as hard as I'd feared, either. It took me two tries to get the right balance of momentum and angle, and the sudden change in gravity direction was more than a little disconcerting. But on the third try I made it, rolling neatly through the opening and even managing to grab the handhold that had been welded onto the deck half a meter away despite my restraints.

I got up on my knees, noting in passing that we were indeed in another sphere, this one crammed with wires and equipment. Selene rolled into view, and I grabbed her arm and helped pull her through. I eased her to the side to clear the space for Tera, and got ready for my next assist.

"Not her," Nask ordered. "Let's see how well she does on her own."

I was still trying to decide whether or not to obey him when Tera rolled smoothly through the opening, doing another half-roll away from the opening to put herself facedown and then using her bound hands to push herself up to her knees and then to her feet. She threw a slightly condescending look at the handhold—which she hadn't bothered with—then looked around her. "You really *do* need help, don't you?" she commented.

I could see her point. The sphere was about twenty meters across, roughly half the size of the one we'd just left, and covered with cables, monitors, and control boards. Some of the cables came in from the larger sphere, clearly put there by the Path, but most of them were apparently original equipment. A mesh lay across the entire inner curve of the sphere, holding the cables in place against the floor, with numerous cutouts to give easier access to the various monitors and control boards set into the surface. Six of the boards and displays were active, showing glowing controls and colored indicator lights, but everything else was dark. Extending out from one of the panels directly across from us was a slender, black-and-silver banded extension arm that stretched out to the center of the sphere.

"Indeed we do," Nask said with surprising humility, especially for a Path. "The question is whether or not you're willing to provide it."

"*Willing* is just the first question," Tera said. "*Able* is the second. This is hardly my area of expertise."

"Come now," Nask said reprovingly. "You've been with Icarus for six years. I can't believe you didn't learn everything there was to know about the system." He nodded toward Selene and me. "Especially when there are lives balanced on the line."

I frowned as a sudden thought struck me. They were arguing about getting a super stardrive running... except that said super stardrive was currently buried a hundred or more meters underground. Tera could get the damn thing up and running tomorrow, and it still wouldn't be ready to join the Path merchant fleet for years. Especially since Tera's friends at Icarus were six years ahead of them and presumably on the cusp of getting their own version on the market.

Unless, as I'd wondered earlier, the stardrive simply didn't work.

In which case, Tera would never be able to get Firefall working, either. No matter how hard she tried, and no matter what Selene and I had to go through.

"Are we boring you, Mr. Roarke?"

I snapped my attention back to the conversation. Nask was looking at me, that intent look back on his face. "Sorry," I apologized. "Mind wandering. I was just wondering if all these extra power cables might be interfering with Firefall's own power system. Maybe you should take them out and see if the thing has some self-diagnostics you could run."

"What makes you think Firefall has a power supply?" Nask asked.

"It's got artificial gravity," I reminded him. "Two sets, in fact, that compete and balance against each other. That not only takes power, but also control." I pointed in the direction of the active control boards. "Are you running those, or is Firefall?"

"Thank you for your advice," Nask said, not sounding very thankful at all. "But this isn't your task."

"I know, I know," I said. "My task is to bleed."

"That's up to Tera," Nask said. "Well?"

"Let me think about it," she said evenly. "Right now, my companions and I need food and rest. Ask me again in twelve hours, and I'll tell you what I'm willing to do."

"You don't get to set the terms—" Geri began.

"Twelve hours," Nask agreed calmly. "Expediter Geri will show you to your quarters."

"And then food?" Tera pressed.

Nask smiled. "Yes. And then food."

Our cell turned out to be only a little bigger than the suite we'd shared aboard Geri's ship, though it felt smaller because it had partitions to allow each of us a private sleeping space. The sleeping cubbies connected to a miniscule common room and even smaller bathroom. I'd been in worse, but the reminder that we might spend less time here than we would in Nask's torture chamber threw a certain pall over the exploration.

I'd assumed Nask would have our food brought to us in the cell, as a way of emphasizing our isolation and confinement. To my surprise, we'd barely had time to look around the suite when Geri and the Iykam guards ordered us out and marched us down the corridor to a surprisingly spacious and well-lit dining room.

Which included several tables currently occupied by groups of Iykams. All of them turned to look at the three of us as Geri ushered us to one of the more isolated tables, and none of them looked happy to be sharing their eating space with alien prisoners.

Apparently, Nask had decided to pass over intimidation by claustrophobia and go directly to intimidation by angry alien.

"Your guards will wait outside the door," Geri said. "They'll take you back to your suite when you're done. Food and drink will be brought to you in a few minutes."

"We don't get a choice of menu?" I asked as we all sat down, noting that we all instinctively chose chairs that offered views of the rest of the room.

"Sure," Geri said. "You can take what's offered, or you can go hungry." He shifted his attention to Tera. "When you're ready to cooperate with Sub-Director Nask, just let your cell guards know."

"Nask gave me twelve hours," Tera reminded him.

"You might want to reconsider," he said. "Patth get annoyed when you make them wait. I don't think you want to see the sub-director annoyed." Throwing her an icy smile, he turned and strode back across the dining room and disappeared out the door.

"This resort leaves a lot to be desired," I commented, doing a quick visual scan of the walls, ceiling, and floor nearest us. Wherever the microphones and cameras were—and I had zero doubt that they were there—I couldn't spot them.

"Microphones shouldn't be a problem," Tera said. "At this range they'll have trouble picking up anything as long as we keep our voices low."

"You might be surprised," I said.

"I don't think so," she said. "Anyway, we have to risk it. We need to figure out what we're going to do, and our cell is much too quiet for any private talk. Just keep your voices low and try not to move your lips any more than necessary."

"And do this," I said, scratching my fingernails gently on the tabletop. "Helps mask the higher frequencies."

Across the room, three Iykams appeared through a doorway, each carrying a tray loaded with a covered dish, a tall glass of clear liquid, and a squat one-liter brown bottle with a gaudy green-and-orange label. They walked to our table, set the trays in front of us, and retreated without a word.

"Any idea?" I asked, tapping the bottle as I lifted the cover from the dish. There were two different meat-like slabs on the plate, plus two servings that looked like vegetables and one that was clearly some sort of grain bread. A typical cross-species selection, and from the smell they were reasonably close cousins of foods I'd had before. I looked at Selene, wondering if the aroma would be too much for her, but her pupils showed more curiosity than revulsion or discomfort.

"Nask talked about alcohol earlier," Tera said. "I'm guessing this is his first offering." She pulled out the cork and gave the liquid a cautious sniff. "Smells like some kind of brandy, or maybe a brandy-fortified wine. Definitely ethanol, so it's probably safe to drink." She lifted the bottle toward her lips—

"No, wait," I said, frowning as I looked around the

room. Every Iykam-occupied table had a similar bottle in the middle, all of them open. "Don't drink it. Put the cork back in and hand it to me."

"Why?" Tera asked as she obeyed. "If they wanted to drug us, there are a lot of easier ways."

"That's not it," I said, taking the bottle, and holding it for a moment while I pretended to read the label. "Selene?"

"Did you want me to open it first?" she asked as she handed over her bottle.

"No, I'll do it," I said. I uncorked the bottle, held it in both hands while sniffing it, then put the cork back in. I did the same with mine, then put all three bottles at the far end of the table.

"I presume there was a good reason for all that?" Tera asked.

"Just planning for the future," I said, picking up the soft plastic fork I'd been given and attacking one of the meat slabs. "Let's talk about the present. What are you going to do about Firefall?"

"Nice, succinct question," she said, digging in a bit more cautiously. "I wish I had a nice, succinct answer. On the one hand, I don't relish the thought of you and Selene being tortured. On the other, this is an important piece of alien technology, and the people I work with wouldn't appreciate me helping the Patth get a handle on it."

"Those people aren't here," Selene pointed out around a mouthful of vegetable. "You are. What do *you* think?"

Tera's throat worked, and not just from swallowing. "Given the growing Patth stranglehold on shipping," she said, "I'm not at all certain the Spiral's economy can survive an operational Firefall in Patth hands. Why else would I have risked myself trying to get to McKell before they did?"

"Okay, different question," I said. "If you decide you want to get it running, *can* you? Not just whether you have the expertise, but will it even be physically possible? There could easily be vital components that are missing or damaged."

"If there are, I didn't see anything obvious," she said. "You're right, though, and there's no way of knowing until I start hooking things together."

"Excuse me, but I see a problem that no one seems to be addressing," Selene said. "A stardrive buried this deeply underground would seem to be useless. They'd have to dig it out, and I would anticipate a good chance of damage or destruction during the process."

"I was wondering that same thing," I said. "It would take months or even years to get the damn thing out, plenty of time for someone else in the Spiral to come here and take it away from them. So what are they *really* up to?"

"One: nobody out there knows where we are," Tera said. "Even if they found out about Firefall, it's a big Spiral to go hunting in. Two—" She hesitated. "Look, there's no way around it. Whether I do what they want or not, in the end Nask is going to kill us. The only difference will be how much pain is involved."

"You're probably right," I conceded. "Personally, I vote for the no-pain option."

"You afraid of a little pain?" Tera asked scornfully.

"No, I'm afraid of a *lot* of pain," I said. "More to the point, working to get Firefall fixed buys us time to find a way out of here."

Tera looked across the room at the Iykam tables. "You have a plan?" she asked, resuming her eating.

"I have the germ of one," I said. "But it's going to have to simmer a bit before we know if it has a chance of working."

For a moment Tera sat silently, taking a few more bites of her food and a couple of sips from her water glass. Selene and I took the cue and continued our own meals. Whether or not Nask was trying to listen in, the Iykams were certainly watching us. "All right," Tera said at last, a clear reluctance in her voice. "How much time do you need?"

"A couple of days to see if what I've got in mind will work," I said. "Realistically, a day after that to come up with a second plan when the first falls through, then a couple of days to develop that one."

"And if you need a Plan C?"

"The same three or four days tacked onto the other end," I said. "As my father used to say, *Plans are like roses—you have to let them grow a little before you can smell anything.*"

"And like roses because they can poke thorns into your fingers?"

"He used to say that, too."

"Your father must have been hilarious to grow up with," she said acidly. "Fine. You said two days before you know?"

"Hopefully, I'll have an idea by this time tomorrow," I said. "In the meantime, as my father used to say, *Never pass up an opportunity to eat. And if possible, always ask for seconds.*"

People who've never left their own home planet never really understand the challenges of switching worlds on a regular basis. Not only are there time zone and biorhythm changes to deal with—which, granted, can also be a problem on a single world—but also the more subtle adjustments needed with a new gravity, new atmospheric mix, even a new sunlight spectrum. Adding in new food, drink, and odors, you have a situation that might realistically take several days to adjust to.

Tourists often had that luxury. Bounty hunters almost never did.

Still, being stuck in an underground warren was probably going to eliminate the atmospheric and spectrum issues, and for me artificial lighting actually made the biorhythm adjustment easier. For the rest, we were just going to have to work it through.

Initially, we would have those twelve hours Nask had promised. Tera clearly intended to run down that clock, partly to take advantage of what little control she had of the situation, partly to give us more time to think and plan. Until then, I decided, my best use of our brief grace period would be to catch up on some of the sleep I'd missed lately. I stripped down to my underwear, stretched out on my sleeping nook mattress, and fell asleep.

Five hours and not nearly enough sleep later, I was brusquely awakened by an Iykam who informed me it was dinnertime and that I *would* be joining them in the dining room.

Apparently, our first meal in our new prison had been lunch.

My truncated sleep cycle had left me groggy, and I could feel myself staggering a little as the Iykams half escorted and half shoved me back into the dining room. Selene and Tera were in better shape, but I could tell neither of them was happy with this scheduled force-feeding, either.

But then I got my first look at the groups of Iykams seated around the other tables, and my fatigue was suddenly gone.

There were roughly the same number of aliens here now that we'd seen at the earlier meal. Once again, in the center of each one of their tables was a bottle identical to the ones we'd been offered at lunch.

Time to find out if Plan A might actually be a go.

I waited until we were seated and the servers had brought our trays—this time featuring a different selection of food—another water glass, and yet another of the green-and-orange-labeled bottles. "I suppose you don't want us to drink these, either?" Tera asked as she reached for hers.

"Hang on," I said, motioning her to stop. "Selene? Are these the same bottles we had at lunch?"

Out of the corner of my eye I saw her nostrils and eyelashes working. "No," she said.

"How do you know?" Tera asked, frowning.

"Gregory handled all of them," Selene reminded her. "I don't smell his scent."

"Oh," Tera said. There was an odd expression on her face, as if she was only now starting to fully comprehend the depth of Selene's abilities.

"Okay, now you can open it," I said, picking up mine and pulling out the cork. "Sniff, but don't taste, then seal it up again. You, too, Selene."

"What now?" Tera asked when we'd all finished.

"Now Selene's going to take two of the bottles to each

of those other tables, tell the Iykams that they smell funny and ask if they'll swap with her. At each table, she'll see if she can spot any of our lunchtime bottles."

"All right," Selene said as she stood up. "Please do keep eating. We don't want them thinking you're overly interested in what I'm doing."

Tera and I watched in silence, mechanically shoveling in food, as Selene went in turn to each of the eight occupied tables. At six of them the Iykams turned her down with brusque words and gestures, while those at the other two added more verbal abuse to their refusals.

But at least no one took a swing at her, as I'd feared someone might. She finished her tour and returned to our table, shuffling along with her shoulders hunched and her head hung low, the perfect image of a beaten alien put in her place by her social and cultural betters. Briefly, I wondered if Tera appreciated Selene's acting abilities as much as she did her olfactory ones.

I took the bottles as she passed me, setting them down on the table away from us. "Well?"

"The first, fourth, and fifth tables," she reported as she sat down and resumed her meal. "All three were nearly empty."

"Perfect," I said, remembering not to smile or in any other way indicate that my gamble had paid off. After all, I was supposed to be a beaten and intimidated lesser creature, too.

"What's perfect about it?" Tera asked. With Selene now safe—relatively speaking—she was showing a little more interest in her dinner.

"Nask promised us the finest cuisine and alcohol available," I reminded her. "I thought it likely that the Iykams would also appreciate the finer things in life.

Certainly the alcohol part—most beings appreciate good liquor. So when we left three untouched bottles of perfectly good hooch on our table, they helped themselves to them."

"So how does that help us?" Tera asked. "Unless you're thinking you can tell on them and get them in trouble, I don't see the point."

I glanced up at the ceiling, wondering again what kind of listening devices Nask might have planted there. "The point," I said, lowering my voice still further as I starting scratching on the tabletop, "is that I've got knockout pills I can drop into the bottles."

Tera sat up a bit straighter. "How many?"

"Four," I said. "Unfortunately, one pill per bottle will leave the drug too dilute to actually floor anyone. But it should at least make them a bit befuddled and unsteady on their feet. In an escape situation that can make all the difference."

"Agreed," Tera said. "So . . . ?"

"Easy, girl," I cautioned. "Growing roses, remember? I first have to figure out the guard schedule and match that to how the bottles get redistributed once we hand them back. It'll be a couple of days at least, maybe more."

"The question then," Selene said, "is how long can you stall on activating Firefall?"

"Not a problem," Tera said. "I can make the repairs last as long as you need without Nask getting unhappy or suspicious."

"Then we've got a plan," I concluded. "Let's finish here, and get back to our cell before I fall asleep in my soup."

"It's a *puree d'rita*," Selene corrected absently, sniffing at the bowl beside my plate. "Not technically a soup."

CHAPTER NINETEEN

———— ❖ ————

The next few days settled into a comfortable, if somewhat boring, routine. Tera was taken away every morning to work on Firefall, while Selene and I stayed in our cell. At lunch, the three of us were reunited in the dining room for a meal and some casual chatting, interspersed with hurried bits of quieter and more clandestine conversation. Half an hour after our arrival we were separated again, Tera going back to work, Selene and I going back to our cell. Dinners followed the same pattern, with Tera working an extra hour or two afterward before being brought back to the cell for the night.

At least once a day I offered to join Tera in Firefall, pointing out that my long experience flying the *Ruth* had given me a fair degree of mechanical skill. But the two Iykam guards who took Tera away each day merely said they'd pass the word along, and the four who accompanied Selene and me ignored the offer completely, and nothing ever came of it.

Still, the three of us had a fair amount of time together, and I could tell Tera was a bit puzzled by that. Traditionally, prisoners were kept apart as much as possible to guard against escape attempts, mutual planning, and synchronization of stories and lies. In this case, though, Nask was apparently willing to take that risk in favor of getting Tera as socially and emotionally tangled up with his sacrificial hostages as possible.

He was probably also hoping to eavesdrop on any nefarious schemes we might be plotting. Hopefully, our dining room precautions were enough to thwart him on that one.

Back in Havershem City, Geri had said that Patth weren't normally very good at distinguishing human faces, but that the possibility of a two-hundred-thousand-commark bounty might inspire them to make the effort. I was equally bad at distinguishing Iykam faces.

But while money was definitely a big motivator, staying alive beat it hands down. Which meant my next priority was learning to identify each and every damn alien in the place.

I started with our guards—there seemed to be two shifts of two guards per prisoner—who stood outside our cell until mealtimes and then escorted us to the dining room. Identifying the Iykams who brought Tera to and from the dining room—again, there were two different pairs—was the next step. Memorizing the ones we got glimpses of at various doors and intersections along our limited journeys came next, and then the pair who bodyguarded Nask on the rare occasions when he passed us by.

After that, all that was left was to track each of the off-duty aliens into the dining room, looking for patterns in seating and especially noting where our rejected liquor bottles ended up.

I couldn't keep sending Selene around the room hunting for those, of course, lest Nask get suspicious. But Tera turned out to have terrific eyesight, and subtle fingernail tears and loosened corners of the bottle labels let us pick them out with reasonable precision. Like most beings, the Iykams had a social hierarchy, and to my quiet satisfaction I discovered that after the first couple of days it seemed that our personal guards—ours *and* Tera's—were getting first crack at the bottles we left behind.

Tera suggested it was probably a picture of dominance or even assault against us. Selene saw their drinking of our liquor as a somewhat more gruesome metaphor. Personally, I didn't care what the psychological basis for it was as long as they kept doing it.

And finally, we were ready.

"The guard shift change happens about an hour before dinner," I told Tera and Selene as we sat in the dining room eating what I hoped would be our final uneventful lunch together. "Those evening guards—the ones at that table over there—eat lunch when we do, then pick up guard duty just before they take us to dinner. They're also drinking the liquor we left behind at yesterday's dinner."

"So if we drug tonight's bottles," Tera said slowly, working through the logic and timing, "they'll drink from them at lunch tomorrow. Will the effect last long enough?"

"It should," I said. "Remember, all we're going to get is a little slowing of thought and reaction time.

We'll let them take us out of the cell, dump them into one of the other rooms along the way—I've already figured out which ones will work—then rendezvous with you as you're on your way here. We then drop your guards and hightail it to the elevator."

"What about the guards along the way?" Tera asked.

I gave a small shrug. "We deal with them."

Her lip twitched. Possibly she'd forgotten that dealing with our guards meant we'd be collecting their corona guns to bring to the next phase of the party. "So you're saying this happens tomorrow?"

"As my father used to say, *Putting off until tomorrow what you can do today just crowds up tomorrow's schedule,*" I said. "Unless you have a reason we should hold back?"

"No," Tera said hesitantly. "But we can't just run to the elevator. There's something we first need to get out of Firefall."

"So bring it with you."

"It's too big for one person to carry," she said. "We all need to be there."

I looked at Selene, saw her nostrils working, and focused on her pupils. As far as she could see, Tera was telling the truth. "Why do we need this thing?" I asked.

Tera paused, either gathering her thoughts or else searching for a way to phrase a lie so that it would slip through Selene's filter. "You haven't yet explained how we're going to get to the elevator and all the way to the surface before Nask can shut everything down," she said. "There's something in the small sphere that will guarantee he has to let us go."

"Like what?" I pressed. "A rare crystal globe? A lamp with a genie inside?"

"I can't explain further," Tera said. "You just have to trust me when I say—"

"No," I cut her off harshly. "I need more than just *you have to trust me*."

"And *I* need more than just *we'll get to the elevator and somehow it'll all work out*," she shot back. "Roarke—"

She took a deep breath, lowering her eyes to her plate. "We're in the middle of an underground research station," she said, her voice so soft I could barely hear her, "in the middle of nowhere, on a planet inhabited almost exclusively by Patth. There's something in Firefall that will guarantee Nask will let us go. That's all I can say. You really do just have to trust me."

I looked at Selene. Her pupils were still not registering any lies.

Still, Tera wasn't exactly being fair. Just because I was being vague about some of the details didn't mean I hadn't worked them out. Because I definitely had.

I had a way to keep everyone away from the elevator long enough for us to get to the surface. If there was a ship waiting we could get off Lacklin that way; if not, I'd spotted at least two air vehicles tucked away in the barn on our walk to the silo that would get us out of the area before Nask could organize an effective pursuit.

And just because Lacklin was Patth-dominated didn't mean there weren't plenty of places we could go to ground until I found a freighter or liner we could stow away on. Especially since Nask couldn't exactly charge in with plasmics blazing if he wanted Tera to live long enough to get his damn alien stardrive working.

Still, if Tera really did have a massive lever to use against him, it might make things a lot easier. And unless Selene had completely lost her touch, such a lever really did exist.

Or at least, Tera *thought* it existed.

"If you're wrong, we all die," I warned.

"I know." Tera looked up and gave me a hard-edged smile. "Ditto."

"Fine," I said. "But if it doesn't work, prepare yourself for an *I told you so* that even your grandchildren will hear."

"Understood," she said, and I saw a little color come back into her face. Whatever was going on, she'd been genuinely afraid I would turn her down.

"In that case, there's no point in taking out the guards on the way here," I said. "We might as well wait until we're taken back out again. That way we won't need to worry about connecting with each other, and we'll get at least one last nice meal."

I looked over at our three bottles, sitting all forlorn and rejected across the table. "And there may be one or two other bonuses, as well," I added.

Beside me, Selene shivered. "I wish you wouldn't refer to it as a last meal," she said.

"Sorry," I said. "But as my father used to say, *Eat, drink, and be merry, for tomorrow you'll get the bill.*"

Tera shook her head as she sliced off a piece of meat with the edge of her fork. "I'm guessing," she said, "that your father was a very lonely man."

We were escorted back to our cell and settled in for the night. I told Selene and Tera they should get a good night's sleep, but I doubted they did. I know I didn't.

The next morning's routine went as always. Tera was led off by her usual pair of Iykams, I again offered unsuccessfully to tag along and help, and Selene and I were then left to our own devices.

Selene spent the next few hours in her sleeping cubby, thinking, meditating, or possibly trying to catch up on the sleep she'd just missed. I mostly sat in the common room, giving Selene her privacy and mechanically playing solitaire with the single deck of cards they'd given us as I ran endlessly through the plan. But if there were any factors I'd missed, or any variations I hadn't taken into account, I couldn't find them.

Lunchtime came. Again, we stuck to our routine: Selene and I escorted by our four guards to the dining room, Tera joining us from Firefall, our food being delivered, our usual sniffing at the open bottles before recorking and setting them aside, and then eating our meal. To anyone observing, it was exactly the way we'd always done things.

Only this time, as I disdainfully sniffed the contents of the bottles, I slipped a knockout pill inside each one. After lunch, we were taken away, and as we left the dining room I watched out of the corner of my eye as the Iykams cleared the table. As far as I could tell, none of them was acting any differently than usual, either.

Every plan included one or more make-or-break points. Our first such hurdle had been passed.

Only maybe a thousand more to go.

I tried to get some sleep that afternoon, but with limited success. After I gave up the effort, Selene and I played a few rounds of poker and double solitaire. But it was strictly for the benefit of the monitor cameras I'd long since spotted and the Iykams presumably watching. In reality, neither of us really had our hearts in the game.

And then, right on schedule, the door was unlocked, and the Iykams outside ordered us out for dinner.

We headed down the corridor, Selene and I walking side by side, the four Iykams as usual forming a moving box around us. As we rounded a corner I looked sideways at Selene, and in her pupils I saw confirmation that the Iykams' odor had subtly changed. The drug was in their bodies, and our next make-or-break point had been passed.

Though whether or not they were sufficiently affected for what we needed had yet to be determined.

Tera joined us in the dining room, and as her guards dropped her off at our table I again got Selene's silent confirmation that those two Iykams, too, had joined their fellows in drinking our leftover liquor. Our dinners were served, we did our usual routine with the bottles, and settled down to eat. I kept an eye on everything and everybody, but could see nothing to indicate suspicion or heightened alertness or any other hint that they were on to us.

Which made it that much more of a shock when Nask and his bodyguards unexpectedly came sweeping through the door and headed straight for our table.

"Don't react," I warned Selene and Tera as I took a sip of water. I didn't dare make the potentially telegraphing head and eye movements necessary to check out their expressions, and I could only hope that neither of them was doing anything to give us away.

"Good evening, Mr. Roarke," Nask greeted me as he came up to the table. "Good evening, Ms. Tera; Ms. Selene."

"Is there anything particularly good about it?" I countered with the barely civil antipathy I always used in our infrequent conversations.

"Of course," he said, sitting down in one of the chairs across from me. "We received confirmation this afternoon that your two hundred thousand commarks has been fully registered into your Xathru account."

"So glad to hear it," I said, throwing a furtive look at Tera. The Path blood money, and I wouldn't be human if I didn't want to check out how the woman I'd betrayed was reacting to the reminder.

To my relief, she was reacting perfectly. She was looking sideways back at me, her throat tight, her eyes cold and bitter. Whether it was all an act or whether she was boosting the visible emotion by channeling her current tension, it was an excellent performance.

"There's other news, as well," Nask said. "You'll be pleased to know that, thanks to Tera's exemplary work, your long wait is nearly over."

"Really?" I asked, feeling a sudden warning knot in my stomach. After all the effort Tera had put into evading the bounty hunters the Path had put on her tail, Nask had to know there was no way she would just meekly hand over Icarus's secrets to him.

"Really," he assured me. "She has one more day to prove that she's serious about activating Firefall. If she fails, the torture will begin."

He said it so matter-of-factly that it took a second for the words to register. When they did, it was like a kick in the teeth. "*What?*" I demanded.

"You heard me," Nask said coldly, his casual tone gone like it had fallen into a bottomless pit. "Tera continues to merely pretend she's working in our interests while in fact working wholly against them."

"You've watched me every step of the way," Tera said, her tone tight. "Did you see anything to suggest I wasn't doing exactly as you asked?"

"I saw many things," Nask said. "I saw you connect circuit boards one day, then reconnect them the next, then completely rewire them the next. I saw you ignore orders to run power to one of the primary panels. I saw you turn one of the displays upside down."

"I've told you a hundred times this isn't my area of expertise," Tera countered in that same stiff tone. "I'm trying to remember exactly how Icarus looked, and where everything goes. Sometimes I need to sleep on the day's work to realize I had it wrong." She flicked a glance at me, then focused on Selene. "Do you think I *want* them tortured?"

"Perhaps more than you realize," Nask said. "They may be the only friends you have, but you surely haven't forgotten that they're the reason you're here."

Tera lowered her eyes. "Hardly," she muttered.

"Good," Nask said. "My decision stands. Unless you make substantial progress tomorrow, their suffering will begin the following day."

"Ours, *and* the Spiral's?" I suggested. "The Talariac Drive hasn't caused enough damage to everyone else's star travel? You need something even faster?"

Nask's eyes narrowed. "You seem like so many others to believe the Patthaaunutth are the source of all evil in the universe," he bit out. "You would be well advised to learn the true history of our rise to economic power."

"You ruined a lot of people and small companies," I said. "That's all I need to know."

"The Talariac opened up possibilities previously undreamt of," Nask shot back. "We've made life better for billions of beings across the Spiral."

"And crushed millions more," I said. "Not sure that was a deal worth making."

"Then you're a fool," Nask said scornfully.

"Maybe," I said. "But *I'm* not the one threatening to torture innocent people to keep that economic machine chugging along."

"You would if you could." Abruptly, Nask stood up. "That will be all the work for today, Tera. You may retire to your quarters to consider your options: activate Firefall, or watch your friends suffer."

"You're forgetting her third option," I pointed out. "One that guarantees you can't torture us."

Nask tilted his head slightly. "What is that?"

"Smothering us in our sleep," I said. "Oh, and I know where the cameras are in our cell, so we can make sure no one's watching while she does it."

"You are an endless source of amusement," Nask said. But there was a brittleness in his voice that hadn't been there before. Maybe he hadn't heard of the Earth philosophy of keeping the last bullet for yourself. "I bid you good night."

"Likewise." I reached across the table, got my hand around the abandoned liquor bottles, and dragged them over to me. "Sounds like this is the time to find out if this stuff tastes as bad as it smells."

"Really," Nask said. "I was beginning to think you didn't drink alcohol."

"Only on special occasions, like when I'm being

threatened with torture," I said. "Alcohol is a traditional human anesthetic, especially when taken internally."

"Ah," Nask said. "I think you'll find your bleak assumptions about Pfistria brandy are wrong, much as your assumptions about the Patthaaunutth. Good night." He smiled slightly. "Sleep well."

We watched in silence as he and his bodyguards strode across the room and out the door. The rest of the diners, who'd been furtively observing our impromptu drama, now returned to their meals, though their conversation seemed a bit more subdued. "You think arguing economics was the smart move right now?" Tera asked, glaring at me.

"It got him to leave, didn't it?"

"I suppose," she conceded grudgingly.

"But you're not *really* planning to get drunk, are you?" Selene asked.

"That depends on how the next half hour goes," I said. "You'd better be right, Tera. About everything."

"I am." She took a deep breath and looked back down at her plate. "You wanted a last good meal," she reminded me. "Eat, drink, and be merry."

We finished our dinner in silence. Then, as usual, we headed to the door and our waiting guards.

Not as usual, I carried two of the liquor bottles, their bases cupped in my hands, while Selene carried the third.

With the subtle effects of the knockout drug still in our guards' blood and brains, they may not have spotted this notable break in our usual pattern. They certainly didn't comment on it. We all headed off together toward our cell, Tera in front, me in the middle, Selene bringing up the rear, all of us walking as close together as we could without stepping on each other's heels. A few steps along the way, I shifted the bottles so that I was gripping them around their necks.

And at the first turn, where I'd long ago noted a blind spot in the monitor camera coverage, I made my move.

The two guards flanking me went first as I swung my arms up along my stomach and chest and then thrust my arms to the sides, slamming the bottoms of the bottles hard against their heads. The impact sent them bouncing off the corridor walls and into a pair of unconscious heaps on the floor. I pulled my arms back in, again tucking them close to my body as I pivoted forty-five degrees to my left, and again shoved the bottles straight out to my sides, this time taking out the Iykam on Tera's right and the one on Selene's left. Selene had already used her bottle to take out her other guard, and as I turned back around Tera threw herself at the last Iykam still standing, grabbing his arm and hand and pinning the limb in place as he fumbled for his corona gun.

He was still trying to pry her hand away when my bottles and I sent him to join his unconscious fellows.

"That went better than I expected," Tera said, her breathing showing the slight raggedness of a person whose adrenal glands had kicked into overdrive. "Casual walk, or a sprint?"

"Pretty sure casual went out the window when the first guard went down," I said, kneeling down and relieving three of the Iykams of their weapons. Having observed even just a partial demonstration of the damn things I was pretty sure it was something I never wanted to use on any living being. But as my father used to say, *Better to have a card you never have to play than watch someone else play that same card out of his sleeve.*

"So we sprint?"

"We sprint," I confirmed, handing each of them a corona gun. I stuffed mine into my belt and retrieved my two liquor bottles. "If you have to shoot, don't hesitate. And try to stay out of my line of fire."

The danger inherent in falling into a routine was never more evident than it was during the next few minutes. We were already halfway to the big work cavern before any alarms sounded, and even then the Iykams clearly weren't taking it seriously. It was only when the three of us actually charged into view that any of them seemed to realize someone hadn't called a drill or accidentally bumped a button.

At which point they did indeed swing into action with an intimidating degree of professionalism. But we had the initiative and momentum, and the fact that everyone was armed with the same short-range weapons slowed any inclination on their part to charge us. On the contrary, their immediate instinct was to shy back or duck around convenient corners to get clear and out of range.

Only the pair of guards at the cavern blast doors showed any willingness to risk their lives, dropping to one knee with weapons drawn and waiting stolidly for us to get close enough to fire. Unfortunately for them, while a kneeling position was good for purposes of targeting, it left them completely unable to evade the liquor bottles I hurled at their torsos.

One of them managed to dodge far enough to the

side to take the impact on his shoulder; the other caught my attack squarely in the chest. Neither alien should have any lasting damage, but both were out of position to stop us as we barreled past them.

Of course, Nask might inflict some lasting damage of his own for their failure. But I couldn't worry about everything.

There was the usual assortment of Patth techs and assistants roaming around the cavern as we entered. Like the Iykam guards, they scrambled to get out of our way as we ran to the lifter. We hopped on, I keyed for the fastest setting, and we shot upward. I waited, the last liquor bottle ready in case the Iykams outside rallied and came charging in to stop us. But again, the sheer unexpectedness of our break for freedom seemed to have caught them by surprise.

Or more likely, the ominous thought occurred to me on our way up, Nask's authorized escape counter was for everyone to rush to the choke point by the elevator, the only way for us to reach the surface. Tera's little side trip to Firefall might very well cost us any chance we had of getting ahead of that response.

Whatever magic wand she was hoping to wave in Nask's face, it had damn well better work.

We reached the sphere, and I spent a few seconds locking the lifter in place. Hopefully, by the time they found a way to bypass the lock we'd have Tera's gizmo in hand and be ready to ride the plate back down. Tera had already reached the entrance to the smaller sphere as I finished, with Selene right behind her. One by one they rolled inside and out of sight; corona gun in one hand and liquor bottle in the other, I followed.

I arrived to find Selene standing by the opening,

her own gun ready, and Tera up to her elbows in one of the alien control panels. "What are you doing?" I called to her. "Let's grab this thing and go."

"We're not leaving," Tera's muffled voice came back.

Selene's head twisted around toward me, her pupils wide with surprise and growing horror. "What the hell are you talking about?" I demanded.

"We're not leaving." Tera peeked out from the panel, a tight smile on her lips. "But don't worry. We're also not staying."

CHAPTER TWENTY

◆◆◆

"Well, *that's* clear," I snarled. What the *hell* game was she playing now? "You want to elaborate before they break in and haul us off to the rack and Iron Maiden?"

"Yes, do try to keep them out," Tera said. "I set things up as best I could, but I didn't dare leave it too close. It'll take me a few more minutes."

"A few minutes to do *what*?"

"I couldn't tell you before," she said. "I wasn't sure whether the Path knew the truth, and I wasn't sure how much they could overhear." She paused in her work to throw me another quick look. "You see, everyone thinks—because we let them think—that Icarus is a stardrive. It's not. It's a star portal."

"What the hell does *that* mean?"

"Exactly what it says," she said. "You step into the launch module—this sphere here—you punch in the address of your destination portal, you grab that shaft"—she nodded her head back toward the black-and-silver extension arm—"you ride it up to the center, and you disappear from here and pop into the center of your destination's receiver module. That's the big sphere out there."

I stared at her. Of all the answers I might have expected . . . "That's insane," I insisted. I looked at Selene. "She's lying, right?"

Selene was staring at Tera, her pupils quivering with shock and disbelief, her nostrils flaring and contracting. "No," she said mechanically. "She's telling the truth."

I looked back at Tera. Or at least, I reminded myself, she was telling what she *thought* was the truth. That could be a huge difference. "We're deep underground," I reminded her. "That won't be a problem?"

"The portal can punch through forty-five thousand light-years' worth of dust, gas, and stars," she said. "I don't think a couple hundred meters of rock will be a problem."

"You've tested it?"

"Yes. Just back and forth between the Icarus launch and receiver modules, but we know it works."

"Is it instantaneous?"

"A few seconds per trip."

I looked over at the striped extension arm, the possibilities and implications bouncing through my mind like tethered balloons in a windstorm. The Talariac Drive, the faster, cheaper transport method that had raised the Patth to economic dominance . . . and now, suddenly, we were sitting on an alternative that could take someone across the stars in the time it took to check for oncoming traffic.

The Patth had offered a hundred thousand commarks for someone who might be able to give them Icarus's secrets. Tera the con lady had suggested she might be able to talk them out of five or even ten million.

Neither number had been even close. Not by at least five orders of magnitude.

I looked one final time at Selene, holding out one last small hope that it had all been a lie. A lie would mean we were in horrible trouble, but at least I would be able to avoid making a drastic upheaval in my worldview.

But it wasn't a lie. As far as Selene could tell, every bit of it was true.

As my father used to say, *Truth is stranger than fiction because fiction has to make sense. And usually tries to leave a better aftertaste.*

A distant sound snapped me out of my tailspin contemplation. Back in the big sphere, the lifter had been unlocked from below and was headed down. "Snap it up," I called. "Company's coming."

"Two more minutes," Tera said.

I looked around. There were dozens of power and sensor cables around, and given enough time I could probably weave them through the sphere's cable-control mesh into something that would at least require a would-be intruder to go get some wire cutters.

But I didn't have that much time, and anyway there were probably cutters and saws lying around the cavern down there. Our only other assets were three corona guns and one bottle of liquor.

One bottle of *flammable* liquor.

When Nask had first described the two spheres' competing gravitational fields I'd suggested a person in the interface could bounce up and down. He hadn't been amused. Now, that arrangement was going to

offer an even better trick, though I was pretty sure
he wouldn't be amused by this one either. Uncorking
the bottle, I poured the liquor into the center of the
opening.

It behaved exactly as expected, its momentum carrying some of the liquid through to the larger sphere
before sloshing back toward me, the splash quickly
dampening out as it also flowed outward to fill the
opening. A screen of bad-smelling alcohol floating in
the path of anyone who might try to get through.
Beyond the rippling barrier I heard the lifter start
back up again—

"Ready," Tera said. She extricated herself from her
work area and started punching an array of glowing
red squares. As she tapped or double-tapped each one,
it changed color to either yellow or black. "Both of
you, get over to the shaft. And be careful—right at
the base gravity changes direction to point inward."

"Right," I said. At this point, even a gravity field
that could change direction in midair didn't seem any
more remarkable than a favorite restaurant suddenly
altering its menu. "Selene, get over there." Taking a
step back, wondering how close the lifter and its pas-
sengers were, I pointed my corona gun at the gently
undulating liquor and fired.

Stardrives and shifting gravity fields might challenge
traditional theories of physics, but at least alcohol sub-
jected to a sudden blast of electrical energy behaved
exactly the way it was supposed to. The floating
puddle ignited into a brilliant blaze, throwing danc-
ing flames in both directions. I felt a wave of heat
from the fire and a more subtle wind at my ankles
as the sphere's air rushed to fill the partial vacuum

and feed the flames, and it belatedly occurred to me that my handy little barrier was rapidly chewing up the sphere's supply of oxygen. Hopefully, we'd be out of here before that became a problem.

If not, at least suffocation would be a faster and easier way to go than whatever Nask had planned for us.

Selene had reached the base of the extension arm by the time I headed that direction. Sure enough, she was now floating slowly upward, her hand sliding along the shaft for balance or stability or just to have something to hold onto.

I looked over at Tera as I ran. Most of the squares on her board were yellow or black, but there were still three red ones, her hand poised over them. "Trouble?" I called.

"Just trying to remember," she said.

"Remember faster," I bit out.

"You just focus on not falling over your own feet," she shot back. With three quick movements she keyed the last three squares to yellow. "Go."

"I'm going."

But not nearly as fast as Tera. By the time I reached the base and my inner ear was screaming the change of gravity to my brain, she was already halfway across the sphere. Clearly, she'd had a lot of practice moving across the mesh and cables coiled beneath it. I grabbed the extension arm and started my own ride, and as I looked upward to check on Selene I saw that the last twenty centimeters of the arm had changed color from black-and-silver to an oddly luminescent gray.

Selene and I were well on our way, Tera was nearly to the base of the arm, and my fire barrier was still going strong. Another few seconds, half a minute at the most, and we'd reach the end of the arm. If the fire held out—and if Tera was right about what this damn alien thing was—

With all the shifting gravity fields, I should have been prepared for anything. I wasn't. Abruptly, my inner ear gave another warning scream as my upward float switched to a full-speed downward fall.

I tightened my grip around the arm, only now discovering how slippery the damn thing was. I got my other hand on it, squeezed hard, and felt myself slowing down.

My relief was premature. A hint of a whimper was my only warning that Selene, with her lesser hand-muscle strength, was sliding helplessly down on top of me. I barely had time to brace myself when I felt her feet land squarely on my shoulders.

She did her best, bending her knees as she hit in an attempt to soften the impact. But she still had all her weight, and all her momentum, and I was nearly jerked off the arm as we dropped like a two-piece rock toward the deck.

Fortunately, I was able to maintain some semblance of a grip. Even more fortunately, we hadn't been too high up when she crashed into me, which meant we didn't have time to build up too much speed before my feet hit the mesh and the tangle of cables beneath it. Tera had managed to stay clear of our path, and I got a glimpse of her staggering for balance off to the side as Selene and I rolled onto the mesh.

I used the last part of my final roll to get back up on my feet, doing a quick mental inventory to confirm nothing was broken or sprained. Selene was getting shakily to her feet, and a quick look at her pupils showed me that she was also not in any pain. I turned to Tera, now standing rigidly, and opened my mouth to demand an explanation—

"Excellent," Nask's voice came from the sphere interface.

I turned back, looking a little ways up the curved hull to see the opening. The fire was gone, vanished like it had never been. Nask was standing just inside the opening, his angle making him tower a little above me. He was flanked by his Iykam bodyguards, and Geri was standing a little ways to the side.

Patth and Iykam expressions were still partially unreadable to me. But Geri's was perfectly clear: a mix of contempt and immense satisfaction. Whatever had just happened, he and Nask had clearly been behind it.

I eyed them, wondering if I could get to either of them in time. Geri responded to my look by slipping his Libra 3mm from beneath his jacket and holding it casually at his side.

"So I was right," I said, looking back at Nask. "The damn thing doesn't work."

"*This* one?" he asked, waving an arm around the sphere. It was hard for such a simple motion to look smug, but Nask pulled it off. "Of course not. But then, working was never its purpose."

"No," Tera whispered.

I turned my head to look at her, something cold running up my back. Her face was rigid, with the stricken look of someone staring at death. Not just her own death, but the deaths of everyone she'd ever known and cared for, the death of every dream she'd ever had.

And with that, the skies seemed to open up and the horrible truth rained down on me.

"I don't understand," I said, dredging up some puzzlement to shine through my dismay. *Getting your enemy to underestimate you . . .* "What do you mean, it was never supposed to work?"

"Are you that naïve?" Nask demanded. "Do you truly not comprehend?"

"He's a bounty hunter, Your Eminence," Geri said derisively. "They're known for their targeting skill, not their intellect."

Nask gave a wet-sounding snort. "Perhaps Tera would be good enough to explain it to him."

But Tera had turned her back on all of us, her shoulders shaking with reaction or possibly silent sobs. Selene stepped close, reached out a hand as if offering to comfort her. Then, slowly, she let the arm fall to her side. "I guess you'll have to do the honors," I said to Nask.

Nask snorted again. "It's incredibly simple," he said. "As Tera and her friends at Icarus feared, the Path have indeed found a portal of our own. Not here, of course, but safely secured on one of our three core worlds." He waved a hand at the board Tera had been working at, the one with the pattern of yellow and black squares. "But like any other form of communication, a lone portal is of little use. One must have at least two in order to make proper use of them."

I looked at the display as if I'd suddenly figured it out. "You needed Icarus's phone number."

"Address," he corrected, the contempt getting a little deeper. "We call it an address, not a phone number. But yes. We needed Icarus's location. Now we have it."

"So you rigged up a duplicate of the portal here in Lacklin," I said. "And then you pretended you needed Tera to hook it up for you."

"No," Tera said, her voice almost unrecognizable. "That's impossible. This *is* the portal. It has to be. The gravity fields—no one in the Spiral has the technology to do that."

I felt my breath freeze in my throat. Slowly, imperceptibly, she'd swiveled slightly to put her left side toward Nask and the others...and from my angle I could see her hand moving to the corona gun tucked away in her waistband.

And in the second horrible revelation in two minutes, I realized what she was going to do. A blast or two of high-voltage current into the control panels, and the whole thing might well be damaged beyond anyone's ability to fix it. If this was indeed the real portal and not just a decoy, that would end the Patth bid for this technology.

There was only one problem. Her weapon was still in her waistband, but Geri's was already in his hand. She would never even get the gun into position, let alone be able to fire, before he dropped her in a bloody heap on the deck.

Not unless something else drew his attention first. His attention, and his attack.

"You had this whole thing set up from the start, didn't you?" I demanded, taking a step closer to Nask. "You grabbed me, then let me run around playing games with cameras and microphones and liquor bottles. And the whole time you were just sitting back laughing at me." I put my hand ostentatiously on my own corona gun, knowing full well that I was still too far away from any of them to use it. "Well, damn you all to hell."

There was nothing like the appearance of a loaded weapon to pique a person's interest, even a weapon that was out of range. Like magic, Nask's, Geri's, and both Iykams' eyes turned to me. Nask's Libra was still hanging at his side, but I had no doubt he could lift it and put two or three rounds into me before I could take so much as another step toward them.

I had no intention of taking that step, or of even looking like I was thinking about taking it. All I wanted to do—all I needed to do—was hold their attention long enough for Tera to get a killing shot into Firefall's heart. After that...well, I could only hope that Nask would recognize the pointlessness of revenge killings. I looked closer at Geri's eyes...

And with the final gut-wrenching revelation of the evening I realized that it wouldn't matter what Nask wanted. Not in the heat of the moment, maybe not even afterward. Geri was looking for an excuse to kill me, and one way or another he was going to find it.

In that single heartbeat I almost shouted a warning to Nask, drawing his attention to Tera and thwarting her desperate last-minute act of sacrifice and stupid bravery. I had no reason to die for her, or for Icarus, or really for anything else. I didn't know why Selene and I were even here—Geri could have recruited any of a hundred other crocketts for this insane search.

And then, out of the corner of my eye, I saw Selene. She was still where she'd been when this whole depressing thought process began racing through my head: barely a step away from Tera, still trying to decide whether to offer comfort or to give her space to work through the emotions of her failure. And I realized that if Geri opened fire on Tera, he might hit Selene, too.

And with that, I no longer had a choice.

"Damn you all to hell," I repeated, taking a diagonal step away from Tera and Selene and toward Nask. I couldn't stop Geri from shooting me, but if I was Geri's first target Nask might be quick enough to stop him from killing Selene along with me. I took another step forward—

Just as Tera yanked her corona gun free and sent a withering blast of high-voltage into the control panel she'd just activated.

I snapped up my own weapon, shifted the aim to Geri, and squeezed the trigger. Even as my own crackling spray of current shot out I could see that it would dissolve woefully short of its target. I braced myself for the crack of his Libra, for the inevitable stab of agony as the slugs blasted their way through my chest. Tera fired a second time—

And then, all was silence.

The miniature electrical storm swirling in front of me dissipated. To my disbelief, I saw that Geri's weapon was still at his side, his earlier death mask replaced by a self-satisfied smirk. Nask and the Iykams were also just standing there, and I could swear the Patth had the same smug look as Geri.

"By all means, Tera, destroy anything you want," Nask said, mock-encouragingly. "Fire again if it makes you feel better. Fire until the power pack is drained. We were finished with this copy the minute you punched in Icarus's address."

Tera spun around, her earlier despondency replaced by fury. "Good luck picking it out of *that*," she bit out.

"Please," Nask said, with all the disdain the Patth were so famous for. "Even locked away in the Icarus research department you must have heard of such things as *cameras.* Be assured we have recordings of every move you made this evening."

He looked at me. "There's no need for any of you to die tonight," he added. "Unless you strongly feel the need to be a martyr."

I took a deep breath, gauging his expression and Geri's. If they were planning on shooting us anyway...

But no. Nask was smart enough to recognize that there was no need to kill helpless hostages. Especially when those hostages might still be useful down the road. "Not really," I said, leaning over and placing my corona gun on the mesh. "Selene? Tera?"

I looked back to see Selene straightening up, her own weapon on the mesh in front of her. "Tera?" I repeated.

For a bad moment I thought she was going to take Nask up on his martyr invitation. But she exhaled a silent sigh, and tossed her corona gun to the side. "So how did you do it?" I asked.

"This?" Nask asked, waving a hand to encompass the whole setup. "A great number of small gravity plates beneath the shell, of course. Extreme heavy-duty, of course, so that they could overcome the planet's own pull."

"Something like that would be pretty hefty," I pointed out. "Lot of equipment, lot of power."

"Certainly," Nask said. "But we had plenty of room to build everything once we'd hollowed out enough space in the rock. You'll have already noted, of course, that the one place where the mass of gravity equipment would be noticeable is at the receiver module entrance, and of course we oriented that so that the planet itself would provide the pull."

"What about the interface between the spheres?" I asked. I could see the puzzlement in Selene's pupils, as she wondered why I was bothering with this now. But if Tera was right about this being the actual portal, with Nask merely bluffing about it being a faked duplicate, it would be useful to find that out before they hauled us away. Not just so that we knew where we stood, but also so that we could maybe do a little more damage on our way out.

"Directed repulsor projectors at opposite sides of the spheres," Nask said, pointing over my shoulder. "You can see the one in here if you know what to look for."

I followed his pointing finger, my heart sinking a little more. It was there, all right, buried in a mass of cables between a pair of glowing light displays whose glare helped throw the projector into shadow. "I didn't know you could focus repulsors that tightly," I said, mostly just to have something to say.

"It *is* quite difficult," Nask admitted. "Not just the directionals and the edge sheerings, but also the tuning and balance. But once we had that perfected, it was easy to simulate a pair of opposing gravity fields."

"And all of that work just to convince us we were in a real portal?"

Nask smiled. "Great efforts bring great reward," he said. "In this case, the reward is indeed great."

I looked at Tera. If she'd had any lingering hopes that she'd smashed the Patth portal, those hopes were clearly gone. "So what happens now?" she asked dully.

"I *was* going to let you spend one last night here

before we left," Nask said. "But on consideration, I
see no reason for further delay. The guards will put
you in restraints and we'll go to my ship."

"And from there to a hidden prison somewhere?"
I asked.

"Hardly," Nask said, a gleam of anticipation in his
eye. "I'll take you to the *real* Firefall." He smiled
maliciously at Tera. "After all, Tera deserves the chance
to say farewell to her Icarus friends."

CHAPTER TWENTY-ONE

------------ ◆◆◆ ------------

The ship Geri had used to transport us from Kashmir had been a nondescript sort of freighter designed to blend in anywhere in the Spiral without attracting attention. Nask's ship, in contrast, was far more fitting for a Patth sub-director: sleek and expensive-looking, plastered with a big Patth diplomatic emblem and all but screaming luxury and privilege. If Nask could have hooked up external speakers to scream that message more literally, he probably would have.

As always, with power and privilege came an entourage. The *Odinn* had a full crew, including no less than three of the cyborgian pilots with their shiny face implants to fly the ship, plus a contingent of Iykam guards to bolster the contingent Nask brought along from Lacklin.

The interior of the ship was just as luxurious as the outside. Naturally, the three of us didn't get to see much of that.

Still, the cell we were locked in was bigger and more comfortable than either the Lacklin prison or Geri's ship's suite. For whatever that was worth.

Nask had said that the Firefall was on one of the three Path core worlds, which didn't tell me anything since no one had more than a vague idea of where those worlds were. He'd also said the trip would take us four days, but with a Talariac Drive cutting us through hyperspace that also told me nothing.

Still, for the first couple of days of our journey I entertained myself by visualizing as much of the Spiral as I could, eliminating the systems owned or colonized by the Commonwealth or any of the other alien species, and trying to narrow it down.

Wasted effort, really. But then, there wasn't much else to do. Tera spent most of her time lying on her bed, her face turned to the wall, not talking to either of us. She only roused herself for our twice-a-day meals, and I suspected she wouldn't have shown even that much liveliness without Selene's quiet but persistent encouragement.

I thought about putting in a reminder or two of my own about the importance of keeping up strength in captivity, but I never found a good place to bring it up. Anyway, given the looks Tera gave me whenever our paths crossed, prolonging any of those interactions probably wouldn't have been a good idea.

Interspersed between meals, sleep, and my speculations on our destination, I tried to think up a way to fix this mess.

As far as I could tell, there wasn't one.

The Path had their own Icarus-type star portal. We were headed there right now with the key that would let them use that portal to send a team across to either capture or destroy their competition.

And they would succeed. Barring something unexpected, there was no doubt about that. Icarus was a sitting duck, with none of the people there having the slightest idea of what was about to come boiling out their back door. Even if McKell had alerted them that Tera had been captured, they had no way of knowing the ace the Patth were holding up their collective sleeve. A small commando team dropped into the Firefall launch module in the dead of night—hell, even a single well-equipped invader could probably pull it off—a quick jaunt to the Icarus receiver module, and the whole project would be theirs, to haul away or wreck as they chose.

Either way, the dust would settle with the Patth holding all the cards. If they could reverse engineer either portal and make more of them, the upheaval in transportation they'd brought about with the Talariac Drive would be nothing in comparison.

And here Tera, Selene, and I sat: imprisoned, incommunicado, and outnumbered. No one out there even knew where we were, let alone had any idea what the Patth were up to.

Could we unlock our cell, overpower our guards, and take over the ship? Even if I somehow pulled off such a miracle, I couldn't fly this thing without the continual cooperation of one of the pilots.

Could we break free somehow once we landed, get off the ship, and call someone? But I didn't have a name or number, and given Tera's current feelings toward me I doubted she would trust me that far. Even if she did, I'd be a human on a Patth world, and I probably wouldn't make it a single block toward any kind of transmitter before I was tackled or shot. Tera wouldn't do any better. Selene would probably do worse.

Could I throw myself at one of the Iykams after we landed, sacrificing my life in the hope that someone would take note of such a bizarre event and start an investigation? Again, a futile waste. A human death on a Patth world wouldn't even be noticed.

The Patth had won. Again.

The Spiral just didn't know it yet.

I was lying in my bed on the last night before our arrival, sleeping as poorly as I had every other night since we'd been hauled aboard, when there was a soft tap on my door and the panel slid open a crack. "Gregory?" Selene's soft voice came timidly.

"Yes, what is it?" I asked.

"I wanted . . . could I come in and stay with you a while?"

I frowned into the darkness. Selene had never, ever made such a request before. We worked well together, and we certainly liked each other. But that was all. We were partners in a business, no more, no less. Besides, I was human and she wasn't, and while interspecies romances were a clichéd staple of star-thrillers I'd yet to see one in real life.

But of course that wasn't why she was here. There might not be much romance in the sordid worlds of bounty hunters and crocketts, but there was more than our fair share of loneliness, fear, and despair. I could understand Selene's need for comfort, especially given our bleak situation.

And to be honest, being able to lie close to another

living being, holding her and being held in turn, sounded like the best the universe was offering us right now. "Sure," I said, shifting over to one side of the bed. "Come on."

"Thank you." She closed the door softly behind her and sidled into the narrow space between the bed and wall. There was a moment of hesitation, and then she gingerly lay down beside me, her long white hair briefly tickling my nose as it brushed across my face. She shifted position awkwardly, moving close to me; belatedly, I wondered how my breath and body smelled to her hypersensitive senses. She'd never complained about my scent before; but then, she normally wasn't this close to me. I wondered if I should turn my back to her and let her snuggle with me that way, or whether that would be seen as rejection, or even if I would smell any better that way.

And then, as I waited apprehensively for her to decide this had been a bad idea, she pressed up against me, her face half buried in my neck, her cheek pressed tightly against mine. "We need to talk about Tera," she whispered, so softly that even with her lips to my ear I could barely hear her. "There's something wrong."

I sighed, adjusting a bit so that my lips were up against her ear. I could understand her wanting to keep our conversation private, and I had no doubt Nask had microphones in here. But the fact that Tera had spiraled into a deep depression wouldn't exactly be a surprise to anyone. "She's lost everything, Selene," I whispered back. "It's perfectly normal for her to feel miserable."

"That's just it," Selene said. "She doesn't."

I frowned. "Doesn't what?"

"Feel miserable," Selene said. "It's an act. All of it."

Abruptly, my fatigue and dejection disappeared. "Are you saying she's come up with a new plan?"

"I don't think she ever gave up on the old one," Selene said. "Back on Lacklin, when the portal failed to work? She looked horrified and angry, but she didn't smell that way."

My mind flicked back to Kashmir and my brief confrontation with McKell. *If it makes you feel any better,* he'd assured me, *there is a plan.* Was this what he'd been talking about?

Only what the hell kind of plan was it to get the three of us captured and tossed into a Patth prison? "Why didn't you say something about this sooner?"

"I wanted to keep watching her," Selene whispered. "I thought it might be denial or delayed reaction. But it's not. Her dejection isn't real. Her reluctance to eat isn't real. Her lying in bed for hours—none of it is real."

I stared at the side of Selene's head, her white hair in stark contrast with the dark metal wall behind it. Like the contrast between what Tera was feeling and what she wanted us to *think* she was feeling.

Or *was* it us? Of course the acting was for Nask's benefit—that much was obvious. But was it for our benefit, too? Surely she remembered how Selene had been able to read her emotional responses via the subtle changes in her body odor. Did that mean she expected us to know or at least suspect that she was up to something?

I didn't mind her having a plan. What I minded was that she might have a plan we knew nothing about but were expected to participate in.

"What do we do?" Selene asked.

"We pretend to believe her," I said. "We help her sell the act to Nask. And we wait."

"For what?"

"For whatever she's got planned," I said. "I'm guessing we'll know it when we see it."

"I hope so." Selene paused. "Do you want me to go now?"

"Only if you want to," I said. "Me, I'm pretty comfortable right like this."

She gave a soft sigh that again tickled my ear. "So am I," she said. "Maybe just a little longer."

Five minutes later, still resting alongside me, she was fast asleep. Five minutes after that, so was I.

EarthGuard and other militaries, it was rumored, had hidden underground landing pads and cradles scattered around the Spiral for the use of rapid-response and DarkOp units. Having never been invited to such a place, and with the sum total of my own travel experiences having been with aboveground facilities, I tended to view those stories with a bit of skepticism.

Not anymore.

"Impressive," I commented as we walked down the *Odinn*'s ramp and turned toward an Iykam-guarded door at one end of the large underground chamber we'd landed in. Across the walkway we were now walking on was another landing cradle, currently unoccupied, a twin of the one we'd put down in. Set up neatly around the empty cradle was a full complement of support gear, equipment carts, and fueling hoses, again duplicating those surrounding Nask's ship. Above us was a flat gray roof, probably metal-reinforced ceramic, that echoed back our voices and footfalls.

There were certainly plenty of footfalls available for that purpose. There had been a good fifty Iykams waiting when our little group emerged from the ship, and they were now marching with parade-ground precision on either side of us.

Personally, I thought it was a bit over the top. Tera, Selene, and I already had our wrists restraint-locked, Geri was walking behind us with his Libra no doubt close at hand, and Nask, who was leading the procession, had positioned his bodyguards between him and his three prisoners. All that the extra troops did was make the whole thing bigger, more unwieldy, and a lot louder.

But Nask was a sub-director, and the local Firefall garrison commander probably felt he needed to put on a show.

"We're glad you like it," Geri said from behind me. "Very expensive, I'm told, but money well spent."

"Hey, when you're looking to take over the whole Spiral, what's a little pocket change?" I said, frowning. In front of me, Selene had half turned her head, and I saw her nostrils and eyelashes going like crazy. Something interesting in the air?

"The Spiral?" Geri let out a small snort. "You think too small, Roarke. I'm thinking we can take the whole galaxy. Maybe even the whole universe, depending on Firefall's range."

I thought about telling him the current record was forty-five thousand light-years, but decided against it. If the Path were hell-bent on conquering everything, they could do the damn research themselves. "It's nice to have goals," I said. "But I'd bet they'll find that taking is easier than holding. Every human empire has eventually figured that out."

"Humans aren't Patth," he countered. "Still, conquering even a single galaxy is a long-term proposition. You and I will be long dead before they find out whether or not it can be done."

"You're always such a wellspring of optimism and comfort," I said. "Do we at least get to see this thing before you lock us away?"

"Of course," he said, as if that was a foregone conclusion. "If for no other reason than Sub-Director Nask wants you to see just how closely the Lacklin decoy duplicated the original."

"Yes, I was curious about that," I agreed, feeling my pulse pick up a bit. So he was going to take us to the actual Firefall portal? Had Tera anticipated Nask's desire to gloat and planned her move around that expectation?

"Naturally, you'll be going alone," Geri went on, as if that, too, was obvious. "Maybe with Selene. We're certainly not going to let Tera anywhere near it."

"After that light show on Lacklin, I don't blame you," I said, my cautiously rising hopes dropping back to ground level again.

"Who would, really?" Geri said. "So where exactly do you stand on all this?"

"On all what?" I asked. "The Patth taking over the universe? Like you said, it's not likely to happen during my lifetime. Makes it a moot point. Of course, even if you figure out how to make new portals, there's the whole problem of getting them to where you want them. Even the Talariac isn't *that* fast."

"I'm sure that question's already being pondered," Geri said. "What I meant was what are you hoping to get out of all this?"

I shrugged. Selene had turned the other way, her nostrils slowing their fluttering but her eyelashes now going double-time. "My life," I said. "Selene's life. A huge pile of commarks would be nice, too, but I'd settle for walking out of here alive."

"I'm sure you would," Geri said softly. "But if I were you, I wouldn't get my hopes too high."

The work cavern we were taken to was very much like the one on Lacklin, with the exception that the entryway into the portal was in the side of the large sphere instead of the bottom. "As you see," Nask said, waving toward it. "Exactly the same."

"Well, so far as we can see from here, anyway," I said.

"You'd like a closer look?" Nask asked. "Certainly." He gestured to one flank of our Iykam guards. "Take the females to their quarters. Follow me, Mr. Roarke."

I set off behind him as he strode toward the entrance, watching out of the corner of my eye as Selene and Tera were escorted away from the cavern down a different corridor. So much for whatever scheme Tera had planned.

Too late, I wished now that I'd taken the risk of trying to get some information from her before we disembarked. At the time, it had seemed more important to keep any such conversation away from eavesdropping ears; but at the time I'd also assumed Tera would get a crack of her own at the Firefall portal. "I'm impressed that you were able to get it here," I commented. "Do you actually have freighters big enough for it to fit inside?"

"We didn't," Nask said. "We do now. Please; join me."

I glanced over my shoulder. Aside from Nask's bodyguards all the rest of the Iykams had dispersed, either heading to various guard positions inside the cavern or support equipment outside or with the group that had escorted Selene and Tera. But Geri was still with us, and he didn't look exactly thrilled with Nask's invitation.

Still, an order from a Patth sub-director was hardly something a person could simply ignore. Picking up my pace, I caught up to him and settled into a spot a couple of meters to his right, making sure the bodyguard on that side was between us. The last thing I wanted was to be close enough to Nask that some innocent gesture on my part might be perceived as an attack. "How much of it have you figured out?" I asked. "If I may be so bold."

"You may," Nask said, eyeing me thoughtfully. "But then, I would say that boldness seems to come naturally to you."

I shrugged. "Some would say it's not so much boldness as pigheadedness."

"The two traits are often confused," Nask said. "But you're far too modest. From everything Geri and Freki have told me, I believe your talents are being wasted."

"Bounty hunting is a dangerous job," I said, feeling my throat tighten at the memory of that last, terrible job. "Trailblazing may not pay as well, but it's safer."

"So it is," Nask agreed. "I wasn't suggesting you return to your old position. I was suggesting you might join the Patthaaunuth as an Expediter."

With half my attention on the portal now only a few steps in front of us and the other half on Geri and the rest of the cavern's security setup, Nask's suggestion caught me completely flat-footed. "I—*what*?" I managed.

"Come now, Mr. Roarke," Nask said with clear amusement. "Having successfully gone up against two of my finest, surely you aren't surprised that I would be interested in recruiting you. The Patthaaunuth have always sought the service of the very best the Spiral has to offer." He stopped at the rectangular opening leading into the portal and pointed inside. "The entrance is a bit tricky. Watch me, and use the handholds."

He reached both hands into the opening and ducked his head and shoulders through. His arms stiffened as if someone was pulling on them, and as his head and torso disappeared inside he lifted first one foot and then the other to the opening's edge and disappeared inside. "A moment for the handholds to reset," his voice came through the opening, "then join me."

I stepped to the opening. From my new vantage point I could see that a framework had been set up inside the sphere with a handhold on either side, the handholds currently sliding back toward me along a pair of tracks.

They reached the bottom and stopped. Bracing myself, I ducked my head and reached inside.

Back on Lacklin, my inner ear had had a field day each time I crossed one of the abrupt gravity change gradients. This place was no different. As my eyes and brain struggled to orient themselves I grabbed the handholds, wondering how I was supposed to activate them.

Fortunately, the designers had that covered. I'd barely gotten my fingers wrapped around them when they started upward on their tracks, pulling me up into the sphere. I put my feet on the edge as I'd seen Nask do, and a moment later I was able to let go of the handholds and step away from the opening onto solid metal.

Nask had watched me from a couple of meters away and now inclined his head. "Nicely done," he said. "Most people have more trouble the first time."

"I had a little practice on Lacklin," I reminded him, turning to look at the interface opening into the launch module and noting that the same handhold system had been set up there. "Thanks for fixing things here so that we don't have to do that whole roll-around-the-corner thing," I added, turning back to him. Geri, I noted, was now halfway into the sphere, his gun in hand, his eyes focused unblinkingly on me.

"It *does* rather bruise one's dignity, doesn't it?" Nask agreed. "Please—feel free to walk around a bit. Get a feel for the place."

I took a couple of steps, and then a couple more. The conflict between my inner ear—which insisted I was walking on flat ground—and my eyes—which insisted just as loudly that the landscape was curving up in all directions—was the stuff of which headaches were made.

But if I could get past that, I could see the subtle differences between this portal and the Lacklin counterfeit. In that one, I'd felt slight discontinuities as I walked along the inside of the sphere—a result, I knew now, of the fact that the interior gravity field was made up of dozens of separate gravity plates mashed together. Here, in contrast, everything was as smooth as polished glass, with no breaks or hesitations in the gravity. However the portal's creators had pulled that off, they'd done an impressive job of it. "Gravity seems a bit lighter here," I commented.

"You're very observant," Nask complimented me. "Yes, the portal's default setting is about eighty percent Patthaaunuth norm, or eighty-five that of your own core world. On Lacklin, since we were using the planet's own gravitational field for the lower part of the receiver module, we had to adjust our gravity plates to match it."

"I'm surprised Tera didn't notice."

"The difference was slight," Nask said. "We've also found indications the gravity levels in the two modules may be adjustable, though we are a long way from learning how to do that. If Icarus has also discovered those controls, she may have thought we had done likewise. Perhaps you'd like to investigate the launch module."

I came to a casual stop, a quiet alarm bell going off in the back of my head. The launch module was where all the critical equipment was located. If I was able to wreck something important, the whole massive thing would be worthless. Surely Nask wouldn't take such a risk.

Unless he knew there wasn't any.

At the moment, as I stood with my back to Nask, Geri was also out of my line of sight. But I didn't need to see him to recognize the trapbox they were trying to nudge me into. The minute I got within sabotage range of the launch module and had therefore proven myself a threat, I would be shot down like a rabid dog.

Geri had already hinted that I might not be leaving Firefall alive. This might be his golden opportunity to make that happen.

"So," I said, my back still to them. "Is this corporate vacillation, or just a private bet?"

"Excuse me?" Nask asked.

"Are you trying to decide whether I'm worthy to be an Expediter?" I explained. "Or is it a bet between you and Geri that I'll be brave or stupid enough to try something destructive?"

I turned back to face them. Nask's face was mostly unreadable, though I was pretty sure there was some amusement there. Geri's, in contrast, was as coldly malevolent as I'd ever seen him. "I'm guessing the latter," I added.

Once again, Nask inclined his head. "A bit of both, actually," he conceded. "Personally, I'm pleased that you passed the test."

"I don't doubt it," I said. "Bloodstains are a pain in the butt to clean up."

"So they are," Nask said. "Time to go. You need to rejoin your companions"—he looked at Geri—"and Geri needs to prepare for his mission."

I felt a muscle in my cheek tighten. "Icarus?"

"Icarus," Nask confirmed. "If you'll precede us out, Mr. Roarke, I believe your keepers are just about to serve lunch."

Our keepers had indeed served lunch in our new cell—no more open dining rooms for us, apparently. A fine lunch it was, too.

A shame I didn't have any appetite for it.

For the next few hours I ran the entire memory over and over in my mind, trying to find a place where some change in my actions might have given me an edge, or a hostage, or anything else that would have led to something besides abject failure.

But I couldn't find anything. I'd been there, close

enough to the heart of Firefall to stab it to death, and there'd been nothing I could do. Not without getting myself uselessly killed.

I went to bed early, not wanting to spend any more time avoiding Tera's and Selene's eyes than I absolutely had to. Fortunately, like the suite aboard the *Odinn*, our cell had sleeping room doors that closed.

I was in the middle of a terrible and depressing nightmare when I started awake to find someone shaking me roughly by the shoulder. "Wake up, Roarke," a familiar voice bit out. "Wake *up*."

I squinted up into the face looming over me. "Freki?" I managed, wincing at the hoarseness in my voice. "When did you get here?"

"Never mind me," Freki growled, grabbing my upper arm and all but hauling me up into a sitting position. "Get dressed. *Now*."

"Why?" I asked, my voice sounding a little more human this time. "What's wrong?"

"I said *get dressed*."

"And *I* said what's wrong?" I repeated, making no move toward my clothes.

For a fraction of a second I thought he was going to hit me. With visible effort, he resisted the temptation. "It's Geri," he said. "He's disappeared."

"Into Firefall?" I asked, snagging my shirt from the hook beside the bed.

"Yes," he said. "Almost seven hours ago."

"My condolences," I said. "What do you expect me to do about it?"

"What do you think?" Grabbing my trousers from the hook, he tossed them viciously at my chest. "You're going in after him."

CHAPTER TWENTY-TWO

------ ❖ ------

Nask and a handful of Patth and Iykams were waiting as Freki hauled me into the work cavern. "There you are," Nask said, as if I'd stopped for a meal or some sightseeing on the way from our cell. "Over there. Get dressed. Now."

I looked where he was pointing. On a chair near the Firefall entrance was a gray combat suit. "What's happened?" I asked as I headed toward it, resisting the urge to point out that I was already dressed and that my outfit was probably a lot more comfortable.

"Geri went into the launch module," Nask said. "He hasn't returned."

"Are you sure he *can*?" I asked, stopping at the chair and pulling off my shirt. "He's got Firefall's address, right?"

"Of course," Nask said. "The arrival and departure addresses should both have appeared on one of the displays upon his arrival."

I paused with my trousers halfway down. "*Should have appeared?*"

"That's how it worked at our end," Nask said. "The displays showed both addresses."

"You didn't know your own address before that?"

"We couldn't obtain Firefall's address until we sent a package to Icarus. Now we know it." He gestured to one of the Patth, who scurried up and handed me a piece of paper.

It was a print photo showing two grids of squares. One grid showed the yellow/black control board that Tera had punched Icarus's address into back on Lacklin, while the grid beside it showed a different pattern, this one in squares of orange and black. "Which is which?"

"Yellow is destination; orange is home," the Patth said. His voice was strained, somewhere between controlled nervous and equally controlled panicked. "But the displays are only lit for ten to fifteen minutes after activation. If he was delayed in moving from the receiver module to the launch module, he won't have any way to return."

I nodded, understanding Nask's nervousness. His big scheme had presumably relied on Geri hitting Icarus a killing blow before they knew what was happening. After seven hours, that plan was looking a little ragged. "Why me?" I asked. "Actually, back up a little. Why was Geri alone in the first place? Why not send a full commando squad? You could at least have sent Freki along."

"The plan was for him to reconnoiter and perhaps lock down a beachhead if the opportunity presented," Nask said. "He would then send back a situation report and a team would follow." He leveled a finger at me. "That will now be *your* task."

"Ah," I said, suppressing a grimace as I finished undressing and started to pull on the combat suit. "Let me guess. You don't have enough human Expediters to put together an assault team, and throwing a bunch of Patth or Iykams at Icarus would be way too provocative."

"There were other considerations," Nask said stiffly.

"Yeah," I said, pausing in my dressing as a new thought suddenly occurred to me. "Speaking of considerations, has the possibility occurred to you that Geri never even got to Icarus? I remember Tera having trouble coming up with the last three digits of the address. What if she got them wrong? What if he ended up on the other side of the galaxy, or nowhere at all?"

"That thought has occurred to us," Nask said. "You asked why Freki was not being sent. That's your answer."

"Right." I looked over at Freki, found him glaring a sort of simmering frustration at me. "Because I'm expendable, and he isn't."

"Yes," Nask said.

"Ah." Carefully, I set down the boot I'd been preparing to put on. "So why again am I agreeing to go?"

"Because if you don't, your companions will suffer," Nask said. "Greatly."

"I thought that would be your answer," I said. I stood up, noting peripherally that all the Iykams within range had suddenly put their hands on their corona guns. "So let's get a couple of things clear. If I do this for you, whether I make it back or not, Selene goes free. Understood? Not in twenty years, not in one year, but right now."

"And if I merely pretend to agree?" Nask asked.

"You're a sub-director of the Patth," I said. "Your people are here, all around you. Do you really want to renege on an agreement in front of them?"

Nask's eyes flicked around the room. Probably wondering what would happen if he just ordered them away.

But it was too late, and he knew it. They'd heard my veiled threat, and whether they heard the rest or not, one or more of them would make sure to follow through on the outcome. I didn't know much about the Patth upper echelons, but I had no doubt there were a dozen sub-sub-directors waiting with quiet eagerness to take Nask's place. "I would never so debase myself," he said stiffly. "Very well, we have an agreement. If you don't return, Selene will be delivered unharmed to—" He looked questioningly at Freki.

"Xathru," Freki said.

"To Xathru," Nask said. "It may take as long as a week for the arrangements to be made, but it will be done."

"I accept," I said, a small part of my mind noting that even now he was deliberately fudging the timing in order to further obfuscate the location of the Patth core worlds. "What about Tera?"

"What are your wishes for her?

"I'd like her released, as well," I said. "Any chance you'll agree to that?"

He pondered the question. "She cannot be released with the same immediacy," he said at last. "But I pledge that she, too, will be released unharmed within the next half-year." He looked around the room again. "If we haven't achieved our goal by then, I think it unlikely we ever will."

"I accept," I said, sitting down again. Leaving Tera

cooped up for the next six months was hardly ideal, but I was frankly surprised I'd gotten that much.

Not that any of it was guaranteed, of course. I wasn't that naïve. Nask could do whatever he wanted on the assumption that a success with Firefall would make him impervious to any political fallout that might come of his having broken an agreement with a stubborn human. Hell, if it came to that, his prestige would probably go high enough for him to simply have all of the witnesses killed.

But my participation had been all the leverage I'd had. Even if in the end that lever turned out to be made of balsa wood.

"Let me get these boots on," I told Nask, "and I'll be ready."

The combat suit, for all its tightly arranged matrix of rigid armor inserts, was light, flexible where it needed to be, and surprisingly comfortable. The helmet was a bit heavier than it looked, and the faceplate and breather mask were cumbersome and tended to fog up. But all in all, it was better than some of the limited-coverage armor I'd occasionally worn over the years. Soon—all too soon, really—I was ready.

"The address has been properly entered," Nask said, nodding toward the glowing yellow-and-black display from his position beside the launch module entrance. "You have the return setting?"

"Yes," I said, my eyes flicking back and forth between the picture of Tera's departure code and the one the Patth tech had just punched into Firefall's destination panel. Nask could say *properly entered* all he wanted, but I had no intention of just taking his word for it.

For a while I'd held out a small hope that Geri's disappearance had been a simple copying error, that some idiot had missed Tera's address by a digit or two. But I'd now had time to compare the two pictures, and had reached the reluctant conclusion that they'd gotten Geri's destination right.

Which didn't allow for the possibility that Tera herself had gotten the address wrong, of course. But there was nothing I could do about that. Going in and messing with the code on pure guesswork would be one of the worst ideas I'd had in a lifetime full of bad ideas.

The tech here had gotten it right, too. Wherever Geri had ended up, that was the same place I was going. "Okay," I said, sliding the picture into the hip pocket where I'd also stored the shot of Geri's departure code. "You going to stand there and wave goodbye?"

"We don't want to risk it," Nask said, motioning his bodyguards toward the opening. "We have no way of knowing whether the launch module is intended to hold more than the designated traveler. When you reach the gray section, get a firm hold onto it and you'll be transported." He gave me a final brisk nod. "Good luck, Mr. Roarke. I hope to see you soon."

I watched as one Iykam, then Nask, then the other Iykam disappeared into the receiver module. Then, with a final look around at the various control and monitor boards, I walked over to the base of the black-and-silver extension arm. The new gravity field caught me as I reached it, and I started to float upward.

I wrapped my hand loosely around the arm for steadiness, a small part of my mind noting the irony of my position. Earlier that day, Nask had tempted me with the opportunity to come in here and raise havoc. Now, I was completely alone, with no one to stop me should I decide to be brave and stupid.

But if I did I would never get out of this facility alive. More than that, my actions would guarantee that neither Selene nor Tera did so, either.

Besides, there was a part of me that really, truly wanted to see if this damn thing actually worked.

The end of the arm had gone luminescent gray. I watched it as I approached, wondering how the Patth on Lacklin had pulled that one off. My sliding hand reached it, closed around it—

I felt a tingle run through me, like I'd touched a low-level electrical wire. A strangely uniform tingle, running through my entire body and not just in the hand and arm touching the gray section. I could feel the hairs on my neck and arm standing up, and even the numbed nerves in my artificial arm roused themselves back to duty long enough to take note of the effect. Also unlike an electric shock, it carried no pain, nausea, or confusion of balance. Somewhere in the distance I heard what sounded like the rippling thundercrack of a too-close lightning strike, and the world around me went black. I counted three seconds—

Then suddenly, I was back, floating in the center of the now-familiar large sphere, the whole area around me lit by a soft glow whose source I couldn't quite locate. As I started to drift toward the inside sphere surface, I craned my neck to see exactly where I'd landed.

Sometimes observations and revelations came in a nice, well-ordered sequence, the facts trotting themselves out with enough time to consider each before moving on to the next. Here, unfortunately, the first five facts slammed into me simultaneously, like a coordinated rugby attack.

Fact one: This definitely wasn't the Firefall receiver module. That one had been full of equipment and devoid of people. This one contained only Geri.

Fact two: Geri was alive and well, crouching down at one side of the sphere with his helmet and face gear off to one side. Arranged neatly around the helmet were pieces of his Libra 3mm, a Victori plasmic, a dart gun, and an Iykam corona weapon. A metal water bottle and a supply pouch were lying a ways farther off to the side.

Fact three: The thing Geri was crouching beside was a large round plate a good two meters across, welded or otherwise fastened to the sphere's surface. From the lack of any other visible openings, it was clear the plate was currently covering the interface that normally provided access to the launch module.

Fact four: Geri had been here seven hours. The plate was still there.

Fact five: We were trapped.

There didn't seem to be any reason to keep my helmet and face gear on, since Geri's current membership among the living showed there was nothing in here that would kill me with any great speed. Anyway, as long as I was drifting slowly downward with no way to hurry up the process there really wasn't much else to do.

I hadn't noticed any sounds when I first popped into the sphere, but with my helmet off I could now hear a series of soft but sharp sounds coming from Geri's direction. He hadn't yet looked up, either because my arrival had been silent or because he was too focused on his work. He might not notice me, in fact, until I landed.

Unfortunately, my current vector aimed to land me behind him and only a few meters away. Given his probable state of mind, that might spark an instinctive and highly unpleasant reaction. As my father used to say, *If you have to wake a sleeping man, it's best not to use a sharp stick*.

Fortunately, there were other ways to announce my arrival. Getting a fresh grip on my helmet, I gave it a gentle lob toward the floor a quarter of the way around the sphere.

Even having seen Geri move quickly once before, his response this time was impressive. As the dull thud of the helmet's impact echoed around the sphere he threw himself to the side in a flat leap, rolling once on his shoulder, and coming up into a crouch with his water bottle in hand ready to throw. A fraction of a second later the crouch went into a sort of twisting spiral as he saw the sound had been a diversion and spun around trying to locate the source. He spotted me—

"The *hell*?" he snarled, rising half to his feet, the water bottle still poised to throw. "How the *hell* did you get in here?"

"Nice to see you, too," I called back, watching the water bottle warily. I was still in free fall, with zero way of ducking an attack if he chose to launch one. "Nask says hi, by the way."

"What are you doing here?" he bit out.

"I broke out of my cell, of course," I said. "Overpowered the guards, wandered around until I found the soldiers' barracks, picked out a nice combat suit in my size, strolled past all the other Patth and Iykams, broke into Firefall, then gave myself a one-way ticket to Icarus. What do you *think* I'm doing here?"

Slowly, he lowered the water bottle to his side. "Are you armed?"

"No," I said, holding my arms out to my sides.

Naturally, the receiver module picked that precise moment to suddenly crank up the gravity and drop me the last meter to the deck. I flailed a bit as I hit, but managed to keep my balance and dignity. "No food or water, either. Probably expected me to die quickly and didn't want to waste the supplies."

"No, that's just Freki's paranoia leaking through," Geri said. "Not the expecting you to die part, but not wanting you to have anything that could be used as a weapon. No tools either, I suppose."

"What you see is what I've got." I pointed toward the plate. "Looks like they were worried about unexpected company."

"I don't know why they would be," Geri said. "They don't even know we've got a portal, let alone that we've got their address. More likely they just wanted to keep their own people out of here."

"Why?" I asked.

"Same reason we've got guards watching Firefall," Geri said with strained patience. "Lot of tech secrets in here, and you don't want random people sneaking in and poking around. Or maybe it was some particular person they wanted to catch in the act."

"Right," I said through suddenly stiff lips. *Secrets . . .*

McKell had told me they had a plan. Tera had only been pretending to be devastated at her reveal of Icarus's address.

Secrets . . . only she'd let this one slip. I hadn't noticed at the time, but Tera had let it slip. *It can punch through forty-five thousand light-years' worth of dust, gas, and stars,* she'd told me inside the fake launch module on Lacklin. *I don't think a couple hundred meters of rock will be a problem.*

How could she possibly know the portals could reach that far?

Geri was wrong. Nask was wrong. The whole damn Patth nation was wrong.

Icarus and Firefall weren't the only portals. The Icarus team had found another one somewhere.

This one. The trapbox Tera had deliberately sent us to.

Maybe she'd assumed that only Patth or Iykams would end up here. Maybe she'd never expected Nask to send me.

Maybe she hadn't cared if he did.

"So if it's a trapbox, how does it work?" I asked.

"Take a look," Geri said, setting the bottle on the deck and walking back to the round plate. "You see how the plate is welded over the interface to keep anyone who came in from getting back out again?"

"Yes," I said, leaning over for a closer look. The plate was a dull gray color, two meters across and about ten centimeters thick. At the four sides, where the north, east, south, and west symbols would be on a compass rose, were the embossed letters ORDW. "What do those letters mean?" I asked.

"They mean that whoever's in charge of Icarus didn't have something this size to use over the access point so he just grabbed a shaft cover from the nearest Volga Industrium plant and slapped it on," Geri said.

"Never heard of them," I said, searching the plate in vain for any other words or identifying marks. "Where does it say Volga Industrium?"

"It doesn't," Geri said. "But I know the company. They're a mid-sized outfit near the Najiki Archipelago, and they're big into inspirational crap. This is one of the *Opportunity-Readiness-Discernment-Willpower* seals they slap all over their factories and offices."

He lifted his finger like a professor lecturing a particularly slow pupil. "Now. If *I* was setting a trap for some troublemaker, I'd make it so you could only open it from the other side. But the Icarus team decided to be cute." He tapped the edge of the plate. "You see these welds?"

"They're a little hard to miss," I said, feeling my stomach tighten. Whoever had been in here with the welding torch had really put his heart into his work. The furrowed marks went around the entire rim where the plate met the sphere deck.

I frowned, leaning in closer and tracing the weld marks with my eye. "Wait a minute," I said. "If they were trying to catch someone in here, welding a plate over the opening doesn't make any sense."

"Comes the dawn," Geri said sarcastically. "About damn time. Because if you look here"—he tapped the middle part of the disk's edge with a slender spine from his plasmic's focusing array—"you can see it's really two thinner plates pressed together. Or I should say, a single plate set on top of a setting ring straddling the entry hole."

"You think the top disk separates from the ring?"

"Has to," he said. "There's no other way for anyone to get in or out of the sphere."

"So the thief sneaks in from the launch module, using some straightforward opening mechanism on that side, and gets trapped," I said. "And then sits here until someone comes by over there and lets him out?"

"Right," Geri said. "Only we can't wait that long." He pointed at the edge of the plate. "So we'll just have to open it ourselves."

I leaned closer. There was a series of small indentations along the line Geri had identified as the connection between the plate and the setting ring. "What are those?"

"Like you said, it's only meant to be opened from the other side," Geri said. "But there still has to be a latch in there somewhere. If we can poke around the edge until we find and trigger it, we should be able to get it open."

"Hence, your little toy there," I said, eyeing the device clearly cobbled together from parts of his various weapons. I could see one of the magnetic accelerator segments from his Libra 3mm with one of the bullets poking out of the accelerator. The powerpack from his plasmic was powering the device, and one of the air cylinders from his dart gun had been hooked up to keep the mechanism cool. "A miniature hammer drill, I gather?"

"Impressed that you even recognized it," Geri growled. "Now get out of the way. I've got work to do."

Obediently, I took a step back from the plate. "How can I help?"

"By staying out of the way," he said, lining up the punch with the intersection line. "Go take a nap or something."

He started the hammer drill, and the sharp sounds I'd heard on my way down resumed. I looked at the remnants of his weapons, wondering if I could put together something of my own out of what was left. Two of us working on the disk would presumably get the job done in half the time.

But it looked like he'd already salvaged everything useful. There certainly weren't enough parts to make another hammer drill. I turned back to the plate, wondering if it came completely apart, or swiveled open, or swung up on hidden hinges. If I could figure out which it was, we might be able to concentrate Geri's work at the critical points.

I scowled at the embossed letters and the subtle mocking embedded in the associated inspirational drivel. *Opportunity-Readiness-Discernment-Willpower.* All fine qualities, but none of them were a damn bit of good without tools. *Opportunity-Readiness-Discernment-Willpower. Opportunity-Readiness-Discernment-Willpower. ORDW. ORDW.*

I stiffened. ORDW...or was it WORD?

A memory flashed to mind: Kashmir and my brief, violent encounter with Jordan McKell. *Just say the word*, he'd said, *and you'll be on your way to a whole new world. Remember that.*

Any particular word you had in mind? I'd asked.

Artichoke is a good one. It's catchy, memorable, and not one most people would ever think of.

For a few seconds I just stood there. No. It couldn't really be that easy. Could it?

On one level, it seemed absurd. Connecting dots that weren't there, or just wishful thinking.

But I had to know for sure. And there was only one way to do that.

Taking another step away from the disk, I walked

around to where Geri had set down his water bottle. It would be a gamble, I knew—a huge, possibly fatal one. There was no guarantee I could get Geri's hammer drill working on my own, and even if I could I didn't have the engineering knowledge to know how and where to use it.

But at this point, nearly any gamble was probably worth taking. I picked up the water bottle, unscrewed the top—

"Whoa!" Geri snapped, the pounding sound stopping. "Hold it, Roarke. That's *my* water."

"I wasn't given any and I'm thirsty," I grumbled over my shoulder at him. "You go back to playing with your toys—"

I was raising the bottle toward my lips when he reached me and snatched it out of my hand. "Like hell," he said firmly. He glared for a moment, then lifted the bottle and took a long drink of his own, underlining his right of possession or possibly just being a jerk. Replacing the cap, he turned and stalked back toward the plate, taking the bottle with him.

He was halfway there when the knockout pill I'd slipped into the bottle sent him sprawling unconscious to the deck.

I waited a moment to make sure he wasn't faking it, then went over and gingerly checked his pulse. Weapons or no weapons, I had no doubt he could kill me without working up a sweat, and if he knew I'd drugged him I'd probably get the chance to watch him do it.

I walked past him to the plate. For a moment I stood over it, gazing down at the embossed W-O-R-D letters and bracing myself for the disappointment that was surely about to come. Then, clearing my throat, I took a deep breath. "Artichoke," I said.

Nothing. I scowled at it, feeling like a fool, and took a deeper breath. "Artichoke!" I said in a louder voice. "I said the word, damn it. *Artichoke.* Open the damn—!"

And without so much as a click or screech the plate split apart right where Geri had said it would, rotating on a hidden post with the speed and precision of a tennis backhand to reveal the same kind of rectangular access hole I'd seen at Firefall. Through the opening I could see the faint radiance and glowing control lights of the portal launch module.

The Icarus people hadn't installed the kind of handholds the Firefall team had been thoughtful enough to provide. But I'd had some practice with the Lacklin version, and I rolled over the edge and into the launch module without any trouble. The small sphere was empty, but otherwise appeared to be completely functional.

I rolled back up to my feet, looking around and savoring the relief flooding through me. It was over, and hadn't ended in either starvation or asphyxiation. All I needed to do was grab Geri, punch in Firefall's destination code, and we'd be back in time for breakfast. I would tell Nask that the disk had opened by itself, without any effort on my part, that the Icarus people had apparently abandoned the project and sealed the portal, and that the whole game had ground to a halt in a stalemate. Nask might suspect this portal wasn't Icarus, but he couldn't prove it, and there was nothing he could do about it even if he could.

Nothing except strap Tera down and start her on a

path of long, slow torture. And probably Selene and me along with her. Nask was determined to have Icarus, and he would kill all of us if that got it for him.

Only it never would.

I'd wondered all along why Tera had been left to run around the Spiral with all that Icarus knowledge in her head. Now, I realized that she hadn't. She'd probably gone through some memory-block or erasure regimens before we left, enough to destroy or at least bury all knowledge of Icarus's address while leaving her the address for this other portal. Nask could torture her all he wanted, and all he'd ever be able to do was pop back and forth between Firefall and here.

Going back to Firefall would mean death by torture. Staying here would mean death by starvation. As my father used to say, *When your only options are frying pan or fire, it's time to rethink your strategy.*

Unfortunately, none of the available strategy was mine. McKell had said he had a plan. Tera, and her capture, had apparently been part of it. From my totally objective perspective, it seemed like one hell of a lousy plan.

Or was I missing something?

I turned to look at the boards that would show the traveler's home and destination. All the squares in both arrays were showing uniform red at the moment. Tera didn't have Icarus's address.

So who did?

Not me or Selene. McKell would have to know we would both be thoroughly searched. Could Tera have stashed it somewhere along our way? Somewhere in the *Ruth*, maybe, where she knew I would find it?

Hopefully not, because the *Ruth* was currently way

the hell over at Kashmir. Could she have whispered it to me when I was asleep, with some kind fancy hypnotic going that would stuff it into my memory, just waiting for a keyword to pull it out?

I cleared my throat. "Artichoke," I called. "The word. Saying the word. Saying the word to McKell. Saying the word to Tera. Saying the word to Tera C. Saying—"

I stopped, growling a curse. Ridiculous. Besides, any kind of hypnotic drug would have left residue that Selene could have picked up ten meters away.

Could McKell have said something during our fight? Something in his words or phrasing that would give me the key? Something besides that damn *say the word* thing? He'd held my left arm pinned on top of my head long enough to deliver most of the Gettysburg Address...

My left arm. My *artificial* left arm.

And that snooping ferret of Ixil's had watched me give the Bonvere seeds to Varsi in the private park in Havershem City.

The combat suit wasn't designed for the wearer to just push up a sleeve. I had to take the whole tunic off to get to the elbow compartment in my left arm.

And there it was. A neatly folded piece of paper with a precisely drawn picture of a portal destination display in colorful yellow and black. My ticket to Icarus, and the way out of here.

But there was more. At the top of the paper was a short inscription: *As your father used to say, there's nothing to end a meal like a good pineapple cake.*

Earlier—a couple of centuries earlier, the way all this felt—we'd speculated that the Patth wouldn't pick up on the subtlety of human-style bounty hunter specs, thus missing the fact that Varsi was quietly calling for Tera to be delivered to him dead rather than alive. Now, McKell had tapped into the same alien unfamiliarity with niche Earth customs and cuisine.

I'd never had a pineapple cake in my life. But I'd had many a pineapple upside-down cake.

Smiling tightly, I turned the paper around and headed for the control board.

I took it slow, double- and triple-checking every square as I tapped it to the proper yellow or black. When it was all done I checked it again, then went to the extension arm and started up.

My last thought before I hit the gray section was that if McKell had screwed this up I hoped Tera would never let him live it down. I hit the trigger section, winced as the tingle ran through my body—it felt easier this time now that I knew what to expect—watched the blackness drop over me, and suddenly I was in the center of yet another receiver module.

Looking down the barrels of six heavy-duty laser rifles in the hands of six armored Kalixiri soldiers who were lying comfortably along the curved deck. "Don't shoot!" I called, holding my hands up with the fingers spread wide.

None of the rifles so much as twitched. But at least no one opened fire.

And then one of the aliens half turned toward the access hole beside him, and with a start I saw it was Ixil. "Jordan?" he called. "Someone get Jordan McKell.

"Tell him Roarke is finally here."

CHAPTER TWENTY-THREE

———— ❖ ————

"That I'm *finally* here?" I demanded, glaring at Ixil as he sat me down in a comfortable conference room chair, eyeing the mug of cola and the selection of snacks set out on the table in front of me. I was hungry and thirsty, but there was no way in hell that I was giving them the satisfaction of touching any of it. "You think any of the timing was under *my* control?"

"My apologies, Gregory," Ixil said, as he sat down in the chair across from me. His ferrets took the opportunity to scamper down his arms to the table, one of them heading to check out the snacks, the other making a beeline for me. He gave me a quick sniff and an equally brief squeak, then joined his friend at the snack bowl. Probably the one who'd shadowed me in Havershem City, I guessed. "I meant no such slight or implication," Ixil continued. "I was mostly acknowledging the fact that Jordan has been quite concerned about you."

"About me?" I asked archly. "Or about Tera?"

"About all three of you," Ixil said. He snapped his fingers twice, and the ferrets returned to his shoulders. "Though I probably wouldn't mention to him that I said so," he added. "Jordan likes to maintain the image of a strong and stoic leader."

I was trying to think up a sufficiently scathing way to phrase my response when the door across the way opened and McKell himself strode in. "Roarke," he said briskly, as if I was an old business acquaintance who'd just happened to drop in for coffee. "The medics check you over?"

"I'm fine," I said, my left arm aching with memory, my right arm itching for a weapon. "All I want—"

"He refused the medics," Ixil put in.

"Did you tell him the admiral ordered it?" McKell asked, sitting down beside the Kalix.

"Did I tell you I don't care a damn what any Earth-Guard brass wants?" I countered. "Selene's a prisoner, I've got a drugged Expediter to figure out what to do with, and there's a Patth sub-director who's going to warm up the rack if I don't get back there soon."

"Relax, Roarke, we're on it," McKell assured me. "The admiral's on his way. In the meantime, let's get you debriefed and start working out our response."

"How about this?" I asked. "Since I don't really want to repeat everything for your admiral friend, how about we instead start by you telling me what the hell is going on?"

"Sorry," McKell said. "That's on a need-to-know basis."

"Trust me, I need to know," I said, putting every bit of quiet menace I had into my voice. "You've been marching me around like your personal marionette proxy and you've put Selene and me in deadly danger. You owe me."

I cranked up the intensity of my glare. "But more than that, you still need me. You want my cooperation? Then convince me that everything you've done to us makes sense."

McKell looked a silent question at Ixil. "We *do* owe him, Jordan," the Kalix said. "I don't think the admiral will object." He considered. "Not overly."

McKell's lip twitched, but he gave a reluctant nod. "Fine. How much do you know about Icarus?"

"It's an alien portal that can send people across forty-five thousand light-years about as fast as it takes to sneeze," I said. "I know a little about how to program it, and I know there are three of them in operation. That's about it."

"Good," McKell said, nodding. "I will note with a certain irony that after six years of studying them we don't know a whole lot more than that."

"Well, you'd better get on the stick, then," I warned. "The Patth have one of their own, and they're pouring everything they've got into studying it."

"Yes," McKell murmured. "Which is really where this story begins... because up until three months ago, they *didn't* have one."

I stared at him. "You're kidding."

"I wish I was," McKell said.

"Though it might be more accurate to say that until three months ago they didn't have it working," Ixil put in.

"Yes, that's true," McKell said. "They may have had it in their possession for years and just taken this long to figure out how to activate it."

I thought about the elaborate setup for Firefall, and the equally impressive base they'd set up around their fake version. "I'm guessing that's the case," I said. "How do you know that was when they got it working?"

"We got what amounts to a ping at that time from the Icarus portal," Ixil said. "A sort of super-electronic handshake letting everyone else know it was up and running."

"How did you know it wasn't someone else in the Spiral who'd found it?" I asked. "Or even someone way the hell across the universe?"

"We didn't," Ixil conceded, reaching up and stroking the backs of his ferrets. "But as we thought back to all the attention and roadblocks the Path had thrown at the *Icarus* when we were trying to fly it to Earth, and the speed at which they'd come after us, we began to realize that even then they knew more about the portals than they were letting on. It was hardly proof, of course, but it was a reasonable working theory."

"Even if they still thought at the time that it was just a super-fast stardrive, they still wouldn't want anyone else having one to play with," McKell said. "Given the means of your arrival, I assume we were right?"

"Well, I damn well didn't get here by bus," I said with strained patience. "So how do Selene and I figure into all this?"

"Let's go back a bit more, to Tera's supposed jumping off Icarus, as you once put it," McKell said. "The decision was made that we couldn't afford to let the Path have a portal. Not because we wanted a monopoly—"

"Not *just* because we wanted a monopoly," Ixil interjected.

"—but mainly because it represented a danger to

our work here," McKell continued, flicking a glance at the other. "We have pretty good security, but if the Path got hold of our portal's address, they could send a sabotage or assassination team directly here."

"Like what just happened," I said, as the dawn suddenly started to glow. "So you figured you'd try to deflect Nask by dangling Tera as bait and letting them talk her into giving them the address to the other portal instead."

"So Nask *is* the one in charge," McKell said, nodding. "I thought it might be. And yes, she gave him the address to the portal we call Alpha. We leaked the story that I'd gone rogue, and that she was trying to find me, and hoped they'd try to grab her."

"Brilliant," I said sarcastically. "And it never occurred to you that they might torture her or just decide to kill her outright? Or did you just not give a damn?"

McKell's eyes narrowed dangerously— "She insisted she be the one," Ixil put in quickly. "Of the three of us—and we were the only three she trusted to do the job—she was the only person who could be memory-blocked to protect Icarus's address."

"What, you two were too squeamish?"

"We were too military," McKell corrected stiffly. "We've both spent time in our respective militaries, and part of the officer commissioning protocol is to undergo procedures to make memory-blocks permanently ineffective. We'd had those procedures. Tera hadn't. That made her the only one who could be safely allowed into Path hands."

"I'd argue about the word *safely*," I said. "So she went on the run, with you and Ixil as, what, shadow bodyguards? What if *you* got caught?"

"We wouldn't," McKell said simply.

I felt a shiver run through me as the full meaning beneath those words penetrated. They would make sure neither of them was taken alive...and as I looked at both of them I had no doubt that the Patth would pay a *very* high price for any such Pyrrhic victory.

"At any rate, we'd been keeping track of her and her progress," Ixil picked up the explanation, "using the StarrComm facilities on Melayse and Pinnkus, as you've already deduced. The biggest complication to the plan was that we needed Tera to be captured, not just by the Patth, but by the *right* Patth."

"They aren't just a single monolithic government," McKell said. "The directors and sub-directors are always jockeying for position and power and the favorable attention of the Director General. If Tera was picked up by someone other than the person in charge of their portal project—"

"They call it *Firefall*, by the way," I put in.

"Ah," McKell said. "Anyway, if she was picked up by the wrong Patth, it could be days or even months before she was negotiated and handed over to the right one. We couldn't afford that kind of delay." He hesitated. "Neither could Tera."

"Fortunately, we had sources of information to draw on," Ixil said. "Jennifer, who you met on Melayse, coordinated much of that and making sure we and Tera were all current on any new developments."

"One of which was the unexpected intrusion of your criminal acquaintance Luko Varsi," McKell said. "For some unknown reason, he suddenly seemed to want Tera for himself."

"Who suddenly wanted Tera *dead* for himself," I corrected.

The ferrets gave a simultaneous twitch. "So we learned," Ixil said. "Fortunately, you'd already been recruited by Geri and Freki. I had Pix eavesdrop on their conversation on the *Ruth*'s bridge when we were doing that circle around Pinnkus, and confirmed they were the ones who could get Tera safely to Sub-Director Nask and Firefall. The other bounty hunter groups had been dispersed by our smoke attacks, and she'd slipped out of their encirclement, so all that remained was to make sure you were in position to capture her and hand her over."

"Right," I said, that whole scene after we brought Tera to the *Ruth* coming back like the repeating of an ill-advised meal. "Only I figured they were going to give her to Varsi and I kicked them off the *Ruth*."

"Yes," Ixil said ruefully. "That one *did* take us by surprise."

"We didn't expect you to go all noble on us at the last second," McKell said. "So we had to scramble to fix it."

"I'll bet you did," I said. "Was that whole *we're con men impersonating the real Tera and Ixil* story part of it?"

"That was more Tera's attempt to improvise," McKell said. "Though to be fair, she was just jumping off your ridiculous conclusion that she was trying to sell Icarus to the highest bidder. At any rate, once you reached Melayse, Tera was able to fill us in on Freki's attempt to force you to Kashmir."

"Why Melayse?" I asked. "Because she'd started from there?"

"And because it was likely the Patth who'd been looking for her still had a presence there," McKell said. "We assumed Geri and Freki would be smart enough to split forces, one going to Kashmir in case their course-lock worked, the other going to Melayse in case it didn't."

"And we were right," Ixil said. "Unfortunately, an Iykam squad had also arrived on Melayse, and we had no way of knowing if they were fully under Freki's command or if they were working for some other director or sub-director. Until that was settled, we couldn't let Freki get hold of you. We certainly couldn't let the Iykams do so."

"I thought Expediters could commandeer any Patth resources and personnel," I said.

"Theoretically, yes," McKell said. "As a practical matter, it mostly means that if some director interfered with Freki he could bring it to the Director General's attention and demand a ruling. It would probably be in his favor, but Tera would still have been sitting around in the wrong place for days or weeks and we'd still be out that much time."

"But eventually Tera was able to persuade you to head to Kashmir," Ixil said. "So that part, at least, eventually worked out."

"Yes," I murmured, something he'd said a minute ago belatedly bouncing up from my memory. *We didn't expect you to go all noble on us at the last second.* And on McKell's note, he'd written *as your father used to say.*

How had he known about my father and his fondness for offbeat aphorisms? And how were any of them expecting anything from me, nobility or otherwise? "You seem to know a lot about me," I said carefully. "Are you saying you pushed Geri into hiring us?"

"I wondered if you'd be able to put the pieces together," McKell said. "The short answer is, yes, that's indeed what we planned to do."

"I'm so terribly honored," I said between clenched teeth. Jordan McKell, who'd tried to kill me once, now blithely having another go at it?

If McKell noticed my sudden bubbling anger, he didn't show it. "You're being sarcastic," he said calmly, "but in fact, you should be. We searched through hundreds of hunter and former hunter profiles looking for someone who could quickly and believably sniff out Tera."

"In your case, quite literally," Ixil said.

"I'm sure you see the balance we had to walk," McKell went on. "Too easy, and Nask would get suspicious. Too hard, and we'd lose time we couldn't spare. Not to mention the risk that Varsi's men might get to her first."

"You could have just asked us," I bit out, knowing full well that I'd not only have turned him down flat but would probably also have taken a shot at him. But right now my sense of logic was teetering on the edge, and I didn't really care about self-contradiction. "I'm sure it's fun to manipulate people, but you could have just *asked* us."

"Easy," McKell soothed. "I said we'd *planned* to nudge Geri. As it turned out, we didn't need to. He found you and hired you all by himself."

I frowned, my anger cooling just a bit. I had no doubt McKell would lie his face off if he thought it would benefit him. But if he *wasn't* lying... "Why would *he* recruit us? How would he even know about us?"

McKell shrugged. "I assume the Patth have the same depth of information sources that we do."

"Though from what Tera said it sounded like you still had to pass an entrance exam first," Ixil said.

I scowled. That stupid money test back on Xathru, with Freki's week-old scent on it. Apparently, everyone out there liked playing marionette proxy with us. "Oh, he tested us, all right," I growled.

"The point is that things worked out the way we all wanted." McKell quirked an almost-smile. "Though I'll concede it probably wasn't the way *you* wanted."

"Oh, yeah, it worked out great," I growled. "I don't suppose it ever occurred to you that Nask wouldn't be happy with just Tera? That he'd want to bring a couple of extra hostages along into oblivion's backyard?"

"Actually, it not only occurred to us," Ixil said, "but it was what we hoped he would do."

"Because we knew he'd never let Tera test his portal," McKell said. "She was far too valuable to let out of his sight. We needed Nask to have someone available who we could get to Alpha, and from Alpha to here."

"Why?" I demanded. "To see if Nask really *did* have a working portal?"

"No." McKell pointed to my side pocket, the one where I'd put all the pictures and papers I'd been given. "So we could get Firefall's address."

I stared at him. With all the rest of the conversation—the secrets and the double-crosses and the revelations of manipulation—that part hadn't even occurred to me. "Why, so you can go there and destroy it?"

"No," McKell said, his voice suddenly low and very, very dangerous. "So we can go there and bring Tera and Selene back home."

I looked into his eyes, letting the simmering anger

there wash over me. Jordan McKell... and now, somehow, we'd ended up on the same side of this battle.

And depending on how serious he was about getting Tera back alive...

"Well, at least there's *something* we agree on," I said, reaching for the cola and one of the snack cakes. "Apology accepted. Tell me more."

They'd barely gotten started describing their assault plan when the admiral finally arrived.

Though it would be more accurate to say he swept in, like some ancient Roman procession or a major weather system. He was dressed to the hilt in full EarthGuard dress uniform, shimmering blue and sparkling white, with gold insignia and rows of ribbons.

I was wearing an elite Patth combat suit, its deliberately subdued design nevertheless exuding power and skill and authority. It was the most impressive outfit I'd ever worn, and I still felt seriously underdressed.

Fleetingly, I wondered if McKell and Ixil were feeling any of my intimidation. Somehow, I doubted it.

"Mr. Roarke, I'm Admiral Sir Graym-Barker," the admiral introduced himself. His voice, measured and casually confident, completely matched his outfit. "I want to first apologize for having put you in this situation, and to also congratulate you on your sterling performance despite the necessity of keeping you in the dark about what was happening."

"Thank you, you're welcome, and it's not even close to being over," I said brusquely. "Selene and Tera are still stuck in there with a bunch of Patth and Iykams"—I gestured to McKell and Ixil—"and from what I've heard so far the extraction plan stinks."

"Agreed," Graym-Barker said calmly. "I'll add that much of the stench comes from our current lack of intel on what exactly their team will be walking into. We're counting on you to fill in those crucial details."

"The crucial detail is that the place is a fortress," I said. "The Firefall portal has a one-man entrance—I believe those are called *choke points*—and opens into a cavern loaded with Iykam guards that also has a single exit."

"How big an exit?" McKell asked.

"Okay, that one's decently sized," I conceded. "But it's also a good solid sprint from the portal, and the minute you charge out with lasers and plasmics blazing they'll seal you in with a set of heavy blast doors. And as I say, it's a cavern, so rock walls all around with nothing except the blast doors for you to punch through."

"I assume Tera and Selene will be on the other side of those doors?" Graym-Barker asked.

"Nask doesn't trust Tera anywhere near the portal, so that would be a yes."

"Then we'll just have to go in without the blazing plasmics," McKell said. "Sneak in somehow."

"You'll never make it," I said bluntly. "Even if you did, how long do you think you could keep your presence secret on a Path core world? They'd know you were there so fast it would—"

I broke off. Suddenly, like a blinding flash of lightning the whole thing had become clear. *Keep your presence secret* . . .

I focused on the others. Graym-Barker was looking thoughtfully at me, Ixil's expression was unreadable, and McKell had the look of a man who was about to be asked to take a card. "When did Tera move from Melayse to Pinnkus?" I asked. "How many days before we brought the *Ruth* into Havershem City?"

"Let me check," Ixil said, producing a pad and scrolling rapidly through the pages.

"Is it important?" Graym-Barker asked.

"Let's find out," I said. "Ixil?"

"She arrived in Havershem City about five days before you did," Ixil said.

"You're sure?" I asked, mentally running the numbers. And damned if I wasn't right.

"Very sure," Ixil said. "And?"

I leaned back in my seat. "I know where they are, and it's not on one of the Path core worlds," I said. "But there's a price."

"Go on," Graym-Barker said.

"I'll give you the name of the world," I told him. "Once you have that, you should be able to launch a two-prong attack from both inside and outside. I'm guessing that's the last thing they'll expect, and I guarantee it's your best shot."

"Simultaneous assaults do usually raise the odds," Graym-Barker agreed. "Your price?"

"I'll do whatever you want to help lay the groundwork and assist with the operation," I continued, ignoring his question. "I'll also give you a map of the areas I've seen. Which, I'll admit, won't be all that complete."

"But certainly better than nothing," Graym-Barker said. "And?"

I braced myself. "In return"—I looked at McKell—"you give me McKell."

Graym-Barker cocked his head slightly to the side. "Excuse me?"

"I have a score to settle, and this seems the best time to do it," I said. "It comes down to McKell or Tera. Choose."

I held my breath, waiting for them to call my bluff or—worse—remind me that if Tera didn't make it out alive neither did Selene. If necessary, I had a plan for Selene, but the odds were worse than anything we could possibly come up with here and I would only use it as a last resort. I waited, counting my heartbeats . . .

McKell stirred in his chair. "All right," he said, his voice steady. "If that's what it takes, I agree."

"Jordan," Graym-Barker rumbled.

"Sorry, Admiral, but you don't have a vote in this," McKell said, his gaze steady on my face. "All right, Roarke. Where are they?"

I let my breath out in a silent sigh. And with that, the die was cast. "Bonvere Seven," I said.

"How do you know?" Ixil asked.

"Three indicators," I said. "One: like you said before, an entrance exam. Geri had already confirmed that Selene could pick up a days-old scent, which she would need to find Tera. But as long as they had us, he figured he might was well see if there were any bits from the Firefall base that might have leaked into the atmosphere where they could be picked up by a crockett probe. If we didn't find anything, odds were no one else would, either."

"Seems a bit dubious," Graym-Barker said.

"Not done," I told him, raising a warning finger. "Two: the Commonwealth did a survey fly-by of the Bonvere cluster sixteen years ago, which is often the precursor to a more thorough study. But then, suddenly, everyone forgot about that whole area. Anybody remember why?"

McKell sat up straighter in his chair. "Lacklin," he said.

"Lacklin," I confirmed. "Suddenly the Patth were swarming around that system, pouring in money and attention and massive amounts of publicity, and the whole Spiral went nuts. They kept it going long enough for everyone to forget about Bonvere, then shut down Lacklin to make everyone go away."

"Seems to me that's also a mark in favor of Firefall being there and not on Bonvere Seven," Graym-Barker pointed out.

"It might," I said. "But setting up a fake portal on the same world as the real one would be stupid and dangerous." I lifted a finger again. "But here's the clincher. Three: we'd just finished our survey when Geri suddenly decided to skip the rest of the survey and directed us to Ringbar. We met Freki there, and he told us Tera had been spotted three days ago in Havershem City. That was *after* we'd left Xathru, and I remember thinking at the time how Ringbar was ideally placed as a jumping-off point for Pinnkus. *"So how did Geri know all of that?"*

For a long moment the room was silent. "There's a private communication array on Bonvere Seven," McKell said softly. "A world that's supposedly only been visited once."

"And supposedly never even been landed on," I said. "In retrospect, I'd have to say taking us there was a huge mistake on Geri's part. But they were so focused on getting to Tera that I guess he assumed I would never make the connection."

"Or if you did, that you'd notice too late," Graym-Barker said. "Ixil?"

"We can have a team there in three days," Ixil said, working his pad some more.

"That fast?" I asked, frowning. "Just how close *are* we, anyway?"

"Not really any of your business," Graym-Barker told me. His voice was civil enough, but I had no trouble hearing the unspoken order to drop it. "McKell?"

"I don't know," McKell said doubtfully. "Three days is a long time to stall. You have any idea where on the planet it is?"

"Not really," I admitted. "The landing cradles are underground, hidden by a ceramic-and-metal roof. I don't think the base is too deep, either. In fact, from the angle, the receiver module may be poking up out of the ground, unless they've disguised it. If that helps any."

"That, plus a communications array on an otherwise uninhabited world, should be all we need," Graym-Barker assured me. "As to the delay, Jordan, I have a few ideas."

He pulled out one of the chairs and sat down. "We have some planning ahead of us, gentlemen. Let's get to it."

CHAPTER TWENTY-FOUR

———————— ◈ ————————

Two hours later, I was back in Firefall with a semi-conscious Geri in tow, my pockets bulging with all the pieces he'd taken out of his weapons, and a water bottle that had been thoroughly purged of the knockout drug I'd given him.

And with one hell of a story to tell.

"I don't know what kind of crystal ball you've got," I told Nask across the table as the Patth medics silently checked Geri's injuries after his face-plant on the Alpha deck, "but your timing was just about perfect. It was four in the morning by the time I got in—there was a clock in the main analysis chamber—and everyone was gone. I didn't want to dig too deep, but—"

"Where was Geri all this time?" Freki interrupted. He'd planted himself behind Nask, hovering there over the sub-director's shoulder like an angry and very suspicious thundercloud. The only times he'd taken his icy stare off me were his occasional glances at

Geri to check on the medics' progress. Fortunately, they seemed to be focusing exclusively on treating his injuries and not checking for drugs in his system.

"I already told you," I said, putting a little impatience into my voice. As my father used to say, *If you've got a story to tell, tell it like you're as excited to hear it as everyone else.* "He'd tripped and knocked himself out on the receiver module deck."

"No," Freki said flatly. "We don't just *trip*. Not ever."

"Maybe it wasn't just a trip," I said. "His Eminence said the gravity in the modules can be changed. Maybe there was a brief glitch that threw him off-balance."

"Did *you* feel anything?" Freki pressed.

"No, but I wasn't really paying attention," I said. "I also wasn't walking at the time."

Freki shook his head. "No," he said again. "That's simply not possible."

"It's an alien artifact filled with alien technology," I reminded him acidly, suddenly tired of this. "*Anything* is possible. But fine—have it your way." I pointed to the red marks on Geri's cheek, forehead, and jaw, spots where he was already raising some impressive bruises. "I walked up to him, right up in front where he could see me, wound up my fists and punched him—*three times*—and he never even tried to stop me. You like that scenario better?"

Again, Freki looked at his partner. "Well?"

"I don't remember anything after I showed him my hammer drill," Geri said. He was trying to be as hard and strong as Freki, but he was still coming out of it and there was more confusion than steel in his voice. "But there's no way he could have attacked me without showing it." He shifted his eyes to me, a little more life and ice in them this time. "Or without being dead."

"Which I'm clearly not," I said, turning back to Nask. "Can we get on with it, Your Eminence?"

"You seem remarkably eager to assist us," Nask said. There was challenge in the words, but to my hypersensitive ears his tone sounded more curious than suspicious.

"What I'm remarkably eager to do is get this over with and move on with my life," I corrected. "I have it on good authority that there are two hundred thousand commarks in my Xathru account ready to be spent. And also—well, we'll get to that. Like I said, it was four o'clock when I finally got the hatch open. I went through the launch module—lot of stuff had been opened up in there; they must be doing some serious work. I went through and into the analysis chamber—"

"How did you get the hatch open?" Geri asked.

"I kept going along the edge with your hammer drill like you'd been doing," I told him. "When I got to the catch it popped, just like you'd said it would, and I was able to swivel the plate around and open."

"You're sure no one spotted you?" Nask asked. "You were in the receiver module for a long time before entering the base. There weren't any guards?"

"There were a couple on the blast doors leading into the analysis chamber," I said. "But they were facing outward, toward whatever work or sleeping areas were in that direction. They never saw me."

"No monitoring devices in the chamber itself?" Nask persisted. "Or in the receiver module?"

"There was nothing in the module," Geri said. He

was sounding stronger now, almost back to his usual smugly annoying self. "I checked when I was looking for another way out."

"There wasn't anything in the chamber, either," I said. "But hang on—here comes the good stuff."

I dug into the pocket where all my portal address photos were stashed and pulled out the artificially-aged flier that Graym-Barker's people had put together. "Geri was thinking the plate suggested Icarus might be somewhere near a Volga Industrium facility in the Najiki Archipelago. Turns out he was right, and furthermore I can now tell you their exact location, right down to the planet and city." I slapped the flier triumphantly on the table in front of Nask.

"What is this?" Nask asked, picking it up.

"A notice about the Bokken Festival in Okan City," I said. "No idea what the hell a Bokken Festival is, but it's got a sword pictured on it, and a lot of the desks I saw had miniature sword racks on their curio shelves. That tells us Icarus must be somewhere in the area."

"A bokken's a wooden replica of an Old Japan sword," Freki said, pulling out an info pad. He peered briefly at the flier, then began punching keys.

"I thought it might be a tournament," I said. "Probably just a marketplace or exchange, then. It still tells us they're near Okan City."

"Yes," Nask said thoughtfully, eyeing the flier. "You say some of the desks had miniature sword racks?"

"Yes, quite a few of them," I said. "That's why I figured it was safe to take the flier. There were at least a dozen of them in the stack, and I figured everyone would just think one of the others took it."

"Indeed," Nask said, still gazing at the paper. "Freki?"

"Okan City's on Hoshshima, Your Eminence," Freki said. "The system's near the south-nadir edge of the Archipelago, as Geri said. Probably an eight-day flight from here. The festival's not just in Okan, either—looks like versions of it take place all across the planet."

He gestured toward the flier. "Unfortunately, it begins in three days and only runs for two. Not enough time."

"Perhaps." Nask reached a hand up toward him.

"Not enough time for what?" I asked as Freki handed down his pad. Nask began punching keys, ignoring my question. "Not enough time for what?" I tried again.

"This is a sword festival," Freki said, sounding a little annoyed that I was butting in. "Some of the Icarus staff are sword enthusiasts. People who take off work to go to the festival won't be in the chamber. You get it now?"

"Ah," I said, as if that had never even occurred to me. As my father used to say, *Never tell someone everything he wants to hear. Let him fill in important parts on his own.* "So if we pick that time to go in, those are people we won't have to deal with."

"Exactly," Freki said. "But as I said, the festival starts in three days, and we're eight days away. We can't get there fast enough to take advantage of the timing."

"*We* can't," Nask said. "But there are two rapid-response teams that can." He handed the pad back to Freki. "Do you know these two Expediters?"

"Only by reputation," he said, peering at the pad. "But they're solid enough. Fifteen Iykams in each team, I see. Roarke? Would sixteen soldiers be a big enough assault team?"

"How should I know?" I asked.

"Oh, I don't know," Freki said sarcastically. "Maybe because you were *there*?"

"One: I told you I only got into the main analysis chamber," I said. "Two: Maybe Expediters can count people they can't see, but I can't. They could have a whole army stashed away down there for all I know. Three: I have no idea what kind of outer door they've got, or how secure it is."

"Pity you didn't take any pictures," Freki growled. "They might at least have given us some parameters."

"I didn't have a camera," I reminded him. "Nothing that could be used as a weapon, remember?"

"*I* had a camera," Geri said, glaring at me.

"That would have been good to know," I said, doing a little glaring of my own. "Next time mention it to me when it might still be useful. Or are you suggesting I should have gone through your pockets while you were sleeping?"

"Only if you had a death wish."

"My point exactly."

"Enough," Nask said. "I'll make sure you have a camera on your next journey. In the meantime, I presume you can draw us a map?"

"Of course," I said, letting my eyes narrow a little. "What do you mean, my next journey? I thought you just said you were sending an Expediter and a bunch of Iykams."

"As you just said, we have no idea of their entrance's security," Nask said calmly. "We'll therefore launch a twin-edged attack, one from the outside, one from the portal itself. I assume you're willing to lead the latter attack?"

"You want me to *lead* it?" I asked, letting my eyes widen. "I'm not a soldier."

"You're the only one who can open the hatch," Nask reminded me.

"It's easy," I assured him. "I can teach Geri or Freki how to do that."

"And if you teach us wrong?" Geri asked.

"Why would I do that?"

"You're human, and the Commonwealth doesn't like Patth," Geri countered. "You said you were eager to end this. Are you, or aren't you?"

For a couple of seconds I looked back and forth between him, Nask, and Freki as if I was weighing the situation and the options. So far, Graym-Barker had anticipated Nask's responses perfectly. All I had to do to help it along was not look too eager about getting volunteered. "Fine," I said at last. "But once I get it open and make sure the path into the chamber is clear, I go back to the launch module and come straight back here."

"I thought you bounty hunters weren't afraid of anything," Geri said scornfully.

"Of course we're afraid of things," I shot back. "We're not stupid. Just because I'm willing to point the way doesn't mean I'm ready to reenact the Charge of the Light Brigade."

"Interesting that you bring up Lord Cardigan's failed Crimean War attack," he countered coldly. The guy who liked sprinkling French and Latin into his conversation apparently couldn't stand being one-upped on anything cultural. "Let me tell you how *I'm* seeing the scenario you're painting."

"I can hardly wait," I said acridly.

Geri leaned forward in his chair, brusquely pushing aside the Patth medic trying to bandage his forehead. "I see you having been caught when you went into Icarus. I see you having made a deal with them. I see you setting us up, then scurrying away like a rat the minute we get there. I see them shooting us at their leisure while we roll out one at a time." He leaned back again. "And then I see *me* blowing your head off."

I looked at Nask. He was watching me closely, clearly waiting for my reaction.

Fine. If he wanted a reaction, I would damn well give him one.

"Interesting little fever dream," I said, turning back to Geri. "Let me tell you what *I* see. I see me *not* getting caught. I see me leading the way in because they know I was snatched along with Tera and they won't just open fire on me on sight. I see me able to distract them by telling them I escaped, and maybe getting their leaders to come talk to me. I see you *not* getting shot because you weren't stupid enough to charge in one by one but lobbed in a few flash-concussion grenades first. And as for working with Icarus—"

I broke off, looking again at Nask. "I was going to save this for later, but what the hell. If you want me to do this, there's going to be a price. Not just Selene and me walking out of here, but a real, actual price."

"Expediter training?" Nask asked.

Freki looked down at him, and for the first time since we'd met back at Ringbar the man seemed genuinely surprised. "You're taking him as an *Expediter*?"

"That conversation's for later," I said before Nask could answer. "Right now, my price is Jordan McKell. I want him."

"Alive or dead?" Nask asked calmly.

"Alive if possible," I said, frowning at him. I'd expected a little more reaction than that. "I'd prefer to deal with him myself."

"Why?"

"That's between him and me," I said.

For a long moment Nask gazed at me. "For now," he said. "Very well. I'll inform the Expediter in command of the ground assault team. If McKell's there, we'll save him for you." He considered. "Assuming he survives the assault from Firefall."

"I'm sure Geri knows how to pick his targets," I said, looking at him.

"Oh, I do," Geri said softly. "Trust me."

I waved a hand. "Then I don't see a problem."

"The problem would be if McKell is unlucky enough to be in the analysis chamber when we arrive," Nask said. "I'm afraid you still think like a bounty hunter, Mr. Roarke. If you wish to become an Expediter, that will have to change. Freki, explain how you'll enter the chamber."

"Flash-concussion grenades are for amateurs," Freki said, giving me an evil smile. "I'm thinking a pair of heavy fire shells—probably hellspawn mortar rounds—lobbed into the center of the room."

My mouth felt suddenly dry. The sheer cold-bloodedness of the idea— "Surely Your Eminence isn't seriously considering letting them do that," I said carefully.

"You object?" Nask asked.

"There are civilians in there," I reminded him, trying to keep my voice calm. If he was going to let Geri have some of those hellish things, he would probably hand them off to the Iykam assault team, too. The thought of someone with hellspawns wandering around the public parts of Okan City... "You don't have to kill them."

"This is a military operation, Mr. Roarke," Nask said, his voice gone suddenly cold. "Icarus is a potential prize of war. You can hardly object to the use of military equipment."

"What about their intrinsic value as Icarus techs?" I countered. "Them and their equipment both."

"Certainly we would prefer to take them and their equipment intact," he said. "But if that's not possible—" He gave an eerily human-style shrug. "We have plenty of our own techs."

I looked at Freki, then Geri. Their faces were as wooden as Nask's. "But they're *civilians*."

"There are no civilians in a field of war, Mr. Roarke," Nask said. "All who stand within such a field are to be considered soldiers."

"That's not how the Spiral Military Conventions see it."

"The Conventions are for the weak and the timid," Nask said contemptuously. "Victory goes to the strong and bold. The Patthaaunutth are both. Perhaps you don't have the fortitude to be an Expediter, after all."

"Maybe he *should* just tell us how to get into the launch module," Freki suggested. "We don't need a coward with us."

"We don't even need *that* much help from him," Geri said. "I got a good look at that hatch plate. A couple of turns of blast cord should take it out."

I took a deep breath. Like it or not, Graym-Barker's plan required me to be part of the assault team. "I'm not a coward," I said. "As for blasting it open, be my guest. *If* you want every eye and gun pointed at you before you're even out of the receiver module."

"They can point all they want," Geri said. "Doesn't mean they'll have time to do anything else."

"Fine," I said. "Just remember you'll need to get all the way to the other side of the launch module before you can fire your mortars into the chamber— there's too much stuff in the way to send a shell through from the receiver. Also remember that the interface opening between the spheres is every bit as much a choke point as the one leading out of the launch module."

Geri shifted his eyes to Nask. "Your Eminence?"

"You'll be in command of the operation," Nask said. "Whatever decision you make, it will be final."

"I still think there are better ways," I said. "Did I mention the valuable data that's probably stored in the analysis chamber that a hellspawn would destroy?"

"You did," Geri said. "But we won't need their data. Once we have Icarus we can generate our own."

"Only if you can get the portal out of there before someone comes along and stops you," I warned. "I don't think fifteen Iykams and an Expediter will be able to hold off any serious effort to take it back."

"Other assets will arrive close behind them," Nask said. "The operation will commence in three days. You have that much time to convince Geri to your point of view. If you can persuade him that the two of you entering will be a better opening move than an unexpected attack, I'm certain he'll modify his plan."

"But don't count on it," Geri said.

"Wouldn't think of it," I assured him. "And if you

think you're coming in with me, forget that, too. Given our recent history, I don't think the Icarus staff would believe you'd been kidnapped, too."

"You think that's what His Eminence is suggesting?" Geri asked mockingly. "Don't be a fool. You said it yourself: Expediters can't count people we can't see. Luckily, we know someone who can do exactly that."

I stared at him, my blood going cold. "No," I said. "Not an option."

"Why not?" he countered. "A couple of sniffs in the launch module and we'll have the whole personnel count. As long as she stays down, no one's likely to blow her head off." He raised his eyebrows. "The hellspawn attack's looking a lot better now, isn't it?"

I looked away, trying to calm my sudden churning fear. Graym-Barker had anticipated almost every other aspect of Nask's tactical thought process. Why hadn't he anticipated this one?

Because of course he hadn't. Selene was a wild card, a factor so rare she would never figure into ordinary military considerations. The real question—the damning question—was why *I* hadn't seen it coming?

But I hadn't, and now I was trapped. If I backed out of my offer to scout the Icarus analysis chamber, they would wonder why I was suddenly okay with letting a surprise hellspawn attack kill dozens of people. But if I somehow managed to talk Nask into dropping Selene from the attack, he would probably bounce me, too. And if he did that, Graym-Barker's whole counterattack plan fell apart.

And if that happened, Selene and Tera would probably die. Not to mention that I probably would, too. Nask's vague Expediter offer was clearly contingent on the Patth successfully grabbing the Icarus portal, and if I backed out there really wasn't any reason to keep me around.

"Mr. Roarke."

I snapped out of my depressing train of thought and looked at Nask. He'd risen from his chair and was looking expectantly at me. "Yes, Your Eminence?" I asked.

"I would speak with you," he said, turning toward the door. "Walk with me."

We left the conference room and turned toward the portal and Firefall's work cavern. Nask's two bodyguards, who'd been waiting out in the corridor during the meeting, now rejoined him, again flanking the Patth and shouldering me to the outside of our little group. "You said your conflict with Jordan McKell was between the two of you," Nask said. "No longer. Tell me about it."

I threw him a sideways look. Of all the things vying for my attention right now, this one was pretty low on the list. "With all due respect, Your Eminence—"

"Tell me."

I scowled. But it hadn't been a suggestion, and I still needed his goodwill if I was going to get Selene out of here. "It was five years ago," I said. "Back when the *Icarus*—the original ship—first disappeared the Patth had put massive bounties out on the four crew members they had names for and every hunter in the Spiral was crawling over all of the others trying to get to them first."

"I remember," Nask said, his voice distant with memory. "I was the one who authorized those bounties."

I looked at him in surprise. "*You?*"

"I'd interacted with McKell and some of the others," he said grimly. "I had him within my fingers, in fact."

"What happened?"

He sent me a hard look. "Let us say merely that if you don't deal with him I will," he said. "You said you were all hunting him?"

"We were hunting all of them," I said. "But their trails just got colder and colder, and none of them were ever very warm to begin with. Most hunters figured that the crew disappeared when the ship did, and after a few months of wasted effort most of them gave up and moved on."

"But not you."

"Actually, we'd dropped out after the first six weeks," I said. "Then, about a year after the *Icarus* disappeared, we picked up a rumor that McKell had been spotted on Rachna. We headed there, found a security video with him on it and used that to find a place he'd recently touched. Once Selene had his scent, there was no way he was going to lose us."

"Unless he left the planet."

I shook my head. "Two ways to get to a ship: walk, or take a vehicle. If he walks, no problem. If he gets a cab or runaround, we'll know where he picked it up, track through the records to find which specific vehicle it was, track through *those* records for the destination, and reacquire him there. Same process if he gets on a ship, just longer and more complicated."

"And yet somehow he evaded you."

With a conscious effort, I unclenched my teeth. "He didn't evade us. We tracked him down, and he tried his damnedest to kill us."

"Really," Nask said. "How?"

"We had him cornered in a warehouse district," I said. "He was upwind, and Selene knew exactly where he was. It was late at night, with no one else around, and we figured we could just run him down and take him."

I took a deep breath. "We were moving in when he opened fire. Not a warning shot, like most people do when they're trying to brush back pursuit, but a straight-up killing shot."

"That was when you lost your left arm?"

I nodded, my throat tight. I'd been able to mostly ignore the continued numbness of the arm for the past few days. But now those memories were flooding back again. "It was pure dumb luck I had my arm up to signal Selene or the shot would have burned out the center of my chest," I told him. "I got off a shot, but it was wild and I missed completely." I took another deep breath. "And then, for no damn reason at all, he shot again. Only this time, it was to put a pair of slugs into Selene's chest."

"Interesting," Nask said.

I turned to him, a flash of fury suddenly boiling up inside me. "*Interesting?*" I snarled, ignoring his bodyguards' sudden alertness. "Is that all you can say? *Interesting?*"

"Interesting in the sense that I now understand your motivations," Nask said calmly. "Interesting in the sense that I now also understand McKell a bit better. So how will you kill him?"

I turned away from him. "Hadn't really thought about it," I muttered. "I just want to look into his eyes over the barrel of my plasmic and let him know that payment has finally arrived. Maybe I won't even kill him. Maybe I'll just burn his arm off, then borrow a gun and pump a couple of rounds into his chest. I had a long time to think while Selene was in the hospital. Thinking is good for a person."

We'd reached the work cavern and Nask had led us between the door guards before he spoke again. "I understand why you don't wish to put her in danger again," he said. "Yet you surely also understand that we must use every resource at our disposal if we're to succeed."

"Sure," I said, looking around the cavern. It was getting late, but there were still over a dozen Patth in the room, working under the muted lighting, bathed in the slightly brighter lights from the various consoles. Tracking, sifting, analyzing, and otherwise trying to squeeze every last bit of data out of the Firefall portal that they could. I looked at the entrance to the receiver module, at the handholds they'd set up to make it easier to get in and out.

And frowned. There was something in the module, I saw now, something small and barely visible, sitting right at the edge of the opening.

My first thought was that it was a tool or handheld scanner that had been carelessly left there, and for a moment I considered pointing it out to Nask as a reminder of how observant I was. But it was really none of my business. I started to look away—

And then, the object moved.

I felt my eyes narrow, trying to pierce the shadows inside the module. It moved again, part of the vague lump now resolving into a small head with a pair of bright eyes. Mice? Rats? Did Bonvere Seven have native vermin, or was this something that had hitched a ride when the Patth set up shop here?

And then, with a rush of adrenaline, I got it.

The creature was one of Ixil's outrider ferrets.

CHAPTER TWENTY-FIVE

———— ❖ ————

My first reaction was disbelief. Graym-Barker was launching his attack *now*, without further planning and with his commando team still three days away? Worse, launching it before I'd had a chance to even get back to Selene, let alone tell her and Tera what was happening?

Following right on the heels of that first flash judgment was the more personal one of professional outrage. Were they checking up on me? Had McKell and the admiral decided that my description of Firefall and the work chamber wasn't good enough and that they needed a look for themselves? Did they just flat not trust me?

And then, reality kicked in. Of course they didn't. Why in hell should they? With Selene's life hanging by a thread, why should they believe anything I said? Hell, I wasn't even sure *I* trusted me.

But that wasn't important. What was important

was that Graym-Barker's perfectly understandable paranoia had now hung the Icarus project over a field of razor knives. If Ixil was hiding in Firefall—and I couldn't imagine him sending his ferrets in alone, not with three long days before he could get back here to retrieve them—then a single Patth tech going in to check on something would bring the whole thing crashing down. Ixil knew Icarus's address, and if Nask was able to extract it from him then everyone at Icarus was doomed.

I couldn't let that happen. Not with Geri gleefully talking about hellspawn shells and mass slaughter.

"But that's exactly my point, Your Eminence," I said, kicking my brain into high gear. The ferret had the look of someone preparing to hop out for a little floor-level recon, and even if no one was looking in that direction right at the moment its movement might draw attention. I had to make sure that didn't happen. "Thinking things through. Geri's hellspawn might clear the analysis chamber, but the sheer magnitude of the blast will alert everyone else in the facility. If instead I go in first, I can draw every eye to me and give him time to move his team into the launch module without being seen."

"I doubt you could draw *every* eye," Nask demurred.

"You don't think so?" I took a step back from him and his bodyguards and filled my lungs. "No!" I shouted, throwing panic and desperation into my voice, cringing back with my hands up as if to ward off some monster looming invisibly in front of me. "No! This is another trick—I *know* it's another trick. Please—just leave me *alone*."

And with every Patth and Iykam staring wide-eyed

at me, exactly as I'd planned, I saw the ferret hop out of the receiver module, pause to adjust to the new direction of gravity, then scamper off toward the nearest line of work stations and disappear behind them.

"I know you're not really here!" I shouted, just in case Ixil wanted to send the other ferret out, too. But the portal entrance remained empty. "I know it's a trick. *Just leave me alone!*"

I held the cringing pose another moment, then straightened up. "And at that point," I continued in a normal voice, "I get dragged away to a security office somewhere to find out who I am, how I got there, and what the hell I'm talking about."

"Interesting performance," Nask said. "And if Selene is with you?"

"The same thing happens, only doubled," I said. "She's an excellent actress, you know. We're dragged out, leaving behind a bunch of analysts talking excitedly among themselves and ignoring their work, and never even looking at the portal."

"I hardly think the guards would ignore the point where you appeared."

"I'd make sure they had their hands full corralling me," I assured him. "Or us, if Selene is there. Though actually, if we get out of the portal quickly and smoothly enough, they may not even realize right away that that's where we came from." I inclined my head, looking toward the portal entry as if I'd just had a thought. "Though if we're going to go that route, I should probably practice going in and out."

"An interesting thought," Nask said.

I shrugged. "Again, just thinking it through. May I have your permission to stay for a bit, Your Eminence?"

"Of course." Nask gestured ahead. "Go."

"Thank you." I nodded to him and headed toward the portal at a brisk walk, sorting through the possibilities. If Ixil was in the receiver module, I should be able to whisper a quick message before I continued farther in to the sphere interface and started my first set of practice runs. If he was instead in the launch module, even better—I'd be farther away from the rest of the Patth working out here in the cavern and wouldn't have to keep my voice quite as quiet.

I was five paces from the portal entrance when I realized that Nask and his bodyguards were right behind me.

"Your Eminence?" I asked, frowning back over my shoulder. "Did I forget something?"

"Not at all," he said. "I wanted to observe your practice."

"Ah," I said. "Yes, that would be most appreciated. I'm sure you'll be able to offer some helpful suggestions."

"Perhaps later. For now, I'll be content to simply watch."

I turned back and kept walking, my stomach doing a slow spin. As my father used to say, *Things are darkest just before they go completely black.* But there was nothing I could do but keep going and hope that Ixil was on top of what was happening out here.

I reached the opening and ducked my head in, giving the receiver module interior a quick look while I waited for my inner ear to catch up with the gravity shift. No sign of Ixil, but as my sweeping gaze reached the launch module I saw his other ferret climb through the interface opening and disappear inside. A bit of good news there, at least.

The handholds loomed invitingly over me, offering the quicker, easier way in. But I was supposed to be here to practice my dismounts. Bracing my hands on the inside edges of the opening, I pushed my torso up into the sphere. I got my legs inside and sat there for a moment, letting myself finish the adjustment. Then I stood up and headed around the sphere toward the launch module.

"I'm curious about one thing," Nask said from behind me.

I looked back over my shoulder. One of the Iykams was already standing guard in the sphere, and Nask was riding the handhold system into view behind him. "You claim to care about Ms. Selene's safety," Nask continued. "Yet the plan you describe would seem to put her into the very heart of danger."

"Not at all," I said, fighting the impulse to nudge up my volume. This was my chance to say exactly what Ixil needed to hear, but I couldn't afford to have Nask wondering why I was suddenly talking as if I had an audience bigger than just him. "Geri can talk all he wants about how she'll be safe in the launch module, but you and I both know that once he fires off his hellspawn shells there'll be some backwash, no matter how well he covers the opening. He and his team might not care about that—they'll all be in full combat gear, with helmets and breathing equipment and everything. But Selene won't have any of that to protect her."

"Of course she will," Nask assured me. "We'll equip both of you the same way."

"You can't," I said. "Not if you want Selene sniffing the air and doing a head count. Well, body-odor count, if you want to be technical. You know what I mean. Her face will have to be exposed, which means she'll take the brunt of any blowback or fumes. Ask Geri how she handled the gas attack on Pinnkus. One whiff of anything strong, and she'll be useless to us."

I reached the launch module and lay down beside the rectangular opening, maneuvering carefully to avoid whacking my head or shins against the handhold supports. "*My* plan, on the other hand, has the two of us hauled out of the Icarus analysis chamber and the blast doors presumably sealed behind us before Geri makes his move. That will keep us safe from his little inferno."

"Safe, perhaps, but also in custody."

"Oh, please," I said scornfully. "Don't make me laugh." Bracing myself, I rolled over the edge, my brain spinning as always at the gravity switch, and came to a stop inside the launch module.

And found myself face-to-face with Ixil. Or, more properly, face-to-face with the muzzle of Ixil's plasmic.

The Kalix was lying flat on his stomach on the cable mesh about three meters back from me, his legs wedged between two of the displays at a spot where their bright red lights threw a slight shadow. His right arm was stretched out in front of him, his plasmic pointed at me, his head slightly tilted to look down the weapon's barrel. The ferret I'd just seen slipping out of the big sphere was on his right shoulder, crouched in attack position like a squirrel who'd convinced itself it was really a wolf. "I'm a bounty hunter who's gone up against some of the best and smartest in the Spiral," I continued, calling back over my shoulder to Nask and raising my voice enough to make sure he could

hear me. "The Icarus guards are going to be a bunch
of would-be soldiers who haven't had a single minute
of excitement since McKell parked the ship there six
years ago. I'll have them for breakfast before they
even know what hit them."

"You're very confident," Nask called.

"I've run into their kind before," I said, gazing
unblinkingly at Ixil, trying to ignore the death pointed
squarely at my face. Couldn't Ixil see that the fact I
wasn't calling down on him meant I was on his side?
"All I need is the chance to prove it."

And then, to my relief, he turned his wrist over,
laying his gun hand sideways on the mesh. Maybe he
hadn't recognized me at first, or maybe he'd still had
lingering doubts. But apparently all was well now. He
lowered his head, laying it flat like he'd done with his
gun hand, and I saw the ferret flatten itself as well.

Apparently, I'd convinced him. Feeling a sense of
relief, I hunched myself over and rolled up onto my
other side to face the opening again—

And found myself eye to eye with one of the Iykams,
his head poking up into the launch module, his eyes
glaring at me from just above the level of the opening.

The relief vanished. Hope vanished. The Iykam was
staring straight at Ixil; and whether Ixil got his shot off
first or the Iykam got his warning shout off first, the only
difference would be how fast and how messily I died.
And then Selene would die, and then Tera. All was lost,
and there wasn't a damn thing all of Graym-Barker's
horses and all of Graym-Barker's men could do about it.

I braced myself, wondering whether the shot or the
shout would come first. That single agonizing fraction
of a second ticked over...

I frowned to myself. I was still lying there, Ixil's plasmic still behind me, the Iykam's face still glowering in front of me, neither of them springing into action.

And with a surge of dissipating adrenaline, I realized what I should have spotted right from the start. The Iykam was glowering at *me*; not at Ixil, but at *me*.

Because with Ixil's head, gun hand, and ferret pressed as far down as they could go the bulk of my body was completely blocking the Iykam's view.

But that moment of grace would last only as long as the Iykam didn't come any farther up into my sphere. "A little room, please?" I growled, waving him back. "I'm trying to get in some practice here."

"Calmness, Mr. Roarke," Nask called up soothingly. "He was merely concerned that you might intend to take leave of our hospitality."

"With Selene still locked up?" I retorted. "Don't be ridiculous. Your Eminence," I added with as much respect as I could muster.

The Iykam made a sort of warning growl at me. "And I still need room," I told him. "So move it."

"Give him room," Nask ordered.

The Iykam gave me one last look and disappeared. I readied myself and rolled back over the edge into the receiver module. "Well?" Nask asked.

"I think it's getting easier," I said. "Let me try a few more here, then we'll shift back to the receiver."

"I would think that interface would be more useful to know than this one."

"Ultimately, yes," I agreed. "But I need to know how to do both. A few more minutes only, I assure you."

I rolled between the spheres another five or six times, then expanded the routine to include the standing up and lying down parts as well. Nask and his two guards continued to watch silently, the Iykams looking impatient, Nask merely looking curious.

Finally, I decided I'd pushed things far enough. "One more time," I told Nask. I paused beside the opening like a gymnast preparing his routine, then dropped to the deck, rolled around the edge, and rolled back up to my feet.

Ixil was still where I'd first seen him. But now something new had been added to the scene: his ferret was crouched close to the opening, a piece of paper with a handwritten note gripped between its teeth.

Which, from my current standing position, I was too far away to read.

Easily fixed. My last few times through the opening had been quick and smooth, drop-roll-stand. Time to add a little clumsiness to the mix. I gave Ixil a microscopic nod, then dropped back to the deck.

And as I positioned myself beside the opening, I bumped my shin against the handhold frame.

"Damn," I cursed under my breath, wincing as I reached down to rub it. Now, from my new position, I could read the note.

Draw attention again when you're at the chamber exit.

"Are you injured?" Nask called.

"Just my pride," I said, giving the shin one last rub and repositioning myself. I rolled over the edge and stood up. "Tried it too fast and bumped my shin," I explained.

"I trust you'll be more focused at Icarus?" Nask asked.

"It won't be a problem," I said. "They don't have any handholds or frames there."

"Foolishly short-sighted of them," he said contemptuously. "But then, humans have so little dignity. Are you finished?"

"One more," I said, gazing down at the opening. Back on Lacklin, I'd asked Nask if a person who jumped into the intersection would bob up and down in the competing gravity fields. Nask had said yes.

But I knew now that the fake portal intersection had been created with dueling repulsor projectors. Would it work the same here with actual alien gravity fields?

As my father used to say, *You really won't know how hot the stove is until you touch it.* "Let me try something." Stepping right to the edge of the hole, I gave a little hop and dropped into the hole feetfirst.

Rolling across the intersection was disconcerting. Jumping in was even worse. My head and inner ear remained untouched, but the sudden back-pull on my feet, legs, and internal organs raised sensory confusion to a whole new level. My momentum carried me in to about chest height, at which point the launch module's pull on all that extra body weight slowed me to a stop and sent me falling—or rising, as my inner ear was currently reading things—back the other direction. I rose to knee level, then dropped back down again. The cycle repeated itself, slowly dampening out, until after about ten bounces I ended up bobbing gently between my navel and hip bone.

Nask had watched the whole thing with some amusement. The Iykams, in contrast, just looked annoyed. "Well?" Nask asked as I got a grip on the edges of the opening and pushed myself back fully into the receiver module.

"If the Patch ever build an amusement park, this

would make a great ride," I said, pausing a moment to let my body adjust once again to a single gravity direction. "Other than that, pretty useless. All right. A few practice rolls at the receiver module exit, and we can call it a night."

"Is the angle here the same as the one at Icarus?" Nask asked as we walked around the sphere.

"Not exactly, but it's pretty close," I told him. "That's a good point, actually—you'll probably want Geri and his team to do some practice runs over the next three days, too. Especially since they'll be in combat suits and carrying weapons."

"And Selene?"

I shrugged. "If you're hell-bent on her coming, yes, she'll need some practice, too."

"Is there a good reason to leave her behind?"

I felt my throat tighten. There was an excellent reason to leave her behind, actually. Unknown to Geri, our little jaunt wasn't going to be to Icarus, but to the distant Alpha portal, where Graym-Barker had instructed me to open the interface hatch plate, roll through, then seal the opening again before Geri could see there wasn't a second opening on the far side of the launch module and realize we weren't at Icarus.

The problem was that the interface opening wasn't wide enough for Selene and me to both roll through at the same time. We'd have to go one after the other, which would give Geri that much extra time to figure out what we'd done to him.

At which point there was a good chance one of us would get left behind with Geri and a whole bunch of angry Iykams.

I couldn't go first, leaving Selene behind in full

range of Geri's anger and frustration. Selene alive was a hostage, but I couldn't rely on Geri thinking straight at that moment.

But I also couldn't go second and risk sacrificing my own freedom to give Selene hers. She would be alone in the launch module, every bit as trapped as I was, with no knowledge of the plan and, worse, no knowledge of Icarus's address. She would sit there until Geri forced the hatch plate open and we returned to Firefall.

Probably to our deaths, because McKell wouldn't launch his attack until I showed up to alert him that Nask had launched his.

So yes, I desperately needed Selene to stay behind. But I also knew there was no way to lead Nask to that conclusion.

As my father used to say, *The best laid plans of mice and men usually involve cheese. Everything else is pretty much a crapshoot.*

Which left me with the weak plan of drilling Selene in the drop-and-roll as best I could and hope we would be fast enough to both get to safety before Geri could react. Maybe we could come up with some sort of distraction at the crucial moment, though I had no idea what that might be.

At least I'd been able to give Ixil a heads-up on Nask's sudden game change. Maybe he and Graym-Barker could come up with something at their end.

Though even if they did I had no idea how they would implement it. It wasn't like they could pass me a note with the details of any updated plans.

Of course, there was always the Plan B that McKell had suggested early on and that Graym-Barker had just as quickly dismissed: popping some commandos into Alpha right behind the Iykams and launching a surprise attack while I pretended to work on the hatch plate. I could only hope that, if Graym-Barker went back to that one, that whoever he sent were *really* good with their sniper rifles.

I spent a few more minutes practicing my dismount from receiver module to cavern, focusing mostly on the transition outward from sphere to ground. The biggest irony, of course, was that while this was an ability I really didn't need to master, it was precisely the one Nask and Geri thought I did. It had been hard enough to maintain a more casual attitude as I earlier worked at the spheres' interface; here, now, I had to really crank up my enthusiasm and determination to match Nask's expectations.

Unfortunately, with the odd angle between the two different gravity fields this transition had always been the harder of the two. I sweated, swore, came close to emptying my stomach at least twice, and picked up a few more bruises on my shins and arms. Finally, as soon as I reasonably could, I declared I'd had enough.

"Your speed has definitely improved," Nask commented as he and his Iykams walked me back across the cavern. "I assume you'll spend tomorrow here as well?"

"As much of it as I can," I assured him. "Once I've really got it down, I can bring in Selene and start teaching her. I'll talk to her about it when we're both together in our cell."

"That won't be possible," Nask said. "You'll be taken to a different cell for the duration of your stay here."

"I'm not going back to Selene and Tera?"

"No," Nask said. "Your focus will be better enhanced by solitude."

So much for passing on even the basics of what had just happened to me. "Fine," I said. "Can you at least tell her I got back safely? She worries about me."

"We certainly don't want her to be concerned," Nask agreed. "It might interfere with her remarkable abilities."

We'd reached the chamber's exit now, only a few steps from the blast doors and the Iykam guards standing watch there. Time to satisfy Ixil's last request. "A moment, if I may, Your Eminence," I said. I took a long step to the side away from him, putting myself out of the direct sight line between the door guards and the portal's entrance. "One last bit of practice."

I filled my lungs. "No!" I shouted, this time waving my arms as if driving away a swarm of invisible gnats. "You aren't real—I know you're not. Just get away from me!"

I had more of the routine ready to go, but I never got to use it. Nask's bodyguards, who hadn't been impressed by the first show, were even less impressed by this one. I'd barely launched into my tirade when they dived at me in unison, slamming their shoulders into my torso and locking their arms around mine, their momentum carrying us along to slam me shoulders-first into the angle between the cavern wall and the blast door on that side. "Enough," one of them snarled into my ear. "You make too much noise."

"Hey, that noise may well keep your friends alive when we all break into Icarus together," I retorted. "Okay, okay—enough. You can let go now."

Neither Iykam so much as twitched a muscle. "Let him go," Nask ordered calmly.

Reluctantly, I thought, they disentangled our arms and stepped back. I made a show of straightening my shirt, and as I did so looked casually back at the portal. For a second I thought I'd missed it; and then I saw the ferret emerge from behind another console, scurry along the floor, and leap through the opening.

Once again, unobserved by everyone in the room. Not only was this madman skit fun, it was pretty useful, as well.

And with that, the day really *was* over. I'd been dragged out of bed early, and wherever Nask planned to put me I was more than ready to be locked away for a few hours. "I trust there will be some food in my new cell," I said as we passed through the blast doors and the glowering guards and headed down the corridor. "I never got breakfast. *Or* lunch."

"There will be everything you need in there," Nask said, eyeing me curiously. Maybe he hadn't been quite as amused by my performance as I'd thought.

"Thanks." Everything I needed, anyway, except for a way out of this mess. But I couldn't exactly tell him that. "And don't forget to tell Selene I'm back. Your Eminence."

The three days quickly settled into a routine. Mornings and afternoons brought Selene and me together at Firefall for a couple of hours of drills, while the long periods of time in between were filled mostly by inactivity and boredom, each of us in our individual cells. We worked hard on our dismounts, both between the portal spheres and between the receiver module and the Firefall cavern, and with each practice run I tried to find even a few seconds of privacy I could use to at least let her know I'd met the Icarus people and that there was a plan underway. But while Nask had been willing to give me a little extra leash when I was alone in Firefall, he wasn't nearly so casual when Selene and I were together.

In retrospect, I should have expected that. I'd said it myself, right to Nask's face: as long as Selene was his prisoner, I wasn't going to make a break for it. Nask had unfortunately taken that to heart, with the result that every one of our practice drills had four alert Iykams hovering over us, plus two more standing at the foot of the launch module extension arm that was our only way out.

But if I couldn't get any information to Selene, I could at least get a little in the other direction. From her guardedly casual comments I gathered that she and Tera were still locked up together in our original cell, which meant that if the plan ever got far enough for McKell's team to get in here I could lead them there.

Assuming I was still alive at that point, of course.

I also kept a close eye out for unexpected company, on the off-chance that Ixil would be crazy enough to send in one of his ferrets with a message or even decide to drop in himself. It would be not only suicidal but useless, given my odds of getting to such a message before one of the Iykams did.

Fortunately, Graym-Barker had apparently run the same odds to the same conclusion. Despite my combined hopes and fears, Firefall remained ferret-free.

With nothing else to amuse me, I also made it a point after each of our practice sessions to offer Nask my assistance in working Geri and his team through their own dismount drills. I didn't expect him to take me up on the offer, and even if he did I was pretty sure Geri would flatly refuse. But as my father used to say, *If they won't let you be helpful, you might as well be irritating.*

Late in the morning on the third day, it was finally time.

CHAPTER TWENTY-SIX

"Sub-Director Nask has convinced me to try your plan first," Geri said as he went methodically through his final checks on the gear and equipment of the nine Iykams making up the first-wave assault team. "The progress you and Selene showed on your exit skills—"

"We call them *dismounts*," I interjected.

"—persuaded him that you have a reasonable chance of making it out of the Icarus portal without being seen," he continued, ignoring my comment. "Assuming you still want to try." He stopped, clearly watching for a reaction.

He would have a long wait. With danger sitting just over the horizon in a dozen different directions I wasn't interested in faking enthusiasm just to calm any lingering doubts he might have. I sure as hell wasn't going to show him any of my *real* emotions. "I do," I said. "I assume that means the Hoshshima commando team is in position?"

He nodded. "They located Icarus's entrance an hour

ago and are preparing to breech the outer doors. The festival's also off to a brisk start. We're hoping at least some of the Icarus people are in the audience," he added, his tone strongly suggesting that if they weren't it would be my personal fault.

"Good," I said, feeling a few lingering doubts of my own. My assumption was that Graym-Barker had picked Okan City because their Bokken Festival would give Nask a reason to delay his attack until the admiral's team could reach Bonvere Seven, and that Icarus wasn't actually anywhere near the area. But that *was* only an assumption. "What kind of communications time delay are we looking at?"

"None," Geri said. "The Expediter is in radio contact with someone parked in a booth in the local Starr-Comm center, who in turn is in contact with someone in our own StarrComm facility. The only time lag will be when the people at the two ends have to relay their messages. Once we're inside Icarus, of course, I'll be in direct communication with the Expediter and his team."

"Sounds good," I said. There was movement at the corner of my eye, and I turned to see Selene walking toward us, escorted by Nask and his bodyguards. Like me, she was dressed in the clothing she'd been wearing when we were snatched off of Kashmir, the better to sell our act of having escaped the evil clutches of the Patth.

"One more thing," Geri said, taking a step closer. "You and Selene are going in first. If your plan works— if they grab you and hustle you out of the analysis chamber—all will be good. If it *doesn't* work—" He tapped the bulky tube slung over his shoulder. "We have the hellspawns, and we *will* use them. Whether the two of you are clear or not."

His eyes bored into mine. "So this is your last chance to stay safe and sound in the launch module and let me clean out the analysis chamber before any of us goes in."

"Understood," I said. "We'll do it my way."

A muscle in his cheek twitched. "Suit yourself." Spinning on his heel, he stalked across the chamber to where the second, third, and fourth waves of Iykam attackers were busy with their own equipment checks.

Selene walked up to me. "Hello, Gregory," she greeted me, uncertainty in her pupils. "I'm told there are no practices today?"

"Rehearsal ends when the performance begins, Ms. Selene," Nask told her. "You're ready, Mr. Roarke?"

I nodded, taking a long look at Selene's pupils. There was nervousness there, along with uncertainty and a little fear. But on top of it all was something I'd both hoped and dreaded to see.

Trust.

Five years ago, I'd failed to live up to that trust. I hoped to hell I wouldn't fail her again.

"Roarke?" Geri called, twitching his fingertips in command. "Time to go."

I took Selene's hand and squeezed it briefly. "Ready?" I asked.

She squeezed back. "Ready."

Even after all their practice it took Geri's team a few minutes to get themselves into the receiver module and from there into the launch module. By the time Geri ushered Selene and me through the opening the address had been punched in and the Iykams were spread out in readiness around the sphere. "Here's the deal," Geri said, gesturing to one of the Iykams as he, Selene, and I headed to the base of the extension arm. "The techs think that you have to be touching the gray tip of the arm to get transported, which only gives us twenty centimeters to work with."

I peered at the end of the arm, which had now turned the familiar luminescent gray. "Do you need to be holding onto it, or will a fingertip touch work?"

"We don't know," Geri said. "I held onto it when I went through the first time. You?"

"The same."

"And this isn't the time to experiment," he said. "We figure that with combat gloves in place only four of us can hold on at once, so we're going across in groups of four." He gave me an ominous look. "Being the math genius you are, you'll have noted that with two of you and two of us, after we transfer you're going to have the best odds you ever will. Let me assure you: they're not nearly good enough."

"And being the tactical genius *you* are, you're not seriously expecting me to be stupid enough to try it," I growled back. "Can we skip the posturing and get on with it?"

"Sure," he said. He stepped to the base of the arm, his feet leaving the deck as the module's reversed gravity sent him drifting upward. I took Selene's arm and walked her over, and a moment later the two of us were floating up after him, the Iykam who was forming the fourth member of our group right behind us.

"Here's where it may get tricky," Geri called down over his shoulder. "I'm going to try to hover near the gray section without touching it. You two do the same until all of us are in position."

It sounded way too complicated to me, especially

since the portal designers must surely have assumed that more than one person would be using it at a time. But as he'd said, this wasn't the time to experiment. I curled my fingers around the arm as I reached the gray area, trying not to touch it and watching the Iykam behind us. He reached the end—

"On three," Geri said. "One, two, *three.*"

I closed my fingers firmly; and with the now familiar tingle and distant thunderclap the world went black. I waited, belatedly remembering that I'd never given Selene any warning as to what to expect and that I really should have—

The universe came back on, and we were there.

For a moment we hung in the middle of the receiver module amid the soft, directionless lighting. Then, we all started drifting in different directions toward the deck. I looked at Selene, watching the confusion in her pupils quickly replaced by excitement and interest. She caught my look and returned it, along with a tentative smile.

And then, I saw the interest replaced again by caution and a frown. Her nostrils worked, and the frown in her pupils went a little deeper.

I sniffed the air. If there was something new here since my last trip, I couldn't smell it.

But I knew that look.

"Well, well," Geri muttered.

"What?" I asked, managing to turn far enough in my current free-fall state to get him in sight. Had he spotted the smell, too? Unlike me, he had an air sampler; maybe something had showed up there?

"Looks like we were right about someone poking around in here," he said, pointing to a spot in the deck across from the interface and its covering hatch plate. One of the hull sections looked like it had been pried partially out of place and then pushed back in, but hastily enough that the edges hadn't quite aligned. "I wonder if the fancy lock trap got him, or if he managed to weasel his way out."

"I'll try to remember to ask," I said, eyeing the misaligned section. Like the smell, that hadn't been there before, either, and I didn't think for a minute that any of it was coincidental. Was the whole setup a diversion, the kind I'd hoped Graym-Barker would arrange, giving Geri something to look at while Selene and I escaped into the launch module? Did the misalignment conceal some kind of monitoring device? Was it supposed to distract Geri from checking his sampler before whatever was in the air did whatever it was supposed to?

"Yeah, I'm sure they'll tell you," Geri said. "Here." He dug a hammer drill out of his pocket—a real one this time, not the monstrosity he'd cobbled together before—and tossed it to me. "Go get set up so you're ready to let us through once everyone's here. And be *quiet* over there— we don't know how well that thing conducts sound."

Selene was looking at me, a mix of question and expectation in her pupils. I smiled reassuringly and mimed a warning about the sudden last-meter drop I knew was coming. She nodded, and I shifted my attention to the deck, concentrating on being ready when the higher gravity kicked in.

Like the teleportation itself, the landing was hardest the first time. This time, I had my knees bent and landed without trouble. Selene, even without completely knowing what to expect, still managed to land more gracefully than I did.

We were barely down when the next four Iykams popped silently into the center of the sphere above us.

I looked around. Geri was squatting down beside the misaligned plate, the other Iykam from our group standing midway between him and us and watching me closely. The four newcomers floating down from the ceiling were likewise focused on me, with their Pickering 6mm full-autos pointed in my general direction.

I sighed to myself. So much for our chances of slipping out while Geri was busy looking elsewhere. Even as I sent yet another reassuring smile at the lads with the guns, the next batch of Iykams appeared in the center behind them, putting a final end to that particular line of speculation.

"Gregory?" Selene asked quietly.

I turned back. She was kneeling beside the plate, leaning over it with nostrils and eyelashes again going like mad. "What is it?" I asked, walking over to her. "Are you smelling something in the air?"

"Yes, but I don't know what it is," she said. "It's volatile and nearly odorless. I may just be smelling impurities."

"Great," I said sourly. There were a whole range of odorless gasses out there, and a lot of them weren't especially friendly to human biology. "Odorless implies it's something they don't want us to notice."

"Maybe," she said. "But here's something they *do* want us to see."

She pointed at the plate. "There's a message here," she said. "Written in Ixil's scent."

"Is there, now," I said, my mind flashing back to the New Sandio Commons and the message I'd traced out on the quick-rent notice board to let Selene know where Tera and I were going to ground. Tera had watched me do that; clearly, she'd passed on the trick to Ixil and Graym-Barker. "What does it say?"

"*Both together feetfirst into opening*," she said. "Does that make any sense to you?"

I stared down at the plate. The message itself was crystal clear. The reasoning behind it was anything but.

Ixil had been right there at Firefall when I'd tried that stunt, and he'd seen firsthand that the trick went exactly nowhere. Even if Selene and I jumped as high as we could before dropping into the interface opening we still wouldn't make it all the way through before the launch module gravity caught us and sent us bobbing helplessly back into the big sphere again.

Could I get my hands on the launch portal deck fast enough to push myself up into a handstand position? But it wouldn't be just a matter of setting my hands—I'd have to raise the whole upper part of my body through the opening, and I doubted my arm muscles were up to the task. Even if they were, it was even less likely that Selene could pull it off, especially not without practice, and even more especially not knowing what was going to happen or what was expected of her.

"Roarke?"

I turned. Geri had finished his cursory examination and was striding around the sphere toward me. The second batch of Iykams had landed and were also on the move in our direction. "Stop daydreaming," he ordered softly, "and get that hammer drill ready."

"Right," I murmured back.

And with that, we were out of time.

I had no idea what the plan was. But Ixil had to

know that, and was presumably ready for it. My choices came down to trusting him and Graym-Barker, and possibly dying here and now, or not trusting them and dying later when Geri realized he'd been betrayed.

Selene was looking at me, that quiet trust still filling her pupils. I took her in my arms, gently maneuvering her as close to the opening as I could, making sure were on the side where the plate wouldn't break our ankles when it did its tennis-backhand snap opening.

"Roarke?" Geri demanded. "What the hell are you doing?"

I took a deep breath. "Artichoke," I said.

And as the plate snapped open, I tightened my arms around Selene, lifted her a few centimeters off the deck, and leaped us both into the opening.

I heard her gasp as we dropped through into the launch module—felt the clashing gravities trying to push me in opposite directions—got a glimpse of Geri's suddenly widened eyes and furious expression—saw the Iykams fumbling for their sidearms—felt my death and Selene's inexorably nearing as our initial momentum began to slow—

And then, something closed viselike around my calves. Before I could even begin to wonder what was happening every bone in my body seemed to creak simultaneously as I was yanked straight up into the launch module. I got a glimpse of large feet beside me; on the other side of the interface I saw Geri raise his arm to point accusingly at me—

The plate snapped closed as quickly as it had opened, cutting off my view. An instant later an additional plate, this one new and shiny and just as fast as the other one, snapped shut on the launch module side.

"Hands on the deck, please," Ixil's calm voice came from above me.

Taking another deep breath, I unwrapped my arms from around Selene—I hadn't noticed until then that I was still holding tightly onto her—and set my palms on the plate now directly beneath us. "Thank you," Ixil said, and eased me down.

"I think the thanks are going the wrong direction," I said as I brought my arms in, ducking my head and rolling off my shoulders as Ixil lowered me the rest of the way down. Selene was being lowered with the same care, and I was finally able to see far enough past her to recognize that our New Sandio Starr-Comm acquaintance Jennifer was working that half of the rescue.

"Hardly," Ixil said, offering me a hand. I took it and he helped me back to my feet. "After all, you were the one who came up with this plan in the first place."

"Well, there *is* that," I said. It hadn't *exactly* been my plan, of course. But on the other hand, I *had* pointed Ixil the right direction. Under the circumstances, it seemed reasonable for the two of us to share the credit.

As my father used to say, *If you're going to get blamed for things you didn't do—and you will—don't be afraid to take credit you don't deserve, either.*

"Nice to see you again, Jennifer," I said, nodding toward her. "Still thinking about shooting us?"

She wrinkled her nose as if she was still considering it. "Probably not. Really, the moment's passed."

"Well, it's best not to focus on past regrets," I said. "Okay. What now?"

"You two head to Icarus," Ixil said. He nodded

toward a newly installed monitor that showed the inside of the receiver module, where a bunch of angry Iykams were crowding around the hatch plate. From the angle, I could tell that the camera was set in or near the misaligned section Geri had been so interested in earlier. "I think we've got things handled here, and Jordan's waiting on you."

"Waiting for me to say *the word*, I suppose," I commented. Not one of my better jokes. "Incidentally, I don't want to worry you, but Geri probably has some blast cord with him."

"He won't use it," Jennifer assured me as she walked to one of the control panels and touched a couple of squares, turning them from red to blue. She returned to the receiver module monitor and pulled a mic from one side of it. "Excuse me a second."

She touched another key. "Attention, Geri and the rest of the Patth force," she called. "Attention. A couple of things you need to know. Point one: you are not, repeat *not*, in Icarus. I've just opened the viewports out there, and you can see for yourselves that we're in deep space, in a portal thousands of light-years away from any known point in the Spiral. We've been studying it for six years, and we still don't know where it is."

On the monitor, the activity had come to a slightly confused halt as the Iykams took that in. The ones nearest the small viewports that Jennifer had opened peered through them, and I saw one of them turn and say something in Geri's direction. "So if you break through into the launch module and wreck anything, you're dead," Jennifer continued. "Not by our hand, but because if you break the portal there's literally no way for anyone to find you and get you out."

One of the Iykams grabbed at Geri's shoulder, and I could see his mouth moving behind his faceplate. Geri said something back, the Iykam responded, and abruptly Geri grabbed his arm and twisted, throwing the Iykam onto his back on the deck. Two more Iykams started to move toward him, backed off as Geri and three of the others snapped their weapons warningly from their holsters.

"Second point," Jennifer went on, a rather mischievous smile playing at her lips. "If you ignore all of this and decide to break in anyway, bear in mind that we've taken the liberty of adding some acetylene to the atmosphere out there. It's not especially toxic, at least not short-term, but I wouldn't recommend lighting up a cutting torch or blast cord or anything of that sort. But if you feel the need to test it yourselves, be my guest."

Our view of Geri's force was suddenly blocked as a fresh batch of Iykams appeared in the center of the sphere. Geri looked up as the newcomers started to drift toward the surface, and while Jennifer's camera wasn't quite good enough to show his expression I had no trouble guessing what it looked like.

"I don't know how many of you are coming," Jennifer said, "but don't worry, there's plenty of room for all. Feel free to sit down, lie down, take off your boots— just make yourselves comfortable. If all goes according to plan, someone from Firefall will be along in a few hours to take you back home. If not . . . well. Let's just hope it all goes according to plan." She started to put the mike back, then stopped. "Oh, and if you want to scream or curse or whatever, feel free to do that, too. I won't hear you, but it's good for the digestion."

She put the mic back. As she did so, and as the

newest batch of Iykams floated out of our line of sight, Geri raised his Libra and send a burst of slugs at the camera. There was a single flicker, and the monitor went black.

"I'm rather surprised he heard you out," Ixil commented. "I assumed he'd be more impulsive."

"Maybe he's mellowing in his old age," Jennifer said, turning off the now useless monitor and walking over to the destination control panel. "Come on, Roarke. Nothing more to see here, and they're waiting on you and Selene."

"What about you?" I asked, looking doubtfully at the inner hatch plate. "If they really want to get in, those plates aren't going to stop them."

"Don't worry, I'll have plenty of time to cut and run if I need to," she assured me. "You, too, Ixil. Icarus, party of three."

"I thought you wanted me to stay with you," Ixil said, his ferrets twitching in unison.

"That was before I saw their limited collection of party favors," Jennifer said with a hint of amused disdain. "Nothing I need to worry about."

"They may have heavier stuff coming in," I warned. "They're supposed to be assaulting a bunker-class facility, remember?"

"Right, but I doubt they'll bring a jackhammer," she said, "and anything nonmechanical will light up their air. If I hear a *whoosh* I'll know it's time to bug out."

"And you've erased the *artichoke* trigger?"

"That was always only keyed to your voiceprint," Jennifer said. "Look, we can chat about this later over a cola. Right now, you need to get moving. We let McKell doze off, and we'll never get him to wake up."

"There *is* that," Ixil agreed, putting one hand on my shoulder and the other on Selene's and gently pushing us toward the extension arm. "I hope that wasn't too frightening for you, Selene," he said. "From the expression on your face, I assume Gregory wasn't able to properly describe the sensations involved."

"I wasn't really given much of a chance," I said, feeling a little defensive. I looked sideways at Selene— "And I probably wouldn't have done a very good job even if I had," I conceded.

"It's all right," Selene assured me. "I'll admit it was confusing. Perhaps a bit frightening."

She leaned forward to look past Ixil at me, and to my surprise I saw a shimmering of sheer delight in her pupils. "But mostly, it was glorious."

CHAPTER TWENTY-SEVEN

———— ◆◆◆ ————

The first time I'd popped into Icarus there'd been six armored Kalixiri soldiers waiting, lying comfortably in the receiver module with their eyes and laser rifles pointed on guard at the sphere's center. This time, the three of us arrived to find the welcoming committee had quadrupled in size. Most of them were standing instead of lying, checking gear or talking earnestly among themselves, but there were still six sentries lying on the deck, ready to french-fry anyone who blundered in.

At least this time there was no need for anyone to call for McKell. He was right there in the middle of the pack, dressed in full EarthGuard assault armor, peering up at us as we started drifting down. I reached over and took Selene's hand, pulling her close so we would land together instead of at different parts of the sphere. Not that I was worried about her, but right now I really didn't want to face McKell alone.

But for the moment, he had eyes only for Ixil. "I thought you were staying with Jennifer," he called.

"She thought you needed me more than she did," Ixil called back. "The trap worked exactly as planned."

"As did the rescue, I see," McKell said, shifting his attention to Selene and me. "Glad to see you both. Any problems?"

"Not yet," I said. "But it's early."

"That it is," he agreed. "Your combat suit is waiting outside."

"Fine," I said, watching the deck as we neared the spot where the gravity would kick back up to full power. Selene already had her knees bent slightly in anticipation of our landing, and I bent my own. "Did you get anything from Ixil's ferret?"

"Pix?" McKell nodded. "Yes, quite a lot. With the visuals he brought back, we were able to figure out the key spots for taking out the lights and alarms and making sure the blast doors stay open. Nice distractions, by the way."

"Thanks," I said. Our gentle drop abruptly became less gentle, and Selene and I landed with a double thud. "Is the other team in position?"

"We assume so," McKell said. "They can't exactly tap into the Bonvere Seven communications array, so we don't have any direct communication with them. But if they're on schedule, they'll be ready as soon as we hit the portal."

"Right," I said, grimacing. As my father used to say, *People who firmly believe in schedules probably also believe in the tooth fairy.* But in this case, there really weren't any alternatives. "You've got someone who can take Selene where she can rest?"

McKell nodded. "The admiral said he'd be honored if she would wait with him."

"No," Selene said. "I have to come with you."

"Not safe," I said firmly. "We'll be using—"

"I have to," she cut me off. "When Nask took me out of the cell he told the others to move Tera."

I shot a look at McKell. "Move her where?"

"I don't know," Selene said. "That's why I have to go. I'm the only one who can find her."

Ixil had joined us in time for that last bit. "Jordan, she can't be with us," he said firmly. "I saw firsthand how the Snowblind gas affected her."

"Is that what you used in Havershem City?" Selene asked.

"Yes, to break up the hunter packs who had Tera pinned down," I confirmed. "Ixil's right. If she's with us we can't use it. Or any other gases."

"What if we give her breathing gear for the first stage?" McKell asked. "She could take it off once we've cleared the work cavern."

I shook my head. "Some of the stuff's bound to leak out into the rest of the complex."

"Is there any chance the receiver module will be empty?" Ixil asked.

"It was pretty damn busy in there when we left," I told him. "Nask had at least four waves of nine Iykams each, and he could have more waiting in line after that. At four soldiers per trip, that's going to take a while."

"They're only sending four at a time?" McKell asked, frowning.

"That was what we saw in Alpha," Ixil confirmed.

"Nask isn't sure whether you have to grab the gray end or can just touch it," I explained.

McKell muttered a curse. "A touch is all you need," he growled. "Not to mention that the launch module seems to recognize how many are on their way up the arm and waits to launch until everyone's in position. We've sent up to twelve at a time without trouble."

"Well, unless you want to send Nask a memo, I think we're stuck with the long line," I said.

McKell huffed out a breath, his eyes on Selene. Then, reluctantly, he shook his head. "No," he said. "If Firefall is occupied and we try to pop in there without dropping a gas cloud first, it's going to degenerate into a slaughter. That's not what any of us want."

"You'll be coming in above them," I reminded him. "They're all standing up, heads pointed at the center. They'll never even see you coming."

"Maybe you missed what I said a minute ago," McKell said tartly. "We don't want a slaughter. On *either* side."

"Then what about Tera?"

McKell's throat worked. "We'll just have to hope we can keep Nask too busy to think about using her as a shield."

I looked at Selene, wincing at the fear and frustration in her pupils. "Please," she said. "I promised Tera I'd look after her. I—" She looked at me, the fear increasing.

I sighed. "Fine," I said. "How are you supposed to signal the commando team to attack? Assuming they're actually there, of course?"

"I have a beacon," McKell said, frowning at me. "I'll trigger it as soon as we hit Firefall."

I nodded and held out my hand. "Give it to me."

"We're going in at the same time," McKell reminded me.

"No, we're not," I said, still holding out my hand. "I'm going in first."

McKell and Ixil exchanged looks. "Excuse me?" Ixil asked carefully.

"You need to clear out the sphere and get Nask out of the way," I reminded them. "You send me in, I'll do that, and you can follow."

"How?" McKell asked.

"As quickly and non-slaughtery as possible," I said, more harshly than I'd intended. Charging in with a hasty and barely half-baked plan wasn't my idea of a good time.

But considering the likely size of Nask's labyrinth, having McKell's team hunt for Tera blind would take a bigger chunk of forever than any of us could afford. "And I won't need that combat suit," I added, "so you can let Selene wear it."

"All right," McKell said, pulling out a small disk the size of a poker chip and handing it to me. "It's ready to go—just squeeze the center and it'll send the signal. Wait a couple of seconds, trigger it a second time, and then rotate the outer ring a quarter turn to turn it inert. That way, if they scan you for transmitters or electronics, they won't see anything."

"Got it," I said, sliding the disk into my jacket pocket. Whatever else McKell might be, at least he knew how to make quick decisions.

Of course, the fact that I was the most expendable person in the room might have had something to do with it.

"I assume you'll want a weapon?" he asked.

"You assume wrong," I said, turning toward the opening into the launch module. "I'll call in the commandos as soon as I arrive. Give me fifteen minutes, then feel free to join me."

I got two steps before Selene caught my hand. "Gregory?" she asked, her pupils now shimmering with fear.

"I'll be fine, Selene," I said, touching her cheek. "You just focus on getting McKell to Tera."

"I'll find her," she promised. She hesitated, then to my surprise moved close for a quick hug. "Be careful."

"I will," I assured her, watching McKell out of the corner of my eye. He was still just looking thoughtful and wary. But then, he wouldn't know that hugging wasn't something Kadolians normally did. Maybe she was overcome with the moment. Maybe she was hoping that kind of human gesture would help inspire me.

Maybe she was just saying goodbye.

I broke the hug, smiled at her, then continued my march around the sphere toward the launch module. "Get her suited up, McKell," I called over my shoulder. "And whatever you do, do *not* be late to the party."

Earlier, the Firefall receiver module had been a hive of activity, with groups of Iykam soldiers checking equipment, getting last-minute instructions, and lining up for their turn to blast their way across the universe. Now, half an hour later, the scene below me was pretty much the same, except maybe more so. As I'd predicted, no one was paying the slightest bit of attention above them.

And really, why would they? The only way anyone could appear up here was if they came from Icarus, and as far as any of them knew Geri and his team had Icarus all sewn up.

Time to disabuse them of that idea. As my father used to say, *When you think about it, really,* most *kinds of awakenings are rude ones.*

I slipped the signaling disk out of my pocket, squeezed it twice, then deactivated it and put it away again. Hoping that no one down there had really extraordinary combat reflexes, I stretched my arms out to the sides, spread my fingers wide to show they were empty, and filled my lungs. "Hey!" I shouted. "Someone down there get me Sub-Director Nask!"

The Iykams had reflexes, all right. Fortunately, most of them were to look wildly around and then twist their necks up to gawk at me. Only two of the responses included bringing weapons to bear, and both of the Iykams behind those weapons were experienced enough not to impulsively fire off any gratuitous shots. "Don't just stand there, you idiots—I need Sub-Director Nask," I called, maintaining my harmless-human pose. *"Now!"*

"What are you doing here?" Nask's voice came from behind me.

I flailed around in free fall and managed to get myself turned around. Nask was standing by the interface between the two spheres, looking up at me. His usual pair of bodyguards was absent, though with a small army of armed Iykams milling around him any extra security would have been pretty superfluous.

"Geri sent me," I said. "I need to talk to you."

"Talk quickly," he ordered. "I'm busy sending him more forces."

"Don't let me stop you," I said. "In fact, you can speed it up—they only need to touch the end of the arm, not grab it. Run them through as fast as you can; I'm guessing you can get eight to twelve across at a time."

"What's the matter?" Nask asked, gesturing the nearest group of Iykams to the interface. "Is something wrong?"

"Is *something* wrong?" I echoed harshly. "No; *everything's* wrong. Geri got the analysis chamber locked down fine, but then someone bumped an alarm or something and a whole swarm of soldiers popped up out of nowhere. He got one of the hellspawns launched out through the blast doors, but that just incinerated the first batch and there was another batch right behind them. Now he's pinned down in the chamber, the second hellspawn misfired—"

I broke off as I landed, grunting a little with the impact. "Bottom line: He needs more troops, and he needs them *now*."

"I already said they were on their way," Nask said, leaning over the opening. "Ten at a time, you say?"

"Ten at a time," I confirmed. "They just have to wait until the last group is out of the way—it won't send anyone else through as long as there's something solid in the middle."

"Ten at a time," Nask called into the launch module. "They just need to be touching the gray." He straightened up and pointed at the Iykams still standing around the receiver module looking uncertain. "All of you—*go*."

"Thank you," I said, shying back as armored Iykams rushed past me on both sides in response to Nask's order.

"What about the other Expediters' attack force?" Nask asked. "Have they penetrated Icarus yet?"

"Yeah, that's the other bad news," I ground out. "Geri hasn't been able to contact them."

"Not at *all*?"

"Not even a whisper," I said. Which wasn't surprising, given that the Hoshshima attack squad was dozens or even hundreds of light-years away from Icarus at the moment, which put them seriously out of range of even the most upscale radio on the market. "I thought you said you were in contact with them."

"We are," Nask said, pulling out his phone and punching in a number. He spoke a few words in the Patth language, then stopped, waiting silently.

I leaned over a little, just far enough to see through the opening into the launch module. The Iykams had taken Nask at his word, and were floating up the extension arm in tight clumps instead of the single-file approach Geri, Selene, and I had used.

"The Expediter reported ten minutes ago that they'd breached the outer door and were going in," Nask said, putting away the phone. "You say you were with Geri at that time?"

I thought back. Ten minutes ago . . . yes, I was still in Icarus. "Yes."

"And he'd received no word?"

"That's what he told me," I said. "But he was pretty busy at the time—it's possible he missed the call. What have they told you since then?"

"Nothing," Nask said, his voice going dark. "There's been no word since that report."

I stared at him, a cold chill running up my back. McKell hadn't said anything about taking out the other Patth force. All that talk about avoiding slaughter . . .

"How do you know only a touch is needed?" Nask cut into my thoughts.

I dragged my mind back from images of dead

Iykams lying twisted on the ground with a gloating McKell standing over them. "It was the second team through after ours," I said. "One of them told Geri that he'd lost his grip on the arm and had just been touching it when they were transported. I tried it on my way back here, just to be sure. It works."

"Good," Nask said. "If we can get reinforcements there quickly enough—" He broke off as a high-pitched trilling wafted up through the opening to the work cavern.

"What's that?" I asked.

"The alarm," he bit out, leaning over the interface opening and shouting more Patth orders into the launch module. Someone in there answered in the same language—

And then Nask pulled out his phone again and rushed past me at a speed I hadn't known he was capable of, heading straight for the opening out into the work cavern. "What can I do?" I asked, charging after him.

He didn't answer, his full attention on his phone and the rapid-fire orders he was barking. I caught up with him as he dropped through the opening, using the handholds only to adjust his balance, and rushed out of view. I dropped to the deck and rolled through the opening, also skipping the handholds, and hit the cavern floor running.

Nask was already halfway to one of the monitor stations along the wall, a station that was flashing a lot of red lights at the moment. His two bodyguards had reappeared from somewhere and were racing along beside him, trying to keep up. As I headed off after them, another eight Iykams appeared from outside the blast doors, also heading toward Nask's target station. The Patth operator seated there was leaning over his controls, rattling off more orders or questions as his fingers darted over the control board. The displays over the board didn't mean much to me, but I was pretty sure that the whole system was announcing the arrival of Graym-Barker's commando squad.

And now came the trickiest part of this whole plan. The part where, if I was going to die today, it would probably happen. Nask had stopped by the station and was talking back and forth with the operator, the rest of the crowd forming up around him. "Let me through," I said in my most commanding voice. "Let me through. I can help."

Nask wouldn't have fallen for it. But Nask was pre-occupied with the invasion of his fortress and didn't have any attention to spare for the supposedly secure area around him. The Iykams, under normal circumstances, probably wouldn't have fallen for it, either.

But these circumstances weren't normal. The wailing alarm had dropped everyone into crisis mode, and the normal reaction of soldiers in crisis mode was to obey any order that came at them with sufficient authority. Like magic, the crowd melted away before my advance, breaking to either side to let me through. I passed between them, coming up right behind Nask—

And as I passed the last Iykam I darted out my right hand, grabbed his corona gun, and twisted it out of his grip. Taking a final step up behind Nask, I wrapped my left arm solidly around his throat and pressed the muzzle of my newly acquired weapon into his back. "Just stand easy, Sub-Director," I said. "Back them off, or die a really horrible death."

He tried to turn around, stopped as I tightened my arm across his throat. "No one needs to die here," I soothed. "I don't want you dead, and I certainly don't want *me* dead. All I want is Tera."

"Tera?"

"Tera," I repeated. "Human, dark haired, smarter than either of us expected. Your other hostage."

"I know who she is," Nask said coldly. "What do you want with her?"

"To leave," I said. "Take me to her, bring us back here, and that'll be the end of it. We'll be gone, you'll still have Firefall, and everyone will be happy."

"What about Icarus?"

"That's in Geri's hands," I said. "I don't really much care what happens to it. Actually, I'd rather enjoy seeing McKell's face as he hands you the keys to the place."

"Then help us."

"I'll help by taking Tera and getting out of your way," I said. "McKell's got his troubles, Geri has his, and you've got yours. Right now, your biggest problem is that your guards are all sporting corona guns, and as long as I'm standing right beside you they can't deep-fry me without also deep-frying you."

"You stand in the same stalemate," Nask reminded me.

"Yeah, but I'm not nearly as important to the universe as a Patth sub-director," I pointed out. "You need to stay alive, if only to keep your enemies from crowing triumphantly over your grave. Tell me I'm wrong."

Nask didn't reply. But I felt a fresh stiffening of his throat against my forearm that showed I had not, in fact, been wrong. Upper-level Patth rivalries were apparently strong enough to even last beyond the grave. "Only the human?" he asked.

"Only the human."

"My guards won't permit you to take me away from them."

"They're more than welcome to tag along," I assured him. "In fact, bring the whole gang if you want. Just tell them not to crowd me."

"They will stay back," Nask promised.

"I hope so," I said. "You might also remind them that I had my left arm burned off with a plasmic and still got off a shot at my attacker. A little story to remind them that there's nothing they can hit me with fast enough to stop me from killing you, too."

"No one will attack you." He straightened up and made an abbreviated gesture toward the blast doors. "This way. I'll take you to the other human."

During our enforced stay in Firefall I'd walked the path between the hangar and the portal chamber, the path between our original group cell and the portal, and finally between my last solitary cell and the portal. Just traveling in those areas had shown that the whole complex was pretty extensive.

I'd had no idea how big the damn place really was.

I'd assumed Nask would head back toward our cells. Instead, he pointed me to a corridor branching off the work cavern, one I'd never been in before. We passed a lot of doors, plus a few open areas equipped with tables and chairs and food service counters. The corridor itself had a fair number of zigzags to it, along with an occasional blind corner.

The doors, the furnishings, and the layout made it clear that we were in the Iykam barracks.

Under other conditions, that could have been a

very bad thing. But as we passed the second lounge area and I noted the disorganized positions of chairs and cups I realized the place had been emptied, the soldiers either gone down the Firefall rabbit hole with Geri or else rushed to the ramparts to repel Graym-Barker's commandos.

Though just because there were no reinforcements to be had here didn't mean I was remotely in the clear. Nask's bodyguards were hovering about a meter to my left and right, the farthest they were willing to go, and trailing along at a respectful distance behind us were every damn Patth and Iykam who'd been in the chamber when I made my move. If I'd ever had any tendencies toward loneliness, this would probably have cured me for good.

"How much farther?" I asked as we eased around the sixth zigzag and I felt some of my tension ease as, once more, we found no one waiting in a blind spot to ambush us.

"Are you tired?" Nask asked in a rather snide tone. Maybe he was getting as tired of having a corona gun in his back as I was of holding it there. "We can stop and rest if you need to."

I grunted. "Just keep walking."

We'd reached and successfully rounded the next corner when I began to hear the sounds of distant weapon fire.

"What's that?" I asked, digging the corona gun a little deeper into Nask's back.

He made a rude-sounding gurgle. "Have you so soon forgotten your desperate and futile attack against us?"

"We're near the exit?" I asked, frowning. "And you stashed Tera *here*?"

"In a barracks, surrounded by the finest soldiers the Patthaaunutth have at their disposal?" Nask countered. "Certainly." He half turned his head. "Do you then fear to approach the scene of a battle?"

I focused on the sounds wafting back to us. Sporadic fire, mostly plasmics but a couple of laser rifles as well. Occasional quiet orders, but no shouts or screams. "Seems to me more of a standoff than a battle," I pointed out. Still, that being said, walking into a situation where stressed people were pointing guns at each other was never a good idea. "Where is she?"

"In a room beyond this blast door casing," he said, nodding ahead to a pair of bulky, coffin-sized boxes sticking a few centimeters into our corridor on both sides.

I craned my neck to the side. Just beyond the casings was another shallow bend, and I could just make out a group of Iykams kneeling behind a barrier firing rhythmic bursts of plasmic fire at something out of sight farther down the corridor.

For a moment I pondered my options. I'd have a better view once we passed the blast doors, but of course then I'd also be open to a stray shot from Graym-Barker's side or a more deliberately aimed shot from Nask's.

But I had no choice but to keep going. "Let's go," I said, nudging Nask forward. We reached the casings and started to pass between them—

My brain had just enough time to see that there were no doors set into the casings, but rather a pair of vertical rows of some sort of spoutlike projectors, when Nask was violently thrown against the left casing and I was just as violently slammed into the right.

The impact wrenched the corona gun out of my grip, sending it flying. An instant later I was pinned to the wall, pressed there like I was lying helpless in the gravity of some gas giant planet.

And then, as suddenly as the sideways weight had appeared, it was gone. I staggered as normal gravity resumed, managing not to fall on my face, and looked across the corridor at Nask.

He was smiling, a happy, beaming smirk that told me everything I needed to know. "Let me guess," I said, panting a little as my lungs recovered. "Directed repulsor projectors?"

"Of course," he said, readjusting his robe and reaching down to retrieve the corona gun I'd dropped. He certainly didn't have to worry about me getting there first—with every Iykam in our impromptu entourage having now sprouted weapons, I wasn't in a position to do anything except continue breathing. Assuming Nask let me do even that much. "We installed them as a defense against a line of invaders," he continued, eyeing the corona gun a moment and then passing it to one of his bodyguards. "Something to interfere with a charge and allow us to counterattack."

"Nice," I said. "Inevitable, really. After you've put enough effort into a new technology, you usually find lots of other uses for it."

"But now, I have a dilemma," Nask said. "Do I let you continue onward, walking into the standoff, as you call it, under the assumption the invaders will hesitate to shoot you and thus make them more vulnerable to our counterattack? Do I continue to hold you hostage, though I'm not certain who would pay for your return?"

His satisfied smile disappeared. "Or do I save you for Geri, who has already expressed a deep desire to kill you?"

"Interesting options," I said. Had that been the faint flicker of a shadow on the wall in the direction we'd just come from? "Let me see if I can help you work through them. Let's start with you. We've already established that a sub-director is one of the most valuable Patth in the whole Spiral, correct?"

His eyes narrowed slightly. "We have."

"Then there are the Iykams," I went on. "I imagine you have a decently large pool of them to choose from. But as you said, these are the best, and trained soldiers aren't something you simply toss away. Also correct?"

Nask's gaze flicked toward the standoff down the corridor. "Dying in the defense of the Patthaaunutth is an honor."

"But surely dying for nothing is just plain wasteful," I argued. "Especially since I assume the Iykams are sort of common property, available to any director or sub-director who needs them."

"You waste my time, Roarke," Nask said. "The invaders won't succeed. Certainly no Iykams will die in vain."

"That's up to you, really," I said. "And you're looking in the wrong direction."

I'd ended up just around the last bend in the corridor, and couldn't actually see anything behind him. But the sudden freezing of his expression told me all I needed to know. Pushing myself off the wall, I crossed to the other side of the corridor for a better look.

They were there, just as I'd hoped and expected: McKell and Ixil in front, kneeling with three other

Kalixiri, their plasmics trained on Nask and the others, with a standing row of soldiers behind them, this group a mix of human and Kalixiri, also with plasmics and laser rifles aimed.

And sandwiched between the front lines and a wary rearguard, almost lost to sight between the crush of large Kalixiri bodies, were Selene and Tera.

"Like I said, dying for nothing is wasteful," I said quietly, stepping over to Nask's bodyguards and holding out my hands. "If they'd wanted you dead, you'd already be dead."

For a long moment Nask didn't move or speak. But he didn't have to. He'd already convinced himself he needed to survive for the good of his people. Lowering his head, he made a small gesture.

Silently, the Iykams set their weapons on the floor. One of Nask's bodyguards dropped his corona gun into my outstretched hand, while the other apparently decided surrendering his weapon was too demeaning and instead simply dropped it on the floor.

"McKell?" I prompted, tucking the corona gun into the back of my belt as I nodded my head behind me toward the still oblivious Iykams in their standoff.

McKell nodded and gestured. The two rows of soldiers behind him dissolved their formation and slipped in single-file past him, the Iykams, Nask, and me, heading toward the standoff. "Don't worry," McKell advised Nask. "Once they're in a pincer and we've disabled the autodefenses we'll call on them to surrender. As Roarke said, there's no need to waste any lives here."

Nask turned his bitter-edged gaze from McKell to me. He wouldn't ask, I knew, but he was dying to know.

That was okay. He'd done a lot of gloating earlier after Tera fed him the wrong portal address. It was only fair that I took my own turn.

"I was pretty sure you'd lead me away from Tera," I said as Ixil began organizing the Iykams for a prisoner march back to the main chamber. "I was also sure you'd bring anyone we happened to find along the way. Between that and rushing all those troops to help Geri, we figured most of Firefall would be empty. Especially with the commando squad out there pinning down everyone else," I added, again nodding back toward the standoff. "With a clear base, and knowing what Tera and I both smelled like, Selene had no problem leading McKell's team first to her and then to me."

"I could have killed you," Nask said, the calmness in his voice somehow scarier than full-blown fury would have been. "When you first assaulted me."

"You could have," I agreed. "But I knew you wouldn't. Why risk your life when you knew you were leading me into a trap?" I waved at the disguised repulsor projectors. "Though I have to admit I never saw that particular trap coming."

"And Geri?" Nask asked. "Was that talk of slaughter merely talk?"

"Not at all," I assured him. "Geri and the other soldiers are alive and well. Unless they've started shooting each other out of pure frustration. You see, Tera didn't give you the address to Icarus. You obligingly sent them all instead to another portal way the hell off at the edge of nowhere. Once we have all of your people here secured—"

I paused, listening. The earlier sporadic gunfire

and occasional Iykam voices were gone. In their place were equally quiet human and Kalixiri voices, and a *lot* of the soft zipping sound of wrist restraints. "Which would seem to be imminent," I continued, "we'll send someone to fetch them. Probably Freki, who I assume is in charge of the rampart defenses. And once they're back, it'll all be over."

Nask's eyes bored into mine. "No," he said. "Not yet."

I looked at McKell, who was walking among the prisoners and double-checking their restraints. "You're right," I agreed, a lump forming in my throat. "Not yet."

CHAPTER TWENTY-EIGHT

—— ❖ ——

It was pretty obvious that Freki was less than enthusiastic about his assignment. But at least he seemed able to look at the half-full part of bringing a fellow Expediter and a whole bunch of valuable Iykam soldiers back alive. McKell loaded him with wrist restraints, gave him the code to get them through the hatch plate into the launch module, and went through the rules for how to proceed from there. Once we'd confirmed that Jennifer was safely back at Icarus, we sent him off to Alpha.

Ten minutes later, they started coming back.

I'd worried a little about this part, given that we had no idea what desperate schemes Geri might have come up with while sitting around seething. His troops had been armed to the ears, not to mention he still had his two hellspawn mortars. If he wanted to go out in a blaze of insane fury, launching a hellspawn from the center of the Firefall portal would be the way to do it. Wagnerian in scope, Ixil called it, whatever that meant. Geri could probably have explained it to me.

But for all my uneasiness, the repatriation went smoothly. They popped in four at a time, as Freki had been instructed, their wrists tied in front of them, their weapons and armor left behind. Ixil had organized a sentry squad of twenty Kalixiri commandos, lying ready in the Firefall receiver module, with another ten ready to check the returning Iykams for concealed weapons and to escort them to one of the holding tanks McKell had set up.

Selene and I were in the Firefall dining room, talking out what had just happened, when the major in command of Graym-Barker's attack force popped in to tell us that McKell and Tera wanted to see me.

We found them in the main chamber, watching from a few meters back as the returning Iykams were helped one by one out of the receiver module by yet another pair of Kalixiri commandos. "Hello, Gregory; Selene," Tera greeted us. She looked tired and a little pale, but the stress I'd seen in her earlier had faded considerably. "We wanted to thank you again for everything you've done."

"No problem," I said. "Granted, most of it wasn't exactly our idea. But no problem." I gestured at the Iykam currently struggling to get out of the opening with his wrists tied together. "We almost done?"

"If you're asking about the Iykams, yes," McKell said. "If you're asking about you and me, I think we still have some issues."

I focused on him, that terrible day five years ago once again flashing back. "Yes, we do," I said softly. "I seem to recall you making an agreement back at Icarus."

"What kind of agreement?" Selene asked.

"Your partner Roarke wants to kill me," McKell said evenly. "Or maybe he just wants to burn off my arm. The provisions of the deal weren't entirely clear."

Selene spun to face me, her eyes wide, her pupils blazing with disbelief and horror. "*Gregory?*"

"He knows what he did," I said, trying to match the calm fortitude in McKell's voice. I'd waited years for this chance, and it was *not* going to slip past me.

And yet, as I thought back over what we'd all been through, and what we'd all accomplished here, I could feel some of that resolve eroding. "The day we almost caught him, he ambushed us, burned off my arm, and nearly killed you."

"Yes, I thought that was probably it," McKell said. "The thing is, I didn't do it. In fact, I wasn't even there."

I snorted under my breath, the fading resolve leaping back again to full strength. Of all the feeble excuses he could have come up with... "Really," I growled, nodding toward the plasmic holstered at his hip. "That's not a plasmic?"

"Oh, it's a plasmic, all right," McKell said. "We'll get to that in a moment. The point is that, yes, you were tracking me. But by the time you reached that corner I'd already slipped away."

"Not a chance," I insisted. "Selene had your scent."

"Yes, she did," McKell agreed. "And by that time I'd heard of you and knew what I had to do." He pulled back his left sleeve and raised the arm. "See that?" he asked, running a finger down a five-centimeter-long patch of skin defined by an oval-shaped ring of scar tissue. "That's where I sliced off enough skin to hopefully keep Selene's sense of smell occupied while I made my retreat."

Tera gasped something. "Is *that* what happened to your arm?" she breathed. "You never told us."

"We had other things to worry about," McKell said, rolling the sleeve back down. "There's one other thing. Once I figured out that was why you'd bargained the admiral for me, I did a little research into the incident. You were shot with a plasmic and Selene with a 3 mil, correct?"

"Yes," I said cautiously.

"What sense does that make?" he asked. "Why would I fire a plasmic at you, then switch weapons in mid ambush and fire a 3 mil at Selene?"

I opened my mouth...closed it again. That question had never even occurred to me. "What are you saying?" I asked. "That there were two of them?"

"That's exactly what I'm saying," McKell said, his voice quiet and earnest. "I think what happened was that I was also being chased by another pair of bounty hunters. I think they got between us, saw you coming, and decided to eliminate the competition."

"Bounty hunters don't shoot each other," I growled. "We might wave off with a warning shot, but we never shoot to kill."

"Then maybe they weren't hunters," McKell said. "Maybe they were someone else. Someone who *really* wanted to grab me. Someone who thought nothing of killing in order to achieve that goal."

At the portal, Geri appeared, rolling awkwardly to the floor. The two Kalixiri stopped to grab him under his arms and help him back to his feet. He shrugged off their hands, spotted the four of us watching...

"And," McKell said quietly, "someone who knew

Selene's tracking skills from that incident, and who knew enough about them to hire you to find Tera."

I stared at Geri, watching his face turn to carved stone, a horrible mix of memories flashing across my mind.

I got off a shot, but it was wild and I missed completely.

You do know you can get models that are way stronger than human bone and muscle, right? Not to mention versions that can hold a knife or even a two-shot plasmic.

Geri in the Firefall receiver module, looking bitterly disappointed that I hadn't given him an excuse to shoot me in the back.

Geri in the Havershem City smoke attack, gripping a Libra 3mm semiauto, the caliber that had been used against Selene.

Geri pointing at me through the interface on Alpha just before Jennifer slammed the plate shut.

And now, Geri raising his bound hands to again point our direction—

"Watch it!" I snapped, my hand reflexively grabbing for the holstered gun I wasn't carrying. Cursing, I shifted my hand toward the corona gun still tucked into the small of my back, knowing full well that I'd never get to it in time, wondering if he would go for a quick kill or try for something more lingering.

Out of the corner of my eye I saw McKell grabbing for his own sidearm. But he didn't have time to bring it up, either. For the briefest fraction of a heartbeat I saw the indecision in Geri's eyes, the question of whether to kill the man who'd cost him his arm or the woman who'd played his game and beaten him at it.

The indecision ended. He shifted his aim slightly, bringing his hidden plasmic to bear on Tera. Beside me, McKell got his plasmic free of its holster—

And in a single smooth motion he hurled it underarm toward Geri's outstretched hand. A brilliant burst of plasma erupted from Geri's palm and slammed into the incoming weapon, blasting it into a blaze of metal and plastic.

Reflexively, Geri flinched back from the explosion, a spasm of pain showing that some of the blast or shrapnel had caught his hand or face. But even as the two Kalixiri at his sides instinctively stepped back and grabbed for their own weapons he was back on balance—

Or even a two-*shot plasmic.*

Once again, I thought he might go for me. Once again, his thirst for revenge against Tera was stronger. He steadied his arm back into firing position, no doubt secure in the knowledge that McKell's weapon was gone and that neither Kalixiri could get to him in time.

Unfortunately for him, in his overwhelming hatred for Tera he'd forgotten about me.

Back in the New Sandio Commons I'd had a taste of what a corona gun could do. Now, I got the full show.

It was every bit as horrible as I'd expected. A bluewhite sheath of electrical flame engulfed him, burning his skin and hair and sending him into a writhing frenzy of pain. For maybe a second he stayed more or less upright, then collapsed into a charred heap on the floor. Distantly, I wondered if he'd tried to scream as he died. But he really hadn't had the time.

I stared at the smoking body, only then aware of the sound of running footsteps behind me. I turned to see Selene racing as fast as she could toward the blast doors and the clearer air beyond them, her hands over her nose as she tried to block out the stench. Tera was right behind her, and as I watched she caught up with Selene and took her arm in support.

"She'll be all right?" McKell asked.

"Eventually," I said, watching as they disappeared down one of the corridors. "Sooner if there's a clean room or biosuit somewhere back there."

"If there is, Tera will find it," McKell said.

"Yeah," I said. "I still need to go help her."

"Of course," McKell said. "When you've got her settled, come back here. We should probably tell Nask about this."

"Wonderful," I said. "You're welcome to tell him without me."

"Thanks," McKell said dryly. "But I really think you should be there, too."

"I thought you probably would." I hesitated, looking down at the corona gun. But I really wasn't likely to need it again. "I'll be back as soon as I can," I said, handing him the weapon. "But really, feel free to start without me."

Nask, to my surprise, seemed to take the whole thing in stride.

"He was always full of hate," he mused as we watched the line of Patth and Iykams trudging into the transport he'd summoned to take them all off Bonvere Seven. A few hundred light-years across the Spiral on Hoshshima, a similar transport was loading the Iykam team that had been caught trying to raid an empty warehouse near Okan City. "Geri never understood that vengeance is a singularly unsatisfying meal."

"Mm," I said. Though that hadn't kept Nask from being willing to help him set the table for his hoped-for feast. "I don't suppose you'd be willing to give me the name of his partner at the time?"

"I don't have that information," Nask said. "It wasn't Freki, if that was your unspoken question. Freki has been with me for nine years, while Geri was only assigned for this single mission."

"Having told you he knew the perfect team to track down Tera, no doubt," McKell said.

"Yes," Nask said, eyeing me. "I would offer you the same advice I did him."

"I appreciate that," I said. And despite all he'd put me through, I found I genuinely did. "But there's no need. Losing my arm was traumatic, but I've long since accepted it. It was Selene's near death I was never able to forgive."

"Really," Nask said. "An interesting ranking of priorities." He shifted his attention to McKell. "As were yours," he added. "Finding Firefall and defeating me, balanced against the possible death of your friend."

McKell shrugged. "Tera thought it was worth it," he said. "Which isn't to say she didn't have to fight tooth and claw to get the rest of us to agree."

"I imagine it was a sight to behold," Nask said dryly. "A shame it was all for nothing."

I pricked up my ears. "What?" I asked cautiously.

"This facility is Patthaaunutth property," he said, waving a hand around the hangar. "The Director General has surely already filed a complaint with the Commonwealth Judiciary requesting that you withdraw your people and return everything to Patthaaunutth control." He smiled. "Including, of course, Firefall itself."

McKell cleared his throat. "Actually, I'm afraid it's the Patth who'll be on the receiving end of any injunctions," he said, sounding almost apologetic. "You see, we own Bonvere Seven."

Nask's face went rigid. "What?" he asked softly.

"We own the planet," McKell repeated. "Three days ago we filed the claimant papers and put the billion-commark development guarantee into escrow. Thirty-six hours ago"—he consulted his watch—"make that thirty-six and a half hours ago we were granted title."

"Nice," I said, my estimation of the whole Icarus team going up yet another notch. "And of course the title includes lands, resources, *and* any unknown alien artifacts to be found within the near-space boundary."

"This facility is *not* an alien artifact," Nask insisted angrily.

"You're absolutely right," McKell agreed. "And we'll be more than happy to either buy it from you or disassemble it and take it wherever you want. But the Firefall portal *is* such an artifact, and as of thirty-six hours ago—"

"Thirty-six and a half," I muttered.

"—thirty-six and a half," McKell corrected, "it's ours."

For a moment he and Nask stared at each other. "This will not stand," the Patth said coldly. "We found the portal. It is *ours*."

"You're welcome to file a complaint," McKell said. "But you need to ask yourself if you really want the rest of the Spiral knowing about these things. Because if you bring it into open court, they will."

"What does that matter now?" Nask spat.

"It matters," McKell said, "because I don't think Icarus and Firefall are the only portals out there. And if there *are* more . . ." He left the sentence unfinished.

"I see," Nask said, his anger and frustration fading just a little. "And you think the Patthaaunutth will simply allow you any such prizes?"

"That's up to you," McKell said. "Personally, I'd look forward to a quiet Easter egg hunt between you and us."

"Perhaps," Nask said. The frustration had burned itself out now, and I could see he was seeing the personal consequences of not only losing Icarus but Firefall as well.

The Patth might indeed not give up on McKell's Easter egg hunt. But Nask knew he was unlikely to be the one in charge of that operation.

The last of the Patth and Iykams had disappeared into the transport now. Freki, who'd been at the end of the line, was standing by the hatch, looking expectantly at his boss. "I offer farewell," Nask said, scraping together all the dignity he could, and turned toward the ship.

I sighed. Nask had threatened to kill me. He'd threatened to let Geri kill me. He'd threatened Tera, and Selene, and pretty much everyone else I knew.

Still, I'd faced enough failure in my life to know how he felt.

And as my father used to say, *Better to keep the enemies you already know than spend a lot of time breaking in new ones.*

"One other thing," I called after him.

Reluctantly, probably expecting a final jibe, he turned around. "Yes?"

"You remember, oh, about four years ago there was talk that the Patth were going to license some non-Patth pilots for the Talariac Drive?" I asked.

"Those were rumors," Nask said stiffly. "There were never any such plans."

"Right," I said. "Or if there were, they were dropped once you realized what you had in Firefall. The thing is, some director or sub-director out there didn't give up on the idea."

"Really," he said. I definitely had his interest now, I saw, enough to show that the alleged plan *hadn't* been just a rumor. "Why do you say that?"

"One of my associates, a man named Luko Varsi, has had some preparatory facial work done," I told him. "At first I thought he was setting up for plastic surgery to alter his appearance, but after getting a closer look at your pilots I realized what the prep work was actually for. If that wasn't authorized by the Director General, I imagine he'd be most interested in finding out who went behind his back that way."

"He would indeed," Nask agreed, a hint of malicious anticipation in his voice. "I'll look into it."

Nodding at each of us, he turned and resumed his walk toward Freki and the waiting transport. "So that's why he was so interested in getting hold of Tera," McKell commented.

"*And* why he was doubling the Patth bounty," I said. "He was poised on the edge of having a unique access to the Talariac Drive and didn't want some newer and better version undercutting him."

"Hence, dead *or* alive," McKell said. "You might have mentioned that part to him."

"I thought about it," I said. "But then I realized that Tera's early demise might have wrecked his plans for Icarus, but would at least have left Firefall in Patth hands."

"Good point," McKell said. "Still, I think Varsi and his organization are in for some hard times."

"We can hope."

We waited until the transport hatch had closed, the roof overhead had retracted, and the repulsor boosts and perimeter grav beams did their technological magic to send the Patth ship into the sky. "So that's it?" I asked as the roof began to close again.

"Yes," McKell said, sounding suddenly very tired. Under the circumstances, I didn't blame him. "Now, it's over."

Only, as things turned out, it still wasn't.

CHAPTER TWENTY-NINE

◆

There really wasn't any reason Selene and I needed to go back to Icarus for a debriefing. McKell already knew most of the story, and any parts he didn't have Tera and Ixil could supply. As far as I was concerned, they owed us a pat on the back, a stack of commarks for our trouble, and a ride back to Kashmir to retrieve the *Ruth*.

But Admiral Graym-Barker had requested our presence, and apparently whatever Admiral Graym-Barker wanted he got.

Still, the EarthGuard ship they sent to bring us to his office was comfortable enough, and the food was good, and it was a good chance to catch up on my sleep. Besides, I'd always wanted to visit Earth.

McKell and Ixil had both managed to avoid the meeting. But Tera's footwork hadn't been as good, and she was waiting when we were ushered into Graym-Barker's office.

"Good to see you again, Mr. Roarke," the admiral greeted us as he motioned to a couple of chairs in front of his desk. "And you, Ms. Selene. I'm honored to finally make your acquaintance."

"And we're just as excited to be here," I said, keeping my sarcasm firmly in check. Most of it, anyway. As my father used to say, *Just because the crocodile is smiling doesn't mean he's your friend.* "I thought everyone was happy with our reports."

"Extremely happy," he said. "Though of course with a project as secretive as Icarus the number of people included in the term *everyone* is quite limited. But no, there's really just one point we need to clear up."

I sighed. And for a single unresolved point he needed to drag us halfway across the Commonwealth? "I'll do my best," I said.

"Actually, it's a question for Ms. Selene," he said, shifting his eyes to Selene. "I understand, Ms. Selene, that when you and the others first arrived at Firefall you presented an odd reaction."

"An odd reaction?" Selene asked, her pupils showing a frown.

"Yes," Tera said. "You were looking around as we walked from Nask's ship, and your"—she wiggled her fingers by her own nose—"nostrils, I guess, were quivering."

"I'm sorry if that distressed you," Selene apologized. "There was an odd smell in the air, and I was trying to identify it."

"Ah," Graym-Barker said, opening a decorative box on his desk and pulling out an old-style fountain pen. "*Were* you able to identify it?"

"Not really," Selene said. "But it was everywhere.

Low-level—very low-level—but I could still smell it if I concentrated."

"Had you ever smelled it before?" he asked, jotting something down on a paper in front of him in clipped, precise motions.

"No. Yes." Selene shook her head, her pupils starting to show frustration. "I don't know. With something that faint, it's very hard to tell."

"Probably something the Iykams had been eating," I put in. Selene didn't have many failures, but she took every single one of them very seriously. "Or drinking. Their choice of alcohol leaves a hell of a lot to be desired—"

I broke off as Selene gave a sudden gasp. "There!" she said, her nostrils and eyelashes going full speed. "There it is!"

"You mean this?" Graym-Barker asked. In that single instant his manner had gone from casual and friendly to something dark and deadly serious. He picked up the open box and moved it closer to Selene. "This in here?"

Selene nodded, still sniffing. "Yes. It's there."

"Oh, my God," Tera said softly.

I looked at her, noting that her expression was plumbing the same depths as Graym-Barker's. Unlike his, though, hers also held an edge of excitement.

"Enough," I bit out. "If you're trying to scare us, you've succeeded. What the hell is going on?"

"Tera?" Graym-Barker invited. "It was your idea."

"Yes, sir." Tera reached to the desk and snagged the box. "Take a look," she said, lowering it so we could see inside.

I frowned. There was nothing inside but a small

folded piece of cloth. "And you think this is *helpful*?" I asked.

"I'm sorry," Graym-Barker apologized, some of his earlier casualness peeking through the solemnity. "I didn't mean to be so mysterious. I certainly didn't mean to alarm you. But Tera had a theory, and it had to be tested."

He pointed into the box. "That cloth is a simple handkerchief that I bought six blocks from my home. Its single claim to fame is that Tera took it and rubbed it on the Icarus portal's outer hull." He raised his eyebrows in silent question.

"No," I said, looking down at the handkerchief again. "No, that's ridiculous. Metals don't smell. Not like that."

"Apparently, they do," Graym-Barker said. "Ms. Selene?"

"Yes," she murmured. "Yes." She looked up at him, her pupils frowning. "But why didn't I smell it when we did our survey of Bonvere Seven?"

"The probes didn't go very deep," I reminded her. "Or we might have been too far away. A second or third probe might have picked it up."

"Or maybe you did," Tera pointed out. "You *did* say you might have smelled it before."

"Perhaps," Selene said, still looking a little uncertain.

"So where does that leave us?" I asked. A strange idea was forming in the back of my head, but I wanted to see if Tera and Graym-Barker had already beaten me to it.

They had. "We want you to work for us," Graym-Barker said. "Our own personal crockett team, searching uninhabited worlds for signs that they're playing host to other Icarus portals."

"What makes you think we'll find them on planets?" I asked.

He shrugged. "Icarus and Firefall were found on planets," he said. "Both buried, but neither too deeply. That suggests that even if they started out in space they didn't fall too long ago, geologically speaking."

"*And* that if they fell, they survived the crash just fine," Tera added.

"Indeed," Graym-Barker said. "The point is that the galaxy is big, and deep-space portals like Alpha might never be found. But if there are any more of them on the ground, you're the team to find them. So?"

I took a careful breath. Searching through the Spiral, visiting new worlds away from the crush of other people. Doing work that wouldn't get us shot at. Probably getting paid way better than the average crockett.

I looked at Selene. "What do you think?"

"I'd like that." She looked back at me, her pupils smiling impishly. "I don't think I need to ask your thoughts."

"No, probably not," I agreed, turning back to Graym-Barker. "We're in," I told him. "Let's talk details.

As my father used to say, *When you find the very best there is, whether it's a job, a partner, or a pizza, grab onto it and never, ever let it go.*

Now, all I had to do was track down that pizza.

The End

At the End of the Journey   HC: 978-1-9821-2522-6 • $25.00

Six mismatched teenagers and their crusty British captain were out at sea when the world ended. Now, they must step up to leadership or face disaster.

THE VORTEX OF WORLDS SERIES

This Broken World   HC: 978-1-9821-2571-4 • $25.00
                             PB: 978-1-9821-9232-7 • $9.99

Fate has plans for Druadaen, a young man destined to become a military leader when he begins to question everything about the world as he knows it . . .

Into the Vortex   HC: 978-1-9821-9247-1 • $26.00

Druadaen remains determined to uncover "the truth of the world"—which might only be gained by travelling beyond it. But powers on Arrdanc don't want him to succeed. In fact, they'd rather Druadaen doesn't return at all.

OTHER TITLES

Mission Critical   TPB: 978-1-9821-9260-0 • $18.00

(with Griffin Barber, Chris Kennedy, and Mike Massa)

Major Rodger Y. Murphy should have died when his helicopter crashed off the coast of Mogadishu in 1993. Instead, he woke up in 2125, 152 light-years from home . . .

Michael Mersault

THE DEEP MAN

TPB: 978-1-9821-2584-4 • $16.00 US/$22.00 CAN

A relic of humanity's violent past, this ancient weapon stands ready for the Emperor to wield. The Galactic Imperium of the Myriad Worlds slumps into centuries of decadent peace enabled by a flood of advanced technology from the mysterious nonhuman "Shapers." Among the great families, only the once-mighty clan of Sinclair-Maru remembers the maxims of the warrior emperor, Yung I, ready to defend the Imperium from any threat. With spies and assassins on every side, trusting only in his considerable skill and the bizarre competence of his companion Inga, Saef Sinclair-Maru must complete his Imperial mission, restore the greatness of his family, and uncover the chilling plot meant to extinguish humanity's light from the galaxy.

And watch for *The Silent Hand*, an original trade paperback, in September 2023.